A FAMILY OF STRANGERS

FIONA LOWE

PRAISE FOR FIONA LOWE

"Fiona Lowe has expertly crafted a world that's easy to spend time in ... If you're looking to lose yourself in a cozy new novel that shines a spotlight on women's lives and stories, then *A Home Like Ours* by Fiona Lowe deserves a spot on your bookshelf." — *Mamamia*

"Rich, thought-provoking, and extremely absorbing, *A Home Like Ours* is yet another incredible read from the very talented Fiona Lowe." — *Better Reading*

"An insightful, warm and engaging story, *A Home Like Ours* is another fabulous novel from award-winning Australian author Fiona Lowe." — *Book'd Out*

"Fiona Lowe's ability to create atmosphere and tension and real relationship dynamics is a gift." —*Sally Hepworth*, bestselling author of *The Mother-in-Law*, on *Home Fires*

"Lowe breathes real life into her characters ... a profoundly hopeful tale, one of re-generation, of the strength gained from women supporting women, and of a community pulling together, one that acts as a powerful reminder of the resilience of the human spirit ... a deeply Australian story that brilliantly captures our own life and times."— *Better Reading on Home Fires*

"Part-Liane Moriarty, part-Jodi Picoult, *Just an Ordinary Family* is a compelling drama about a seemingly 'ordinary' family that implodes after a domino effect of lies, betrayals, disappointments and regrets ... set to be the next *Big Little Lies*."— *Mamamia*

"Fiona's insight into the fickle nature of life ... and how best intentions can so easily come undone makes it simple to identify with her characters and lends an authentic resonance to this rollercoaster story." — *Australian Country on Just an Ordinary Family*

"Lowe weaves character development and complexity with stunning finesse ... this story is not a light read, but it is one that proved difficult to put down."— *GLAM Adelaide on Just an Ordinary Family*

"Drama, upheaval and family secrets feature in the latest novel by Fiona Lowe, the undisputed queen of Australian small-town fiction ... a moving character-driven tale that steadily draws you into its thrall."— *Canberra Weekly on Just an Ordinary Family*

"*Birthright* is a complex story that seamlessly intertwines many story lines. It is full of interesting characters that reveal more and more as the story progresses. It is raw, incredibly engaging and reads beautifully."— *The Big Book Club*

"Lowe is a master at painting believable characters with heart and soul that contribute to creating such an addictive read." — *The Weekly Times on Birthright*

ALSO BY FIONA LOWE

Daughter of Mine

Birthright

Home Fires

Just An Ordinary Family

A Home Like Ours

Coming in 2023

The Money Club

Join My Newsletter

For a free novella, *Summer of Mine;* Doug and Edwina's summer of 1967, please join my VIP Readers newsletter. You'll also be the first to hear about new releases, book sales, competitions and giveaways. Register at

fionalowe.com

Did you know **BookBub** has a new release alert? You can check out the latest deals and get an email when I release my next book by following me at

bookbub.com/authors/fiona-lowe

A FAMILY OF STRANGERS

First Published by Harlequin Australia in 2022
This revised edition published in 2022 by Fiona Lowe
© 2022 by Fiona Lowe
All rights reserved.
www.fionalowe.com

A FAMILY OF STRANGERS
Cover Design by Barton Lowe

Published by Fiona Lowe

To Norm, with love.
It's been all the feels across the years!

CHAPTER ONE

IT'S THE RIGHT DECISION, Addy Topic told herself as the clank and clang of the *Spirit of Tasmania* berthing at the Devonport dock woke her at the criminally early hour of 6:30 A.M. The overnight crossing from Melbourne had been blessedly calm, not that it had induced sleep. She was very familiar with the pattern on the cabin's ceiling.

"You've got this," she said as she drove off the ferry and immediately found a café with a five-star coffee rating. Never a morning person, she chugged her espresso fast then sipped a latte, taking her time to savor the brew while she scanned *The Advocate*. Not a lot had changed since she'd last read it—it was still a mix of traffic offenses, mostly petty crimes, agriculture wins and losses and ongoing housing issues.

"Anything to eat?" the waitress asked.

"Why not?"

A move to the island state was why not. Addy ought to be maximizing her time and getting settled before starting her new job. But knowing she should seize the day didn't touch the part of her that was in no great hurry to reach Rookery Cove. "I'll have a poached egg with the avocado cup, thanks."

Three hours later, after driving along the rocky coast and taking a detour through Penguin where she dodged cell phone-wielding tourists snapping photos of the cute decorative penguins that lined the Esplanade, she eventually drove into the cove. Then she turned away from the main drag and up the hill before pulling into her parents' driveway.

My driveway.

Addy shrugged the words away. Four years after Ivan's and Rita's deaths, the house still felt very much theirs.

She turned off the ignition, took a deep breath and got out of the car. Despite the weeds on the path, the bulging orange rose-hips and the peeling paint—travesties her mother would never have allowed— she still expected Rita to step out onto the veranda, give her sadness-tinged smile and say, "Aida, you are home."

But Addy hadn't called the cove or the house home in twelve years; and since Rita's death, no one had called her Aida.

After her mother's funeral—six months to the day after her father's —Addy had left the fully furnished house in the hands of a realtor and flown back to her life in the state of Victoria. When people had asked if she'd ever live in Tasmania again, she'd replied "possibly Hobart" while privately thinking *not the north-west coast and never the cove.* But the universe was wily and the gateway job for a long-awaited career move had turned up two towns away from her childhood home.

Leaving her boxes and suitcases in the car, she walked up the steps and fished a bunch of keys out of her handbag. As she slid the old key into the front door, she got a memory flash of a brass key on a piece of orange wool that had once hung with great weight around her neck.

"Tell no one," Ivan had sternly admonished each time he gave it to her.

"No, Papa."

It wasn't until Addy was nine and had been visiting friends after school that she learned no one else in Rookery Cove locked their houses. But Rita and Ivan had escaped a civil war that had turned security into something ephemeral and not to be trusted.

Turning the door handle, Addy got another flash. This time she was fourteen and standing on the porch watching Rita turning the door handle left, then right, then left, after having previously checked eight times that the windows were closed and locked.

Knowing they were already late and that all eyes in the school auditorium would turn to them when they walked in, Addy had screamed, "For God's sake, Mama! It's locked!"

The memory faded and regret tightened her chest. Addy wished she'd understood more about obsessive-compulsive disorder and post-traumatic stress when she was a teen. Although her parents had talked of their childhoods in Dubrovnik, they'd never discussed the war. Whenever she'd asked about it she'd been told, "It's not important. We are Australian now." But the kids at the local elementary school, with their white-bread Vegemite sandwiches, had disagreed when they saw Addy's lunch of salami, cheese and olives.

Now the glass front door swung open and the cloying artificial scent of gardenia hit her nostrils. She gagged. Beating down the nausea, she took another breath and got a lungful of the sweet smell of marijuana with a fried food chaser. So much for the reliable tenants the realtor had promised.

Stepping inside she girded herself for anticipated filth, but apart from the walls being brown and sticky with nicotine, everything looked much the same as it had when she'd left at eighteen eager for a different life. The same wide rust-brown velvet sofa sat on its rotund feet, although minus Rita's crocheted doilies. The same framed photo of the old walled city perched on a shimmering bay hung on the wall, except instead of being fastidiously straight it tilted to the right. Addy automatically straightened it as she'd done each week as a child when it was her job to dust.

Her gaze slid to the upright piano, but with its closed lid and mahogany sheen dulled by layers of dust it lacked familiarity. Despite rising reluctance, her hands overrode her head and she pulled up the lid. She stretched her fingers, struck a chord and flinched at the off-key sound. The piano had been Rita's pride and joy and it had never been allowed to fall out of tune.

A stubborn streak of teen rebellion filled her and she played a ragtime riff from *The Entertainer*. The defiance evaporated and she dropped the lid.

"Sorry, Mama."

She inspected the rest of the house. The kitchen's exhaust fan was coated in grease, the shower was host to a colony of mold, and there was a stain of unknown origin on the carpet in the master bedroom. Nothing that sugar soap, bleach, eucalyptus oil and elbow grease couldn't shift. By the end of the weekend, the house would still be stuck in its nineties-decor time warp but it would sparkle.

Addy paused in the narrow hall outside her childhood bedroom and stared at the single bed, remembering its ruffled pillowcases and detested quilt bedcover. At fifteen, she'd begged for a quilt with a surfing design but had instead been given one with a grand piano design. With it had come the full weight of Rita's expectations. From that moment, her mother's hopes and dreams, which had already cloaked Addy all through the day, became inescapable at night.

Stepping into the room, she opened the freestanding wardrobe Ivan had built for her, including a special wooden box to lock away her "treasures." She was surprised the tenants hadn't torn down the smiling face of surfing champion Layne Beachley and the other surfing posters she'd pinned there between thirteen and seventeen.

Was her board still in the storage shed? Her gaze slipped to her belly and she sucked it in. If it was, she was probably too heavy to use it.

If you lost some weight ... If you drank less ... If you were nicer to me ... tidier ... worked less ...

"Go away, Jasper."

She released the catch on the window, threw up the sash and leaned out, stretching her arms wide. Cool salty air tingled her nostrils and she gazed down at the half-moon bay with whitecaps flashing across a moody and unwelcoming gray sea. An unexpected shaft of sunshine suddenly pierced the heavy cloud cover and golden rays lit a narrow band of water, taking it from steel gray to translucent tropical blue.

Addy smiled, savoring the water's familiar pull. How many times had she climbed out of this window and run to the moonlit beach? To parties at the surf club? To surf at dawn? Triple the number of times her parents had discovered her gone.

If Rita and Ivan still lived, what would they make of her return to the cove? Would they be pleased? Confused? Frustrated?

Addy was still coming to terms with it herself. When she'd accepted the teaching job at the community college two towns away, the plan had been to live close to campus and get fit by cycling to work. After all, the point of living in a small city was to integrate exercise into her lifestyle. The plan didn't include living in tiny Rookery Cove— population three hundred—and making an eighty-minute round trip each day. But she hadn't anticipated her tenants moving out and no one else moving into her old family home. After weeks of no activity, the leasing agent had suggested she turn the place into a vacation rental.

Although a good idea, it wasn't without overhead costs. When she factored in the seasonal nature of vacation rentals, it made financial sense to live in the house for a few months and redecorate it on the weekends. She could still get fit, drink less and eat better living here. She'd get up earlier and exercise with a run along the beach before leaving for work. She'd carve out an hour from her weekend redecorating schedule to prepare tasty and healthy lunches, dinners and snacks for the week ahead. She'd sleep better with the tang of salt in the air. Living here was the change she both needed and wanted.

Addy's fingers itched to crack open her first bullet journal. So far she'd only gotten as far as caressing the leather cover and smelling the crisp clean pages. She'd bought it, along with decorative washi tape, markers, colored pencils, paints and stickers, to help her plan each week so her new job, her new healthy lifestyle, the house renovations and she herself got all the attention they deserved. This was her year of living intentionally. No more floundering. No more wasting time—she was taking charge of her life. But first, all the windows needed throwing open so the sea breeze could blow through and freshen the house.

She'd just reached the bedroom door when her cell rang.

"Addy, it's Grant Hindmarsh."

Surprise tumbled with anxiety—Grant was her new boss for her new job. "Oh! Hi! I've just arrived on the island." Did that sound accusatory? She quickly added, "I'm really looking forward to Monday."

"Excellent! I'm calling to touch base and to say again how thrilled we are we tempted you back from the mainland. The students are lucky to have someone of your caliber."

"Thank you." A flutter of appreciation warmed her. "I'm looking forward to meeting them."

"That's what we want to hear. I know Lyn's already been in touch. Thanks for uploading your course work before your official start date. Others in the department could take a page of your playbook."

She smiled. Grant had just given her more praise in two short sentences than she'd received in three years at her previous job.

The line was suddenly silent. Considering the cove's sometimes iffy cell phone reception she said, "Grant, are you still there?"

He sighed. "Yes, sorry. I'm a bit distracted. Our media lecturer was in a car accident yesterday."

"Oh, no. Are they okay?"

"Sienna's fractured her pelvis so she's off for the semester."

"That sounds nasty."

"It is." Grant sighed. "As you can imagine, it's thrown us into a spin. She teaches social media marketing and touches briefly on website design. Her class has a waiting list and it's one of our biggest earners so we're loathe to cancel it."

Addy knew all about the pressures of funding and the appeal of courses that generated income. "It all sounds very tricky."

"How would you feel about taking it on?" Grant asked.

The question caught her by surprise. "I, um ... I've never taught it."

"But everything's new the first time, right?"

"That's true—"

"And you're a digital native so a lot of it's intrinsic," he said.

Addy doubted it—she knew enough HTML to be dangerous and almost nothing about SEO. What she did know was that she'd spend the entire semester barely staying one step ahead of her students. She already had a full teaching load, but was saying no to her new boss the best way to start?

She sought some clarification. "So this would be a load reshuffle? Which subject am I handing off to someone else?"

Grant sighed again. "Ah, no, which is why I'm asking you. Judging by your interview and references, I get the impression you're the type of person who steps up. Am I wrong about that?"

She thought about her employment terms. Three months' probation, and if she aced that, permanency and a shot at the promotion she'd been chasing for a couple of years. "Not wrong at all."

"I didn't think so." His tone was reassuring. "Obviously it's not ideal and it's a big workload for you, but as we say here in the northwest, there's no 'I' in 'team.' I promise we'll give you all the support you need. Lyn will get Sienna's teaching notes to you asap, so really it's just a matter of delivering ready-made content. So what do you say? Can you help us out?"

Addy's previous job had been fraught with never-ending budget cuts and infighting. The idea of being surrounded by a committed team all rowing in the same direction was as exciting as it was reassuring.

"Absolutely, I can help you out," she said.

"Excellent," Grant said. Addy heard the clicking of a keyboard as he added, "Just be sure to send me the content, skills requirements, and metrics for grading by four o'clock Sunday."

Her hand tightened around the phone. "I thought you said that had already been done."

"I'm sure Sienna has it all ready to go. Talk to Lyn. She'll sort it. Meanwhile, thanks so much, Addy. See you on Monday at 8:oo."

He rang off, and an email immediately pinged onto her phone.

She opened it, scanned the brief contents and rang Lyn.

"Thanks for the email," Addy said.

"No worries," Lyn said. "I've sent you everything Sienna gave me."

"Right." Addy focused on channeling calm. "The thing is, this reads like an ideas list rather than course content."

"That's why the students love her," Lyn said. "Sienna prefers participation learning rather than setting out specific content."

Addy's stomach clenched, but there was no point having a pedagogy discussion with the administrative clerk. "What about the online platform? Has Sienna uploaded the learning, assessment and grading guides there?"

"I'll check." Addy heard the click of keys and then Lyn was saying, "As anticipated, it's not here."

Stay calm. Breathe. "Why not?" Addy asked.

"It's a new course," Lyn said breezily.

What? Addy's brain froze at the full implication of four small words. She finally managed to splutter, "That's not what Grant told me."

"That'd be right." Lyn sounded sympathetic. "He probably thought it was the same as last semester. He focuses on the budget and enrollment numbers and leaves the teaching to the teachers."

Addy knew it was a sensible management style, but it didn't help her today. "Can you put me in touch with Sienna so I can ask her some questions about the course?"

Lyn tsked. "The poor thing was airlifted to Hobart. She doesn't need any more stress."

It appeared Addy's stress didn't count. "So just to clarify, I'm creating and teaching a new course. Please tell me the first class is on Friday."

Lyn laughed. "You're funny. No, it's nine o'clock Monday morning, straight after the faculty meeting at 8:00. See you then."

The line went dead and Addy stared at her cell phone, completely nonplussed. What the hell had just happened?

Anxiety rose in a wave, swamping all her plans for a weekend of washing walls and steam-cleaning carpets. *Move!*

She ran outside to the car, grabbed her "emergency supplies" box, slung her laptop across her shoulder and returned to the kitchen. First, she pulled out a cloth and the antibacterial spray and wiped the sticky residue from the chunky pine table and chair. Next, she opened a large bag of almonds, popped out two protein balls, sliced an apple and refilled her water bottle. Healthy brain food and staying hydrated was key to concentration.

Bypassing the pristine bullet journal, she plugged in her laptop then transferred the documents Lyn had sent her from her phone to her computer. She reread them carefully. Calmly. Mindfully.

Addy cut and pasted Sienna's headings into a new document, numbered them, stared at them, then swore. She needed to consult the government training body website.

She opened a browser, typed in the URL, then cursed the spinning rainbow ball of death as her computer valiantly tried to find her phone's hotspot. While she waited she ran through a list of her former colleagues, wondering who might be able to help her.

The internet is not available appeared on her screen.

"Are you freaking kidding me?"

She checked her phone. One bar. She walked around the house seeking a stronger signal, finally finding it in the bathroom.

Dragging a chair down the hall, she held her breath while a blue line crawled inexorably across the top of the screen. She typed in the URL and the rainbow ball appeared again. Every part of her clenched. This would take forever.

She dumped the computer on the chair and marched straight to the kitchen and her emergency box. She pulled out a notepad, pen, a plastic wineglass and the bottle of red she'd been saving as a treat to drink with dinner. A quick twist of her wrist and the seal broke with a reassuring click.

Addy poured half a glass, took two big gulps and refilled it.

Opening the wine early was not only easy, it was absolutely necessary.

CHAPTER TWO

STEPHANIE GALLAGHER HAD two seams left to sew on the bucket hat she was making for her soon-to-launch online children's clothing store when she heard Monty singing. Damn! He'd woken from his nap half an hour early.

Since Monty's bedroom was closer to Henry's office—a dedicated space—than it was to her office—the kitchen table—she kept sewing, hoping his father would go to him. Over the whirr of the overlocker she heard Monty's singing turn into cries of frustration.

"Henry!" Her call broke her own rule of "don't yell from three rooms away." Don't yell period. But she was close to finishing the hat, and once Monty was up, she wouldn't get any more sewing done unless she put him in front of a screen. She tried to limit those occasions to emergencies.

Henry appeared in the doorway, his cell phone pressed to his ear and his hand indicating he was on a call.

Of course he was on a call—he lived on the phone. For an IT professional he seemed to spend more time on the phone than the computer. Then again, Steph had no clear picture of what was involved in being a senior manager of a cybersecurity company. No one outside of IT ever understood much beyond the blanket terms "software developer" and "virus protection."

Henry mouthed the name of their telco.

With a spurt of irritation, Steph abandoned the hat. This scenario wasn't quite what she'd envisioned on their idyllic vacation fifteen months earlier.

Having never visited Tasmania and in desperate need of a break, they'd accepted the offer of a beach "shack," after being assured this was actually a vacation house. But when they had arrived at the turnoff to Rookery Cove—two cypress pines, a rusted half of a water tank on its side and some motley hay bales—Steph worried they'd made a mistake. The feeling stayed with her as Henry drove the winding eucalyptus-lined road. Just as she was convinced they should have gone to New South Wales, a curve of blinding white sand came into view, followed by the sparkling phosphorescence of a calm turquoise sea.

"Oh, Henry! It's Queensland without the jellyfish."

He grinned at her. "Or the cassowaries."

A blissful week followed. Monty napped every afternoon. Henry reconnected with his daughter, Zoe, who lived full-time with her mother. They took walks together, counting the steps in a mile and then calculating how many steps to Melbourne and to the moon. Steph didn't understand their fascination with numbers, but she loved the joy it gave them.

She and Henry team-parented, ate out, read the papers and took turns having some alone time. Henry took up surfing. Steph had a couple of massages to undo the rigid knots the year had tied inside her. She wished Fern, the masseur, lived in Melbourne.

At the end of their week, Steph was reading on the beach under the shade of a Norfolk pine when a shadow crept over the page. Henry lowered himself next to her.

"We bought you licorice," he said.

Steph accepted the proffered ice-cream. "Thanks! This *is* a day of treats! I didn't think they sold licorice."

"I fudged the truth. I was saving it for the last day."

She rested her head on his shoulder. "Don't say last day."

Zoe snuggled in-between them. "Daddy, I don't want to go home."

"Neither do I, kiddo."

Zoe's eyes—an almost perfect match for Henry's—widened. "Can we stay, Daddy? Pleeease?"

"We can come back."

"When?" Zoe demanded.

Henry pulled a brochure out of his pocket and handed it to Steph. It showed a photo of Four Winds, the cream Federation clapboard with a high pitched roof, decorative gables and a half-turn veranda that both of them had admired during the week. Positioned on the top of a hill, its back faced tree-covered mountains and its front overlooked the crooked line of colonial Georgian cottages clinging like mussels to the cliff. Beyond them lay a view of the bay, and farther north, Bass Strait and the far horizon.

"It's for sale?" Steph asked.

"It went on the market today."

She studied the photos, ignoring the dated carpets and wallpaper and concentrating on the wooden mantelpieces, the Arts and Crafts lead light windows, the pressed-metal ceilings and the bare floorboards that promised to gleam with some love.

"We could buy it and renovate," Henry said.

"How? We're already maxed to the hilt." She handed back the brochure. "Besides, it's too big for a vacation house."

"Not as a vacation house. As *our* house."

Zoe squealed. "Living here would be awesome!"

"Dig?" Monty waved a sandy spade in their faces.

"Zoe, can you please help Monty make a sandcastle?" Steph asked.

The request had as much to do with removing her eleven-year-old stepdaughter from what needed to be a private conversation with Henry as it was about keeping Monty entertained.

Zoe happily obliged, taking her half-brother's hand and leading him down toward the wet sand.

"Henry, we can't just move to a tiny town in Tasmania," Steph said.

"Why not? We want to forget last year, and Melbourne's full of reminders. Besides, how many times have you said we need to slow down and simplify our life? The cove's perfect for that. No stress, no commute, no traffic noise—just clean, fresh sea air."

"And Monty hasn't needed his inhaler this week." Steph couldn't remember the last time that had happened.

"See? Another reason to move." Henry flung his arm out toward the sea. "Imagine how incredible it would be to start and end each day at the beach."

Monty's whoops of delight as he stomped on sandcastles made Steph's heart sing. Living here would give him an idyllic childhood built on the sort of freedoms that were impossible in a big city where danger lurked on every corner. Was the cove the place to raise him and his yet-to-be-conceived younger sibling?

"Again, Zo! Again!" Monty yelled.

The soaring peaks of Steph's anticipation took a hit.

"If we moved, what about Zoe?" she asked. "There'll be a body of water separating you."

Henry grimaced. "There may as well be that now. It's not like she's allowed to spend much time with us and we only live four suburbs away. I'll continue to FaceTime her and we'll fly her down for the school vacations." He tapped the brochure. "She'd have her own room at Four Winds."

Steph was usually the ideas person—the one spinning castles in the air—not Henry. He was the math and IT guy, the practical one who consulted the numbers and spreadsheets. Not that he didn't have his own idiosyncratic superstitions, but they didn't include changing their lives completely by moving to a tiny town on an island.

"Aren't jobs in Tassie hard to find even in the bigger population centers, let alone here?" she asked.

He shrugged. "My job's portable. All I need is my cell phone, computer and the internet. And you're aching to start your own online business, but we've needed your income to pay the mortgage. If we sell the house and move down here, it frees you up to take the plunge."

She looked at the photo of the kitchen and imagined a long oak table with her sewing machine at one end and Monty opposite her, busy with his own craft. Monty playing in the old-world garden. Henry building a treehouse in the huge oak tree—or at least helping someone to build it. Possibilities spun like golden rays of sunshine.

Fifteen months later, their recent move to the seaside, wasn't quite going according to plan.

Monty shrieked again, the decibels easily penetrating the walls of the old house. Steph pushed back her chair, brushed past Henry and marched down the hall. The moment she opened Monty's door his screams ceased. He beamed beatifically and offered her his beloved stuffed toy penguin.

Henry had bought him and Zoe identical penguins to celebrate their move to Rookery Cove. When he'd presented the toys to the children saying, "Welcome to our new home," their responses could not have been more different. Monty had squealed in delight and "Pen" lived almost permanently tucked under Monty's arm, going everywhere with him.

Zoe, on the other hand, was less impressed and had rolled her eyes with all the drama of an exasperated actor. "Jeez, Dad. I'm thirteen. I need a cell phone, not a stupid penguin." She'd thrown the toy at Henry and stomped to her room.

Henry had tried valiantly to mask his hurt, but Steph had seen his shock at Zoe's rejection of the toy. It was the first sign that the happy-go-lucky and enthusiastic girl who'd adored their vacation at the cove had vanished. In her place was a stranger.

Now Monty raced out of the bedroom, his feet thundering along the hall carpet runner, and straight into Henry's office. Henry swung around on his office chair, his dark brows drawn down hard, and indicated the phone by jabbing the air with his pointer finger.

Steph grabbed Monty's hand. "Daddy's working. Let's get your hat and go outside."

The previous owners had been more "interested" in the flower garden than in the house so although the interior had required a complete makeover, the yard had only needed a new fence to make it child-safe. Full of established trees and shady nooks, it was an idyllic secret garden and the perfect spot for hide and seek and imaginative play. Monty would live outside if he could.

He handed her a bucket filled with sand and tapped the top with his yellow plastic spade. "Castle, Mummy."

Steph swallowed a groan and upended the bucket.

"Zah! Mummy," Monty instructed firmly.

Apparently it was impossible to make a sandcastle without the incantation.

"Hazzah," Steph said.

"Again!"

Monty was on a waiting list for part-time childcare in three nearby towns, and as a result, Steph had made more sandcastles in the two months since moving to the cove than she'd thought possible. What had been fun and joyful on vacation was now a mind-numbing chore.

She'd just upended the bucket for the tenth time and was digging deep for an enthusiastic "ta-dah," when Henry came walking toward them. His straight black hair was sticking up in wild spikes plowed by frustrated fingers. An hour on the phone to a call center and being transferred from person to person would do that.

Their internet connection, so vital for remote working, had been an issue since day one. Used to fast internet in Melbourne, they had never stopped to think that speed and reliability weren't standard across the country. After all, weren't billions being spent on the National Broadband Network so Australia would have the gold standard in telecommunications? The rollout may have started in Tassie but it sure as hell didn't work very well at Four Winds. The connection was slow, intermittent, and on a windy day—and there were many of those—frustratingly absent.

"Did you get it sorted?" Steph asked.

Henry shook his head and she noticed the fatigue lines carved in deep around his eyes. "They're sending out another technician to look at it."

"Hopefully that will do the trick."

"Hopefully." But he didn't sound like he believed it. "The only other solution costs the big bucks."

They didn't have many big bucks to spare, having used a large chunk of the profit from the sale of their Melbourne house to renovate their new one. The rest was a nest egg for vacations, emergencies and —she hugged herself as she did every time she thought about it—the baby. In seven months, they'd be welcoming a new addition to their family. After a year of trying in Melbourne, she'd conceived within a week of arriving in the cove. The pregnancy more than made up for the dodgy internet.

"Sandcastle, Daddy!" Monty held out his bucket.

"Good idea." Steph rose to her feet and dusted her hands on her jeans. "Ten sandcastles will give me enough time to finish the hats and put away the machine."

"Sorry," Henry said. "I've got the weekly on-line meeting."

She checked her cell phone. "In an hour. Surely you can spare me ten minutes."

He grimaced. "I would if we had a freaking internet connection, but we don't. I have to drive to the library to use their internet and if I don't leave now, I'll be late."

At this time of day it was a forty-minute trip. Steph's thoughts flew straight to the afternoon's plans as recorded on the whiteboard in the kitchen. They included Henry taking Monty to the beach at 4:00 to give her an hour of uninterrupted time to work and afterwards all of them cooking dinner together. Now, he'd be home too late to do either. This wasn't the evenly divided parenting they'd discussed.

She breathed deeply, reminding herself of all the positives that came with living in the cove. Of the baby that would complete their family. This moment was just a tiny crooked stitch in the fabric of their lives.

She smiled at Henry and gave his arm a gentle squeeze. "We always knew there'd be teething problems."

He raked his hair. "Yeah, but I thought they'd be confined to the renovation and the move. Not still haunting us two months in."

And neither of them had anticipated that Zoe would be living with them full-time.

"At least you'll still be able to pick up Zoe from the bus stop," she said.

Henry shook his head. "I won't be back in time for that. Can you do it?"

It was a rhetorical question. They'd moved just before Christmas, when all the yearly activities had finished for the January summer holidays, so they didn't know anyone in town well enough to ask. But someone needed to pick up Zoe because she'd only been at the school for a couple of weeks and had yet to make the steep mile walk home on her own.

"Of course I'll pick her up," Steph said, but she couldn't help adding, "After all, it's so much fun strapping a tired Monty into his car seat to meet the bus."

"You're the best." Henry kissed her on the cheek. "Love you and you." He patted her barely perceptible pregnant belly before bending down to kiss Monty. "And you. Be good for Mummy."

And then he was striding toward the car without a backwards glance, leaving her uncertain—had he chosen to ignore her sarcasm or missed it completely?

As predicted, Monty was unimpressed by being forced into his car seat to meet the bus. He had back-arching down to a fine art and Steph struggled to avoid being kicked as she snapped the straps into the lock.

"Pen wants to see Zoe and the big bus," she said with faux cheerfulness. "He'll be sad if you don't hold him up to the window."

"Want Zoe," Monty said with toddler stubbornness, as if he was being denied her.

Monty adored Zoe, and during the recent summer vacation, Steph would have said they were a mutual admiration society. But since Zoe's unexpected return to the cove less than a week after she'd left to start school, the adoration between the half-siblings was only flowing in one direction.

Steph didn't fully understand what had precipitated Zoe's sudden move to Tasmania. Hell, she didn't understand it at all. One minute she'd been snuggled up on the sofa half-asleep, having given in to the glue-like exhaustion of early pregnancy, and the next minute Henry was saying, "Joanna wants Zoe to come and live with us for a bit."

Steph had sat up so fast, the room spun. "What's a bit?"

He'd shrugged. "She didn't specify."

"Did you ask her to?"

Henry had sat and pulled Steph's feet onto his lap. "Zoe needs to go to school and it's too disruptive for her education to chop and change. It has to be the full year, doesn't it?"

Does it? It wasn't that Steph didn't want Zoe living with them, it's just she'd always thought of her stepdaughter in terms of a visitor. When Steph met Henry, Zoe had been seven. Six months after their first date when Steph had moved in with him, she'd made the decision to stay out of the Joanna–Henry parental access arguments. Zoe had a mother and a father—Steph didn't need to weigh in and add to an already complicated triangle.

"I don't understand," she'd said. "Why now, on the eve of the new school year? Zoe was so excited about starting high school. It's all she talked about this summer and she has her uniform, books, everything!"

"To be honest, I don't care about the why, just that she's coming. And you know how much she loves being a big sister. She'll be falling over herself to help." Henry had rested his hand gently on Steph's belly. "With Monty and this baby, I've been around from the start. I never had that with Zoe."

"It's not your fault," she'd said hotly, hating how Joanna called the shots, demanded money and deliberately limited Henry's time with Zoe. "You've been around as much as Joanna allowed."

Zoe was the result of a drunken one-night stand after a university ball back when Henry was twenty-one. For the first two and a half years of Zoe's life, Henry hadn't even known he'd fathered a child.

"How did that make you feel?" Steph had asked him when he'd told her on their second date.

"Shocked, furious, bewildered, angry, sad. All that pretty much played on repeat in random order for a long time."

It didn't matter which way Steph came at it, she couldn't fathom Joanna's behavior. "Why did she wait so long to tell you?"

"In Joanna's perfect world, I doubt she ever planned to tell me."

"So why did she?"

"She wanted money." Henry had sighed. "I was no longer a poor student and when Cyberdragon got written up in the *Herald Sun,* she saw my photo and called me up. I've pondered this for a long time and I honestly think she looked at the photo and thought 'Asian.' She expected me and my parents to be so worried about saving face that we'd pay for her and Zoe to stay away."

"So she got a shock when you wanted to be more of a hands-on dad than just a cash cow?" Steph had said.

"That's understating it. Joanna miscalculated wildly. I'm an ABC, not fresh off the boat."

"You're a what?"

Henry had smiled. "Australian-born Chinese, and so are my parents and their parents. Instead of being horrified, Mama and Baba were over the moon at being grandparents."

Phillip and Li had been amazing grandparents and Steph wondered if that boundless love had been their secret weapon with the ever-prickly and obstructive Joanna. Their tragic deaths two years earlier had left a weeping hole in their small family. Steph missed their generosity of spirit and their loud and enthusiastic love for them all.

She wiped away a tear as the school bus lumbered around the bend. Hopping out of the car, she waved as Zoe stepped down off the silver step. "Hi."

Zoe's once sunny smile was lost under an almost permanent scowl. "Where's Dad?"

Hello to you too, Zoe. "He had to go to Burnie for work."

"I thought the point of moving to Hicksville was so he could work from home." Zoe tossed her bag into the back of the car. "If I had a cell phone, he could have texted me. Then I could have caught the bus to the library and done my homework where there's internet."

The thought of not having to "help" Zoe with homework almost made Steph agree about a phone. But she and Henry were hiding behind the excuse of poor reception at Four Winds to delay the inevitable cell phone purchase for a bit longer. With Zoe's current bolshie behavior, Steph felt like they were already saying no a lot without adding cell phone rules.

"Zo, Zo, Zo!" Monty called from the back seat, but his half-sister didn't respond. Instead, she slumped into the front passenger seat and pulled her seatbelt so violently it locked up.

Monty kept calling her name and when she continued to ignore him, he pummeled the back of her seat with his feet.

She turned around. "Stop being a brat!"

Monty blinked in surprise and his bottom lip quivered.

Steph's patience snapped. "How about you listen to your own advice."

Zoe slumped farther into the seat and Steph sighed, regretting her words. She reached out and touched Zoe's arm. Zoe immediately shook her off.

"Zo, Monty just wants you to say hi."

Zoe sighed and turned around. "Hey, kiddo."

Monty proffered Pen—the absolute sign of forgiveness. Zoe took the toy and walked it across the headrest before giving it a push so it dropped into Monty's lap. He laughed in delight.

Steph turned the car toward home. "How was netball practice?" she asked cheerily, hating how forced it sounded. Hating that every conversation with Zoe was a masterclass in tiptoe.

"Okay."

"Did you try out for center?"

"No."

Don't ask why. "Do you have much homework?"

"Math. Which totally sucks."

Steph remembered all the counting games Henry and Zoe had played over the years. "But you love math. Math and maps."

Zoe threw her a look that would freeze water. "No, I don't. Math is lame."

Steph didn't dare mention reading in case that voided another joy. "The weekend's coming up and we don't have any plans. Would you like to invite a friend over? There's the Saturday market and surfing. You could cook dinner on the campfire and roast marshmallows."

She waited a few beats for a reply. "Zo?"

"What!"

Steph's fingers tightened on the steering wheel and she had to actively relax them. "I asked you a question."

"Don't you want me to have any friends?"

Don't react. "I do, which is why I suggested it."

"If I invite someone over and we do lame stuff like a campfire, everyone will think I'm weird or a loser."

Steph was about to say "I doubt that," but wondered if it was worth pushing. At times, Zoe could be as stubborn as Henry. "So that's a no to inviting someone over?"

"What do you think?"

Steph thought that she was going to have a long talk with Henry.

CHAPTER THREE

BRENDA HUMMED as she tapped hot scones—golden and firm—before tumbling them into a tea-towel-lined basket. She set it on the table next to the bowls of homemade raspberry jam and cream.

One of the things she'd worried about when she'd moved off the farm and into this new house in town was the loss of her wood-fire stove. They'd been simpatico for thirty-eight years, probably far more of one mind than she and Glen had ever been. Together, she and her oven had won many blue and red ribbons at the Burnie and Devonport agricultural shows. Although she could give up winning ribbons, she'd wanted the security that she could still knock up a sponge cake, scones and frosting-filled yo-yos for the grandchildren. The hours she'd spent researching stoves and ovens had been worth every minute.

She heard a loud clunk and sighed. That due diligence should have extended to the washing machine.

"They look good." Marilyn stood by the island counter, a dog lead in her hand.

"Take one with you," Brenda said.

"I'm tempted, but I really shouldn't." Marilyn patted her hips. "I didn't realize the perils of sharing a house with an excellent cook who keeps the cookie jar full."

Brenda gave a wry smile. "It's habit after years of filling them for the insatiable appetites of teens, Glen, and work breaks for the vegetable pickers. I forget I'm no longer feeding a crowd. Take the coconut jam bars to school tomorrow for Justine's birthday."

"That would be fabulous, thanks. I'm not a baker, probably because I'm not great at playing by the rules. Sticking to a recipe seems so restrictive."

Brenda laughed. "What you lack in baking skills you make up for in exotic and tasty meals. Since you moved in, I feel like I've eaten around the world."

Marilyn smiled. "Massaman curry tonight. I'm just taking Clyde for a walk and grabbing the ingredients."

"Don't get any fresh veggies because Courtney—"

As if on cue Courtney tumbled into the kitchen, a trail of dirt leaking out of the bags she was carrying. "Hi, Mum. I've brought carrots, onions and— Oh! Hello, Marilyn."

"Hi, Courtney. I'll leave you and your mum to catch up."

"You're not staying?" Disappointment dimmed Courtney's bright eyes. "We haven't sat down together since we chatted at the interview."

"We will, I promise, but sadly not today," Marilyn said. "Enjoy the scones." The back door slammed shut behind her.

"Back in a sec, Mum. I've been holding on since I left home." Courtney disappeared toward the bathroom, as she did almost every time she visited.

Brenda wondered if she should mention pelvic floor exercises to her daughter, but in ways she'd never truly understood, Courtney could be both touchy and embarrassed about things like that.

Brenda was pulling the tea cozy she'd knitted to match her new kitchen over the pot when Courtney returned.

"Marilyn keeps her room neat, doesn't she?" Courtney said, sliding into a chair.

"Didn't I teach you about twenty-five years ago that it's rude to snoop?" Brenda carried the teapot to the table.

"I wasn't snooping. I have to walk past her room on my way to the bathroom and her door was open."

"And you just happened to glance left?"

"Of course." Courtney broke open a scone. "If she's that neat, I'm surprised she's lasted living here for six weeks without breaking out in hives."

"Thank you, darling, for that endorsement of my housekeeping."

"Oh, come on, Mum. We Lambecks are clean but we're not neat."

Brenda waved the butter knife. "Look around."

Courtney swung her head, taking in the large open-plan living space, the stacked books on the coffee table, the carefully folded throw-blanket over the back the sofa and the lack of general clutter.

"It must be Marilyn's work," she said. "Home never looked anything like this."

"The farmhouse was never tidy because you, your father and your brothers all lacked the "pick up" gene and left a trail of disarray behind you. I spent years asking, commanding and pleading for you all to put things away with little success." Brenda sighed at the memory. "Then one day I worked out how much time I spent clearing up after you all and it shocked me into stopping. After that, I made the piano room mine."

"Is that why you banned us from entering unless we were empty-handed?" Courtney dolloped cream on her scone. "I used to sneak in there when Colin and Rick gave me the shi— pip and I'd lie on Nana's throw-blanket and read. It was such a calm room."

"It was." *And now I have calm here.*

Glen's unexpected and sudden death from a heart attack had activated the next step of succession planning for the farm and changed Brenda's life. Not that Colin had pushed her out of the house or off the farm. He'd even suggested they swap houses as a compromise if she wished to stay on the property.

But the previous year Glen had surprised everyone by purchasing a tract of land in town. "Retirement planning!" he'd told Brenda.

"You've got five years to think about what you might like in a new house."

Brenda had bitten off the words "doesn't planning mean consulting?" and had said instead, "You should plant fruit trees now so they're producing in five years."

After Glen's death, Brenda had built the house on the tract of land. Although the cost of the house had been factored into the farm's succession planning, the build had coincided with a trade war with China that left the farm with a glut of vegetables. To help with the mortgage and to reduce some of Colin's stress, Brenda had decided to take in a boarder.

"You don't have to do this, Mum," Colin had told her at the family meeting. But his drawn face and bitten nails had said otherwise.

It had been difficult to know exactly what her younger son, Richard, thought. He'd joined the family meeting by video link from Hobart and the internet kept freezing. Eventually he'd texted: *Do what you need to do so you wake up every morning feeling calm*

Courtney had said, "I don't like the idea of you sharing the house with a man."

"Why not?" Brenda asked.

"Because it's not safe!"

"I hardly think I'm in any danger except being expected to cook and clean for him," Brenda said.

"Mum, you're always in danger with a stranger. No one in the cove needs to rent a room so we won't know whoever it is who moves in. What about putting up a notice at the community college? Plenty of students need a room."

"I'm done with mothering," Brenda said emphatically.

"Gee, thanks a lot!" Courtney huffed.

Brenda swallowed a sigh. "I meant I'm not sharing with a teen or a twenty-something. I want a fully fledged adult."

"So not a man," Courtney quipped.

Colin glared at his sister. "Are you absolutely sure about this, Mum?"

"Absolutely."

"It might take the edge off your loneliness, Mum," Colin's wife, Lucinda, said. "The farm's quiet without Glen so I can't imagine what the house feels like."

The farmhouse had felt vast and empty after Glen's death, but the new house didn't echo in the same way. Perhaps because it was untouched by Glen—he'd played no part in its design and construction. From the moment Brenda had moved in, it had felt like hers in a way the farmhouse never had.

Courtney had insisted on being at the interview for a housemate, and Brenda, who was working hard on improving her relationship with Courtney, had chosen not to object to being treated like she was eighty-five instead of fifty-eight. Marilyn was the only applicant. She'd moved in with her Scottish terrier, Clyde, a few weeks after Brenda.

"So what have you found out?" Courtney asked now, leaning forward, her eyes bright with interest.

"About what?"

"About Marilyn! Why is she here?"

"You know why," Brenda said. "She's taken a twelve-month contract at the elementary school."

Courtney waved her hand dismissively. "I know that. But I meant has she always been single? Is she divorced? Is this a midlife-crisis sea-change or does she have a tragic love story? It has to be something. Why else would she leave Hobart for the cove?"

Brenda tried unsuccessfully to stifle a sigh. "Why does she have to have a story?"

Dissatisfaction settled over Courtney and the set of her mouth reminded Brenda of Glen's mother. In a time when there was little entertainment in small town Tasmania, Elaine had thrived on gossip. Granted, the north-west coast today was hardly Hobart, but Courtney had a smartphone and Netflix to bring the world to her. Perhaps that was the problem.

"Honestly, Mum! I don't think you have a romantic bone in your body. When a stranger arrives in a small town there's always a story."

"Well, I'm sorry to disappoint you, darling. Why don't you write a novel and create the story you want to hear? It will be far more interesting."

Courtney sighed and dolloped jam and cream on a second scone.

"What do you and Marilyn talk about then?"

"The usual things people who share a house discuss. Who's doing what on the cleaning schedule, who's doing the shopping and whose turn it is to cook."

Courtney snorted. "That sounds like dinner with you and Dad."

Brenda thought about all the meals she'd shared with Glen after the children had left home. How they'd struggled to make conversation unless she asked about the farm, the football club or tractor restoration.

"I don't believe your father ever cleaned anything inside the house," she said. "I know for a fact the only time he cooked was when I was in the hospital for my hysterectomy."

"And he gave us food poisoning, remember?" Courtney laughed, then wiped away a tear. "Dad was old-school, but I miss him."

Brenda squeezed her daughter's hand. "I know you do."

Glen's definition of fatherhood was being a good provider and a disciplinarian, but when pressed he'd taken the kids out to work with him on the farm. Those occasions had forged a bond between him and Courtney that appeared to be far stronger than the connection Brenda had established driving her across the district to play netball, supervising homework, ironing clothes and providing meals.

"When I was helping you pack up the farmhouse, I noticed all the photos of Dad were faded, and you haven't put any up here, so ..." Courtney plucked a shiny silver photo frame out of a bag. "It's the photo you always loved of the two of you at Dove Lake."

"That's very thoughtful, thank you." Brenda studied herself and Glen and saw only strangers. She quickly changed the subject. "How's Livvy?"

"Oh my God! Middle School!" Courtney rolled her eyes. "I

thought when she finished elementary school all those theme days would stop, but no. They still exist to stress out parents."

Brenda had hoped that with Olivia making the transition to year seven, Courtney would be less involved and hover less. "Isn't it up to teens to organize themselves?"

Courtney snorted. "This sort of thing doesn't make it easy. Tomorrow's epilepsy awareness day and she has to wear purple. The only thing Livvy owns that's remotely purple is an old T-shirt with a unicorn and a rainbow."

"Sounds perfect."

"It's far from perfect, Mum! Unicorns and rainbows are fine when you're nine, but at thirteen she may as well wear a sign that says, "Bully Me." She'll be called a baby—or worse, a lesbo or a gayby. Anyway, it's too tight on her now she's getting boobs. Do you want your granddaughter sexually harassed by the boys?"

Brenda counted silently to ten, then said calmly, "Does Livvy think any of those things might happen?"

Courtney's cheeks tightened. "*I* know they'll happen and I intend to protect my daughter."

Unlike you. The criticism stretched between them like a paddock of sunflowers concealing landmines. Brenda knew whichever way she stepped, she'd detonate a bomb.

She loved Courtney and she'd walk over hot coals and enter burning buildings for her, but it didn't mean she understood her.

In contrast, Courtney's brothers seemed blissfully uncomplicated, although Brenda had lived long enough to know that was a far too simplistic view.

"Would Livvy like to wear my purple velvet cloche hat?" she offered.

Courtney dug into her bag and pulled out a purple dress. "I found this at the thrift shop."

Brenda shook it out, taking in the cut, and wondered if she'd lost touch with what young girls wore. If the unicorn T-shirt was too babyish, this dress was definitely too mature.

"Obviously, it needs alteration," Courtney said. "I know it's short notice, but ..." She left the words "you don't have anything on tonight" unsaid.

Brenda thought of the cellophane-wrapped, 1000-piece jigsaw she'd planned to start—but saying no wasn't an option. "I guess Livvy's coming over after netball practice for a fitting."

Courtney smiled. "Epilepsy awareness thanks you."

Do you? But there was no point asking. Brenda knew she still had many amends to make before Courtney thanked her for anything.

Brenda stood and stretched her aching back, pleased with what she'd achieved. Her granddaughter's dress was ready to be picked up in the morning.

Olivia had whizzed in after netball practice and been so excited by Brenda's suggestion of a handkerchief hemline that she hadn't objected to the tulle and satin placket on the bodice. It removed the plunging neckline and made the dress suitable for a young teen.

"Oh, Mémé!" Olivia had breathed in wonder. "I can't wait to show Zoe."

Brenda hadn't heard Olivia talk about a Zoe before, but unlike Rookery Cove elementary school, the middle school and the high school were large, two towns away and drew students from far and wide.

"Is she a new friend?" she asked.

"Yes." Olivia suddenly swung around. "What smells so good?"

"Curry," Marilyn called from the kitchen. "Would you like a bowl?"

"Yes, please! Mum never makes stuff like that."

"Just a small bowl," Brenda cautioned. "Your mum will have cooked dinner."

Marilyn spooned out a decent amount of curry. "I thought the job of grandparents was all care and no responsibility."

"Yeah, Mémé!" Olivia laughed. "You had to be strict with Mum, but you can relax with me and let me have whatever I want."

Brenda thought about Courtney's response and the likely angry phone call if Olivia came home full of food and refused dinner. She mustered a half-smile. "Do you want to get both of us in trouble?"

"Just a small bowl, please, Marilyn," Olivia said.

After Olivia had left with her father—Ben had also accepted a small bowl of curry—Brenda had started work on the dress. Now, she glanced at the clock and was surprised to see it was after ten. As much as she twitched to vacuum up the mess so she could start tomorrow fresh and tidy, Marilyn would already be in bed and possibly asleep. Brenda picked up her empty tea mug, turned off the light and closed the door.

The tick of the kitchen clock and the hum of the fridge were the only audible noises in the house, and automatic nightlights glowed a soft yellow. She stowed the mug in the dishwasher and walked down the hall to her bedroom, reveling in each picture on the wall, the soft carpet under her feet, and the light fixtures. After thirty-eight years of negotiating with Glen, and the farm winning nine times out of ten, it had been a heady experience having carte blanche with the interior decorating and garden design. Sometimes the delight that sparkled inside her felt almost criminal.

When she'd married Glen, they'd moved into a fully furnished cottage on the farm. Ten years later, when they'd taken possession of the farmhouse, Brenda had tried her best to persuade her in-laws to take their furniture with them, but Elaine had refused. "It belongs here," her mother-in-law had said firmly.

Now Brenda understood. Elaine had waited forty years for new furniture and she wouldn't allow anything to stand in her way. When Brenda had moved out of the farmhouse, her daughter-in-law Lucinda had made her the same offer—excluding the long red-gum table—but the only thing Brenda had taken was the piano.

The moment Brenda left, Lucinda had sold or given away most of the furniture and told Colin it was time to modernize the kitchen and bathrooms. Unlike Glen, who'd always raided the "farmhouse renovation fund" whenever the farm needed cash—leaving it frequently empty so Brenda couldn't draw on it—Colin hadn't hesitated in obliging his wife. Perhaps growing up, Colin had sensed the frosty détentes between his parents and didn't want to live that kind of life. There was also the fact that whereas Brenda's employment had been unpaid domestic work, farm work and volunteering, her daughter-in-law worked off the farm at a bank in Devonport and enjoyed a steady income. Either way, the long-overdue farmhouse renovation had happened and Lucinda now enjoyed a modern bathroom and kitchen, and a beautiful outdoor deck with a view of Bass Strait. Brenda was happy for her.

Familiar with the layout of her new bedroom, Brenda didn't turn on a light to get undressed. After pitching half her clothes into the laundry basket, she laid the rest on a chair positioned for that purpose, found her nightie under her pillow and slipped into bed. The pillow-top mattress welcomed her aching hips. Unlike her many years of insomnia in the farmhouse bed, sleep would come quickly in this one.

Adjusting her pillow, she snuggled into Marilyn's reassuring warmth, closed her eyes and gave herself over to sleep.

CHAPTER FOUR

THE SPARKLING MORNING sunshine found every gap between the glass and the ill-fitting blind and streamed unapologetically into Addy's bedroom. Her eyes hurt and she groaned, pulling the covers higher. Why hadn't she fixed the damn blind? Every morning for a month she'd promised herself she would, but every evening she forgot.

The alarm on her cell phone sounded, playing the quiet and soothing sounds of violin and flute. She ignored them and rolled over. Her temples throbbed in objection. Hell, her entire body objected, demanding more sleep.

Bells tinkled, followed by the moody tones of the French horns and then the sharp metallic beat of a snare.

White pain flared behind her eyes. She flailed toward the nightstand, seeking her phone, but only managed to knock her water bottle to the floor.

The tubas boomed and the high pitch of a clarinet chimed, before the trombones enthusiastically commanded the melody. Then the full orchestra joined in, blasting off the walls, and "Building the Crate" hit its crescendo in all its agitating glory.

Addy's head pounded in agony.

Where the hell was her cell phone? As soon as she found it, she was changing her alarm to Pachelbel's "Canon in D."

Except she wouldn't. On mornings like this, the soundtrack from *Chicken Run* was the only thing that roused her out of bed. It was a complicated choice, but everything to do with her mother was complicated. Rita had approved of the film because of the orchestral soundtrack, so growing up Addy had watched it *ad infinitum*.

She sat up and the room tilted and spun. Her dry mouth tasted of sour grapes and she ran her tongue across her teeth, feeling their thick fuzzy coating. Ugh. How much had she drunk last night?

There'd been drinks at the pub after work to celebrate Lyn's birthday. Addy would have preferred to drink sparkling wine, but she'd downed two beers to avoid unwelcome comments about "girlie drinks." She hadn't wanted to attend, but she knew it was important. As the new team member, and a woman in a male-dominated environment, she needed to work twice as hard to fit in. So far Ravi was the friendliest of her colleagues. Addy couldn't decide if that was a case of keep-your-enemy-close—she got the impression Ravi would apply for the promotion she intended on landing—or if he wanted an ally to stand with him against Jett, Derek and Tim. She was cautiously feeling her way and trying to stay impartial.

Her boss, Grant, who'd so far impressed her, seemed to have the special knack of being in charge at work and still warmly welcomed at staff drinks. In a relaxed way that Addy could only dream of replicating, Grant had moved easily from group to group. They were an eclectic faculty staff group who taught everything from auto mechanics to visual art and design and he'd chatted to everyone about their families and hobbies.

He'd asked Addy a couple of questions about the social media marketing course, which she'd cheerfully answered, but when she'd sought clarification on the budget he'd apologized for "talking shop."

Addy, who preferred talking about work to anything personal, had said, "I don't mind," but Grant had shaken his head. "Drop by my office tomorrow," he told her, then he'd turned to Jett, who was asking him about his new sailboard.

Knowing she had a stack of papers to grade and that socializing in big groups stressed her, Addy had declined the general invitation to stay on for dinner and driven home. She'd read one page of a stack of first essays for the pre-college class she was teaching, sighed, and poured herself a glass of wine from an already open bottle.

God, how she'd needed that drink—the standard of the essays was appalling. She needed to teach them how to structure an essay before she could deliver any more content.

When she'd finally finished grading, she'd opened another bottle and settled on the sofa. That was the drink she deserved—the one to relax her after a long day. She'd sipped wine and watched a couple of episodes of a Netflix show she'd downloaded at work, because the cove's internet was seriously dodgy. After that, she'd scrolled through Facebook just before bed and ...

Her inward breath stalled. *No. No. Please no.* With fumbling fingers, she opened the Messenger app on her phone. She stared at the messages she'd sent—poorly spelled, incoherent, needy and undeniably desperate. Oh God! She had to fix this.

Under the onslaught of a vicious hangover and the tremors of anxiety, her sluggish mind struggled to think. It took her a second to notice the blue ticks next to the messages. Relief rushed in—Jasper hadn't read them!

She was stabbing clumsily on the option to remove the texts when the circle with Jasper's face appeared underneath them. Her entire body cramped. She was ten-seconds too late—he'd just read the messages.

Now, three horrifying wriggly dots appeared on the screen.

More than anything she wanted to look away, but couldn't tear her gaze from it. She reassured herself that Jasper would just take a shot at her grammar. He'd always enjoyed pointing out her failings.

I turn my cell off at night now because your bullshit upsets Ainslea. I've been patient but drunk text me again and I'll block you

Ainslea? She must be the new girlfriend. Of course she was. Before Addy, Jasper had spent a year with an Alyson. The man had an A fetish.

I concede drunk texting unwise, she typed. *I wish you and Ainslea every happiness. Deposit that $5000 you owe me and you won't hear from me again*

Jasper's reply was instant. *You gifted me that money*

I did not!

Like a lot of things you say and do, Addy, you were too drunk to remember. We're done

Fury rose so fast it brought bile to the back of her throat. Why the hell had she texted the bastard last night? Despite what the texts implied, she didn't want him back—hell, she'd moved states and put a body of water between them. And granted she only had hazy recollections about last night, but she remembered word for word their conversation the night she'd lent him the money. How he'd promised to pay her back in three days' time. How he'd shown her the invoices to prove money was coming from clients into his account. How he'd told her he loved her. How she'd foolishly believed him.

"It's just four days, Ads," Jasper had said when she'd suggested they sign something. "Think of the environment. It's not worth wasting paper. The money will be in your account before the ink's dried."

Addy might do dumb things when she was drunk, but the night she'd made the stupid mistake of lending Jasper money she'd been stone-cold sober.

Despite her headache and the nausea churning her gut, her fingers flew. *Deposit the money or I'll involve the law*

She waited for the wiggly dots but they didn't come. Instead of the ticks next to the message being bright blue—meaning it had been delivered—they were faded out.

Jasper had blocked her.

"Bastard!"

Her cell phone's alarm sounded in her hand, this time Stravinsky's *The Rite of Spring,* and she knew she'd lost her window to exercise.

Hauling herself out of bed, she staggered to the shower. Some of her male colleagues might turn up to work looking like they'd slept in their clothes or arrived straight from working in the garden, but she'd learned early on in her career that particular latitude didn't extend to women. If she wanted to be taken seriously in the workplace she needed to dress the part from top to toe.

The noise of the hairdryer—a thousand blades slicing into her brain—almost made her call in sick. But that wasn't an option. She had a full day of teaching, a faculty meeting and two student conferences. Rescheduling that load would only ramp up her stress.

Leaning over the basin, she peered at herself in the old chipped mirror and liberally applied concealer under her eyes to hide the ravages of lack of sleep. After perfecting her make-up, she riffled through her work clothes looking for something clean and pressed.

When she'd arrived back in the cove, the plan had been to wash on the weekends and iron on Sunday nights so she had a week's worth of ready-to-wear work clothes. The plan had also been to paint the interior of the house, but she was yet to crack open a single can of the four sitting on the living room floor. The last five weekends had been consumed by writing the damn social media marketing course. Should she add a section on not drinking and texting?

All she knew was that she needed coffee. Sven's coffee. She found a blouse she'd relegated to the "emergency only" section of her closet— it bulged slightly at her bust, revealing a flash of bra. She swallowed two paracetamol, grabbed her handbag, laptop and car keys, and texted Sven's cafe.

The usual. Addy

The thumbs-up emoji came straight back. If Sven hadn't been married to Gloria for thirty years, Addy would sleep with him for his double espressos and butter-laden raisin toast alone.

An hour later, Addy was surprised to see Grant Hindmarsh walk into the faculty lounge. As she'd turned her car into the parking lot at 7:50 A.M., she'd gotten an email notification from Lyn advising that the early faculty meeting had been shifted to Friday afternoon. She'd assumed it was because Grant wasn't available.

"Morning, Addy. I just emailed you the information you asked for last night to save you a trip to my office."

"That's great, Grant. Thanks." Addy was already reaching for a mug for a much-needed second cup of coffee. "I'm making coffee, would you like one?"

"Thanks, but I can make my own." He smiled his easy grin. "Shame you couldn't stay for dinner. You missed a good night."

"Bad timing. I'd promised my pre-college students I'd hand back their essays today."

"I don't miss the grading," Grant said.

"I bet." But Addy wondered how much grading he'd done as she'd heard from Ravi that Grant had gone from "on the tools" as a working plumber to a management position within a year. Then again, Ravi wasn't as much of a Grant fan as the rest of the faculty so the comment could have been sour grapes.

"By the way," Grant said, "I meant to say last night, I'm hearing good things about the social media course."

"I'm glad." Really glad. She was half-killing herself writing it, teaching it and refining it. "I'm learning a lot too."

"Win-win then." Grant, who was taller than Addy, reached over her head and into the cabinet for a mug. Startled, she leaned sideways, intending to get out of the way, but somehow she managed to swing her chest into his arm. His eyes widened and he pulled back fast, as if he'd made contact with flames. "Sorry about that. I wasn't expecting you to move."

She laughed, wishing she could drop through the floor. Why hadn't she just gotten the damn mug for him and then she wouldn't be in this embarrassing situation.

"I'm not the most coordinated person in the world," she said, trying to cover her clumsy hangover movements.

"So I've noticed." His gaze fell, thankfully avoiding the gap caused by the strain on her blouse buttons, and landed on her legs. "What did you walk into to get that?"

Addy glanced down, uncertain what he was talking about, then noticed the large bruise on her shin. It hadn't been there the day before and she couldn't remember walking into anything. Then again, she was always getting bruises.

"The stepladder and I don't always get along," she fibbed.

He put a pod in the coffee machine and pressed the button. "How's the renovating going?"

"It's not. Work's taking priority at the moment."

"Oh, dear." His mouth quirked up on one side. "I suppose that's my fault."

She rushed to cover, not wanting him to think she was complaining. "Not at all. The blame lies with the drunk driver who ran into Sienna."

"Thank you. Not everyone here would see it that way." He sipped his drink. "And you'll have a lot more time in second semester for your renovations."

More time? Despite her dehydration, Addy's mouth managed to dry further. She'd changed states for this job. Pinned everything on it. Was working insane hours proving herself. How had she stuffed it up in four short weeks?

"You okay, Addy?" Grant asked. "You've just gone white."

Somehow, amidst her panic, Addy managed to say, "Did you just tell me I won't have a job next semester?"

A stricken look crossed his face. "Is that what you thought? Hell, no wonder you've gone pale. Here ..." He grabbed the sugar and stirred some into her drink. "Get that into you."

"Thanks." She took a big sip, needing the hit to soothe her agitation. "So if I have a job next semester, why are you so certain my renovations will get done?"

"Because you'll be teaching less."

That did nothing to dispel her fears. "So you're cutting my hours?"

"Type A personalities ..." Grant shook his head indulgently. "Addy, stop stressing. I'm not cutting your hours. I want to promote you to 2IC, which means less teaching so no weekends spent doing prep."

"Second In Charge, really?" Happiness tapped a soft-shoe shuffle, but her fuzzy head struggled to keep up. "But I'm only a quarter of the way through my probation."

"We both know that's a standard safety clause neither of us was ever going to act on. You hit the ground running and took on the new course without batting an eyelid. We need people like you. The promotion's yours if you want it, but—" his face sobered, "—I think it's only fair to warn you it can be lonely in administration. It's almost impossible to be friends with your colleagues when you have to make the hard calls like not renewing contracts and cutting unprofitable courses to balance the budget."

Addy had watched Grant's interactions with the teachers and, with the exception of Ravi, most of them respected him and his role. There was no reason to anticipate that same respect wouldn't extend to her.

"I haven't really been here long enough to make friends," she said, "so I doubt that will be too much of an issue."

"Well, if there were any issues, you can depend on my support," he said.

"Compared to my last job, that's both reassuring and refreshing."

Grant smiled. "We might be small, but we've been inclusive long before it became a buzzword and a legal requirement. There's no place for big egos here. It's our job to give the students the best possible experience and outcomes, and that means we work as a team. Of course, we do have to operate under the umbrella organization and meet targets. Moving forward, there are some big changes coming from the top, starting with an audit and the implementation of a new quality assurance system."

Addy's mind finally shook off the last vestiges of her hangover and started firing. "That sounds exciting."

He laughed. "Anyone else would be daunted by the enormity of the task. It's why I want you to take the job. We'll be working closely and I'll be depending on you to make sure all the departments are audit-ready while I keep the wheels turning wrangling the budget and course planning. There'll be some long days, but I promise you the weekends will be all yours." He shoved his hands in his pockets. "If I haven't put you off, are you in?"

The chance at a promotion like this had been a big driver in her relocation. That and the need to put distance between her and Jasper. "I'm so in."

"Excellent."

Excitement bubbled. "When's the new job official? From the start of next semester or ...?" Addy crossed her fingers, hoping it was earlier and she could pass over the social media course to Ravi.

"About that ..." Grant's friendly smile dimmed. "Sorry, but to satisfy the bureaucracy, you'll have to jump through all the application hoops."

"Don't be sorry," she said hurriedly, wanting to show she knew how to operate inside the rules. "Of course everything needs to be done by the book. It would be difficult to do the job well if I was battling accusations of favoritism."

"And believe me, that lot would bray if they got even a hint of this conversation." Grant dumped his empty mug in the dishwasher, concern lining his face. "We probably should have talked in my office."

"I'm a vault," she reassured him.

He smiled. "Another reason you're perfect for the job."

"Thank you. I'm really looking forward to the challenge." She started accumulating a mental list. "I haven't seen the job advertised on the portal yet."

"Don't worry. I'll send you the link the moment it's live. Meanwhile have a look at the key selection criteria, and if you want to discuss any of them, I'm free after 6:00."

Addy's previous bosses hadn't shown any interest in her career aspirations. "That's generous."

"Hardly. It's in my best interests to have the right person for the job. Feel free to ask me anything, Addy. Communication is key."

"Thanks. I will."

"Right, well, I better go and tackle my inbox. You have a good day."

"You too."

Addy walked back to her office smiling. For the first time since she'd returned to the island she allowed herself to relax. All her hard work was paying off and the craziness of the last few weeks would soon be over. She'd finally be able to do more than just think about her goals —exercise, eat healthy, drink less and paint—and actually start kicking them.

The only dark cloud on the horizon was getting her money from Jasper. Well, she could be proactive about that too. She opened a browser and typed in *How to recover money from my ex?* then clicked on the link that said *Recovering a small debt in state of Victoria.*

CHAPTER FIVE

THE NEXT COUPLE of days raced past and suddenly it was Friday. Addy had taught two classes before lunch and her break had been consumed by a difficult student. She'd only just managed to wrestle down the ins and outs of copyright and ethics in website design before teaching it, and as soon as the class finished, her cell phone pinged with a reminder—the shifted faculty meeting.

To stay both awake and alert in the meeting she needed food. By the time she'd bought a four-berry smoothie and shoved a protein ball into her mouth, she slid into her seat with a second to spare. Even so, Lyn clicked her tongue.

Ravi gave Addy an eye-roll, which she almost returned but stopped herself. She couldn't afford to be caught mocking the woman's officious timekeeping. Especially not with the upcoming audit when she'd be the one increasing Lyn's workload.

"Before Grant starts, I've got some housekeeping," Lyn said. "We started the year well, but kitchen standards are slipping. The coffee machine was left in a bloody mess at lunchtime today, Tim."

Tim held up his arms under her glare. "Not me this time, Lyn. I've been on the farm all day supervising AI."

Lyn extended her scowl to include everyone. "If you use it, you clean it. Also I'm throwing out all unlabeled food on Fridays at 5:00. You've been warned."

"Thanks, Lyn," Grant said genially. "We appreciate you keeping us on the straight and narrow. A round of applause for Lyn by way of thanks and a promise to improve."

Everyone clapped and then Grant started the formal part of the meeting. After they'd all been updated on the recent announcements from the state offices in Hobart and each section had given their reports, he said, "All of you are working hard in your own little worlds but we're a diverse bunch. I've realized IT don't know what Building and Construction's doing, who don't know what Hair and Beauty's doing, who don't know what Primary Industries—"

"They're doing Artificial Insemination," Jett joked. "Tim's had his arm up a cow's cunt all day."

Addy flinched, but the men laughed.

"My point is," Grant continued, "we need to celebrate the good things, and to that end Ravi's set up an 'Isn't It Great' page on the portal. Addy's kicked it off with one of her digital marketing students' Instagram posts that went viral for Blue Hills Honey." Grant smiled. "But I know Addy's not the only one of you doing excellent work, so don't be shy. Share it with the team."

Jett looked straight at Addy. "Not all of us spend our life glued to our cell phones."

A spurt of anger raised goosebumps on her skin. She'd posted a piece of student work that had nothing to do with her phone.

"If you're uncomfortable with taking photos, Jett, I'm sure when one of your students kicks a course goal they'll happily take a selfie in front of the car or engine or ..." She had no clear idea what they learned in Auto Mechanics, which was the point of the project. "I'm happy to show you how to load it on the portal."

Jett ignored her.

"Thanks, Addy," Grant said. "Great job, team. Anything else?"

"There's a sign-up sheet for paintball," Derek said. "Bit of fun for everyone. Just let me know by next week."

Addy glanced at Lyn, Bettina and Jodi to gauge their reactions, but Bettina was looking at her cell phone and Lyn was riffling through papers.

"In that case, class dismissed," Grant quipped. "Have a good weekend."

The room emptied quickly. Addy returned to her office with the intention of getting out the door as fast as everyone else for a change. It was a glorious evening and she intended to go for a long beach walk and try to enjoy the cove rather than resenting its distance from work.

Just as she was about to log off, a vitriolic email arrived from the student she'd met with at lunchtime. She swore and checked if he'd copied in anyone else. The space was empty but it didn't reassure her —he could have blind-copied many people. Picking up her laptop, she walked down the now quiet corridor, hoping Grant hadn't been part of the Friday-at-5:00 mass exodus.

"Thank God," she blurted when she saw him at his desk. "I thought you might have gone home."

"And waste the most productive ninety minutes of my working week?" He must have caught her confusion because he added, "No interruptions. Come Fridays at 5:05, this place is quieter than the morgue."

"Oh, right. Sorry to be the interruption then."

"Don't be." He stood and cleared away an assortment of papers and what looked like hair dye samples off a chair. "Take a seat and fill me in."

She sat. "Thanks. I had a student conference at lunchtime with Rylie Kendall. He's in my pre-college class and he just sent this email." She turned her laptop around so Grant could read it.

Grant pulled on some reading glasses and scanned the contents. "He sounds like a man-child."

Addy let go of the breath she hadn't realized she'd been holding. "That's exactly what he is. He believes he's too smart for the course and needs to be exempt from the assignments. I gently pointed out that the awarding of a diploma was dependent on him completing a certain number of core subjects that couldn't be skipped, and if he found the work easy then the assignments shouldn't be a problem for him. I explained I couldn't offer him the final assessment early, but he was welcome to sit in on the next unit and decide if he could handle doing both concurrently."

"Students have changed, Addy," Grant said. "Many arrive with a sense of entitlement you and I would never have dreamed of at their age. None would have survived my apprenticeship, that's for sure. Not that things didn't need to change there—they did." He leaned back with a shudder. "No apprentice needs their head shoved down a toilet. But we've got the other extreme here. It sounds like you handled this perfectly and Rylie needs to grow up. But students like this can be a pain in the ... You've done the right thing letting me know."

"Thanks. That's reassuring. Since the college offers the students a variety of ways to resolve complaints, including talking to you, I thought you should know."

"Absolutely. Very wise. Perhaps give Kat in student welfare down in Hobart a heads-up too."

She nodded. "And I'll reply to Rylie's email outlining his resolution options and offering him a chance to talk again."

"Sounds good, but do it on Monday. Don't give him the pleasure of knowing he's made you work on the weekend." He closed her laptop. "So how's your job application coming? You nailed those key selection criteria yet?"

She bit off that she'd had no spare time during the week to open the document, let alone work on it. "It's on my list for Saturday."

He frowned. "We can't have that. Especially when tomorrow's weather forecast is great; a day out of the box. Do you have any plans tonight?"

She thought about the long walk she'd promised herself so she could fall asleep without a drink. "Nothing specific."

"Let's tackle it now."

As tempting as the idea was she heard herself saying, "I can't ask you to do that on a Friday night. It's not exactly a quick process."

"You're not asking. I'm offering." Grant swiped his cell phone. "Do you like Vietnamese?"

The question caught her by surprise "Um, yes."

"Great. Binh delivers, so we can eat while we knock over the questions and both be out the door by 7:00, free to get on with our evenings."

Her already flimsy resistance flatlined. "Sounds like a plan—as long as I'm paying for dinner."

"Too easy."

Everyone in town must have ordered Vietnamese too, because the food arrived just as Addy finished typing in her answers to the final question. As it turned out, the key selection criteria were very straightforward and she hadn't needed any help, but it was good to bounce ideas off Grant. As he cleared a space on his desk for the rice paper rolls, satay chicken and pak choy with oyster sauce, Addy saved the document. She closed the computer just as Grant opened a can and the crack of aluminum and the whoosh of carbon dioxide filled the office.

Grant handed her a black can of cider. "Cheers to a job well done today and in the future."

"Thanks. Cheers." She touched her can to his, then took two long drafts. As she hadn't eaten much all day, it didn't take long for the alcohol to caress her with its sweet promise of peace—it was exactly what she needed. Even so, the speed surprised her.

"Wow. How strong is this?" She searched the writing on the can.

Grant laughed. "6.9 percent. I find it hits the spot fast after a big week."

"Absolutely. I'll have to buy some." The subtle aroma of the food suddenly reminded her she was starving. "This all smells amazing."

"Dig in."

At first the conversation centered on the food, but then they were exchanging stories about their vacations to Vietnam—the breathtaking scenery of Halong Bay, the French influence in Hanoi, and the long history of Hue.

"My marriage hit the wall in Hue," Grant said matter-of-factly.

Full of food and floating on the effects of the hard cider, Addy was only half-listening. She suddenly realized what he'd said. "As in it ended?"

"Yeah. The humidity proved too much for it."

Addy laughed and immediately regretted it. "Oh God, sorry. That was thoughtless and heartless."

Grant shook his head. "Nothing to be sorry about. If I'd known that was all it took, Angie and I should have visited five years earlier."

"Do you have kids?" The question was out before she realized, but Grant didn't look like he thought she'd just crossed a line. She reassured herself that he'd been the one to volunteer the information about his marriage and by default that invited questions.

"No kids. That was part of the problem. We tried IVF but it was a nightmare; Angie didn't cope very well with the drugs." He plowed his hand through his hair as if the memory pained him. "The trip to Vietnam was supposed to be us embracing our childfree life, only while we were there, Angie decided she wanted to keep trying."

"That sounds tough."

"In the end, we both agreed the break-up was a relief." He offered Addy the last of the satay. When she declined, he emptied the container onto his plate. "What about you? Do you have kids?"

"God, no."

His brows rose. "That's emphatic."

"Not really. It's more relief I didn't have one with my recent ex."

"Ah. So that's why you left the mainland?"

"Jasper's only part of the reason. I grew up here and for reasons I can't fully explain, it felt like it was time to come home."

She fought a sudden wave of melancholy for her parents, especially her mother, and picked up her can but it was empty. *Damn!*

"Another one?" Grant's fingers reached for the ring-pull on an unopened can.

"I want to say yes, but I have to drive home."

"So say yes to a quarter. And in the half-hour it takes for your body to get back to 0.05, we can exchange notes on being teens in small seaside towns in the nineties."

She laughed. "Speak for yourself. I was a noughty teen."

He poured cider into her empty can. "I bet you were."

CHAPTER SIX

BRENDA SWUNG her feet onto the footrest of the two-seater recliner sofa she and Marilyn had chosen together and a long and contented sigh rolled out of her. It was Friday night and the promise of the weekend stretched ahead.

"Why are you grinning like a clown?" Marilyn sat down next to her.

Brenda leaned over and kissed her. "Because, my darling, it's the weekend and I have you to myself."

Marilyn laughed and slid her hand into Brenda's. "Almost. It's market weekend."

After years of involvement in many community activities—from the Country Women's Association and the elementary school's PTA, to the cove's seven-day town makeover project—Brenda had scaled right back, giving herself plenty of time to focus on Marilyn. But she'd kept the role of hall management president, because Marilyn had joined the committee. Their most time-consuming job was organizing the fund-raising community markets.

"I'm looking forward to it," Marilyn said. "Life's been a bit quiet lately."

Had it? Brenda couldn't remember a time when she'd been happier.

"I was thinking, if it's a nice day on Sunday we could drive to Stanley and have a picnic," she said. "I can show you the historic Highfield House and you can tick off another north-west experience."

"It might be nice to do it with some other people," Marilyn said.

The comment caught Brenda by surprise. Before she could completely process it, Marilyn added, "We could invite Colin and Courtney."

Goosebumps raised so fast on Brenda's skin, the tingle hurt. "It's a bit short notice."

"At least ask. You never know, they might be free." Marilyn swiveled to face her. "Brenda, I've been here since mid-January. It's time they know I'm far more to you than someone who rents a room."

"You don't rent a room!" Brenda said indignantly. "This is *our* house."

Marilyn sighed. "I know that, but no one else does, and they won't know unless we tell them. We need to start by introducing me to your family as your life partner so we can finally tell the cove."

Brenda's gut spasmed. "I can't tell them without Richard in the room."

"So ask him to come up next weekend," Marilyn said lightly— almost too lightly.

Brenda's heart thumped hard. "You make it sound like I haven't tried."

Marilyn's well-shaped brows rose.

"It's not my fault the government's gone into crisis mode over the housing scandal," Brenda said. "The Premier's cancelled all leave indefinitely."

Marilyn withdrew her hand. "So yet again we find ourselves at the whim of forces beyond our control."

Brenda was suddenly thrown back in time. She was standing at a hot-water urn in a community hall and reaching for the water spigot at the same moment as a striking woman with the greenest eyes she'd ever seen. They both said, "After you," simultaneously, then laughed.

Brenda had found herself blushing, her body electrified by sensations she hadn't known in years of marriage. She put it down to perimenopause and the exhaustion that comes from being a farmer's wife and a mother of three. But by the end of a weekend of talking, laughing and touching, she couldn't deny an overwhelming attraction for Marilyn's mind and body. Her feelings pushed her toward Marilyn and the heady, exhilarating sensation of being alive for the first time in years, but her mind had pulled her back. She'd teetered on a life-changing cliff, torn between two very different worlds.

Brenda had never anticipated she'd be a woman who had an affair and she'd been left floundering by the depth of her feelings. With each passing month, she fell from animal lust into love with Marilyn; but even when she acknowledged that reality, she struggled to call herself a lesbian. Hell, why did her love for Marilyn even need a label?

Besides, being "out" as a couple was impossible—too much was at stake. The children were still at school, and all Brenda's income was tied up in the farm. Glen would fight her for custody and probably win; and she couldn't even start to predict the cove's reaction. She could lose her home, the kids, her community—everything.

Back then, Marilyn had held a senior role in the Catholic Education Office in Hobart and it was a dead certainty she'd lose her job if the powers-that-be found out she preferred women over men. She hadn't made any demands on Brenda other than the one weekend a month they spent together and their weekly phone call. Brenda had never considered any of it a demand—more of a much-needed lifeline —even though the precious weekends meant a cycle of euphoria the week prior and deep misery the week after. Glen had put it down to hormones. Brenda hadn't disabused him. But despite the lows, overall the affair had saved her from almost unrelenting depression.

For years, Brenda and Marilyn had worked around the forces at play and their relationship had not only survived, it had deepened into an abiding love only soul mates share. It was ironic that their dream of finally living together was causing far more ripples in their relationship than the many years apart.

Brenda sighed and gave Marilyn an encouraging smile. "I know it's disappointing we can't tell the family next weekend, but in the grand scheme of things, what's another few weeks?"

Marilyn's moss-green eyes met hers and Brenda glimpsed more than just disappointment. This time, the steely fire of determination glowed in their depths. A lump of dread clogged Brenda's throat and she swallowed, trying to force it away.

Desperate to reassure Marilyn, she picked up her hand and gave it a gentle squeeze. "It will happen and soon. I promised, didn't I?"

And she had. She'd promised it after Glen's death, and again when Marilyn had offered to leave Hobart and relocate to the cove so they could finally be together every day. But from the moment the words had tumbled from her lips, Brenda had wanted to snatch them back.

The thought of telling the children—of telling Courtney—terrified her.

The next morning, Brenda was in the hall bright and early, baking for the market café and setting up chairs and tables covered in cheery gingham cloths. Experience had taught her they enticed the morning-tea and lunch crowd to sit and enjoy her scones, quiches and lemon tarts. She'd also learned that "eat now" frequently resulted in "buy some for later," so the community cake stall was located in the same area.

Most people had delivered their cakes early, but there was still one outstanding donation. Brenda crossed her fingers that the woman who'd texted her after seeing the notice in Sven's window would arrive with the promised carrot cakes.

The hall was a buzz of activity with stallholders setting up, and through the serving window Brenda watched Marilyn and Olivia organizing the trash and treasure. All monies raised were going into the hall's roof fund. When the amount reached ten thousand dollars, a grant would cover the rest and two local roofers had offered their labor for free. So far, the committee had held a trivia night and a movie evening, but the summer markets were their most successful idea. Sadly, as soon as Easter was over, the tourists would vanish until some warmth returned in October. Brenda and Marilyn had been trying to think of other ways to generate funds without always hitting up the locals, but so far they'd drawn a blank.

The hall doors banged open and a woman rushed in, followed by a teenage girl with a "kill me now" look. Both held cakes.

Brenda wiped her hands and came out of the kitchen. "Hello."

The woman, who had what looked like a small blob of cream cheese in her hair, gave a wan smile. "Sorry we're late. Things didn't go quite as planned this morning. My two-year-old wanted to help."

Brenda laughed. "When it comes to kids, help's always a relative term."

"Tell me about it."

As the woman put down her cakes, Brenda noticed Olivia was talking to her daughter. Brenda extended her hand. "I'm Brenda Lambeck and this is my granddaughter, Olivia, and one of our elementary school teachers, Marilyn Rennie."

"It's lovely to meet you. I'm Stephanie Gallagher, but please, call me Steph. And this is Zoe." She motioned the girl forward.

"Mémé!" Olivia's excited bouncing was in stark contrast to Zoe's almost bored look. "Zoe's my friend from school!"

"It looks like you and your mum have baked up a storm," Brenda said.

"Steph's not my mum," Zoe said.

"Oh!" Brenda glanced between the girl and Steph. "I'm sorry, I shouldn't have assumed."

"Don't be sorry," Steph said. "Zoe's father's my partner, Henry. We don't like to use the word stepmother. Thanks to fairytales there are too many nasty connotations." She gave Zoe a pointed "be nice" look that combined frustration and pleading.

Brenda recognized it. She'd used it often enough with teenage

Courtney. Who was she kidding? Occasionally she slipped up and used it still.

"Zoe, it's lovely to meet one of Livvy's friends," she said.

"Mémé, can Zoe stay and help?" Olivia asked hopefully.

"If she wants to and it's okay with Steph."

"Help with what?" A flicker of interest broke through Zoe's mostly disdainful demeanor.

"The trash and treasure," Marilyn said. "Here's an idea. If you girls run the stall, I can help Brenda in the kitchen. Just write list the items you sell with the price, and there's a calculator if you need it."

"We won't," Olivia said. "Zoe's a beast at math."

Zoe shrugged away the compliment. "Okay."

Steph blinked, clearly surprised and relieved. "Great! Have fun."

When the girls had run off to the storeroom to heave out more treasure, she said to Marilyn, "Oh, thank God. I was starting to think Zoe hadn't made any friends."

"Starting middle school's a big transition," Marilyn said. "They go from a small pond to a giant pool. It can take a while for them to find their feet."

"It's been harder for Zoe. She's always lived with her mother in Melbourne and was enrolled to go to middle school there, but—" Steph's eyes widened as if she'd just realized she was sharing too much. She gave a nervous laugh. "Now Zoe has a friend, I'd better find myself one."

Brenda heard the younger woman's stress. "How long have you been in the cove?"

"Since Christmas. But between moving, getting Zoe settled and pregnancy fatigue, I've only just managed to get Monty into a playgroup."

"Why don't you stay and help on the cake stall?" Brenda offered. "I'm cove born and bred so I can introduce you to some of the locals."

"I'm new to the cove too," Marilyn said. "We can meet people together."

Steph gave both women a grateful smile. "Thank you. That sounds wonderful."

The morning whizzed past with the usual crush between 10:00 and 11:00 for Devonshire teas and coffee and cake, and then came the needed lull before the lunchtime crowd. Steph had slipped easily into the role of cake-preneur, promoting "home-made" and "free-range" to the tourists, who'd bought three-quarters of the stock before mid-morning. Marilyn and Steph had clicked and chatted easily. Brenda smiled, loving how she could now watch Marilyn out in the world; although, if she was honest, part of her missed the excitement of their secret meetings in the gorgeous colonial Georgian Airbnb in Longford.

"Looks like the girls are having fun *and* selling things." Brenda pointed to a man holding a little boy who was clutching a stuffed toy penguin to his chest.

"That's Henry and Monty," Steph said.

"Ah! So that's why the girls have just made a big sale."

Steph groaned. "Henry has a love affair with old books. I could understand it if they were first editions, but the paperbacks he buys smell like dust and the glue's always brittle, which means the pages fall apart the moment you start reading them." She stepped out from behind the trestle. "Seeing it's quiet right now, I might just go and see if I can halve that pile in his hands."

"And I'll take a loo break," Marilyn said.

"Mrs. Lambeck?"

Brenda turned. At first, she didn't recognize the younger woman with the short but chic hairstyle, who was wearing a black top tucked into a vivid, multicolored waistband. But when her chin lifted and she smiled—self-consciousness mixed with bravado—she looked exactly like her mother.

"Addy Topic!"

"Guilty."

Brenda rushed to embrace the daughter of a woman she'd considered a friend. "Are you visiting?"

Addy returned the hug. "No. I'm working at the community college."

Back in the day, when Brenda had young children, Addy's mother had been the cove's choir conductor. Brenda had loved Tuesday nights, although she wasn't sure if it was the singing and the camaraderie she loved, or the fact that she'd got to hang up her apron and drive away from the farm and all of her responsibilities.

Brenda stepped back and took in Addy's white sneakers and the riot of color that made up her stunning culottes, before coming to rest on her face with its perfectly applied make-up. It was a far cry from the gangly teenage girl who'd spent every minute she could at the beach surfing or partying. "I can't believe you're here."

Addy's smile was wry. "Neither can I."

"So why haven't I seen you before now?"

"Work's been intense, but I'm treating myself today to celebrate my promotion."

"Congratulations!" Brenda tugged Addy into the kitchen. "Talk to me while I make you ...?"

"Coffee, thanks."

"And ...? There's chocolate-peppermint bars, hedgehog, scones and cream, or lemon tart with cream. All worthy celebration foods."

Addy patted her belly. "Coffee's enough of a vice, Mrs. L."

"Call me Brenda," she said automatically. "And you're hardly overweight."

"I'm hardly underweight either."

"Mémé!" Olivia rushed into the kitchen, her face flushed. "We just found some really old stuff in the storeroom and—"

"Livvy," Brenda said, with a hint of warning in her voice. She loved Olivia's enthusiasm, but at the same time her grandchildren never noticed they interrupted other people's conversations—probably because Courtney dropped everything every time to give them her undivided attention. "I'd like you to meet Addy Topic. Her mother and I used to play duets together at the cove Christmas concert."

"Hi," Olivia said, her eyes widening. "Your pants are deadly."

Addy smiled. "Thank you."

"Mémé, come and tell us what we can sell."

"I'll be there in a minute. I'm just making Addy coffee."

"You go, Brenda," Addy said. "I can make my own, and serve anyone while you're away."

"Are you sure?"

Addy laughed. "I might have been gone a long time, but I haven't forgotten how things work in the cove. Besides, you've written down all the prices and if anyone short-changes me, we know where they live."

"Cheeky! You'll be surprised at how many people you don't know. I'll be back soon."

Brenda followed Olivia back to the stall. Henry, Steph and Zoe were watching Marilyn, who was down on her knees using her apron as a duster on something. Going by the wire on the back, it was a wall-hanging of some sort.

"What do you have there?" Brenda asked.

"It's pretty dusty, but I'm starting to see some gold," Marilyn said.

"I think it's an honor board of some sort."

"It's hard to imagine there's one missing." Henry swung his arm around, indicating the memorial hall's list of past presidents of the Veteran's League, the Country Women's Association and the now-defunct tennis club.

Marilyn rubbed a bit harder, then read, "*Rookery Cove Choir Eisteddfod.*"

Stunned, Brenda stared at the board. "I think this is synchronicity."

"What's that?" Zoe asked.

"Synchronicity is meaningful coincidences," Henry said. "Carl Jung—"

"What's a coincidence about us finding it?" Olivia asked.

"Well, Addy's just moved back to the cove and the eisteddfod choral competition was her mother's passion project."

"We have to do a passion project for school," Olivia said.

Marilyn had cleaned enough of the board to make out most of the writing. "Wow. Most years the cove fought it out with Burnie for top honors, although Penguin and Stanley wrested it away once each." She glanced up at Brenda. "I can't imagine the cove ever being big enough to field a choir, let alone hold an eisteddfod."

"Oh, it was a pretty big deal!" Brenda smiled as memories flooded back. "We held it in the biggest beach cave—the acoustics are brilliant. Choirs came from all over the north-west and it was always a fabulous weekend. The sun usually shone, although one year it was wet and we had to relocate to the hall."

"That sounds amazing," Steph said. "Do you still run it?"

Brenda shook her head. "Rita was the driving force, and when she got sick there wasn't anyone confident enough to take it on."

"Please tell me the choir still meets," Steph asked hopefully.

"No, it was years ago. We tried to keep it going, but Rita's illness came at a time when people's lives were changing." Brenda found herself glancing at Marilyn for a moment before returning her gaze to Steph. "Other things took priority."

Marilyn rose to her feet. "A choir would be great. Steph and I have been talking about the challenges of being new to Rookery Cove and meeting people."

The challenges of being new? Brenda blinked at Marilyn, unable to put the wildly rolling words in her head into a coherent sentence. Since Marilyn's arrival in mid-January, they'd been living in an intoxicating bubble of two. For the first time in their lives they'd been able to luxuriate in each other's company without the threat of time ticking down and the inevitable call back to the real world. Hadn't they said over and over how the new house was their sanctuary? How it was everything they needed? And it wasn't like they were hermits and didn't see people—they helped at the market. But now Marilyn, who met parents at school all the time, was saying she wanted to meet people?

Resistance gripped Brenda. She didn't want to commit to anything that invited the world in to stake a claim on their lives.

"I'm not sure there's anyone in town with the skills to run a choir," she said.

"Don't sell yourself short," Marilyn said firmly. "I've run school choirs, and you've just told us you've sung in one that competed in eisteddfods."

"Yes, but—"

"This is so exciting!" Steph clapped her hands like a toddler. "And singing is so good for mental health."

Zoe rolled her eyes. Olivia laughed. Henry smiled.

More than anything Brenda wanted to say to Marilyn, "Stop! Think about the time running a choir will steal from us." But even if their relationship had been public knowledge, it wasn't a conversation they could have in front of a crowd.

"I'll post on the cove's Facebook page, and mention it in the school newsletter," Marilyn said. "And we can pin up flyers around town asking for expressions of interest."

"I can do that on my afternoon walk with Monty," Steph said.

"It all sounds great," Henry said genially. "Just don't have rehearsals on Wednesday nights."

"Tuesdays work well for me," Marilyn said. "Oh! I just had an idea. This might just be the winter activity the town needs to raise money for the hall roof."

"I'm not sure a small concert will pull in much," Brenda said, desperate to keep a lid on the whole choir idea.

"Probably not," Marilyn agreed.

Brenda's lungs emptied in a rush of relief. Thank goodness Marilyn had realized what she'd been about to commit them to. This afternoon, in the refuge of their garden, they'd brainstorm an easy exit from the choir idea.

Marilyn's face suddenly lit up—full of sparkle and enthusiasm. It immediately took Brenda back to the day they'd met.

"A choir concert wouldn't raise much, but an eisteddfod would," Marilyn said, glancing around to include everyone. "This is something we can do together that's fun *and* good for the cove."

No! A project like this would pull her and Marilyn out of their private bubble and plonk them in the middle of the cove's prying eyes.

But Marilyn was beaming, and Steph was nodding enthusiastically.

Brenda's stomach plummeted, leaving nausea in its wake.

CHAPTER SEVEN

Steph and Henry sat on their new veranda chairs wearing their puffer jackets, determined to enjoy their view despite the chill of the autumn evening. After the excitement of the market and an afternoon on the beach, Monty had sacked out early and Zoe and Olivia were inside.

When the market had finished, Steph had invited Olivia to Four Winds. When the girl rushed off to ask her parents' permission, Zoe's dark eyes had flashed bright with fury.

"Why do you do that?" she'd demanded.

Steph had been momentarily thrown. "Do what?"

"Interfere with my life!"

Interfere? Her mind had spun with possible responses: "I'm trying to help you settle into the cove, you selfish ...!" "We're stuck with each other so work with me!" But she'd reminded herself that she was the adult and it was up to her to rise above the teen self-centeredness.

She'd sucked in a deep breath. "You and Olivia have been having such a great time together, I thought you might enjoy her company a bit longer."

Zoe had crossed her arms and pursed her lips. "You don't know what I enjoy."

Steph was tempted to say "I think we just found something we agree on," when Olivia returned, burbling something about meeting her mother. Steph had wondered if Olivia ever noticed that her excitement was inversely proportional to Zoe's indifference.

Now, faint music and giggles floated down from Four Winds' gable windows.

Steph tucked her hand into Henry's, not just out of affection, but to warm it up. "Today's been a great day."

He kissed her. "It has."

"I'm so glad I offered to bake for the cake stall."

"Me too," Henry said. "Although first thing this morning, when Monty was throwing flour around the kitchen and Zoe was refusing to get out of bed, I wasn't convinced it was your best idea."

She raised her brows. "But?"

"You were right and I was wrong." A look of wonder crossed his face. "I saw Zoe smiling at people."

"A happy Zoe and a choir!" Steph laughed. "If I wasn't pregnant, I'd crack open some champagne."

Henry grinned. "Even the third degree by Olivia's mother was worth it. For a moment there I thought she was going to ask us to produce a background check."

After Brenda's warm greeting, Steph had been a little taken aback by Courtney's intensity. "I suppose she was just being cautious. After all, she doesn't know us."

"Sure, but we don't look like axe murderers."

"Speak for yourself." She tousled his black mop. "You need a haircut."

He snuck a hand under her puffer jacket and nuzzled her neck. "What I need is—"

The sound of someone clearing their throat made them look up. A man stood at the bottom of the veranda, clearly embarrassed.

"Sorry to interrupt," he said.

Steph and Henry scrambled to their feet, their words tumbling over each other: "You're not interrupting", and "No need to apologize" and "Please, come up."

"I'm Ben." He shook Henry's outstretched hand. "Olivia's dad."

"Henry, Zoe's dad."

Steph heard Henry's pride and pleasure at being able to say such an ordinary thing in an everyday situation without seeing surprise on the face of a parent who'd assumed Zoe didn't have a father.

Henry continued: "Great to meet you. This is my partner, Steph."

"Hi, Ben." Steph shook his hand. "Um ... it's not that you're not welcome, but did we misunderstand? I thought Henry was dropping Olivia home at 9:00."

"I'm not sure." Ben shrugged and gave them a wry smile. "To be honest, I just do what I'm told."

Remembering Courtney's intensity, Steph deliberately avoided Henry's gaze, knowing they risked laughing out loud. Since it was only 8:00 and the girls were playing happily, she seized the chance for Henry to chat with another bloke.

"Do you have time to stay for a drink, Ben?" she asked.

"A beer sounds great. I'll go and get—"

The gate squeaked and they all turned. Courtney was walking quickly up the path. As Steph stepped forward to greet her, she wondered why Courtney hadn't come in with Ben.

"Hi, Courtney. We're just about to have a drink. Ben's accepted a beer, so what can I get you? We've got just about everything from herbal tea to a hundred and seventy percent proof."

Courtney glanced at Ben, who shrugged—the action saying that declining would have been impolite. She smiled at Steph. "One drink would be lovely. What are you having?"

"Tonic with lemon." Steph patted her belly. "But if I wasn't incubating this one, I'd have gin in the tonic."

"Oh, wow. Congratulations. How far along are you?" Courtney sat in the wicker chair Steph had lovingly restored.

"I'm about to hit the twelve-week mark and I'm hanging out for the energy burst. Would you like to sit inside? It's getting a bit chilly."

Courtney shot to her feet, looking like a completely different woman from the one they'd met at the market that morning. "I'd love a tour. I can't wait to see what you've done to the place."

Part of Steph groaned. Saturday nights were kick back and relax time and the house was never in its cleanest or tidiest state. "As long as you excuse the mess," she said, knowing it was futile. Despite saying "don't worry about it," many women judged others by the state of their home.

Steph led the way through the open front door and into the living room—one of her favorite rooms in the house. The evening light streamed through the lead-light windows, turning the fresh white walls an inviting peach. The polished floorboards glowed, and the rich colors in the intricately carved oak mantlepiece combined to give the room a warm and welcoming feel.

Courtney stopped just inside the door. "Oh my God!"

"What?" Steph glanced around frantically. Had Monty drawn on the walls? Had the cat thrown up?

"This room ..." Courtney shook her head. "Wow! It's unrecognizable."

Steph relaxed. "So you know the house?"

"Everyone in the cove knows Four Winds. For starters, it looks over the town so whenever you glance up, you see it. And the Dentons were a cove institution. Mrs. D taught violin and Mr. D the piano and singing. This room was their studio, only back then it had dark velvet wallpaper and heavy curtains that were never opened so the students weren't distracted by the birds in the garden. It smelled of wet wool and cats."

"The wallpaper was pretty horrendous," Steph said. "Did you have music lessons here?"

"Not for long. I couldn't see the point of staying inside and practicing when I could be outside helping Dad on the farm. And to be honest, this room gave me the creeps."

"I hope it doesn't now."

"Not at all. You've done an amazing job."

Steph warmed to Courtney. "Thank you. Come and see the rest of the house."

After Courtney had popped her head inside all the downstairs rooms, including the bathroom complete with a full potty, they arrived in the kitchen. Henry and Ben stood around the island counter, beers in hand. Henry had even thrown some cheese and crackers onto a board and found some quince preserve.

"Courtney, I've poured Steph a tonic and lemon," Henry said.

"Would you like a splash of gin in yours?"

"Why not?"

The four of them chatted easily. Ben mentioned that he and Courtney grew up on neighboring farms and had known each other all their lives.

"Courtney wasn't like the other girls," he said proudly. "She just mucked in."

Courtney elbowed him gently in the ribs. "I had to ask him out though."

Ben grinned. "In my head we were already dating."

She laughed. "At least I didn't have to propose."

"I got that right," Ben said. "Surprised her on her twentieth birthday. It's probably the only time she's been speechless."

Steph had to hide her shock at how young Courtney had been when she married. She quickly reminded herself she was living in a small town now.

"You two must have gotten started pretty young too," Courtney said.

Steph glanced at Henry, wondering if he'd respond. He gave her an almost imperceptible nod.

"We met six years ago," she said.

Courtney glanced between them, her eyes lighting up with interest. "So Zoe's Henry's daughter?"

"Best accident ever," Henry said. "Until recently, Zoe's always lived with her mother so I'm loving the chance to be her full-time parent."

"It's not the easiest time to take over though, is it?" Ben said.

"Livvy's pretty easygoing, but lately ..." He shook his head as if he couldn't quite fathom the change. "The other day I caught her screaming in the greenhouse. I told her Woolies supermarkets wouldn't take the berries if her shrieking bruised them."

Everyone laughed. Steph made a fervent wish that Henry and Ben would become friends so they could share stories from the trenches about parenting teen girls.

"Dad's stepping back from the farm and Court and I are starting to put our stamp on things," Ben went on, enthusiasm lighting up his face. "With Tassie being a fave tourist destination, this year we've planted some pick-your-own plants and we're expanding the farm-gate stall into a proper store and a café. We'll use our own jams on the pancakes and sell them too, so people can take a bit of their vacation home."

"That sounds like a great idea," Steph said.

"I have to up my jam-making skills," Courtney said. "Sometimes mine won't set."

"Your mum can help," Ben said. "You know she'll do it if you ask her."

Courtney scrunched up her face, then caught Steph's quizzical look. "I was always closer to my dad, but he died eighteen months ago." Her voice cracked and Ben gave her waist a quick squeeze.

"Mum and I have ... Well, things have always been ... it's hard to explain. She's won just about every cooking prize possible in the north-west, not to mention the Royal Hobart Show, but she never taught me to cook. She says I wasn't interested. I say every time I asked, she'd shoo me out of the kitchen as if I was invading her space. I ended up teaching myself."

"I taught her everything I knew. Boiled eggs and toast," Ben deadpanned.

"We depend on the Thermomix," Steph said.

"Not a wok?" Courtney asked.

Henry laughed. "I do a mean stir-fry, but wontons and dumplings are too fiddly and time-consuming. I buy those."

"I'm determined to take more of an interest in my kids than Mum took in us," Courtney said tightly. "I've been involved right from the start. I was the nursing mothers group president, I ran the playgroup and was on the pre-school committee. When they started school, I became a classroom helper and I'll keep doing that until Jesse finishes elementary school. I've never missed one of Olivia's netball matches, and now she's at middle school I'm on the local school council so I know exactly what's going on. The research says if you get involved in your kids' education they value it too. Not to mention how important it is when they're teens that you know their friends and their friends' parents. It's such a vulnerable age. I mean, you wouldn't drop your toddler off at a house without vetting the parents first, right?"

Courtney's vehemence rocked into Steph like an aftershock and she found herself instinctively leaning back. Part of her was looking forward to Monty starting pre-school so she could get a bit of a break and have some one-on-one time with the baby, but an internal warning said not to verbalize the thought.

Ben was rolling Monty's little wooden tractor back and forth along the counter, the action contemplative. "Come out to the farm sometime so Monty can sit in a real tractor," he said.

"Thanks," Henry said. "He'd love that."

"He really would," Steph echoed, liking Ben and grateful for the invitation.

"You know, these tractors might be something we could sell at the farm-gate store." Ben turned it over and studied it.

"Oh, good idea." Courtney smiled at Ben as if he'd just solved world peace.

"Any idea where they're made?" Ben asked.

"Right here," Henry said.

Ben's brows rose. "Is woodwork a hobby to get you away from the computer?"

"Not me, mate. Steph's the toymaker."

"Yeah?" Ben sounded impressed.

"I made the tractor and an old-fashioned dancing bear from patterns I found in my great-grandfather's shed years ago," Steph said. "Monty loves them."

"Could you make a couple and paint them the same colors as the ones on our farm?" Ben asked. "If we sell them, we could order more."

"That's a great idea," Courtney said. "And paint the name of the farm on them too so it's advertising."

"Steph's focus is on inventory for the online children's clothing store she's launching soon," Henry said. "The toys are just something fun for Monty."

"We're not talking selling on consignment," Ben said. "We'll buy them from you."

"I'm not set up for mass production," Steph began, but the Burtons were looking at her, expectation clear in their eyes. She got a ridiculous urge not to disappoint them. "Sure, I can manage two. Message me a photo of your tractor so I know the colors."

Ben's grin was as wide as a kid's. "Awesome."

"We should get going," Courtney said. "Ben has to be up at 5:30. Can you call the girls?"

"Sounds like they're coming down," Henry said.

Courtney smiled. "Going by the laughter, they're having a good time."

The girls walked in chatting, but fell silent the moment they saw the adults.

Steph did a double take. Their faces were covered in make-up—three shades of bright glitter eye shadow, heavy mascara, lollipop lips and dramatic brows. She recognized the glitter eye shadow as her own, left over from a disco-party charity event a couple of years ago. It probably meant Zoe had plundered all of her make-up.

"Hi, Mum. Dad?" Confusion crossed Olivia's face. "I thought Henry was driving me home?"

Courtney's gaze was glued to Olivia, her face was taut. "*What* have you got on your face?"

"It's the Asian glam look," Olivia said. "We did a YouTube tutorial and—"

"You're not Asian," Courtney said, the words barely escaping from her rigid jaw. She pulled wipes out of her handbag and advanced on Olivia. "Take it off. Now!"

"Mum!" Olivia dodged the wet wipe. "Stop!"

Steph glanced at Henry, who was blinking furiously as if that was enough to change the scene. But she wasn't sure if he wanted to change the image of Zoe looking twenty instead of thirteen or Courtney in full-on tiger mother mode.

"Zoe, why don't you and Olivia go upstairs and wash it off," Steph suggested. "There are make-up remover wipes in our bathroom."

"This is art," Zoe said stonily. "My face is the canvas."

"Zo," Henry said softly, "we're glad you've had fun but now it's time to—"

"Fun?!" Courtney whirled around to face Henry. "You think them making themselves look like sluts is fun?"

Henry flinched.

"Steady on, Courtney," Ben said. "Liv, take it off, please."

Courtney glared at Steph. "Did you know they were doing this?"

"No—"

"So they've been unsupervised all evening doing God knows what!"

The hairs on Steph's arms stood up at the unfair criticism. "They've used my make-up without permission and we'll be discussing that with Zoe later, but don't you remember experimenting with make-up?"

"They're twelve!" Courtney said.

"I'm thirteen," Zoe said coolly.

"Mum!" Olivia's tone was pleading and her eyes glistened with tears.

"And you've given them unfettered access to YouTube!" Courtney said.

"Actually our internet isn't good enough to—"

But Courtney wasn't listening. "Olivia, out to the car. Now!"

Olivia looked at her father, her eyes begging, but he gave her a quick nod. She looked at Steph and Henry, then said in a wobbly voice, "Thank you for having me."

"You're welcome anytime," Steph said.

But the fury etched on Courtney's face said it was unlikely Olivia would be visiting Four Winds again.

After an unrepentant Zoe had stormed off to bed still wearing a full face of make-up, and Steph had climbed into bed exhausted, she said to Henry, "My glorious golden day took a massive nosedive."

Henry snuggled her in close. "We got a surprise is all. The girls were just upset we didn't ooh and aah, and Courtney didn't help by overreacting. It was rocky all round."

"No argument from me."

Henry gave a wan smile. "I know Zoe should have asked before using your make-up, but you have to admit, in its own way it's art."

"She has pretty impressive brush skills that's for sure." Steph rested her head on Henry's chest. "But if she wants to do make-up as art, we can't afford for her to experiment with my pricey MAC."

"I'm sure tomorrow morning she'll apologize for using your make-up and for being so rude."

Steph didn't share his confidence. "Let's hope so. By the way, you'll need to soak her pillowslip before you wash it or the make-up will stain."

Henry yawned. "Remind me tomorrow."

She opened her mouth to say "I shouldn't have to remind you," but Henry's fingers were doing wondrous things so she closed it.

Ribbons of pleasure streamed through her, quieting her thoughts about the last hour and reinforcing that today was the first of many wonderful days to come. She rolled into Henry and kissed him.

CHAPTER EIGHT

THE SUN SHONE, the sea glistened and, despite Addy's fully loaded timetable, happiness flowed through her, dampening the low-grade anxiety that was never far away. She'd been feeling content since the Saturday market a couple of weeks ago—and she was holding fast to it. It was a turning point in her new life.

With her job application tweaked to cover every core value, and floating on Grant's approbation that she was a shoo-in for the promotion, she'd treated herself and visited the market. Walking along the row of white tents in the crooked main street had been weirdly familiar yet utterly strange. There was so much evidence of time having passed. The coffee truck with its state-of-the-art machine, the hemp products stall, the wax candles and the organic body washes had all left her feeling discombobulated. In this tourist-friendly market, her father's eclectic second hand household electronics table would have stuck out like a sore thumb. It wasn't until she'd stepped inside the hall, seen the trash and treasure and Mrs. Lambeck's lemon tarts, that she'd truly felt she was in the cove.

During her time helping in the kitchen, she'd met a few of her parents' friends and all of them had greeted her warmly. She hadn't expected that. Mind you, most were elderly so perhaps they'd forgotten her more public teen rebellions—the beach parties and the rowdy dawn walks home? Or perhaps the cove forgave those who ran away if they eventually returned? All she knew was that she'd walked home from the market feeling lighter than she had in weeks. She'd sat on her peeling balcony with its glimpses of the sea between the trees, eaten Brenda's quiche and enjoyed a crispy sauv blanc. Bathing in the sunshine, she'd daydreamed about similar days in the future when work didn't dominate her life. Days when she could relax.

Only you can make it happen, Addy.

That thought had propelled her out of her chair and into action. Using all her new pens, stickers and decorative tapes, she'd enjoyed a wonderful few hours finally setting up her bullet journal. In big sweeping letters she'd calligraphed *I own this year* on the title page so it was the first thing she saw when she opened the journal. Then she'd created the key, recorded her goals, her focus, and her dreams and affirmations, before attacking the calendar.

She couldn't decide if writing an entire year out by hand was mindful or just bloody annoying. By the time she got to September, she'd lost interest and justified that she had months to transcribe the last four months of the year. Since it was already March, she should have started there, but leaving out the first two months of the year went against her need for order. She'd written out summer's January and February, and drawn a house on the move date and noted the day she'd started work, but they were just pointers to the main game. On the date Grant had offered her the promotion, she'd added starbursts and written *The first day of my new life.* Then, in a celebratory mood, she'd opened a bottle of sparkling wine and cooked herself fish.

She'd enjoyed another bottle watching the movie she'd downloaded at work. Not even waking up the following morning with a thumping headache and having to work all day Sunday had dented the feel-good effect that her year was now in order.

Each morning as her feet hit the floor, she reminded herself she was on top of things and could handle her current teaching workload.

The knowledge that there was an end date to her long workdays buoyed her.

Today, as she crossed the parking lot, she hugged the prospect of her promotion close to her chest and was still smiling when she walked into the administration office. Even if Addy hadn't felt like smiling, she'd have made herself smile at Lyn. It was possible the woman wielded more power on campus than Grant, and Addy already had enough on her plate without upsetting her.

"You look happy," Lyn said.

Addy couldn't tell if this was a compliment or a criticism. She went with compliment. Why open herself up to negativity? Just this morning, she'd written *Embrace positivity* in her bullet journal. Sure, she was yet to open a can of paint, but she'd decided it was more important to map out the plan for *all* the parts of her life rather than obsess over one.

"I am happy," she said.

"Any particular reason?" Lyn asked. "Have you got a man tucked away in the cove we don't know about?"

Addy laughed. "What if I told you I'm happy because I don't have a man?"

"I hadn't picked you for a lesbo."

Addy was offended by the pejorative. "I'm man-free at the moment."

Lyn's eyes narrowed with keen interest. "By choice?"

The intrusive questions weren't work-appropriate. "Long distance rarely works," Addy said lightly then changed the conversation. "I'm happy because I'm two classes ahead with my social media marketing class and one of my pre-college students just wrote something worthy of an 'A'."

"Hah! You sure they didn't plagiarize it?" Lyn said.

Addy swallowed a few choice responses, including "I'm good at my job," and "Haven't you heard of Turnitin?" Instead she settled on the safe "You're hilarious."

"I am," Lyn said. "By the way, you've probably worked out by now this place is pretty blokey. Us girls need to stick together."

Us girls? Lyn had never shown any interest in Addy before.

"Right," she said vaguely.

Lyn nodded. "We have a meal together every Thursday night at the Commercial. You should come tonight."

The few times Addy had tried to chat with Bettina and Jodi in the staffroom, it had been hard to move the conversation beyond celebrity gossip and reality TV. Not that she was averse to a bit of royal scandal, but two hours of it? Addy would rather slice open a vein.

"Sorry, but I teach on Thursday nights," she said, hoping she sounded suitably disappointed.

"Classes finish at 7:30," Lyn said. "We're usually there till 8:00."

People who didn't teach never understood that straight after class was when many students chose to stay behind and ask the question Addy wished they'd asked earlier. It meant she always finished closer to 8:00.

"Fingers crossed no one will stay back." She picked up the documents Lyn had prepared for her. "Thanks so much for these. I'd better run."

At 8:10 that night, Addy was powering down her laptop after teaching back-to-back classes since 4:00. After the last one, Rylie Kendall had delayed her. Again. He frequently hung back, wanting to talk in more detail about the class discussion. At first it had frustrated Addy—why couldn't he have offered this sort of insight during the lecture instead of sitting in musclebound silence? But she'd noticed that after their chats he became far more cooperative and she'd decided it was worth fifteen minutes of her time once or twice a week if it made things easier for everyone, including her. The brilliant essay he'd handed in validated her choice.

She was turning off the data projector when Grant popped his head into the lecture room.

"You're here late. Not going to bitch drinks?"

Bitch drinks? Should she be offended? Then she remembered it was Lyn who organized the "girls-only" drinks, which meant Addy and Grant were on the same page.

"It's a bit hard on a teaching night," she said.

He propped his hip on a chair. "You're welcome."

"Sorry?"

He laughed. "My timetabling's saved you from that particular indignity. Believe me, those women feast on gossip like ravens on roadkill. They'll circle you, then drain you of all your secrets. Best to steer clear unless you want them raising the specter of that rat bastard of an ex of yours when you're least prepared."

"Goodness. That sounds both heartfelt and angsty."

"Yeah, well ..." He gave a tight smile. "Let's just say I learned that lesson the hard way and I don't want you suffering their brand of care and concern. Besides, with your promotion, keeping a polite distance is probably a good idea."

His thoughtfulness circled her. "You might be right."

"No might about it." He laughed. "But seriously—and I speak from experience—your job will be easier if you make friends outside of work."

She slid her computer into its satchel. "By the way, thanks for the email with the job link, but when I tried to upload my application I got an error message."

He sighed. "Bloody HR. They couldn't organize a piss-up in a brewery. Sorry about that. I know you hate being all ready and not able to tick it off your to-do list."

An image of a black dot—the symbol representing tasks in her bullet journal—rose in her mind with the neatly written words *Job application* next to it. Grant was right: she desperately wanted to draw an X over the dot and mark it as complete. But admitting her perfectionist tendencies didn't come easily, especially when Jasper had been the king of the not-so-subtle dig— *why are you so anal about work but you're fine gaining twenty pounds?*

"Really, I'm not bothered," she said.

Grant raised his brows, but his smile was warm.

"Okay," she conceded with a sigh. "You got me."

"Hey, nothing to get. I love that you're so on the ball. Seeing HR stuffed up, email me the document and I'll get Ken to input it into the system for you. Hell, they could do with someone organized like you, which is what I wanted to talk to you about."

"A job in HR?" she asked, confused.

"God, no. I have no intention of losing you to another department. It's the audit. The preparatory stuff's arrived earlier than expected. I feel bad asking you this, especially before your new job's official, but ..."

Panic fluttered as Addy's mind slid to her already overloaded schedule. She couldn't fall at the first hurdle, but how could she take on working on the audit unless Ravi took over at least one of her classes?

Grant's voice penetrated the roar in her ears. "... go to Hobart and do the two-day training."

Addy tried to sound as if she'd heard every word he'd said. "Sure. When is it?"

"Next week? Week after?" He shrugged. "I'll get Lyn to email you everything. Fill in the forms and send them to me and I'll approve the accommodation and travel expenses." He fiddled with his cell phone, then rose. "I better let you get home so you're bright-eyed for the first audit meeting tomorrow morning."

"Sorry? I think I got distracted by thoughts of visiting Hobart," she fudged. "What time was that?"

"7:00."

"7:00?" Her voice squeaked and she cleared her throat. "That's early."

"I thought a breakfast meeting was best. That way you don't need to organize for anyone to cover your classes." Her cell phone pinged.

"That's the pre-reading I just sent you," Grant added. "Really looking forward to hearing your thoughts. Night."

He jogged up the steps and out the door.

"Night," Addy said to the empty room. She swiped her phone and opened the document he'd sent her. Her gaze went straight to the number of pages: ninety-seven.

Dear God. She'd be reading till midnight.

She needed a drink.

On Friday afternoon, Addy was shattered after working a fifty-hour week so she did something she rarely did and left early.

It was a real autumn evening in the cove—clear blue skies, sunshine and an Antarctic nip in the air. She pulled on her Tassie tuxedo—her puffer jacket—and walked down to the beach. The surf lifesaving club's parking lot was full of trucks and the sea was dotted with black wetsuit-clad surfers. Trades peoples' early starts meant the working day was done by 4:00, giving them time to surf after work.

Addy's muscles twitched in memory—arms paddling furiously, then gripping the board hard as she pushed to her feet. The sweet spot of balance. The way her weight turned the board and how she was at one with the wave, riding it into shore. It occurred to her that if she'd become an electrician like her father, she could be surfing every afternoon.

The moment the thought hit, Addy heard her mother's voice: *Don't waste your talent, Aida.*

Even if her mother had allowed her to sign the apprenticeship papers, her father would have objected. Although Ivan had hoped to work in Australia as a journalist, he'd eventually retrained as an electrician at the now closed paper mill in Burnie.

I learned electrics so you can play, sing and bring us joy. The world needs joy, dragi.

When she'd abandoned music, her parents had worn their disappointment in the set of their shoulders and the extra shadow that had joined the ones already in their pain-filled eyes.

Sorry.

Addy had a sudden desire for a drink. A big one.

She turned away from the beach and walked toward the surf club's café. As she approached, a woman with flyaway blonde hair was valiantly trying to pin a poster to the noticeboard while a dark-haired kid wriggled in her arms, desperate to be put down.

"Beach. Now!" the little boy demanded, his legs kicking his mother.

"Ouch! Stop that!" the woman said. "Or there'll be no beach."

Addy stepped forward. "Can I pin that for you?"

The woman relinquished the paper with a grateful smile and hoisted the little boy more firmly on her hip. "Thank you. I really shouldn't try to do things at arsenic hour."

Addy had no idea what she was talking about. "What's arsenic hour?"

"Every minute between five o'clock and seven o'clock when he goes to bed." She gave a strangled laugh. "Tonight, his dad's on the water and Monty thinks he should be out there too."

"It's a pretty nice swell," Addy said.

"Oh, you're a surfer too?" Disappointment clung to the words.

"Once, but not for a long time." Addy glanced at the seductive curve of the bay and longing wound through her. "I really should get back on the board. It's a great stress buster and I need something."

"That's what Henry says. It's part of the reason we moved from Melbourne," the woman said chattily. "We needed to de-escalate our stress. I'd been trying to get pregnant for over a year and as soon as we arrived in the cove—" she snapped her fingers and grinned, "—I was knocked up."

"Congratulations." Addy wondered at the amount of personal information the woman was sharing when they didn't even know each other's name. "The cove's a great place for little kids, although it's tougher for teens. But you've got years before you need to worry about that."

The woman's grin faded. "Not really. Henry's thirteen-year-old daughter's living with us."

"Thankfully, most teens in the cove aren't like me," Addy joked, trying to shift the worry off the woman's face. "And even I came back, so all good."

The woman's eyes lit up with interest. "Are you Addy Topic?"

Addy startled, wondering if her adolescent misdemeanors had preceded her. "I'm sorry, have we met before?"

"No. I'm Steph Gallagher." The woman shot out her hand. "Brenda Lambeck mentioned you the other day."

"Oh, dear, that sounds ominous."

"Not at all. She said your mum was the choir conductor back in the day and you have a beautiful voice." Steph tapped the poster. "It's exciting about the choir, isn't it?"

Choir? Addy's mouth dried as she read the poster.

Rookery Cove Community Choir

Do you sing in the shower? Hog the karaoke mike? Dream of singing in a choir?

Now's your chance!

Come along on Tuesday nights 7.30pm at the hall for singing, fun and good company.

Treat yourself! No experience necessary. Everyone welcome!

For more information call Marilyn.

A phone number followed.

"Who's Marilyn?" Addy asked. In some ways, coming back to the cove was like arriving in a new town.

"One of the elementary school teachers. So far there's Marilyn, Brenda, Vera, Fern, Morgan and me."

"Not Courtney?" Addy asked. "She always sang in the school musicals."

"I don't know." Steph gave an uncomfortable shrug. "I've really only met her once and ..." She sucked in her lips as if working out what to say. "Well, it was all a bit tricky."

Addy laughed. "Sounds like some things haven't changed."

"To be honest, I think choir might be more relaxing without her," Steph said.

"Beeeeee-ch!" Monty wailed and threw his hat on the ground.

"I don't suppose you want to come for a walk and talk on the beach?" Steph asked.

Addy was close to the café door and thoughts of a drink pulled hard. The smooth feel of wineglass against her fingers. The heady moment of anticipation just before the first sip; the promise of relaxation and the quieting of her mind. And the blessed moment the crisp, fruity taste hit her tongue, then took its warmth streaming into her body.

It's Friday night. Say no to the walk. You deserve this drink.

After her huge week, a walk along the beach with a kid calling the shots didn't sound close to relaxing. But despite all of Addy's valid reasons, the loneliness in Steph's voice echoed inside her—familiar with a twist of pain.

"Look! Doggy!" Monty announced.

A West Highland terrier tore past, its little legs working furiously. They watched, horrified, as a truck backed out of a car space straight toward it.

"Heel!" Addy commanded.

The dog didn't slow but slid sideways, thankfully dodging the vehicle. Then it crossed the grass verge and leaped onto the road.

Addy ran. A screech of brakes pierced the air. She gasped and held her breath as if that would soften the coming thud.

"Beach!" Steph yelled behind her.

Addy swung her gaze and spotted a flash of white. The runaway dog was now on the sand, chasing seagulls and arcing back toward the road.

She ran and caught the dog by the collar. Panting hard, she fell to her knees on the sand. "Do you have a death wish, you silly mutt?"

Eyes as round as brown buttons stared back at her from under a shaggy fringe of hair, and then a wet tongue licked her hand.

Steph arrived with Monty and supervised his patting of the unknown dog while Addy checked the collar.

She was about to call the number when she heard a woman's voice say, "Clyde! Oh, thank goodness."

"Is he your dog, Marilyn?" Steph asked.

"He is and he just gave me a heart attack. Thanks for catching him. He slipped his leash as we came down the hill." Marilyn clipped the lead onto the collar and checked the fit. "First thing tomorrow, I'm buying a new one."

"Marilyn, this is Addy Topic," Steph said. "She caught him and she's going to join the choir."

What? Stunned, Addy missed a conversation beat and by the time she opened her mouth to object, Marilyn was speaking.

"That's wonderful! Brenda told me all about your mother and her passion for sharing her love of music. You must be so proud of her legacy."

Addy's heart cramped and she nodded, thankful it was a rhetorical question. Of course she was proud, but that didn't mean the emotion wasn't tangled up with anger, hurt and pain.

Marilyn's round face was creased in a wide smile. "Brenda also said your mother had very high standards, which is a bit daunting. But don't worry—we'll give it our best shot. It's great to have you on board."

Addy finally found her voice. "About that. I think Steph's misunderstood. I'm sorry, but I can't join the choir."

Steph's face dimmed. "But I thought you were keen."

"It's not that I'm not keen," Addy heard herself saying, trying to satisfy the argument in her head. One side posed that she was a bad person for disappointing Steph. The other countered that Steph's happiness wasn't her responsibility. A grip of anxiety tightened Addy's chest. *You do not want to join a choir!*

"It's just work's flat-out at the moment," she said, relieved it was the truth.

"Is your job why you said you needed a stress buster?" Steph asked, far too perceptively.

"Yes, but—"

"You know, Addy, if you're looking for stress relief, choir is it,"

Marilyn said. "They've done studies and proved that singing lowers stress and tension, relieves anxiety and improves our sense of wellbeing. It's also incredibly mindful, because you're focusing on your breath and the song."

Create time to be mindful. The words Addy had written in her bullet journal wove through her mind, tempting her. But a choir? No, it was a bad idea.

"Perhaps later in the year when work's—"

"Last year, the only way I managed to leave work early was on Wednesdays," Steph said randomly. "I'd tuck a yoga mat under my arm and walk out the door. People would see it and say "Have a good one." Any other night, I'd be stopped halfway to the elevators and asked to do something for someone, because going home to my family was considered less important than missing a yoga class."

Addy thought about how when she left the office there was rarely anyone else still working to notice her. "I'm not sure of your point."

"Join the choir and at least you'll leave work on time on Tuesdays."

Clyde barked, straining at the leash, desperate to chase a grazing wallaby.

"I'd better take him home," Marilyn said. "See you both Tuesday."

As the school teacher walked away, Steph said, "I've been in town three months. I work from home and I've hardly met anyone. Meanwhile, Henry gets to surf, which is great for him, but I need something just for me. Choir is it, but Marilyn says we need at least eight singers." Steph looked straight at Addy, her gaze clear and direct. "It sounds like you need something outside work that's just for you too. Why not the choir?"

So many reasons. But Addy wasn't about to share any of them with a stranger when she'd never told the people she loved.

"Please," Steph said.

Please, Aida. If not for yourself, for me.

Addy hadn't heard her mother's voice in a long time, but here on the beach it was as loud and clear as if Rita was standing next to her.

For you? Why? What do you ever do for me?

She cringed at the memory of the unforgiving words she'd flung at her mother when she was sixteen and OCD was stealing Rita from her. Regret draped itself around her like a lead-lined shroud. Was joining the choir a way to do penance? Make amends?

"Okay," she heard herself say.

"Fantastic!" Steph proffered her phone. "Let's swap numbers."

"Great." But her voice cracked on the word.

The moment Steph handed back her phone, Addy said goodbye and power-walked up the hill. By the time the front door slammed shut behind her, she was already at the fridge door and grabbing a bottle of wine.

CHAPTER NINE

BRENDA SCANNED the cloth-covered trestle table in the hall and did a quick inventory: hot water urn, mugs, tea, coffee, sugar, milk, teaspoons and a mixed platter of dessert bars including lemon, jam and chocolate-peppermint. As a nod to healthy eating, she also had a bowl of hummus with some carrot and celery sticks. Still, something was missing, but what? Water! She returned to the kitchen, filled a jug and carried it and some glasses back to the table.

"That looks lovely." Marilyn came up behind her and squeezed her shoulder. "Thank you."

As much as Brenda had wanted to convince Marilyn the choir was a bad idea, each time she'd tried to steer the conversation in that direction she'd faltered. Whenever Marilyn talked about the choir her face shone with excitement and Brenda couldn't bear to burst her bubble. If Marilyn wanted to do this, the least Brenda could do was support her. Making refreshments was the easy part.

"I learned a long time ago that a cuppa and something sweet sets the scene for a good meeting," she said.

Marilyn glanced around the empty hall. "We need all the help we can get."

"It's only just 7:30 P.M.," Brenda reassured her.

A cold blast of air swept in around their ankles and Steph tumbled through the door, quickly followed by Addy.

"Hi!" Steph walked straight up to them, her face shining. "I'm here! I can't tell you how good it was walking out the door and leaving Henry to deal with homework and the dishes."

"I remember that feeling," Brenda said. "Although I always returned to a messy kitchen."

"It's great you've joined us, Addy," Marilyn said.

Brenda was about to say "You look so much like your mother," but the taut look on Addy's face held back the words. Perhaps the choir was bringing back memories of Rita and loss? Brenda was intimate with how grief snuck up unannounced and kicked hard.

Instead she said, "Now you're back living in the cove, I'm hoping you'll get involved in all sorts of things."

"I'm only in the cove for as long as it takes to get the house ready to be a vacation rental," Addy said. "I need to live closer to work."

Sadness fluttered in Brenda's chest. The lifeblood of the town ran through the permanent residents, not the itinerant vacationers. Although if she was honest, of all the people who'd left the cove over the years, Addy wasn't someone Brenda had ever expected to return. Small-town life didn't suit everyone and it hadn't suited Addy. Before Rita and Ivan had arrived in the cove they'd lived far more cultured lives in Europe, and Brenda had often wondered why they'd settled here rather than Hobart or Melbourne. Then again, everyone had their own reasons for doing things that weren't always apparent to others. She ought to know.

Brenda had always had a soft spot for Addy. As a child, she'd accompanied her mother to the choir rehearsals, sitting cross-legged on the floor and listening intently. Although choir had been Brenda's night off from the farm and the kids, she'd often found herself watching the little girl. Her fingers always moved in time to the music as if she was conducting, just like her mother. By the time Addy turned ten, she could play the piano well enough to fill in if their rehearsal pianist was unavailable. Back then, Addy had lived and breathed music, but when puberty had hit, the teenage handbook said: dislike anything your parents enjoy.

"I hope we can change your mind about moving," Steph said to Addy.

"Help yourselves to something to eat and drink while we're waiting for the others," Brenda offered.

"Thanks! I came straight from work and I'm starving." Addy picked up a plate and loaded it with desserts. "Is there anything other than tea and coffee to drink?"

"Water," Brenda said.

"No wine?"

"We can't have alcohol in the hall unless it's an event with a specific license."

"I was just kidding," Addy said.

Other people drifted in, making a beeline for the drinks and food while Marilyn and Brenda pulled the cover off the old piano. Brenda noticed Steph was having an animated, albeit one-sided, conversation with Addy. Her sparkling excitement contrasted starkly with Addy's wary face and silence.

"Addy looks exhausted," Brenda said to Marilyn.

"She said the other day work was flat-out. Do you know what she does?"

"No idea. Something at the community college."

Marilyn checked her cell phone. "We should start. I don't want them thinking we're not organized."

Brenda called out, "Can everyone please take a seat."

The conversations died away, replaced by the scraping of chairs on wood and anticipatory silence.

"Welcome, everyone," Brenda said. "You all know me, but unless you have kids at the elementary school you may not have met our choir conductor, Marilyn Rennie. Marilyn's conducted school choirs in Hobart so we're fortunate she's here to lend us her expertise. Before we start, there are a few housekeeping things. We need to cover the heating costs and the refreshments, so a five dollar donation each week would be appreciated or whatever you can manage. Just pop it in the jar. I'll shut up now and put you in Marilyn's capable hands."

There was a smattering of applause and Marilyn said, "Thanks so much for coming out tonight. I hope you're as excited as I am about the choir."

"Unless anyone else is coming, we're more of a group than a choir," Fern said.

"Is it just a choir for women?" Morgan glanced around. "I was hoping to meet someone. Kidding! But seriously, won't we sound better if we have a deep rumbling baritone?"

"We're open and inclusive," Marilyn said. "We just need to get the word out so people know about us. How about we start with a quick show of hands. Who's never sung in a choir before?"

Steph's hand shot up. She glanced around and the edges of her smile wavered. "I didn't think I'd be the only one."

"A long time ago, I sang backing vocals in a band," Fern said.

"Church choir for me and of course Rita's choir," Vera said. The elderly woman waved at Addy. "You look so much like your mother, dear. Same sense of city style."

Addy shifted in her chair. "Thanks, Mrs. ... Vera."

"As a kid, I went to the Friends' School in Hobart," Morgan said. "We had choir competitions, which I loved. These days, I mostly sing in the shower."

"I belonged to a choir in Hobart and we always entered the Festival of Voices," Heidi said. "Since moving here I've been driving to Stanley. It would be awesome if we could make this happen in the cove."

Addy hadn't volunteered any information so Brenda asked, "Addy, what about you? Been singing lately?"

"No."

The blunt response startled her, but by the time she thought to say something, Marilyn was talking. "Does anyone play an instrument?"

Vera smiled. "I'm a virtuoso with the triangle."

People laughed, and while most were shaking their heads, Fern said, "Ukulele."

Brenda couldn't work out why Addy was shaking her head. "No need to be coy, Addy. I know you play the piano beautifully."

"I haven't played in years." Addy shoved a large piece of lemon bar into her mouth, ending the conversation. The action reminded Brenda of Courtney.

"Who's our rehearsal pianist?" Vera asked.

"Brenda," Marilyn said. "Although the hall piano has a few sticky notes. I thought we'd start the night with some vocal exercises and when we're warmed up we can try a simple harmony. If everyone's in agreement, I'll pop a video up on Facebook to encourage others to join us next week."

"Sounds perfect," Steph said.

"As long as we sound good," Fern said. "We don't want to drive away prospective singers."

"We can always upload a photo." Marilyn smiled. "Right! Everyone on their feet. If you think you're a soprano stand to the right, and if you're an alto to the left."

People moved and then Marilyn said, "Now close the gap and form a circle."

Addy moved next to Steph, connecting the sopranos to the altos. Everyone shuffled until Vera and Fern closed the circle.

"Let's start by loosening our bodies. First the shoulders." Marilyn talked them through their body parts, then demonstrated the dragon curl. "Do it twice. You'll feel longer," she said. "It's fine to bend your knees."

"Am I in the right place?" a male voice said. "Thought this was the choir, not tai chi."

"Come in, Brian," Brenda said. "We're warming up."

Brian Jolly was a retired farmer and a friend of Glen's. They'd met as young men at the Burnie tractor pull, and over the years had shared their love of tractors both old and amped up. Since moving into town, Brenda had found herself running into Brian a couple of times a week.

"Now I want you to sigh," Marilyn said.

"Why?" Brian asked.

"All these exercises help you engage your thoughts, focus the mind, and tone and warm up the voice," Marilyn explained calmly.

Brian looked skeptical, but the women were sighing with gusto.

Long haahs filled the hall, followed by some embarrassed laughter.

"Everyone feeling calmer?" Marilyn asked.

"Yes!" Steph said. "I should do this at home, although the family will think I'm nuts."

"I've told you about the benefits at the end of every massage," Fern said.

Brenda found herself glancing at Addy, hoping the exercises would have softened the young woman's aura of tension. She couldn't tell if they had or not.

"Now we'll sing ascending and descending major scales. I'll sing and then you repeat." Marilyn's voice, clear and strong, rose and fell singing nine "lahs."

Everyone responded.

"Sounding great," Marilyn affirmed. "Now let's give your brain a workout with numbers. We'll sing one, then one two one, then one two three two one, and gradually go up the numbers. You get the idea."

"Crikey," Steph said. "Numbers aren't my strong suit."

"You'll be fine," Brenda reassured her. "And if you're not, we'll laugh with you not at you."

Marilyn led off and everyone sang—some frowning in concentration more than others. When they got to four, Marilyn said, "Stomp your foot on five and clap on two."

Heidi and Addy didn't skip a beat, but as they got higher up the numbers, people faltered, stomping and clapping at the wrong time and stumbling over the numbers. Eventually, laughter took over.

"That's a good one for warding off the Alzheimer's," Vera said.

Marilyn smiled. "And I've got lots more, but if everyone's feeling warmed up, let's start with a round of 'Kookaburra Sits in the Old Gum Tree.'"

"You paid royalties for that?" Brian quipped.

The younger women gave him blank looks, but Brenda remembered the controversy around the Men at Work's anthem, "Down Under."

"We're not performing it publicly so we're fine," she said. She struck an A on the piano and Marilyn got everyone to sing the note.

"Brenda will play the note again and Addy, Heidi and Fern will lead. Watch my hands so you know when to join the round." Marilyn raised her hands. "Ready, Brenda?"

"Ready." She played the note and the trio sang.

Heidi and Fern had perfectly fine voices but when Addy's rich timbre joined them, theirs sounded thin in comparison. Steph did a double take at Addy's voice and missed her cue. She caught up on the second line of the song. Brian's voice boomed in, overwhelming Morgan's and Steph's, and suddenly song became noise.

Marilyn stopped it at the end of the second round. "Okay then. Not bad for a first go," she encouraged.

Brenda's heart swelled with unexpected pleasure and pride as she watched Marilyn working with the choir. Her arms itched to hug her and tell her how amazing she was, but instead she picked up the sheet music and passed the pages around.

"We thought we'd kick off with the Beatles as most everyone's familiar with them," she said.

"Belting out the Beatles is my specialty," Brian said.

"I love 'Blackbird,'" Morgan said as she read the title.

"Thanks, Brenda," Marilyn said. "Now we're going to split up for a bit and learn a simple harmony, then regroup. Sopranos, come with me."

Brenda watched Marilyn walk away with the confidence of someone who knew what they were doing. She swallowed her rising anxiety. Playing piano had always been her private pleasure—a chance to escape her life when physically leaving the farm had been impossible. She'd played less since she'd moved into town, the need to escape having vanished. But now she needed to play in public and that stressed her and fumbled her fingers.

"Who can read music?" she asked.

They all shook their heads.

"No problem," she lied. "I'll play it once so you can hear and then we'll have a crack."

She wiped her sweaty palms on her jeans and managed to get through the chorus without making a mistake.

Steph's shoulders slumped. "That doesn't sound like the song."

"The sopranos carry the melody and the altos add the harmony," Morgan said.

"When it's combined, it will sound familiar." Brenda crossed her fingers that would happen. "Let's give it a shot. Ready?"

She counted them in, but found she couldn't play and sing. And Brian's singing came a close second to yelling.

She tried to channel Marilyn's positive approach. "I love your enthusiasm, Brian, but unless you're singing a solo part, a choir's about melding voices so everyone shines."

Brian gave her a blank look. She groaned inwardly, regretting she'd let Marilyn talk her into this.

"You're singing too loud, Brian," Morgan said easily.

"Just knock the volume back a bit," Brenda said gently, not wanting to hurt his feelings.

Brian touched his forehead with his forefinger. "Will do. You're the boss."

You're the boss, Bren. For the first time in months she heard Glen's voice. It unsettled her and she couldn't work out why.

"Let's take it from the top," she said.

Two hours later and back at home, Marilyn handed Brenda a cup of tea before sitting next to her, nursing a glass of whisky.

"Well, that was interesting."

Brenda gave Marilyn's thigh a gentle squeeze. "I think the Facebook video idea was probably overly ambitious."

"It shouldn't have been," Marilyn said defensively. "Four of them have previous choir experience."

"Unfortunately, their experience is no match for Steph's off-key enthusiasm or the volume of Brian."

Marilyn laughed, but it was strained around the edges. "Well, we got there in the end, even if it was only the chorus. Hopefully, it will bring people in." She sipped her drink. "Talking of people, I thought Courtney would come."

"Music's not really her thing."

Marilyn frowned. "I thought you told me once she'd been in *Little Shop of Horrors*."

A prickling tingle shot along Brenda's spine. She had no recollection of telling Marilyn that, but over the years, cozied up during their special weekends together, things about the family had inevitably slipped out.

"That was high school. She hasn't done anything since."

"What did she say when you told her about the choir?"

"I don't know."

Marilyn sat up. "What do you mean you don't know? You talk to Courtney almost every day."

Brenda's gut cramped at the hint of accusation. "We haven't discussed the choir."

Disbelief crossed Marilyn's face. "For two weeks we've done everything we can to get the word out and you haven't even mentioned it to her?"

The prickling sensation turned to heat, making Brenda itch. She pulled off her cardigan. "I doubt Courtney wants to sing in a choir with her mother," she said briskly, needing to kill the conversation. "What daughter would?"

"God, Brenda. She's thirty-four, not thirteen!"

Brenda wanted to say that often Courtney's actions were

reminiscent of a teen, but stayed silent because that would only point the conversation to places she didn't want it to go.

Marilyn pivoted slightly to stare straight at her. "I can't believe you didn't invite her when you know we're chasing numbers. The choir's important to me, and for it to work it needs more people."

"We have nine. Considering the size of the cove, it's a good start."

"You're playing the piano and I'm conducting. We have seven." Marilyn crossed her arms. "You need to ask Courtney."

Brenda didn't want Courtney in the choir before she'd told the family about Marilyn. And before she could do that, she needed to feel Courtney out and see some signs that she wouldn't fall apart and completely freak out. But Marilyn's mouth had lost its softness and was flattened in an unfamiliar hard line. The tug of opposing forces pulled so strongly that pain radiated from deep in Brenda's solar plexus.

The lie rose swiftly in an act of survival. "I'll talk to Courtney."

"Thank you."

Marilyn leaned forward and kissed her—lips soft against her own—and Brenda's world steadied.

CHAPTER TEN

Steph arrived home from choir at 9:30. After a night of freedom from the responsibilities of being a parent, she found the kitchen exactly as she'd left it. Cooked food was still in the wok, dirty dishes were stacked haphazardly in the sink and on the counter, and the fully loaded dishwasher hadn't been switched on. Monty's toys lay scattered around the house instead of away in their basket. Zoe's homework stretched across the table, her school hoodie lay where it had been thrown on a chair, and what looked suspiciously like the remains of a bowl of ice-cream with caramel topping was balanced precariously on the arm of the sofa. Half a load of clean laundry was strewn next to the laundry basket as if someone had chucked out the contents until they'd found what they were looking for.

Irritation jabbed Steph as she snatched up the scattered laundry and stuffed it back into the basket. Her hand stalled on a white pillowcase with black stains. Did the washing machine need a clean? She studied the marks more closely—it was mascara! Henry hadn't soaked it as promised.

Frustration morphed into anger, sucking the lightness from her post-choir happy bubble. She balled the material and threw it hard into the basket.

"Henry?"

There was no reply.

After checking all the downstairs rooms she eventually found him upstairs in their bedroom.

His face lit up when he saw her. "Oh, great, you're home. Do you know where my lucky socks are? I want to wear them to the ultrasound appointment."

"Second drawer."

She'd learned long ago not to question Henry, or any of the Suns, on their family's need to surround themselves with things she considered superstitious nonsense when in most situations they only trusted numbers. She accepted it was a cultural difference. Besides, she quite liked Henry's idea that they build a koi pond, even though for her it was more about aesthetics than believing koi brought good fortune and prosperity.

"Thanks." Henry retrieved the socks, then crossed the room to kiss her. "How was choir?"

"It was fun." She knew she should elaborate and tell him all about it—from Addy's phenomenal voice and Brian's need to question everything to Marilyn's calm and unflappable manner—but the shambles downstairs was firing resentment along her veins. "What happened here while I was gone?"

Henry glanced around their bedroom, clearly confused.

"Nothing."

She clung tightly to the leash on her temper. "I meant downstairs."

"What about downstairs?"

Steph didn't know where to start. "Dinner's still in the wok. Zoe didn't pack up her stuff—"

"Oh!" Henry gave a rueful grin. "By the time we finished her bloody history homework and set up her cell phone she was knackered, so I let her off the hook. When did seventh grade get so hard?"

"Wait, what?" Steph thought she must have misheard. "Did you say phone?"

"Yeah." It came out on a long sigh.

Steph took a breath, trying to keep her indignation at bay. "What happened to the 'no cell phone until eighth grade' rule?"

Henry grimaced. "Joanna bought it for her and mailed it to the school along with a note to the principal saying I was preventing her from talking to her daughter."

Rage ignited, giving Steph heartburn. "You are joking!"

Henry grunted. "I wish. But when have I ever joked about Joanna?"

"How can she afford to buy Zoe a cell phone?" Steph asked.

"It's not the latest one."

"But they're still expensive! And Zoe doesn't need a cell phone. Joanna rings her on the landline, which is way more reliable than the mobile."

"At Four Winds it is, but not anywhere else," Henry said.

Steph was struggling to make sense of Joanna's train of thought. "But at school cell phones have to be switched off and put away, so she can't call her there anyway."

Henry's hands plowed through his hair and he threw her an aggrieved look. "It's power play. Pure Joanna. It means she can bypass Four Winds completely and not talk to me."

"But she sent her down here to live with you—us!" Steph crossed her arms, suddenly ticked off with Henry's inability to stand up to Joanna. "You should have told Zoe she can't have the phone."

"Be fair! How could I?" Henry implored. "It's the first time I've seen her excited and happy about something in weeks. Me saying no would have been like slapping her." He sat down on the bed, shoulders slumping. "Besides, the principal already thinks Joanna sent it because I'm being difficult. Imagine what Zoe would tell him if I said she couldn't use it."

Fatigue suddenly hit Steph like a train. "Okay, fine, but there have to be rules. She can't be on it all the time."

Henry barked out a laugh. "She's lucky to get one bar of reception here, and Joanna's not stupid. She bought her a prepaid SIM, so guess who's the sucker paying for it from now on?"

"Make sure you limit her data."

"Of course."

"And to earn the monthly recharge, she can't just sit up in her room all the time. She needs to participate in our lives, which includes picking up the mess that's currently trailing between downstairs and her bedroom."

"It's hardly a trail." Henry caught Steph's hand and kissed it. "Come on. Let's go and tidy up so we can go to bed."

"No!" It exploded without warning and she was horrified to feel tears prickling the backs of her eyes.

Henry's brows rose. "Is this a pregnancy thing?"

"No. It's a ..." Her brain grappled to find the right words.

"A what?" His eyes scanned her face, seeking clues. "I don't understand. We always clean up together."

He sounded so reasonable and yet all she wanted to do was scream at him. "Yes, but not tonight!"

"Because you're tired?"

"No, because I've been at choir and choir's *my* thing."

He frowned. "I'm not following."

She puffed out a breath. "Surfing's your thing. When you surf, I deal with things on my own. Tonight you were supposed to deal and not wait for me to come home and help!"

"I didn't wait for you to come home. I told you—the homework was a nightmare made more complicated by the cell phone thing. Zoe only got into bed ten minutes ago."

Steph opened her mouth to say "I help with homework while I'm clearing up," but Henry continued talking. "And to be fair, when I surf you come to the beach with Monty and relax."

"Only on Fridays." Her voice rose on a wave of aggravation. "And building sandcastles isn't relaxing!"

"Okay." He held up his hands. The action wasn't surrender—more like indulging an overtired child. "Why don't you have a nice warm bath and I'll bring you up a cup of tea?"

She wanted to tell him that she wasn't tired, she wasn't being irrational and that he was totally missing her point. But whether it was the adrenaline of the fight or the time of night, exhaustion now dragged at her.

A sigh as long as the choir exercise blew out of her. "Thanks. That sounds great."

But she didn't make it into the bath. By the time Henry returned with the promised mug of tea, she was fast asleep.

During the first choir rehearsal, Steph learned that Marilyn ran a very tight ship, which left virtually no time to chat or get to know anyone. Of course she'd joined the choir because she wanted to sing, but she was also desperate to make friends. Addy, with her chic haircut and sense of style, had captivated Steph at their first meeting, and when Addy wore linen pants and a silk blouse to choir, Steph had audibly sighed. She remembered a time when she'd worn those natural fibers, but once Monty had arrived she'd stopped. One-second of holding him on her hip crushed the fabric and one sticky handprint on her blouse meant the silk required dry-cleaning.

Her desire to befriend Addy wasn't wholly driven by her need for a friend or their similar ages. There was something about Addy that reminded Steph of herself before she'd had Monty. Freedom? A career? She quickly told herself she was starting a business, even though many days it felt like that plan was treading water. Whatever it was about Addy, Steph was determined to kickstart the friendship. With that in mind, she texted Addy a couple of days before the second choir rehearsal suggesting they have dinner together at the surf club and go straight to rehearsal from there.

Addy had called her with a counter offer—catch up after rehearsal because she worked until 6:00. "I'll only just make it back to the cove in time for choir."

"But nothing's open at 9:00." Steph couldn't hide her disappointment. Ideally, she wanted to spend time alone with Addy, but was it better to invite her to her home even if it risked them being interrupted by the kids and Henry? "We could come back to Four Winds—"

"No."

Addy's firm reply left Steph wondering if the woman was genuine about catching up. "Um, okay. What about your place?"

"I don't think so. It's a nineties time warp and I work a minimum of fifty hours a week."

"I'm not Courtney Burton," Steph said with far more tart than irony. "I won't arrive expecting a tour."

"Even so, I'm not sure ..."

Steph desperately wanted to make this work. "I won't judge you if you have dishes in the sink and your bed's not made."

Addy made a choking sound. "I'll hold you to that. My office is in better shape than my house."

"So that's a yes?"

Addy had sighed. "Sure. Why not?"

So after their second rehearsal, Steph drove Addy to her Finch Lane house and followed her inside. Busy glancing around, she almost tripped over a container of sugar soap. Then she noticed cans of paint, a brand new roller and tray, a sealed drop sheet and two cases of wine. One appeared to be doing double duty as a coffee table with the TV remote and a mug sitting on top. The swirly brown carpet, the wallpapered feature wall and the faded furniture combined to give the house a melancholy air. Steph shivered as if tendrils of sadness were wrapping themselves around her. If she had to come home to this every night, she'd be in a pit of despair.

Once in the kitchen, she was delighted to find brochures for blinds on the countertop along with some tile samples.

"You're renovating! How exciting." Steph fingered a tile and laughed. "Well, mostly exciting. Henry and I almost got divorced over bathroom tiles. We eventually found one we both liked, but there were a few weeks there when I doubted it would ever happen."

"That's one problem I won't have." Addy was holding up an almost empty bottle of sauv blanc. "This okay? I've got a great red if you'd prefer. Happy to open another bottle."

Shocked surprise made Steph blink. How had Addy forgotten she was pregnant? "No need to open another. The baby's not a fan of either."

"Oh, right. Sorry."

For a second Steph thought Addy looked disappointed. Was her pregnancy triggering sadness in the other woman? After all, they were both in their thirties—a time when the biological clock shrieked as insistently as a whistling kettle.

She quickly filled the silence. "Water's fine, unless you have peppermint tea?"

Addy set the wine bottle on the counter, then opened the pantry and stared into it. "I've got detox tea."

"Detox?" Steph had never heard of it. "What's in it?"

"Not sure. I bought it as part of my healthy eating plan." Addy studied the box. "Sweet fennel, lemongrass and verbena. No caffeine so baby-friendly."

"Maybe I'll stick to water."

"Are you okay with me having a glass of wine?" Addy asked.

"Of course! It's not like I'm not drinking because I have a problem."

Addy laughed. "I've heard that the first four months with a baby is enough to drive you to drink."

"It has its challenges that's for sure, but totally worth it. Are you interested in having kids?"

But Addy's head was back in the fridge and she didn't appear to have heard her. When she turned back she was holding a bottle of mineral water. "I hope Australian's okay. I try to buy food based on the least number of global transport miles."

Guilt prickled Steph. "Good idea. I need to get better at that, but in the middle of winter I get tempted by out-of-season fruit."

Addy pushed the bottle of mineral water and a tumbler across the counter for Steph. Then she emptied the remains of the wine bottle into her own glass.

"It's handy I'm not drinking," Steph said. At Addy's blank look she added, "Saves you opening another bottle."

"True." Addy lifted her glass to her nose like a wine connoisseur, breathed in deeply and took a long sip.

It took Steph a moment to realize there wasn't going to be an invitation to return to the other room and sit on the sofa, so she seated herself on a kitchen stool. Despite the fact that Addy had already sampled her drink, Steph held up her wineglass, wanting to mark the occasion. "To new friends."

Addy smiled and clinked Steph's tumbler. "As long as it doesn't include Brian."

Steph embraced the moment of simpatico. "Oh my God! The man's a nightmare! Why does he have to question *everything*? If I was Marilyn, I'd have brained him by now."

"He's a man of his generation," Addy said.

"Thank goodness our generation's got a better quality of man," Steph said emphatically.

Addy's mouth twisted. "I'm not sure we can agree on that."

Anticipation fizzed in Steph's veins. Was this the moment Addy would open up and share? Up until now she'd been really vague about her relationship status—past and present.

"Are you coming out of a bad break-up?"

Addy cracked the seal on the bottle of red wine and for a moment the only sounds were the hum of the fridge and the glug-glug of the ruby red liquid.

"I can't say that any of my break-ups have been good," she replied, and took a deep drink as if it was water rather than wine.

Steph tried not to be distracted by the fact that Addy hadn't used a clean wineglass. "I think it's easier when the break-up's your decision, don't you?"

"I wouldn't know."

Steph, who'd done her fair share of dumping men, couldn't believe Addy had never ditched a bloke. "Sorry."

Addy shrugged. "Perhaps I'll add 'dump him first' to my bucket list."

Steph felt the need to caution, "Only if he's a dick."

"Highly likely. I seem to be attracted to those." Addy spun the glass. "What are Henry's redeeming qualities?"

"He's hands-on with the house and the kids."

"Cleans the bathrooms, does he?"

"He dusts and vacuums."

Addy's brows rose. "Because he doesn't clean the bathrooms to your standard?"

Steph chuckled, but her chest felt a little tight. "There might be something to that. I read once that if you keep criticizing they stop altogether."

"Well, I'm no expert on relationships, but in the workplace if someone refused coaching in areas they needed to improve, they'd lose their job."

"Maybe," Steph mused. "Then again, I've worked with people who appear to take suggestions on board and then cheerfully do their own thing. Henry and I work to our strengths."

Addy laughed. "Not sure I'd describe cleaning toilets as a strength, but we do what we need to do to make it work, right?"

Steph wasn't certain she understood what Addy meant, only that it made her prickle with discomfort. She picked up a tile from the counter and changed the subject. "I like this one. We've just finished renovating Four Winds, so if you need the names of any tradesm—people—"

"Thanks, but the point is to spend as little as possible," Addy said. "I'm doing the bulk of it myself."

Steph couldn't help glancing around at the very dated décor and appliances. "Wow, it would be a big job even if you weren't working crazy hours."

Addy grimaced. "Ask a busy person ..."

"If you need a hand with the painting, I've got skills,' Steph added. "I did the decorative friezes at Four Winds."

"I'm not doing anything fancy," Addy said. "Just cool whites, but first I have to wash down the ceilings and the walls."

An idea burst into Steph's mind. "Why don't I come over on Saturday afternoon for a couple of hours? We could crank up the music and get the living and dining room prepped."

Addy stared at her. "I can't ask you to give up your weekend."

Should she confess that she wanted some time away from Zoe and Monty and the only way to get it was to walk out the door?

Or that she really wanted to get to know Addy better? No. Both confessions made her look needy. "You're not asking. I'm offering." For the first time, Addy's smile lost its restraint. "Well, if you're sure, that would be great."

Steph almost said thank you, but stopped herself in time. "Do you need me to bring a ladder?"

CHAPTER ELEVEN

STEPH WAS HUMMING "BLACKBIRD" as she used her scroll saw to cut out the pieces for Ben Burton's tractor toys. After the Burtons' abrupt departure two weeks earlier, she'd wondered if they still wanted the toys. But Ben had texted her a photo of his tractor and today had unexpectedly fallen into place, providing time to do the small job.

The hospital had rung at breakfast to reschedule her ultrasound for the second time—two weeks earlier the machine had broken down, and today the radiographer was sick. Steph had to stop herself from telling Henry his lucky socks didn't seem to be on top of things. The rescheduling didn't bother her unduly. Of course she wanted to see the baby sucking its thumb and floating in its safe cocoon, but the ultrasound would happen eventually. And unlike the early weeks with Monty, this pregnancy was much easier. She'd thrown up less—which could only be a good thing—but the fatigue was much the same.

Dovetailing with the ultrasound cancellation was a miraculous five hour vacancy at the cove's day care. Monty had happily toddled into the hall, which looked very different from the set-up for choir rehearsals. There was a fenced-off area for the ride-on toys, a story-time mat, beanbags for resting and a snack corner. Monty had made a beeline for the food-truck toy. She'd left him chattering away and making hamburgers, and had grabbed a chai latte from Sven's before coming straight to her shed.

The plan was to have the tractors assembled and ready for painting by the time she picked up Monty. Her humming changed from "Blackbird" to "Down on the Farm," a song from her own childhood, and she laughed. Since joining the choir, she was singing and humming a lot. She'd sung on the afternoon she helped Addy wash down the walls, although Addy had turned the music up so loud she'd barely heard herself.

It had been a great two hours and as they'd worked she'd told Addy about the difficult year that had triggered her and Henry's move to the cove. Addy was yet to share the reasons behind her move—in fact she'd hardly said anything—but then again, had Steph let her get a word in? Probably not. She'd been too excited about one-on-one time with a girlfriend and had taken advantage of being in the company of a good listener. Next time, she'd do a better job and it would all be about Addy.

"Bugger!"

Lost in her thoughts, Steph hadn't turned the wood in time. Now she had a wheel with a flat edge. She turned off the scroll saw, drew another wheel, switched on the machine and tried again.

Although she'd slept soundly last night and Monty, bless him, hadn't woken at 3:00 A.M., she felt sluggish for some unknown reason. She wished she could down an espresso and spark up, but for the sake of the baby she was avoiding caffeine. She rubbed the ache in her lower back that always came with using the scroll saw.

It's important to stretch, Steph. She heard Fern's voice in her head. She slid off the stool and did dragon curls until her fingertips brushed her toes.

Feeling better, she returned to the tractor pieces, did a quick count and started the assembling and gluing process. As she squirted plastic glue, her mind wandered to her never-ending to-do list. Due to pregnancy fatigue, the baby preparation list was growing faster than her ability to complete tasks. She was itching to get busy in the nursery and as soon as her second trimester energy levels kicked in, she'd start sketching the frieze. She smiled, remembering the joy she'd experienced painting Monty's room in Melbourne three years earlier.

She'd offered to paint a beach-themed motif throughout Addy's place to give what was essentially a residential home a vacation vibe.

"People don't want to vacation in a house that reminds them of their own," she'd told Addy. "Working off a template of sea green, sky blue and sand yellow will bring the beach inside. Then you can add in white furniture and bright cushions. With the stenciling, it will pop on Airbnb as a must-stay place."

Addy had glanced around the tired house with a bewildered face, as if she couldn't picture it ever looking fresh and enticing. "I'm not great at decorating ideas."

Steph had grinned. "Lucky for you, I am."

What about Zoe's room? The thought landed so hard, Steph winced.

During January, when they'd all thought Zoe's room would only be a vacation retreat, Steph had discussed the different ways her stepdaughter might put her stamp on the decor. Zoe had not only been enthusiastic, but overflowing with great ideas. Steph had even drawn some preliminary sketches for a frieze of dolphins and one of turtles. But those collaborative sessions had taken place before hormones had kicked in and replaced bright and chatty Zoe with sullen and difficult Zoe. Steph had a strong suspicion that dolphins would no longer cut it, but she was loath to discuss decorating with the girl in case she insisted on the room being painted jet black.

Steph clamped the glued pieces of the tractor cabin together so they'd bond. When the glue set, she'd sand the wood and the next day she'd paint. Did she have the correct blue? She was checking her paints against the photo Ben had sent when her phone rang. Henry's name lit up the screen.

"Hi," she said.

"Hi. I've got good news!"

"The internet's finally working like it should?"

"Nah, not that good, but close. I forgot to tell you the range-hood company rang while you were dropping Monty at day care. They've okayed Gerry to deal with it. He's coming in five minutes."

"Yay!" They'd spent a fortune on a "quiet" range-hood, except theirs sounded like a jet engine. There'd been almost as many phone calls about it as the internet. "Hopefully he can fix it on the spot and we can finally tick it off the list."

"Fingers crossed. Can you keep an ear out for Gerry and let him in?" Henry asked.

"Um, why? I'm in the shed and you're inside."

"Actually, I took a walk to the point to clear my head after a pretty confronting conference call."

Steph's hand tightened around her phone. Why had he gone for a walk if he knew Gerry was coming? "Why didn't you tell me?"

"I didn't want to interrupt you."

Every muscle in her body tightened like a pulled bow. "But you're letting Gerry interrupt me."

"Sorry about that." Henry sounded sheepish. "I got the call just before Sam threw a tantrum about his testing snafu and it pushed Gerry's coming out of my head."

Henry's apparent inability to write things down on a sticky note or throw them onto their shared digital calendar drove Steph nuts.

"Where are you now?" she asked.

"Sven's. How about I grab one of Gloria's chicken, avo and camembert paninis for lunch?"

"That sounds great." She appreciated he was solving lunch and forgave him his forgetfulness. Hopefully Gerry would be late as usual so Henry would be home to meet him and she'd finish the gluing. "See you in five."

There was silence on the line then Henry cleared his throat. "Um ... I didn't bring the car."

Resentment smashed so hard into her, she shook. The distance from town to Four Winds was at least a twenty-minute walk.

"Walk fast," she managed to get out between gritted teeth.

"Coo-eee," Gerry's voice called out.

"Oh, great, now Gerry's here so there goes half an hour at least," Steph said. "You'll need to pick up Monty so I can finish the tractors."

"What time's that?"

"2:00." She made a mental list of all the things she needed to do before then.

"Sorry," Henry said. "It's Wednesday." He had recently dusted off his school trombone and joined the Burnie Brass Band.

"You don't have band till 7:00," she said, trying not to sound as ticked off as she felt.

"I'm going to Burnie to use the library's internet to run the training," Henry said. "It makes more sense for me to do another hour's work after that and go straight to band. I put it on the calendar."

The bloody calendar! He never remembered to put his activities on it. A flinty feeling made her ask, "When did you put it on the calendar?"

There was a beat of silence. "About five minutes ago."

"Henry!" So many words crowded her mouth, she couldn't decide which to fire first. "Why does your job always come ahead of mine?"

"It doesn't. It's just you're a bit more flexible at the moment because you're not meeting deadlines."

"I have a deadline for the tractors!"

"No, you don't," Henry said amicably. "Ben's happy for whenever."

"What about making hats? I never get to—"

"Anyone home?" Gerry called out.

"Gerry's calling—I have to go."

She stabbed the red button on her phone so hard she jarred her finger. Yet again, working in her childfree window was completely shot.

♫

Addy drove into Hobart, took the turn onto Sandy Bay Road, passed the university and smiled. The first time she'd arrived in Hobart on her own it had been by bus. Eighteen years old and filled with equal parts excitement and anxiety, she'd hopped off at the university stop, only to discover the residence halls were seven hundred yards away at the top of a very steep hill. She'd lugged her suitcase as far as the Herbarium when a family had pulled over and offered her a ride. Initially grateful, Addy had quickly regretted getting into the car.

"And your parents let you come all on your own?" the mother had inquired, judgment clear on her face.

"I insisted," Addy had said.

It was the truth. When the university offers had come out and her parents realized the reason Addy hadn't been offered a position at the Conservatory of Music was because she'd withdrawn her application, Rita's silent anger and Ivan's sadness had filled the house to breaking point. Addy hadn't wanted their sorrow accompanying her to Hobart. She'd craved freedom from their weighty expectations, from the intensity of her mother's illness, and the ever-present disappointment that she'd let them down. She craved freedom from the cove.

Her university years were a blur of study, hall parties, inter-college sports and college raids. She laughed, remembering the time they'd driven to the summit of Kunanyi, filled a student's pickup truck with snow and brought it down the mountain. They'd built a snow wall in the middle of College Drive, then sat back and enjoyed the shocked surprise on drivers' faces, fast followed by the grumpy realization that they couldn't drive any farther.

When she graduated, real life had intervened. She'd gotten a job and moved into a house that wasn't student digs and where she no longer woke up to find random people sleeping on the sofa. It had taken longer for her to lose the habit of waking up to random men in her bed.

Addy pulled into the Wrest Point conference center's parking lot, checked her hair and make-up in the rear-view mirror and touched up her lipstick. She toed off her driving flats, slid her feet into heels and gotten out of the car, checking her skirt was straight and her blouse was buttoned correctly. Gripping her work satchel, she followed the signs to the conference room.

As she approached, she took some long, slow, deep breaths. Walking into a room full of people she didn't know was a certain type of hell. Although she experienced it at the start of every semester with new students, it was worse when she wasn't the one in a position of authority.

You can do this.

When she entered, her heart leaped into her throat. She swallowed hard to budge it. People stood in groups, chatting, holding cups and saucers and juggling sandwiches. Addy found her name tag—the only one remaining—on the table and made a beeline for the lunch set-up. God, she wished it was five o'clock and she could have a drink. With a slightly trembling hand, she shoved an espresso pod into the coffee machine and stared at it as if that would make it brew faster.

"Addy! You made it."

She spun around and was suddenly facing Grant. Her heart rate slowed at his familiar face. "Hello!" Confusion immediately followed. If Grant was attending the conference, why hadn't they shared the four-hour drive? "I didn't know you were coming too."

"They've tacked the audit training onto the end of the annual management conference. I've been here since Monday." He smiled. "You'll be at the conference next year."

"Is it always in April?"

He laughed. "You're going to put it in your calendar now, aren't you?"

She laughed too. "I like to be prepared."

"I know. Come and meet some of the Hobart people before the first session."

♫

The first session outlined how the Australian Skills Quality Authority, ASQA, was changing to student-centered auditing.

"This shouldn't be an issue for us," Heather, the presenter, said. "We've always prided ourselves on delivering quality education, not just compliant coursework."

Heather pressed her remote clicker and a photo of worried-looking people appeared on the screen. "But change ramps up anxiety and that's where you come in. Your job is to prepare the teachers for the audit, as well as to highlight areas requiring improvement before ASQA shows up. Ideally there won't be many holes, but each campus is encouraged to undertake a self-assessment."

Grant leaned in and said quietly, "And you're the perfect person for this because you're new. You'll notice the things we've missed."

"Noticing is one thing," Addy whispered. "Forcing change is another thing entirely."

"You're not alone," Grant said. "Together we'll make the Bass campus shine."

As Heather discussed how the audit followed the student's experience, from their very first contact with marketing material to enrollment and through to completion and certification, Addy relaxed into Grant's words. She had a gut feeling she'd need his support with at least one staff member. Jett struck her as someone who did his own thing regardless of what ASQA expected.

After talking for fifty minutes, Heather split the attendees into small groups to workshop a variety of different scenarios. Addy noticed Grant and the other campus heads were separated into their own group. Her group was a mixed bag—one woman who voiced her disdain for the endeavor, a bloke who kept gazing out the window at the yachts sailing on the Derwent, and two other people who looked to Addy for guidance.

Unlike in social situations, at work she was happy to lead. She uncapped a marker pen and smiled. "Let's do this."

CHAPTER TWELVE

After Gerry left Four Winds, it was time for Steph to pick up Monty, and the rest of the afternoon was consumed by mothering and domestic tasks. That evening, when she was cuddling Monty in the rocking chair and reading him his current favorite book—*The Big Book of Tractors*—she struggled to stay awake. Weariness dragged at her limbs and her back continued to ache from sitting on the stool in the shed. Perhaps she should look for an adjustable bar chair on Facebook marketplace—one that gave some lower back support.

"Want the red tractor!" Monty's chubby fingers tried turning back the page.

"You can go back to the red tractor, but that means there won't be time to see the green tractor."

Steph loved Monty dearly, but after his few hours at day care he was totally wired, overtired, and had been testing her patience since two o'clock. By dinner, he'd worn her down to the point of screaming and she had no intention of allowing him to draw out the story and prolong the day any further. All she wanted was to kiss him goodnight and close the door, knowing a happier and more compliant child would wake in the morning. She also had the kitchen to deal with—Monty had thrown more food than he'd eaten.

"Green tractor!" he demanded.

Steph smiled and turned the page. Reverse psychology still worked on him like a charm—unlike his half-sister.

They finally reached the last page and after Monty had lovingly touched every single tractor, she tucked him in, told him she loved him and escaped. As she reached the landing, she heard the television. Zoe must have finished her homework.

Steph walked into the family room and saw Zoe's binder books and the contents of her pencil case spread across the table along with her now empty dessert bowl. Her school backpack lay beside the chair and Steph glimpsed the turquoise of the insulated lunch bag inside. Zoe was supposed to put the dirty lunchbox on the kitchen counter and the cold pack in the freezer as soon as she got home so everything was ready for the morning.

Steph's gaze moved to Zoe—she was on the sofa with her cell phone in her hands. It was always in her hands, especially at night, because for some reason—be it cool temperatures, thermal currents, who knew—they often got two bars of reception.

Steph sighed. Henry was at band rehearsal so she had to deal with Zoe. "You got all your homework done?" she said brightly.

Zoe rolled her eyes. "No. That's why I'm sitting on the sofa."

Don't react. Steph tried a deep breath. Her backache intensified and she rubbed it with her knuckles. "Now you've finished, I need you to pack up, please."

Zoe didn't look away from the screen. "I'll do it later."

"Now, please. You know the deal: we tidy up before we sit down and relax."

"Geez, Steph, calm your farm."

What horrible beast had swallowed up the delightful and compliant little girl and left this sarcastic and obnoxious person in her place?

"I'll be calm when you've tidied up." Steph glanced at the

television, checking what Zoe was only half-watching. With their internet issues, local over-the-air television was their only option and the show looked like a repeat of something from earlier in the week. "You can do it in the next ad break if you like."

Zoe's mouth flattened into a stubborn line. "I'll do it when I'm ready."

A red light flashed in Steph's brain. As exhausted as she was, she knew this was a line-in-the-sand moment. She'd noticed that when Henry asked Zoe to do things, she grumbled but eventually carried out the task. But since Zoe had returned to live with them full-time, she'd become increasingly resistant to most of Steph's requests.

Steph moved in front of the television screen. "This isn't open to negotiation, Zoe."

"You're not the boss of me."

And I don't want to be. The thought struck like a sniper's bullet, shocking her.

She'd known Zoe for almost as long as she'd known Henry. She liked the child, but during the long periods when Zoe hadn't been around she'd never given her much thought. She'd considered the arrangement pretty simple and straightforward—Zoe was Henry's child, ergo his responsibility. On the occasions Zoe had visited them in Melbourne and come on vacation with them, Henry had been in charge.

Now, as much as Steph wanted to continue being the hands-off adult, moments like these took away her choice and forced her to parent. Hell, she hadn't been given any choice about Zoe moving into Four Winds.

She took a steadying breath. "While you're living here, you're subject to the rules of this house just like Monty, Henry and me. That means packing up before you sit down to watch TV or play on your cell phone."

Zoe didn't look up from the phone. "Dad doesn't make me."

Steph knew Henry had packed up for Zoe the night of the first choir rehearsal, but was he continuing to do it? Lately, she'd fallen into a pattern of putting Monty to bed, then staying upstairs to sort clean laundry or steal some reading time, only coming downstairs as Zoe went to bed. If she was honest, she did it so Henry helped Zoe with any outstanding homework not completed before dinner. The homework Steph found herself supervising, along with wrangling a tired and fractious Monty and cooking the evening meal, on the many nights Henry surfed. By the time she came downstairs, Zoe's things were usually cleared away.

"I'm not your father—"

"You think!"

The muscles in Steph's back spasmed and a bolt of pain corkscrewed down her thigh. She sucked in her lips, forcing her gasp down deep. Getting angry wouldn't help.

"Zoe, I'll overlook the attitude if you tidy up now. In fact, let's do it together and then we can have hot chocolate and watch *Letters and Numbers*."

·"That show's lame."

God! For years it had been Zoe's favorite game show. Steph didn't have the energy for this. Why wouldn't Zoe meet her halfway? Why wasn't Henry home and dealing with her?

She blew out a breath. "We can find a show you want to watch, but if you don't pack up now the consequence will be no phone and television."

"Ooooh, consequences." Zoe waved her hands for extra emphasis. "Dad's not here and I need the cell phone to talk to *my* mother. You're not her so you don't get to tell me what to do." She turned up the volume on the television.

Anger bloomed in Steph's chest, severing the bonds of restraint as fast as a blade. It quickly spread into every cell, fanning the ache in her back around to her belly. She fought the urge to sit down and instead grabbed the remote and turned off the television.

"Look at me," she demanded.

Zoe kept her gaze fixed on her phone.

Steph's barely stitched-together patience snapped. With the skill born of wrangling a toddler she swooped and grabbed the device off Zoe. "I have *never* pretended to be your mother! But if you want to continue living in this house, you'll live by the rules and do as you're told."

Zoe stood, her height almost a match for Steph's. She glared at her, her eyes full of loathing. "Make me."

"Pack. Up. Your. Things!"

"Give. Me. My. Phone!"

"Stop being such a brat!"

Zoe lunged for her phone. Steph instinctively ducked, but she overbalanced and fell backwards, knocking into the corner of the coffee table. She rarely swore, but as pain ripped through her an expletive bounced off the walls.

Zoe paled, her eyes suddenly huge in her face. "I ... Are you o—"

"No!" Steph rubbed the tender space between her ribs that had connected with the corner of the table. "It bloody hu—"

Her belly contracted, the spasm bringing her knees up to her chest. She instantly stilled, not daring to move in case it intensified the pain. Eventually, the cramp eased and she tentatively relaxed, slowly blowing out a long breath. As she opened her eyes, she felt a sticky dampness between her thighs.

No!

Another cramp hit, stronger than the first. She refused to name it, but it didn't care whether it was named or not. It was staking a claim on her body and overruling her wants and needs.

A different kind of pain assaulted her and the pull to lie down and rock almost overwhelmed her. *Stay there, baby. Stay!*

Move. Get help. She rolled over onto all fours, preparing to stand.

Zoe screamed. Then in a barely audible whisper said, "There's blood. On your ... your pants."

It will look worse than it is, Steph reassured herself, but her body didn't believe her. Her heart pumped giant waves of panic, making her limbs shake.

She forced herself to her feet. "Find ... my ... phone."

Zoe stared at her for a second as if she hadn't heard, then she ran to the kitchen.

Steph made it to the bathroom and pulled down her pants. She gasped at the amount of bright red blood and immediately tensed her pelvic floor. A sob rose to the back of her throat and stalled, cut off by the eviscerating cramp of her uterus.

Stay there, baby. Please stay.

"Steph?" Zoe's voice was muffled by the closed door. "Dad's coming home."

But Henry was half an hour away. What should she do? Call an ambulance? It occurred to her that an ambulance would probably come from Burnie, just like Henry.

"Give me my phone!"

The girl cautiously opened the door, silently shoved the device at her and retreated.

Sitting on the bathroom floor, Steph called the hospital and spoke to a midwife. She was advised to clean herself, put on a pad, go to bed and wait and see.

"If the pain or bleeding worsens then come straight in," the midwife said. "Otherwise, we'll see you at 9:30 tomorrow morning for an ultrasound."

"So you think the baby's okay?" Steph managed to ask, craving reassurance.

There was a quick beat of silence. "I know it's scary and hard, but right now all we can do is wait and see. Is there someone there with you?" the midwife asked.

Steph caught a glimpse of Zoe hovering just outside the bathroom door. It was enough to fan the flames of her fury. "No one I can depend on."

"Then call a friend to come and sit with you until your husband gets home."

As the midwife rang off, a text came in. *Tried to call. On my way. Love you. Henry xx*

Steph bit her lip, trying not to cry. Henry should be here. If Henry had been here all evening instead of leaving her alone with Zoe, none of this would have happened!

She wished her own mother was still alive. Wished she wasn't all alone.

Call Addy!

Addy who listened and nodded her interest at all of Steph's stories. Addy who'd accepted her offer of help. Addy would come.

With fumbling fingers, she pressed the woman's name and raised the phone to her ear. *Pick up. Please pick up.*

"Lo." Addy's voice sounded muffled.

"Addy, it's Steph."

"Steph!" Addy had never sounded this animated during any of their conversations.

"Can you come over? Henry's out and I don't want to be alone."

Her voice cracked. "I'm bleeding."

"Bleeding?" Addy sounded confused. "Call reception for a band-aid."

"What? No, I'm ... it's the baby." Tears spilled, running fast down her cheeks. She swiped at them with the back of her hand. "Please come over."

"Where?"

"To my place."

"What room's zat?" Addy's voice slurred.

Room? Was Addy drunk? "I live at Four Winds, remember?"

There was a long silence, eventually broken by the clinking sound of glass on glass.

"Addy, are you there?"

"Hmm."

Steph hated asking again, but desperation drove her. "Addy, can you come to Four Winds? Please."

"I'm in a room with a view." Addy giggled. "Not Florence. Ho-bit."

Steph's anxiety ramped up. "You're in Hobart?" Addy hadn't mentioned a trip at choir or when they'd been washing walls.

"Work conference. Wrest Point. Come see my view. It's room

three um ... wait! I know!" There was a crashing noise and a thump. "Fuck! That hurt. Bring chips and chocolate, okay?" The line went dead.

Steph stared at the phone in disbelief as dread swirled inside her. Addy was partying in Hobart. Who else could she call? She had Fern's number, but for all the woman's prayer flags, incense and soft lyrical voice, she always managed to make Steph feel like it was her own fault she was stressed. God knows what Fern would say about a threatened miscarriage.

Loneliness circled her, tightening its bonds and blurring her vision. Somehow she managed to press Henry's number, but it went straight to voice mail, meaning he was in the mobile dead zone. She was on her own.

Sucking in a deep breath, she tried to steady herself. She could do this. Henry would be home soon. What had the midwife said?

She grabbed a washcloth and cleaned herself up, and pressed a clean pad into her underpants so she could gauge the blood loss. Not that there was going to be any more, because the cramps had thankfully eased. She'd panicked for no reason. She knew a bit of bleeding in pregnancy was common; she'd had spotting with Monty. It didn't mean disaster.

Snuggle in, baby. Sit tight.

Steph sat a little longer, anxiously checking her pad. Nothing.

Thank you!

The bolt of relief momentarily slumped her, stripping her body of strength. The midwife had said lying down was best so she needed to go to bed. Rising cautiously, she crossed the bathroom.

Just as she reached for the door-handle, a heavy dragging feeling filled her vagina and then it felt like a lump of jelly rolling out of her. She gasped, intimate with the feeling—she often got blood clots with her period—and she clenched her muscles tight against it, desperate to hold it back. To keep it inside her.

But nothing would stop it. There was a gluggy plop, then a gush and warm liquid ran a river down her legs.

She fell to her knees, hearing the agonizing sounds of an animal in distress—keening and wailing.

"Steph!" Zoe opened the door. "Are you ... is the baby ...?"

"Go to your room!" Her precious baby was dead and all she wanted was to be alone.

Zoe hesitated, her eyes wild with fear. She took a hesitant step forward. "I want—"

"Get out!"

Zoe's face crumpled and she turned and fled.

Monty's cries drifted downstairs.

Steph lay on the gray and white bathroom tiles she'd lovingly chosen and sobbed.

CHAPTER THIRTEEN

AT THE END of the training, Addy was pleased with the work her group had contributed to the session. She was rolling up the butcher paper when Grant walked over.

"Coming to the bar, Addy?"

"Sounds great, but I should check into my room first and freshen up for dinner."

"Still plenty of time for that and I want you to meet Jessie Chin. She's your counterpart in Hobart, but she's wrangling kids tonight so she isn't coming to the dinner."

He guided her out of the room and along an enclosed walkway.

In high heels, she struggled to keep up with his long strides.

After about two hundred yards she said, "This place makes you work for a drink."

Grant laughed. "Almost there."

Addy heard the swell of noise and then they were in the bar and Grant was introducing her to Jessie and taking drink orders.

"I can get my own," Addy said.

"Let him battle the line," Jessie said.

Addy fished ten dollars out of her wallet. "Sauv blanc, please."

Grant pushed the money back at her. "You buy the next round."

As he walked away, Jessie said, "Don't look so worried. He'll hold you to it. Grant's one of the good ones."

"What do you mean?"

"Put it this way. I wouldn't accept a drink from every bloke I work with," Jessie said. "Some of them would automatically assume it meant something more, but not Grant."

"That's good to know." Jessie's words reassured Addy that for once in her life she'd made a correct assessment of a man.

"He tells me we lured you back from the mainland," Jessie said. "And you're kicking goals with social media marketing."

"Really?" A puff of pride flattened some of her anxiety. "Most days I feel like I'm barely one step ahead of the students."

"You're not. After Grant talked you up, I checked out your course components. Your brand awareness tactics are impressive. I'd love to pick your brain, because we need to tweak our program. Perhaps we can video chat next week?"

"Absolute—"

"Here you go." Grant handed her a glass of white wine. "Cheers."

"Cheers!" Addy closed her eyes, took a hefty sip and sighed.

When she opened her eyes, Jessie was laughing. "That sums up today perfectly. Everyone needs wine after Heather's training sessions."

Addy joined in the laughter. "God, I needed this during the role-play."

"You aced that," Grant said.

"You really did," Jessie said. "I was just grateful you took one for the team."

Between the wine unravelling her tension from the day and the warmth of the praise, Addy relaxed into the conversation. The three of them chatted easily and after Jessie left to pick up her kids, Addy and Grant were absorbed into another group. There was plenty of shop talk, which Addy appreciated and enjoyed. She bought Grant a beer and herself a second glass of wine.

She was about to excuse herself so she could check in when Heather called out, "Our table's ready."

Stunned, Addy said, "It's barely six o'clock."

Grant nodded, his smile rueful. "Be thankful we managed to convince her 5:30 was too early."

They moved as a group to the restaurant. Addy found herself seated opposite Grant at the end of a table. Rob, from Launceston, was next to her, taking up more than his fair share of space. Her left shoulder was pressed against the wall to avoid touching his beefy arm, and his leg kept brushing hers. At first, Addy wondered if he was going to be handsy, but it appeared the touching was more of a manspreading issue, because apart from a polite hello, he mostly ignored her. Usually after she'd enjoyed a couple of drinks, Addy's sense of humor was on fire and appreciated, but Rob was immune—he didn't crack a smile at any of her jokes.

Grant did his best to include her in the conversation, but it was hard going as Addy knew nothing about building and construction and Rob seemed determined to always swing the conversation back to his area of expertise. At least the bottle of red wine she'd bought to share was as big and bold as the description notes promised. Rob had stuck to beer, although Grant had accepted a beer glass. While she ate her tender-as-butter steak, she mentally ran through the best way of introducing the Bass campus faculty to the new audit process.

Addy was still savoring the cabernet sauvignon when dessert arrived. It was bad enough being forced to eat at an hour that belonged to young children and the elderly without being rushed through two courses. She intended to finish her wine, then eat her Pavlova.

She was just taking the last sip when there was a scraping of chairs and everyone rose at once. Calls of "better get home", "must call the wife" and "see you tomorrow" filled the room, then Addy found herself left alone at the table with Grant.

She rolled her eyes. "The big night out's over by seven o'clock? I guess that marks us as the singles of the group."

He laughed. "You're not that different. I bet you're about to head to your room to do Heather's suggested pre-reading."

That was exactly what she'd intended, but something about the way he said it made her reply, "Actually, I'm going to squander twenty dollars at the casino."

He leaned back in his chair and studied her. "This *is* a new side of Addy Topic."

She tossed her head. "Why waste Hobart?"

He laughed. "That's the spirit!"

They settled at a roulette table and Addy chose a Banker from the cocktail menu—Kahlua, tequila, Galliano and coffee—to inspire her. Grant ordered a rum and cola and, in keeping with the drink, stuck to betting on black numbers. Addy alternated between red and black and played a street rather than risking all on one number. Expecting to go down in four straight bets, she clapped in delight when she won on the second throw.

"I can't believe it! I always lose."

Grant rubbed her arm. "Pass on some of your good luck to me."

She laughed and held his hand as they placed their bets. This time she chose red for fun and seventeen for her birthday.

The croupier pressed the button and the roulette wheel spun, the white ball bouncing wildly. She held her breath. Grant squeezed her hand.

The ball landed on red seventeen. "Oh my God!"

"Congratulations!" Grant hugged her as his chips disappeared under the croupier's stick. "You're buying the next round."

"Too easy."

As if on cue, a waiter stepped forward inviting drink orders.

Addy placed some chips on his tray. "Two 'Lark Cask 58%'."

"Addy, that's too much," Grant said.

"Only if you don't like whisky and then it's a waste. Do you like it?"

"These days you can't call yourself a Tasmanian if you don't," he said.

"In that case, we're spending my winnings on something we'll both enjoy."

His grin lit up his eyes—all smoky sex appeal. "Well, what's a guy to do if you insist?"

She leaned in and dropped her voice. "He goes along with whatever I say."

He saluted her, then closed the gap between them. "Yes, ma'am."

She laughed and returned her attention to the table, choosing her next numbers. She won on the next two throws and her squeals of delight drew a small crowd around them. Glowing under the attention, she bantered with the croupier, Grant and the bloke next to her.

By the time the whisky arrived, Grant had won thirty dollars and lost ten and Addy was up another seventy.

Grant picked up the glasses. "Whisky of this caliber deserves to be enjoyed somewhere quiet and with a view."

"You can't leave in the middle of a winning streak," the man next to Addy said.

But as much as the game was exhilarating, the whisky was calling. She downed the last of her Banker and stood. The room spun and she swayed on her heels. Her hand shot out and she gripped the edge of the table, steadying herself before taking a step.

"Miss! Your chips," the croupier said.

"Oh God!" Addy facepalmed and turned to collect the small stack. "I'm not used to winning."

Grant kissed her on the cheek and whispered, "You're a winner tonight, baby."

His breath teased her ear and she shivered in delight, holding on tight to the riot of feel-good sensations pumping through her. She was hot. She was sexy. She was a winner. She could do anything!

Grant handed her a glass and proffered his arm. "Come on!"

"Bye, roulette!" She was teetering on her heels so she happily linked her arm through his. "That was so much fun!"

"Still plenty more of that to be had."

Grant led her out of the casino and outside to the boardwalk.

The nip of night air and the wind off the water lightened the fuzz in her head.

"The lights are pretty," she said.

Grant pointed to a tower. "That's Saint George's Church in Battery Point."

"You know your convict Hobart landmarks."

"Just that one." He sipped the whisky, savoring it. "God, Addy, thank you for treating me. It's amazing."

"Right?" She laughed. "I worked at Lark when I was a student and developed tastes far beyond my means."

He snorted. "Middle-class trauma."

Thoughts of how a war had deprived her parents of their culture, careers, status and money tried to sneak in under her euphoria. She took a big slug of whisky to keep them at bay.

"My father worked at the paper mill. I'm a working-class girl."

Grant rolled his slightly unfocused eyes. "You've got more class in your little finger than everyone we work with, including me."

"It's all show." The words were out before she could stop them.

Grant stroked her cheek. "If it is, it's a bloody good one."

She could feel herself slipping toward the darkness she drank to avoid, and refused to go there. Not tonight. Tonight was about enjoyment and fun and kicking back. It was definitely not about talking about herself. She didn't want sympathetic Grant; she wanted party Grant.

"Forget that bastard, Jasper," he said softly, his fingers curling into her hair.

Jasper wasn't who she needed to forget but she didn't disabuse him. "Good idea." She drained her glass, set it down on the railing, then wrapped her arms around his neck. "And I think I know exactly how to do it."

"I like the way you think."

He lowered his mouth to hers and, despite the sloppy kiss, her body lit up. *I'm hot. I'm sexy. I'm a winner. I'm in control.*

She returned the kiss, hot and urgent, and his hands were all over her, but she didn't care, she wanted them there. It was proof she was desirable and it had been a long time since she'd been adored.

Grant's mouth was on her décolletage and his hand well under her skirt when she heard a male voice saying, "Excuse me, sir. Madam."

Panting, she broke away and tried to focus on the figure in the shadows.

"May I suggest you retire to your room," the security guard said.

Addy giggled. "I forgot to check in!"

The security guard frowned. "I'll call you a taxi."

"I've got a room," Grant slurred. "Kindly direct us to the elevators."

Addy's legs seemed to have lost all strength and she leaned against Grant. He ran an arm around her waist and they set off, zigzagging behind the security guard.

"Not this bloody walkway again!" Addy stopped, kicked off her heels and almost fell over when she bent to pick them up. "Oops!"

"You're short," Grant announced. "I didn't know you were short."

"Power package." She tapped his chest with the stiletto of her shoe. "Remember that."

"Know it already."

The security guard indicated the bank of elevators across the foyer.

Addy carefully pressed the up button four times. The doors opened and she walked in and sat on the floor, patting the space next to her. Grant joined her. The doors closed. Her eyelids were so heavy she gave up trying to keep them open.

The elevator doors opened and so did her eyes. "We're here!"

Grant stared out the open door. "Nope. Not our floor."

"Okay." The doors closed and opened again. "Did you press the button?"

"Good idea!" Grant stood and pressed level five. The elevator started to rise. "Lift-off!"

Addy thought this hilarious and laughed so hard she cried. There was a ping and then the doors opened.

"The eagle has landed." Grant hauled her to her feet. When they stepped out of the elevator, he stopped, looking left and right before announcing loudly, "This way!"

But Addy had seen the twinkle of lights at the end of the corridor and she took off toward the window. "Look at the view!"

Grant wasn't interested. He was busy crossing back and forth and peering at the room numbers.

Addy heard a cell phone ringing and realized it was hers. She opened her handbag and rummaged under tissues, pens and her wallet until she found it. "Lo."

A woman was talking about blood.

Addy shuddered. "Call reception for a band-aid."

"Found it!" Grant called out.

By the time Addy walked into the room, the woman was jabbering on about her coming over. "What room's zat?" she asked.

But she didn't hear the reply because Grant was popping the cork on a bottle of champagne. God, she loved champagne and tonight was perfect for it. He handed her a glass. She knocked it against the phone on the way to her mouth.

"Addy, are you there?" the voice was saying.

"I'm in a room with a view." Addy giggled. "Not Florence. Ho-bit."

"Why are you in Hobart?" the voice asked.

"Work conference at Wrest Point. Come see my view. It's room three um—wait! I know!" She spun around to ask Grant, but the room tipped and she was suddenly on the ground covered in champagne. "Fuck! That hurt. Bring chips and chocolate, okay?"

Grant took the phone out of her hand and tossed it onto one of the beds before picking her up. "Let me kiss you all better."

"Yes, please."

And then her back hit the mattress and suddenly all she wanted to do was sleep.

. . .

Jagged pain behind Addy's eyes woke her with a start. Her head pounded as loud as a rock band. Knowing from experience that moving would send waves of agony crashing through her, she lay perfectly still and slowly became aware of the softness of the sheets against her skin. Two thoughts collided—her sheets weren't usually this silky, and if she could feel them was she naked? She didn't usually sleep naked, because the cold woke her. She lifted a hand to her belly and her fingers touched bare skin, not the cotton of her pajamas.

Cracking open one eye, she saw floor-to-ceiling curtains. Where the hell was she?

She cautiously stretched out her left leg, but it moved unimpeded to the edge of the mattress. The same thing happened when she moved her right. Relief rolled in. She was alone in a bed—that was something at least.

Sucking in a fortifying breath, she opened both eyes. Pain skewered her, but she glimpsed another queen-sized bed before she snapped her eyes shut again.

Think! It took a few seconds but she recalled the long drive to Hobart and the training. Her anxiety tumbled down a few notches. She was supposed to be in a hotel room—she was at Wrest Point.

Agitation skittered through her. God, what time was it? Thankfully early if her cell phone's alarm hadn't gone off yet.

She patted the bedside table but couldn't feel her phone, so she risked a quick squint to read the bedside clock. It was just coming into painful focus when she heard someone whistling. Her body tensed so fast she got whiplash.

She strained her ears, desperate to convince herself the sound was coming from the corridor, but she knew luxury hotels specialized in heavy doors and plush carpet to help absorb extraneous noises. Someone was whistling in the bathroom.

Who?! Think!

She remembered having drinks in the bar with Jessie, the excruciating dinner, and then winning at the casino. After that, nothing.

"Morning, sleepyhead," a male voice said and the bed moved as he sat on the mattress.

Her stomach lurched and an acrid taste hit the back of her throat. Oh, sweet mother of— She'd spent the night with Grant! Her boss. It took everything she had not to pull the covers over her head and hide. She didn't know which bothered her most: the cliché of sleeping with her boss or the fact that she didn't remember anything about it.

"Morning," she croaked.

"I'm heading down for breakfast, but can I make you a coffee before I go?"

"Coffee sounds wonderful." *And necessary.* "Thank you."

"Too easy."

While he was busying himself with the coffee machine, she looked around for her clothes. She eventually spied them out of reach on the floor, so she wrapped herself in the bedsheet and scurried to the bathroom.

The face that greeted her would have scared a young child. Her hair was a mess of flat and spiked strands, her mascara was smeared across her cheeks and her eyes were red-rimmed. She breathed in fast at the sight and caught a whiff of stale champagne and the musky scent of a body that needed a shower.

Had they had sex? Probably. She had no memory of it, but the dampness between her legs hinted at another story.

Hoping Grant would leave her coffee and go down to breakfast, she turned on the shower, but when she shut off the water, she could hear him talking on the phone. She wrapped herself in the fluffy bathrobe and her hair in a towel and returned to the room.

Grant was clean-shaven and neatly dressed. The only thing that hinted at a big night was some slight puffiness around his eyes. How could he look this good when she looked like she'd been pulled through the wringer backwards?

He smiled and handed her a coffee, a blister sheet of paracetamol and a container of fruit salad. "Caffeine, sugar and drugs always help me."

"Thanks." She swallowed the tablets with some water, then took a mouthful of coffee. "So, last night ...?"

He laughed. "You know how to party."

"Right." She glanced at the other bed, which was rumpled.

His eyes twinkled. "We let our hair down for some well-earned relaxation. I blame the whisky. Up until that point, I was in complete control."

There'd been periods in her life when she'd specialized in waking up in strangers' beds or in her own bed with a stranger, but since she and Jasper had gotten together neither scenario had happened. A flash of memory hit her: Grant's hands in her hair, his throaty voice in her ear saying, "Let me kiss it better," and his mouth on her breasts. She couldn't remember much else after that, but it was a non-existent leap from foreplay to sex.

Grant smiled at her. "It's the best drunk-sex I've ever had. I appreciate your adventurous spirit."

Adventurous? God, what did that mean? She tried to conjure up something, anything about them having sex, but it was a blank. She was hazy on the details of arriving in the room, let alone what had followed.

Trying to stall her rising panic, she laughed. "Adventure's my middle name."

He stroked her arm, then picked up his jacket. "Before you stress out, I want to say I've always lived by the adage of what happens at conference stays at conference. We're both adults away from home, we let off some steam and had fun. There's no harm in that, but when we step out that door, it's like it never happened."

Grant's one of the good ones. Jessie's words from last night wrapped around her like a soft blanket.

"That's good to know. Not that I regret what happened," Addy said, rushing to reassure him. Past experience had taught her men didn't like being unmemorable. "It was a fun night, that's for sure."

"It was a *great* night. Thanks again." He turned for the door.

Her brain coughed up a cogent thought. "Before you go, could you do me a favor?"

"Of course."

"My suitcase is still in my car." She fumbled in her handbag for her car key. "Rather than do the walk of shame in yesterday's clothes, could you get it for me? The porter could bring it up to save you a return trip."

He frowned and checked his phone. "I'd love to help, but I've got a meeting I'm already late for because I wanted to make you coffee and check you were okay."

"Oh, right. Of course ... Thanks." She bit her lip against a traitorous prickle of tears and tried to kickstart her fuddled brain.

"Talking of being late, Addy, aren't you giving a short presentation in thirty minutes?" He didn't wait for an answer. "Just a tip. Heather hates latecomers and she's got a memory like an elephant. You don't want to get her off side."

"Right. Good to know." She barely heard her words over the roar of panic.

"Anytime. See you there."

Before she could utter another word, he was disappearing out the door.

As it clicked shut behind him, the full significance of her situation hit her. She had no clean clothes, no make-up, no hair products and no way of getting back into this room. Without her name on the room, reception wouldn't issue her with a new key, and anyone who was having breakfast in the restaurant would see her dressed in crumpled and champagne-soaked clothes. Even if she managed to get to her car without being seen, it would be impossible not to be caught getting dressed in the public restrooms. That left the car.

Yesterday's delight at getting a parking spot so close to the conference center now turned to horror. The Hobart staff would be arriving and able to see her getting changed. Whatever option she took, she was screwed. She fell back on the bed, tempted to text in sick.

But she couldn't do that. Especially when Grant was functioning despite a hangover. And she prided herself on not only being able to party hard, but showing up on time ready and raring to go. Right now though she'd never felt less ready, let alone raring. Was this what being thirty-three meant? Less stamina?

Get moving!

She hauled herself to sitting and almost threw up. Gulping in air to shut off the gag reflex and keep her coffee in her stomach, she got dressed, finger-styled her hair, and rummaged through her handbag for powder and lipstick. It wasn't her usual put-together look, but it was better than nothing. If she could just make it to the car unseen and get dressed lying flat on the back seat, she could touch up her make-up in the restroom, then everything else would fall into place.

She pressed her palms on the vanity and leaned close to the mirror. "I promise you, I'll never drink during the week again." She heard the faint echo of a laugh. "Shut up. This time I'm serious."

CHAPTER FOURTEEN

BRENDA AND CLYDE were heading to the beach for a well-earned break after Clyde had spent two hours visiting the elementary school's lower grades with Brenda as his handler. They were just passing Sven's when Henry Sun called her name.

"I'm about to grab a coffee," he said. "Would you like one?"

Brenda tried to limit herself to one coffee at breakfast, but there was something about Henry's demeanor that made her say, "Lovely. Can you bring it to the beach? Clyde's desperate for a run."

Five minutes later Henry joined her under a Norfolk pine and handed her a coffee. "I heard Clyde was a big hit with Monty. He's usually scared of dogs."

"I imagine when you're little and not used to animals, big dogs are terrifying," Brenda said. "Clyde's a lot closer to Monty's size."

"Steph and I promised the kids we'd get a dog when we moved here, but with the house and ..." He sighed. "Are Westies good pets for kids?"

"They're rather independent souls." She thought of the farm dogs and Glen's dictum: "They're not pets, they live outside." Of the many times she'd craved the unconditional love of a dog and how she'd promised herself she'd have one of her own one day. "Golden retrievers and Labradors make lovely family pets," she said. "They're playful and loyal, and they look at you with such big and adoring eyes you lose your heart."

Henry made a strangled sound and Brenda scanned his face. "Are you okay?"

He blew out a long breath. "Steph lost the baby."

Brenda's heart sank. She'd wondered why Steph had missed choir last week. "Oh, Henry. I'm so sorry."

"Yeah. Thanks."

"How are you both?"

"I'm sad, but part of me thinks if there was something wrong it's better it happened early. You know, before we felt it moving. Before it was born with a disability." He fiddled with the lid on his travel mug. "Steph's absolutely gutted and I don't know what to say or do to help her. I was wondering ..." His eyes implored her. "Could you possibly visit? She's saying she doesn't want to go to choir this week, but I think getting back to normal is what she needs."

"It's early days, Henry. She probably just needs some time."

"I think she needs the wisdom of an older woman."

Brenda cut off a rueful laugh. "Believe me, old doesn't mean wise."

"Lucky my mother's not alive to hear you say that. She'd have taken you down." Henry's smile wobbled. "Once, I would have turned to family for help, but neither Steph nor I have living mothers and I'm floundering. I've made her Mama's chicken and wonton soup. I've taken the kids out so she can sleep. I've suggested a drive to Table Cape, and a shopping trip to Launceston, but she's refusing to leave Four Winds. She's making herself sick with crying."

Brenda knew that feeling. *For Pete's sake, Bren! Get up and face the day. It will make you feel better.* She pushed away the memory of dark days when getting out of bed was almost impossible.

"Me talking to her is no guarantee she won't stop crying."

"I know, but it's worth a shot. Please?"

Despite her own misgivings, she couldn't ignore his desperate plea. "Okay."

Henry moved to hug her, then stopped himself. "Thank you."

"When's a good time to visit?" she asked.

"As soon as you can."

"I've got lunch plans but I'll pop in before the school bus."

Henry grimaced. "Zoe's pretty cut up about the baby too. She was at home with Steph when she miscarried and I think it terrified her. Not that I can get her to talk about it. My two best girls are struggling and it's killing me. I could do with some tips on dealing with teens too."

Brenda thought about the difficult years with Courtney. Who was she kidding? The difficulties continued. She stifled a sigh. "Just keep loving them and hope for the best."

Henry's face fell into disappointed lines at the non-specific advice and Brenda's skin pricked in irritation. It dove deep, weaving itself around old hurts and failures, and anger swept in fast and furious. Bloody hell! What had Henry expected? Especially from her!

"I told you older doesn't mean wiser," she said crisply. She called Clyde, excused herself and strode up the hill.

Courtney arrived soon after Brenda had hung up Clyde's lead. She rushed into the house in her usual whirlwind way with her arms full of produce, which she dumped on the kitchen table.

"Hello, darl—"

"Back in a sec, Mum. I'm busting."

As Courtney ran to the bathroom, Brenda swallowed a sigh and stowed the vegetables and the berries into the refrigerator. She had just plated the baguette sandwiches when Courtney returned and sat down.

"Yum! I'm starving. How did Clyde go at school? It was all Jesse could talk about this morning."

"He was a hit. He featured in the reading, writing and math activities. As we left, the second graders were creating an enormous collage to accompany the stories. We've been invited to return next week."

"I wish we'd had an integrated curriculum when I was at school." Courtney bit into her turkey, cheese and avocado baguette. "Hmmm, this is good."

Brenda stopped herself from saying "You sound surprised" and said instead, "Have you tried the strawberry jam recipe yet?"

"I've just bought the jars so you can show me how to make it this afternoon."

"Oh, I wish you'd told me earlier. I've got something on this afternoon."

Courtney frowned. "But you never do anything on Thursday afternoons. It's why I came."

Brenda was long used to Courtney's task-driven visits but she held on to hope that one day her daughter would visit just to spend time with her. "Sorry, darling, but I'm not a mind-reader. I've promised to visit Steph Gallagher this afternoon."

Courtney's baguette hit the plate. "Why are you going to see the woman who let Livvy cover her face in so much make-up she looked like a sex worker?"

Brenda had heard Olivia's version of events. "I'm sure Livvy—"

"What really gets up my nose is neither Steph or Henry saw the problem. Worse than that, they said so in front of the girls! I'm Livvy's mother. She needs to listen to me, not a woman who's happy to let her stepdaughter look like a slut. It's bad enough Olivia's all starry-eyed about Zoe and willing to follow her over a cliff without her idolizing the rest of the Sun family too. She's begging to visit again, but I've said no. If she finds out you've been to Four Winds, it will undermine my authority."

Brenda wanted to say that experimenting with make-up was normal teenage girl behavior and suggest to Courtney that she was overreacting. But if she did that her daughter would leave in a huff, shattering months of relative harmony.

She decided to appeal to Courtney's compassion. "Steph's had a miscarriage."

"That's unfortunate and sad," Courtney said. "Mind you, without a pregnancy and a new baby distracting her, she'll have time to sort out Zoe."

"I'm not sure that's how life works," Brenda said.

But Courtney had a mouthful of food, and when she eventually swallowed she said, "It seems I have to make an appointment to see you these days. When are you free to teach me how to make jam?"

"Tomorrow or any day next week." With Marilyn working full-time, Brenda was selfishly determined to keep the weekends as free as possible.

"What about Saturday?" Courtney's eyes lit up. "That way you can teach Ben and Livvy too and Jesse can be involved. Saturday afternoon works best. We can be here at two."

"Saturday's—"

"Hi." Marilyn walked into the kitchen. Clyde rose from his basket and trotted over to her, ever hopeful of a dog treat. "Sorry to interrupt. I just popped back for the popsicles for the kids. I was in such a rush this morning, I forgot them."

"You should have called," Brenda said. "I could have dropped them over."

She shrugged. "I'm not on yard duty and sometimes it's nice to duck out."

"Can you stay for lunch?" Courtney asked. "There's half a baguette, right, Mum?"

Brenda's heart raced. "We don't want to make you late."

"You won't. I've got twenty minutes, and a baguette and a cup of tea sounds perfect." Marilyn switched on the kettle. "Did I hear you two making weekend plans?"

"Mum's teaching the Burtons how to make jam," Courtney said.

"Oh! I need that lesson," Marilyn said. "I only tried once and it didn't set."

"Mine's hit and miss too, but I have to master it. Ben's super keen to sell our berry jam at the farm gate." Courtney smiled. "You should join us. The more the merrier."

"There's only so much room in this kitchen," Brenda said, desperate to cut the idea off at the knees. "Besides, Marilyn will have plans for Saturday."

"The only thing I can think of is working on the arrangement for choir." Marilyn set the teapot on the table. "That leaves loads of time for jam."

"I didn't know you were starting a school choir," Courtney said. "There hasn't been anything about it on the school app."

A wave of nausea rolled Brenda's lunch to the back of her throat.

Marilyn shot her a look that clearly said, if you don't tell her I will.

"Marilyn's starting a community choir." Brenda forced brightness into her voice. "Isn't that great?"

Courtney clapped. "That's awesome! I'd love to sing again. When are the auditions?"

"No auditions necessary," Marilyn said. "Just enthusiasm and a love of singing."

"I've got that," Courtney said. "Count me in."

"Excellent. We've started with seven, but we need more. Do you know anyone else who'd like a weekly sing?" Marilyn asked before biting into her baguette.

"So the choir's already started?" Courtney frowned. "Why didn't you tell me, Mum?"

Above the boom of blood pounding in her ears, Brenda heard the accusation in her daughter's voice. She swallowed to moisten her dry mouth and tried channeling calm. "Ben has soccer training on Tuesday nights and I know you don't like leaving Livvy and Jesse alone on the farm."

"Soccer training's Wednesday nights," Courtney said with a hint of exasperation. "It's always been Wednesdays."

"Has it?" Brenda feigned confusion.

"God, Mum. I hope this is a grief memory-loss thing, not Alzheimer's." Courtney turned to Marilyn. "I might need you to keep an eye on her and tell me if she's leaving the stove on or losing her reading glasses."

"The glasses are already a lost cause," Marilyn quipped.

"I'm right here, thank you very much," Brenda snapped.

"Mum's never been great with teasing," Courtney confided, leaning in toward Marilyn. "Which is crazy, because Dad teased her all the time. You'd think she'd be used to it."

Brenda caught Marilyn's quizzical look and mustered a wan smile. She'd deliberately kept marriage and family stories out of her relationship with Marilyn, desperate to keep the bubble of love and romance—her great escape—unsullied by the rest of her life.

She gulped hot tea, welcoming the scald along the length of her esophagus. It was a lot less painful than watching her two separate worlds of lover and daughter colliding in front of her.

That night, after Brenda had picked Jesse up from elementary school and taken him to hockey training, then met Olivia at the bus and helped her make a corset as part of her history project—women's fashion and women's rights—she finally sat on the sofa with Marilyn.

"I dropped in to see Steph today. She lost the baby."

Marilyn wrinkled her nose. "That's pretty common in the early days, isn't it? I wonder if she regrets telling everyone she was pregnant."

Brenda loved Marilyn, but unlike herself she'd never wanted children or sought motherhood in other ways. Sometimes that difference snuck up on Brenda and hit her over the head.

"When you want a child, just imagining it feels real," she said. "Once you see the pink line on the stick, you love it and weave dreams around it. Miscarriage is a real grief."

"Hopefully she'll get pregnant again quickly so she can put this behind her," Marilyn said pragmatically.

"It's not like getting a new puppy when your dog dies. It took her over a year to conceive with this one and that stress isn't helping."

Marilyn was quiet for a moment, as if considering everything Brenda had said. "In that case, it sounds like she needs the choir more than ever."

Brenda laughed and Marilyn said defensively, "What? You just told me it's real grief so I'm trying to be supportive."

"You are being supportive." Brenda kissed her on the cheek.

"Only someone who cares would be actively encouraging a tone-deaf woman to be part of the choir."

Marilyn joined the laughter. "Why is it that the most enthusiastic members are always the worst singers? Between Steph and Brian, it's going to take all my skills to hide their voices. What's Courtney's singing voice like?"

Brenda tried to keep a lid on her discomfort around Courtney joining the choir. "It's not in the same league as Addy's but her range is pretty good. Or it was. It's been a long time since I heard her sing."

"I'm so glad she's joining."

"Hmm." Brenda tried for non-committal and sipped her tea.

"I really want to get to know her," Marilyn said.

Brenda sighed. "I want you to get to know her too, but please be careful what you say. I want to prepare her for our announcement so it's not a shock."

Marilyn's brows rose. "Like you've been preparing her for the last few months?"

A flash of panic or anger, Brenda wasn't sure which, sent heat scudding through her. "Trust me to know my own daughter."

"I do." Marilyn's tone was worryingly cautious. "But I think you look at her and see a child. I look at her and see a grown woman, wife and mother. She loves you, Brenda. She'll want you to be happy."

A hysterical laugh bubbled in the back of her throat and she pushed it down. Of the two of them, Marilyn was the one who wore rose-colored glasses. "Courtney adored her father. She won't find this easy to accept."

"You don't know that."

I do.

"In fact," Marilyn continued, "the longer you wait, the more problems you imagine and the further from reality you get. With things like this it's best to rip off the band-aid. And it's well past time. I didn't move up here to live in limbo."

Brenda hugged herself. "But it's not just Courtney. What if I lose Olivia and Jesse?"

"You've got other grandchildren," Marilyn said.

"They're not interchangeable! And I've got no idea how Colin will react. All I know is there's lots at stake. The worst thing we can do is rush things."

"Rush things?" Marilyn's voice rose as the sofa shot upright from the recliner position. "Brenda, it's been years!"

"No," she said firmly, knowing an important distinction must be made. "It's not been years. From the start we both agreed we wanted the affair to be secret because of your job and my family. Why are you pushing me so hard now?"

"Because the obstacles have vanished!" Marilyn's arms rose in the air, vibrating with frustration. "Glen is dead. Your children are adults. I've left the Catholic Education Office and changed my life to be with you. I've been here since January. It's time, Brenda. It's long past time."

But time wasn't only an interval, it was a social construct. "But we're happy," she implored.

"We can be even happier." Marilyn slid her hands into Brenda's and gazed into her eyes. "I want the world to know we're a couple. I want to stand up in front of our family and friends and say 'I love you.' Surely you want that too?"

"I do."

But every time Brenda visualized telling the boys and Courtney, she found it difficult to breathe. Visualizing any of them at a wedding was impossible.

CHAPTER FIFTEEN

"Have fun at choir." Henry kissed Steph on the cheek, then pushed open the car door for her. "No need to hurry home. I've got everything under control."

Steph doubted it, but she lacked the energy to say so.

The next minute she was standing at the bottom of the hall steps, hesitant to enter. For the past six weeks she'd been unable to contain her excitement about the pregnancy and she'd told everyone she met. Now, the thought of telling the choir she'd miscarried made her want to curl up in a ball and howl.

She'd cried so much recently she should be bone dry. But her tears for a lost life and lost dreams still came easily and often. After she and Henry had viewed her silent and almost empty uterus on the ultrasound screen, and she'd woken from the light anesthetic, she'd retreated to their bed and slept. A few days later, when her thoughts were slightly more ordered, she'd realized Addy should have returned from Hobart and she'd expected her to drop by. But Addy hadn't visited. Nor had she called.

When the doorbell eventually pealed, Steph had rushed to answer it. Disappointment had slammed her so hard she'd needed to grip the door-handle to stay standing.

"Henry told me," Brenda had said, sympathy etched on her face.

"I'm so sorry. You must be devastated."

Steph had collapsed into her arms and pretended Brenda was her mother.

Later, after scones and tea, Brenda had said, "Do you want me to pave the way for you and mention the miscarriage to the choir?"

"No," she'd said sharply.

But now, standing and staring at the flaking green paint on the hall door, Steph wondered why she'd been so adamant. If she'd given Brenda permission to tell everyone, it would have been one less hurdle to clear. It was bad enough dealing with the shame of losing the baby without adding in the humiliation of having told people about the pregnancy too soon.

When she'd been pregnant with Monty, the doctor and the mid-wives had carefully outlined all the possible things that could go wrong before twenty weeks. Accompanying that information was the implied warning: keep the news to yourself until it's safe. But this time, after taking so long to get pregnant, she'd bubbled with excitement. It had been impossible not to share her joy. It had never occurred to her that anything could go wrong—Monty had been a textbook pregnancy—but Zoe hadn't been living with them then and causing chaos.

Causing miscarriages.

Steph flinched at the unfair thought and tried not to cry. Again.

Every part of her wanted to turn from the hall steps and run. But even if it wasn't already dark and she could have walked home to Four Winds, she'd have to deal with Henry's sadness and his disappointment in her desire to hide from the world.

"You're working from home and you need more than just Monty, Zoe and me for company," Henry had said ten different ways over the last two weeks.

She'd barely been working—her concentration was almost non-existent—and she could happily live without seeing Zoe. Fortunately, outside of school hours the girl spent most of her time in her room. Steph no longer demanded she come down and participate in family life.

"Hi, Steph."

She turned to see Addy. The woman was beautifully turned out as usual, although today her linen pants pulled at the pockets, bulging them out, and her blouse gaped at the button on her bra line. Was her face rounder? Steph's hurt and disappointment that her new friend hadn't called or visited morphed into schadenfreude—Addy had gained weight.

As they stepped into the hall Steph noticed Courtney chatting to Fern. Her stomach dropped. Had Courtney joined the choir? The last thing she needed on top of everything else was Courtney's judgmental manner. She'd take Addy over Courtney any day.

Pushing away the unkind thoughts about her friend, she asked, "How was Hobart?"

"Yeah, okay. You know how full-on work conferences can be."

Addy gave a tight laugh. "Where have you been? I missed having someone to trade eye-rolls with over Brian's antics.'

Steph's breath rushed out of her lungs so fast she coughed.

Addy poured her a glass of water. "You okay? You look a bit pale."

Steph's hand shook, spilling water. "Are you for real?"

"Yes! How have I offended you by showing some friendly concern?" Addy asked.

"Concern?!" Steph heard the shrieked word bounce around the hall. Saw Brenda glance in her direction and Courtney's mouth tighten in disapproval. She dropped her voice. "Where's your concern been since you got back from Hobart?"

Addy's brow creased in confusion. "I feel I'm missing a vital piece of information."

Steph's fingernails dug into her palms as tears burned the backs of her eyes. "I called you the night I was bleeding. I thought you were in the cove, but you were at Wrest Point."

Through the fog of despair that clouded that dreadful time, Steph suddenly remembered what Addy had said. Anger roared in, flattening her grief. "You told me to put on a band-aid. Really helpful advice when someone's having a miscarriage!"

"No! I wouldn't have ..." Addy's face drained of color. "I ... It was noisy in the casino. I must have misunderstood or misheard what you were saying. I'm so sorry. I ... Oh God!"

Addy hugged her so hard Steph's glass of water spilled down her back, but still Addy didn't release her. Steph gave in to the hug, soaking up the care of a much-needed friend.

"Hugs are so important. They feed our souls." Fern wrapped her arms around them both and laid her head on Steph's shoulder.

Steph caught Addy's eye-roll and for the first time in days experienced a momentary lightening of her grief. It gave her the strength she needed and she disengaged herself from Fern.

"Actually, my soul's taken a battering," she said. "I'm no longer pregnant."

A hush descended on the group and the silence pressed in on her.

Eventually Brian broke it. "At least you've got the other kids to keep you busy."

But I wanted this baby. Her heart twisted painfully in her chest. Was this why people didn't talk about miscarriage?

"Not helpful, Brian," Morgan muttered. "Sorry for your loss, Steph."

"They're pretty common though, right?" Brian was saying to Vera. "Nature's way of getting rid of the duds, I reckon."

"Doesn't make the loss any easier." Heidi hugged Steph. "I had a couple of misses before Sammy and Nick. I still have moments when I think of them and imagine."

"Thanks for sharing that," Steph said. "It's completely sideswiped us. Henry and I were so excited when we conceived down here. It was like the baby had reinforced our decision to move and—" Her voice broke and tears spilled. She hastily brushed them away with the back of her hand.

Addy squeezed her other hand. "Are you going to plant something special in the garden?"

Gratitude filled her, washing away the hurt from their misunderstanding. "That's a lovely idea. A way of remembering."

Fern pressed her hands together. "I could do a healing ceremony and banish the bad energ—"

"Henry and Steph might want to do something private," Addy said.

Fern bristled. "I think that's up to Steph."

"It is."

♫

Addy had little time for touchy-feely New Age claptrap or for people intruding on other people's grief. But she knew her unexpected urge to protect Steph, who currently didn't look capable of making a decision about tea or coffee let alone a healing ceremony, was driven by guilt. She was racking her brain, but that night in Hobart was a series of blanks. She had no recollection of Steph calling her. Then again, she didn't remember much about sleeping with Grant, but passing out during lackluster sex was barely a sin compared to telling a woman who was miscarrying to use a band-aid. When Steph had told her, Addy had wanted the floor to open up and swallow her in big, painful, jagged bites.

Thankfully, she'd covered fast. Steph had accepted the story about the noise in the casino and had given her such a look of appreciation for the plant idea that Addy was certain she was home free. But stress lingered in the dampness of her armpits and the churning of her gut. *This* was why she didn't usually put in the effort to make friends. This was why she avoided joining things like choir—they always turned into emotional minefields. God, she could do with a drink.

That's what got you into this mess.

No. Two glasses of sauv blanc, three-quarters of a bottle of red, two cocktails and one whisky got me into the mess. One drink is fine.

"Does the 7:30 start mean arrive and chat and the singing starts at 8:00?' Courtney asked. "If it does, I won't rush next week."

Addy suppressed a wry smile. So much had changed in the cove in the years she'd been away, but not Courtney. At school, the girl had been a mix of fun and strict adherence to the rules—perfect prefect material. The principal had loved her. Back then Courtney had always insisted musical rehearsals start on time, whereas Addy was content for them to start late as that meant they were shorter, or better yet, didn't take place at all.

"Let's make a start, shall we," Marilyn said. "I'm excited to welcome Courtney, and we were expecting Kieran, but he doesn't appear to have made it."

Morgan's eyes lit up. "Who's Kieran?"

"Someone who made contact through the Facebook page," Marilyn said. "If you don't know him perhaps he's new to town too?"

"Fingers crossed he makes it," Morgan said.

"You're not the only single woman," Courtney said. "You might have to fight Addy for him."

Morgan laughed. "You happy to share, Addy?"

"You never know," Addy said. "Brian might be more his type."

"Steady on, love," Brian said. "I'll have you know I'm a one hundred percent red-blooded man."

"Pretty sure gay men have red blood too, Brian," Heidi said.

Courtney said something Addy didn't hear. Vera and Brian laughed, which meant it was likely politically incorrect and possibly homophobic. After all, she was back living in a small town and Courtney had never been shy about saying what she thought.

Addy glanced at Brenda to check if she was smiling at the joke too, but she wasn't looking at Courtney. She was handing sheet music to Marilyn and Addy caught a hand squeeze pass between the two women. She blinked in surprise. Was Brenda being kind to Marilyn because the school teacher was gay? Come to think of it, Marilyn with her short spiky hair and propensity for wearing checked shirts and trousers certainly had a bit of a "butch look" about her. Although the dangly earrings, shellac nails and long bright cardigans muddied the waters.

Addy moved her gaze to the women's faces and glimpsed a flash of something that was far more than just empathy. Deep affection?

Love?

Don't be ridiculous. But as the thought landed she was already looking around at the other choir members, hoping to see something on their faces that would confirm what she thought she'd just seen. But everyone's gaze was firmly on Fern and Courtney.

"Choir is open and inclusive, Courtney," Fern said in a steely tone. "A safe space."

"Of course it is," Courtney said. "But that doesn't mean we can't have fun."

"It isn't fun if some people feel—"

Brenda crashed a loud raft of chords on the piano. Everyone fell silent. "Let's focus on our breathing so we can start singing."

As Addy watched the straight-shouldered, no-nonsense farmer's widow, grandmother, agricultural show judge and old friend of her mother's pull the ragtag group into line, she decided her own work stress was messing with her ability to read people. Brenda being gay was as unlikely as a fly-free picnic. Besides, no one could keep that sort of news secret in the cove.

Marilyn led the warm-up. When everyone fell apart laughing on the clicks and claps singing down from eight, she crossed her arms and brought the choir to order.

"As you know, as well as singing, the ultimate plan is to host an eisteddfod later in the year to raise funds for the hall roof."

"Can we compete if we're hosting?" Morgan asked.

"We can, or we could sing to open and close the competition. But before we're able to make an informed decision, we need to sing in public. It's a very different beast from singing in the hall to one another. And as every choir needs a challenge I've entered us in the Community Choir Crush. Penguin's hosting this year so we don't have to travel far."

"Do we really want to do this?" Addy asked, fighting memory flashes.

"When is it?" Morgan asked.

"In a month," Marilyn said.

Brenda looked incredulous. "A month?"

"But we don't even have a piece," Heidi said.

"I think it's a great idea," Steph said, sounding like herself for the first time.

"Thank you," Marilyn said. "And if we rehearse Tuesdays and Thursdays, we'll be ready."

"What's the piece?" Courtney asked.

"'This Is Me' from *The Greatest Showman*," Marilyn said.

Steph pressed her hands to her chest. "Oh, I love that movie."

Heidi laughed. "The movie or Hugh Jackman?"

"A bit of both."

Marilyn handed out the music. "I chose it because it suits a range of voices and people will know it. In a competition like this it's best to go with a crowd-pleaser."

Addy wasn't familiar with the movie, but she read the music, humming it in her head. Then she looked at the lyrics. As she read each word, her heart rate picked up.

She'd just reached the fourth line when Marilyn said, "Addy will sing the lead, ably supported by everyone with the harmonies."

Icy dread chilled Addy, making her shiver. "This song suits Heidi's or Courtney's voices better."

"I disagree," Marilyn said firmly.

"So do I," Steph said. "Your voice is amazing. You'll do an awesome job."

"They're right," Heidi said. "I could do it, but your voice has that extra something."

"But I thought the point of a community choir was to sing as an ensemble," Addy said, desperate to avoid the lead. "Not to showcase anyone over another."

"Since when have you suffered from false modesty?" Courtney

said. "The only time I got the lead at school was when you were sick. If Marilyn says you're the best voice for the part, then you are."

"It's not false mod—"

"Why join a choir if you don't want to sing?" Brian interrupted.

The question was simple, but the answer was as complicated and tangled as a ball of knotted fishing line. God, she hadn't wanted to join the bloody choir. She'd let guilt and Steph's friendly puppy eagerness draw her in. Now she was expected to step up when all she wanted to do was run.

"I teach late on Thursdays," she tried.

"Not a problem," Marilyn said. "We'll work on harmonies then."

"See?" Steph squeezed Addy's arm. "It's meant to be."

Marilyn smiled. "And, Addy, it's not often the lead has the full support of the choir. Normally, there's someone else desperate for the limelight."

"It's a sign of the positive energy that flows through this group."

Fern shot Courtney a look. "Energy we need to harness so we thrive."

Steph rolled her eyes at Addy, but Addy was too stressed to see the funny side. Every part of her screamed to quit choir on the spot, but she needed to live in the cove for a few more months yet. She could just imagine the negative energy Fern would hurl at her, not to mention the strong possibility of Courtney, Vera and perhaps Brenda raising the specter of her rebellious teenage self and some of her less social activities. She was stuck between the choir and the cove, and sharp edges dug into her on all sides.

"So it's settled." Marilyn beamed. "I promise you, it's going to be great!"

Addy gripped the music so hard it crumpled in her hand.

CHAPTER SIXTEEN

When Brenda walked through the back door after choir and switched on the kettle, agitation was still jumping through her like fleas on a rat. After Courtney's "joke" and her own intervention, the choir had thankfully settled. There'd even been half a dozen bars when they'd sounded like a choir before Brian had boomed a low G, swamping the other voices, and Steph had sung sharp. Considering how much non-singing stress the choir was causing her, Brenda was taking those few harmonic bars as a sign it might all be worth it.

Marilyn walked into the kitchen as Brenda was pouring boiling water over the tea-leaves. "I was just coming to do that."

"I know. But I needed to do something." As Brenda lifted two cups out of the cabinet she tackled the beast in the room. "You heard Courtney tonight."

"You mean her lovely voice or the questionable joke that might offend some people?" Marilyn said.

"Might?" Brenda stared at her. "She offended Fern and she's not even part of the LGBTQI community." The letters sounded clumsy in her mouth.

"Yes, but Fern's part of the PC police. Her mission in life is to be offended then react."

"So it didn't upset you that it was my daughter who made that joke?"

Marilyn calmly turned the teapot. "Would you be this het up if she'd made a joke about a priest not being able to tell the difference between a bishop and a queen? Or any of the "an Englishman, Irishman and Australian walked into a bar" jokes? All of those are predicated on stereotypes and I've heard you laugh at them."

Brenda didn't want to be sidetracked. "You didn't answer my question."

Marilyn shrugged. "I've heard a lot worse delivered with malice and so have you. Courtney was probably a bit nervous and trying to fit in."

Brenda doubted that but she didn't interrupt.

"We all know it's not easy walking into an established group," Marilyn continued. "And Courtney hasn't seen Addy in years. Why aren't you cross with Addy for raising that Kieran might be gay when it's irrelevant? Or with Morgan for treating the unknown bloke as a piece of meat that she and Addy can share? If you view their comments through the same lens, they're equally offensive."

Usually, Marilyn's sunny and optimistic personality, and her determination to see the best in people, buoyed Brenda's tendencies toward melancholy. But as much as she wanted to agree that Courtney's joke was borderline rather than offensive, she knew her daughter. Her hand rubbed the fire in her stomach.

Marilyn sighed. "Making yourself sick is *why* you need to tell Courtney and the boys, so we can come out to the town. The longer you keep us a secret, the more you read too much into what everyone says about the community." She wrapped her arms around Brenda. "Darling, what I've learned is there are allies everywhere, but they often don't appear until you're out. Look at my family. They love me and want me to be happy. Give your children some credit. They love you and want what's best for you."

Brenda closed her eyes and breathed in Marilyn's fresh citrus scent. She remembered the love and care the children had shown her in the early days after Glen's death. How Courtney called her more often now than she ever had when Glen was alive. That was love and care. Was Marilyn right? Was she underestimating Courtney?

Marilyn stroked her hair. "You've put your family ahead of your own happiness for far too long. It's time for you to live an authentic life."

An authentic life? Their usually unnoticeable eight-year age gap rose up and thwacked her. Marilyn's generation and the following one were all about putting individual needs first, whereas Brenda had almost always been pulled by duty and the needs of others.

The past stirred. Her mother's and Elaine's voices spoke loudly in her head, accompanying a memory from a few months after Richard's birth. Brenda had been miserable and barely coping, and the older women had arrived to "sort her out."

"It's not just about your happiness, Brenda," her mother had said. "You're a wife and a mother. Janice Elliot told Cynthia van Lange you have postnatal depression. I told her she had the wrong end of the stick and the reason you haven't been off the farm is due to the harvest. But unless you want everyone in the district talking about you as if you're a mental case, you need to get out of bed and deal with your responsibilities."

Elaine had folded diapers with determined precision. "I really don't know why you had a third."

Brenda knew there was no point explaining to her mother-in-law that the pill raised her blood pressure to dangerous levels, that Glen, who'd refused to have a vasectomy, still expected to have sex whenever he felt like it, and condoms and diaphragms failed.

"Glen always wanted three," she said instead.

"He's such a good father, but he works too hard. Buck up, Brenda! He deserves to come home to a hot meal and some semblance of order."

Brenda's depression had run headlong into her family's wants and needs—their authentic life. But she'd also chosen marriage and children. Even today, almost forty years later, she still remembered the relief that had flooded her body when Glen had asked her out. How his proposal to her had silenced the unsettling thoughts she'd been having since she was fifteen. She'd flung her arms around his neck with more relief than passion. From that day, she'd tried her best to honor her choice, despite the constant feinting and sparring with an ever-present cloud hovering over her—some days light gray, many days inky black. When the children had arrived they'd cleaved her in half—love and despair.

Brenda stepped out of Marilyn's embrace and concentrated on pouring tea. "You don't have children."

Marilyn's shoulders squared. "Neither do you. You have adults."

"I have children who view me solely in terms of being their mother and what I can do for them."

"Courtney's very good at that," Marilyn said drily. "And you let her use you."

"Establishing rapport with my grandchildren is not being used! Neither is rebuilding what's always been a rocky relationship with Courtney."

"It's only been rocky because you've lied to her for years!"

The black years spun around Brenda like a lasso, ready to snap tight around her and pull her down. "That's unfair! You know how much I struggled—"

"I'm sorry," Marilyn said softly. "I do know, but it's the past. This is now!" Her contrition vanished. "I've been here months and nothing's changed. All I hear are words without action."

Their different needs collided, rolling panic through Brenda in tumultuous waves. "Don't push me!"

"Push you?" Marilyn slammed down her mug. "You can't be serious?"

"I am." Tremors racked her. "I promised you I'd tell the family. I will tell them, but it has to be on my time and my terms."

"Now who's being unfair? I've bent over backwards trying to be patient and understanding. I've given you plenty of time to organize getting Richard, Courtney and Colin in the same room, but nothing's happened. Meanwhile, I'm being forced to act a part I don't want. I can't get to know your family. I can't hold your hand in the street, and I'm dodging endless probing questions from the good citizens of the cove who assume I'm single when I'm not single at all. I'm committed to you! I've always been committed to you!"

Marilyn threw the dregs of her tea into the sink and vigorously rinsed the mug. "We've moved beyond a long-term affair, secret assignations and protecting *your* marriage. I happily gave up Hobart for you, but we had a deal. I've been incredibly patient but the well's empty. This situation's not fair to me. Hell, it's not even close to fair to *us*. Unless I see something that shows me you really do intend to tell your family, I'm starting to wonder if we have a future together."

If we have a future? The ultimatum pressed so heavily on Brenda's chest it was difficult to breathe.

"Of course we have a future. How could we have come this far together if I didn't believe in that? I love you, Marilyn."

"And I love you too, but love's not the issue."

Heartache echoed in Marilyn's words, making Brenda break out in a cold sweat.

"I'll call everyone and set up a family lunch," she said.

"When?"

Brenda's dread coalesced with anger, forming a hot and heavy brick in the pit of her stomach. The terror of Marilyn leaving her was equal to the task of telling the family.

"It's too late to call people tonight. I'll do it in the morning."

Marilyn raised her brows, the action screaming "I don't believe you."

Brenda reached for her cell phone, brought up Richard's number and texted: *What time tomorrow's a good time to call?* After she'd pressed send and the word "delivered" appeared under the text, she shoved the device at Marilyn.

"Happy?" she demanded.

"Not really."

"What then?"

"Relieved," Marilyn said heavily.

At least that made one of them.

Richard called at 8:00 the next morning. "Hi, Mum, what's up?"

"Nothing in particular," Brenda said. "I just realized we haven't talked in a while."

Despite their rocky start when Richard was born and the fact that he was the only one of her three children who'd left the cove, she felt closest to him. She didn't know if this was because he was the youngest and they'd spent the most time together in recent years, or if it was Richard's temperament—probably a bit of both. There was a lot more of her in Richard than in Courtney and Colin.

"We've both been busy," Richard said. "How's the flower garden coming along?"

"Faster than I expected. We had a damp summer and autumn so it's a riot of color at the moment. A last hurrah before winter."

"Send me a photo."

Brenda gazed out the window at the iron garden sculpture Marilyn had bought her—two bronze interlinking circles—and took in a deep breath. "A photo won't do it justice. Come and see it."

"I will. On your birthday."

Her birthday was far too many weeks away for Marilyn to see it as a sign of her commitment to tell the family.

"By then the garden will be winter brown. Come up this weekend or next?"

"I'd love to, Mum, but work's crazy."

Since Glen's death, and more so recently, she'd let Richard get away with that excuse, but not this time. Too much was at stake.

"You worked through the March long weekend and Easter, so the last time you came home was Christmas. I've just read in the paper that the Premier's leaving on a two-week fact-finding mission so

Hobart can spare you for one night. I'll invite Courtney and Colin and we can have family lunch." Static buzzed down the line. "Richard?"

"What if I sneak up and just see you and the garden? I promise I'll come again for your birthday and the full family catastrophe."

Hot and cold flashes raced across her skin—the conversation was fast veering off script. She heard herself say tartly, "Is it too much to ask for you to be in the same room as your brother and sister for *one* lunch?"

Richard sighed and a couple of beats passed before he spoke. "I know you miss Dad, and that you dedicated thirty-odd years to motherhood so it's important to you that we're one big happy family. But just because we share some DNA doesn't mean we have anything in common. I'm about as interested in berries and broccoli as Colin and Courtney are in government policy development. Believe me, catching up twice a year works best for us all."

Although she knew her children weren't close, his words stung. And where did she start to even try to unwrap any of what he'd said? She avoided the topic of missing Glen, his reference to happy families and his misguided notion that she was a career mother. Instead, her mind danced on which was the worse sin—lying to Richard or lying to Marilyn? Could she agree to Richard's plan of "just the two of them," then ambush him with a family lunch when he arrived? Agitation splashed through her.

"This year, I'm asking you to make an exception," she said. "Perhaps three times will be a charm."

"Mum!"

Brenda could imagine him raking his hand through his hair exactly as Glen had done whenever his frustration levels rose.

"You're making it sound like I'm the unreasonable one in this scenario," she said.

"Do you have any idea what it's like for me when I come back to the cove? Courtney peppers me with questions, and the least intrusive one is, am I dating anyone."

Brenda totally understood how uncomfortable it was to be

interrogated by Courtney, but too much was at stake. She pushed aside her natural inclination to side with Richard.

"Is your sister taking an interest in your life really so outrageous? Besides, it's six months since you and Sara parted." Brenda still grieved for the lovely violinist who'd seemed so perfect for her younger son. But Richard had broken Sara's heart by breaking up with her when everyone had been expecting an engagement. "Or are you regretting that decision? Perhaps give her a call—"

"God, Mum!" Richard laughed, the sound oddly harsh. "Why do you think I moved to Hobart?"

The question came out of nowhere and seemed rhetorical, but she answered it anyway. "Initially for uni. Then you stayed for work."

"It's more than that."

Growing up, Richard had worked on the farm for pocket money but, unlike his father and siblings, he'd never shared the same love of living on the edge of the wilderness.

"For the galleries and the Tasmanian Symphony?" she asked.

"That's only part of it." His voice had dropped and he suddenly sounded exhausted.

"Darling, are you okay?"

"I'm fine." A long sigh rattled down the line. "Actually, I'm more than fine, Mum. I've met someone."

"I'm so glad. What's her name?"

"*His* name's Aaron. We've been together seven months."

Brenda sat down hard on a chair as his words clattered in her ears. Was this yet another failing as a mother—that she didn't know her younger son was gay? She rubbed at the sharp pain in her temples.

"Mum? You still there?"

"Yes. I ... You ... That's wonderful, darling." She hauled in a deep breath, trying to slow her racing heart. "Falling in love's the best feeling in the world. I'm glad Aaron makes you happy. Thank you for telling me."

"Thanks, Mum. Sorry it was on the phone." His voice rumbled

with relief. "I'd planned to tell you in person, but whenever I come up, the family gathers en masse and ..."

"Do your brother and sister know?" she asked, already sensing the answer.

"Not yet. I'll tell them when I'm ready."

A sudden surge of aggravation hit her—its target centered on Marilyn. "It's your news, Richard. It's up to you when and who you tell."

"Thanks, Mum. You're being remarkably cool about it. I wasn't sure—"

"I just want you to be happy!"

He laughed. "I can promise you I am. Hang on a sec." She heard the muffled rumble of male voices and then Richard was back on the line. "I don't want to put you in a difficult position with Colin and Courtney, but if we do family lunch, can Aaron come too?"

Her first thought was safety in numbers. Richard's news would take the spotlight off her. "Yes, of course. It will be great to meet him."

"Awesome. We can be there on the tenth."

It was a month away and she could picture Marilyn's reaction to the delay. "You can't manage it any earlier?"

"No, sorry. Aaron's a chef and that's his next weekend off."

She swallowed her disappointment, which she couldn't deny was tempered by considerable relief. The delay gave her more time with Courtney before the news broke.

"The tenth it is then. I'll let the others know." She heard the nervous quiver in her voice. "And it's funny that you want to introduce someone to us, because there's someone I want you and your brother and sister to meet."

"A special someone?" Richard's tone wavered between shock and delight. "Neither Courtney or Colin have even hinted you have a special friend. Hang on, it's not Brian Jolly, is it?"

"It's definitely not Brian Jolly!"

"Okay, Mum. Keep your hair on. Who is it then?"

Unlike Richard, she was not coming out over the phone. "Like you,

I want to keep it a secret until the tenth. You know how your sister is about your father and I want to be the one to tell her."

"How on earth have you kept it secret from Courtney, let alone the cove?" he asked.

"You're not the only person in this family capable of keeping a secret."

"Fair enough. Love you, Mum. See you on the tenth."

"See you then."

Buoyed by the conversation, she immediately texted Colin and Courtney, inviting them and their families for lunch. Not inviting their spouses or the grandchildren would generate far more questions than she wanted to answer. When it came to the after-lunch conversation, Olivia could take the cousins for a walk while the adults talked.

Colin replied with *Check with Lucinda.* As Brenda was texting her daughter-in-law, Courtney sent a thumbs-up emoji and *Can't wait to see Rich.* Lucinda replied within a minute, texting *It's on the calendar. What can I bring?*

The speed of the replies stunned Brenda, but she took it as a sign that the gathering would be a success.

Clyde trotted into the kitchen, his nails clacking on the tiles, quickly followed by Marilyn.

Brenda stood and pulled her in for a kiss. "We have a date for family lunch."

Marilyn leaned back and studied her face. "When?"

Brenda tensed at her tone, uncertain of how she would react to the month's wait. "I pushed hard for next weekend, but Richard's first available date is the tenth. Everyone can make it."

"Thank you." Marilyn returned her kiss. "You seem remarkably calm."

"I am."

And it was the truth. For months she'd been tying herself up in knots about telling the children about Marilyn, but now she had an unexpected ally in Richard. His news was wonderful and welcome, but also serendipitous. Courtney loved and adored her younger brother and forgave him anything.

For the first time since Brenda had agreed to come out, she got a real sense that everything was pointing in her favor. Not only was it time; everything would be fine.

CHAPTER SEVENTEEN

Henry was eating an apple and staring at the big calendar on the wall. "So we'll need to leave at 5:00 on Thursday night."

Steph paused in wiping down the highchair, her mind with her baby as it often was. "What's happening on Thursday?"

"Parent-teacher conferences for Zoe."

Steph's hand tightened around the cloth. She and Henry had already argued about his offer to pay for Joanna to fly over and attend. "When you say 'we' you mean you and Joanna, right? Please tell me you didn't invite her to Four Winds."

Henry grimaced. "I haven't, and I doubt she's flying down. She hasn't replied to my emails or my texts."

Steph thought there was every chance Joanna would demand Henry book her a last-minute flight when fares were sky-high. "When did you last talk to her?"

"Not since Zoe got her cell phone."

"Henry! That's weeks ago."

"Don't say it like that. It's not like I haven't tried, but you know what she's like."

Steph did, and sadly there was a lot of manipulative Joanna in Zoe.

"But either way, you're coming, right?" Henry asked with a hint of entreaty.

"I hadn't planned on it."

His eyes widened in surprise. "Considering how vocal you've been about the passion project, I thought you'd not only want to be there but first in line."

The passion project was one of those behemoths that not only challenged the students but completely drained the parents. Zoe was yet to choose her "passion," let alone research it, interview experts and decide on the creative way she would present it on the presentation night. Before the miscarriage, Steph had tried guiding Zoe toward something involving numbers, but the response had either been apathetic or explosive. Now she didn't care if the girl did the project or not. It was Henry's problem.

"It isn't that I don't want to come," she lied, "but we don't have anyone who can babysit. Besides, it's choir rehearsal and getting back in time will be tight."

"Choir's Tuesday."

"For the next three weeks it's twice a week so we're ready for the Community Choir Crush."

Henry turned back to the calendar and squinted at the boxes. "There's nothing on the calendar."

"Really?" She was suddenly confused. "I was sure I'd written it all down."

"Not even the concert." Henry grinned, then made a fist and pulled down his arm. "Woohoo, Monty! Daddy's normally the one getting into trouble for forgetting to put things on the calendar."

My baby died.

Steph threw the cloth onto the sink, wiped her hands and stomped over to the calendar. Plucking the pen from Henry's hand, she wrote in the extra rehearsals and circled the concert date in red.

"I hope you can come," she said.

"Zo, Monty and I will be there with bells on and we'll cheer the loudest." Henry gave her a gentle squeeze around the waist and kissed her. "With band and choir, midweek's getting busy. Hopefully I can still sneak in a surf."

Since they'd moved, Henry's surfing had increased from once or twice a week to whenever there was an easterly. Just lately that had been up to five times a week. What had been easy on their vacation—everyone lazing on the beach while he surfed—hadn't translated to everyday life with its demands of work, school, kids and housework. Lately, Steph found herself flinching whenever Henry mentioned surfing. Far from being relaxing for her, it meant she was the adult in charge, juggling dinner and kids and reminding Henry to rinse out his wetsuit.

She decided to tackle it. "Ben Burton rang this morning. The tractors have sold and he wants five more."

Henry dropped his apple core into the overflowing compost bucket and closed the lid on it. "Have you got time to make them?"

"I do if you don't surf this week and you cook dinner three nights." She stopped herself from saying "the three nights you agreed to."

"But surfing's my exercise and relaxation. It's part of why we moved here."

Her simmering frustration boiled over. "And working from home and being a team is why we moved here too. But the dodgy internet means half the time you're working elsewhere and my work time gets whittled away by childcare!"

Monty startled at her raised voice and his bottom lip trembled.

"It's not my fault we have a mountain between us and the tower." Henry scooped up Monty. "And raising our children is hardly childcare."

Our children? *My baby died.*

"We agreed I was starting my own business."

"You are." He glanced at the overlocker that she'd hardly touched since the miscarriage. Making baby hats hurt way too much. "But with the—" He paused. "With everything that's happened, perhaps you need to give yourself some time."

"Miscarriage, Henry! Our baby died. Don't lessen it by not naming it!"

He grimaced at her shrewish tone. "Sorry. I was trying not to upset you."

Shame and anger swirled together before smashing into grief. Tears threatened and she blinked fast. She didn't want to cry again—she'd been crying on and off for weeks. She wanted some respite from thinking about her baby all the time, but she feared if she moved her focus she'd forget. That hurt as much as the miscarriage. But somewhere in the middle of this contradictory mess of failure, she had a driving desire to achieve something.

"I don't have time to take time," she said hotly. "I have a commission from Ben. When that's finished, I'm going to make an acrobatic penguin from Gramps's patterns and some stacking circus people."

Henry rubbed the back of his neck. "So you're moving away from kids' clothes and into wooden toys?"

She had no idea what she was doing, just the urge to do *something* and fill the empty space inside her. Suddenly she was saying, "I'm launching the online store of Steph's Retro Toys by the end of the month."

"Ah, Steph, the end of the month isn't very far away."

She hated his gentle tone. "I'm aware."

"How's it all going to work when half the time our internet doesn't?" he asked in the business tone he usually directed at his interns.

She glared at him. "I'll do what you do and go into town or to Wynyard."

"How will you manage it on top of choir and the kids?"

Their vacation conversation under the Norfolk pine came back to her. "Just like we planned. Sharing everything fifty-fifty."

A pained look crossed his face. "That was when we assumed the internet was reliable and childcare was available. Until we get that sorted, I think you should wait."

My baby died.

"No! I need a go-live date or my business will never have a chance of getting off the ground. I need you to take it seriously."

"I do take it seriously!" Indignation flared red on his cheeks. "I'm behind you all the way, but you don't seem to know what you want. First it was kids' hats, now it's wooden toys. What will it be next week? Outdoor playhouses? Do you even have a business plan? A website designer? A photographer?"

His questions pummeled her, but before she could say "Yes! Me! All me!" his phone rang.

"Whoever it is, call them back," she said. "We need to talk about my business."

"And we will, but right now we need my income to support whatever the hell your business is." He hand-balled Monty to her. "This call's important. I have to take it."

"Of course you do," she muttered to his retreating back. "It's always bloody important."

With Monty in the carrier backpack, Steph was panting slightly as she hiked back around the point with Addy, but it felt great to be outside and exerting herself. It was Friday afternoon and Henry was surfing before the sun dropped below the horizon. Zoe had refused his invitation to join him; she'd barely spoken a word since getting off the bus. Before the miscarriage, Steph would have pushed Henry to try harder to get Zoe to surf with him, but since that awful night she lacked the energy. She no longer engaged with Zoe much beyond "dinner's ready" and "please tidy your room." If Henry had noticed he hadn't commented and that suited Steph—it was one less argument.

When Zoe had flounced off to her room, Steph had blown off preparing dinner, called Addy and arranged the walk. Sure, it meant in a couple of hours she'd have to deal with a tired and hungry Monty, but so would Henry. Zoe would be sullen and difficult with or without food.

Up until the steep section of track on their way back from the cave, Addy had been unusually chatty, asking Steph about her week. She was enthusiastic about the acrobatic penguins—"My father made me a bear and I loved it. It's probably still in the house somewhere." She'd also listened attentively to Steph's idea of planting a white rhododendron bush close to the house in memory of the baby.

But as they reached the top of the climb, Addy sank onto the ground and gulped down water. "God, the world's spinning."

"At least it's from exercise," Steph said. "I still remember the one and only time I got so drunk the world spun and I couldn't stand up. I was gripping the porcelain as if it was the only thing stopping me from sliding off the edge of the world."

Addy raised her brows. "You've only been seriously drunk once? You're putting me on."

"It's true!" Steph shuddered at the memory of vomiting so hard she felt like her stomach would follow. "I was so sick I vowed I'd never let it happen again. Don't get me wrong—I'm no puritan. I enjoy a drink, but I hate the feeling of not being in control. You know what I mean?"

Addy grimaced. "Control's an illusion."

Steph thought about the miscarriage. How long she'd taken to get pregnant only to lose the baby. Was Addy right? Was all her and Henry's planning worthless? Did they exist only to be buffeted by forces far beyond their control? The thoughts unsettled her, shaking the feel-good effects of the walk.

Addy lurched to her feet. "I think we should start a tradition of celebrating Fridays with a walk and a whine and a wine. After all, we've both survived another week without killing Brian—"

"Or Courtney!"

Addy laughed. "True, but at least the girl can sing."

Steph gave a begrudging nod. "You're our ace though. I get shivers when you sing that line about scars."

Addy suddenly bent down to retie her shoelace, and Monty, who'd been chattering happily, banged Steph on the head. It was a sure sign he'd had enough time in the carrier and was approaching meltdown. The pleasant interlude was over.

Steph felt the pull of responsibilities, but at the same time she was loath to fully give in. "Do you want to come back to Four Winds for a drink?"

"I don't have my car, which makes it complicated afterwards,"

Addy said quickly without looking up. "How about I buy you a glass of wine at the surf club and Monty can explore the play equipment?"

Monty was likely to crack it from exhaustion, but the playground might just keep him going so it was worth a shot. "Great, but I can't stay too long so just one glass."

"One glass is all I can have too. I have to work after dinner."

"That's too bad on a Friday night," Steph said.

Addy shrugged. "Short-term pain for long-term gain. It's going to be worth it."

"Sounds like I should be buying the wine and toasting your promotion."

"I won't argue with that," Addy said with a laugh. "Race you to the bar."

An hour later, when Steph walked into Four Winds holding a screaming Monty, she found Henry in the kitchen dicing ingredients for a stir-fry.

He gave her a kiss and lifted Monty out of her arms. "Where have you been? I was calling."

"I went for a walk with Addy to check out the cave."

"But it's been dark for an hour."

"We had a drink at the surf club."

Still screaming, Monty reached for the capsicum. "Mine!"

"He's hungry," she said.

"Hardly surprising since it's an hour past the time you normally feed him."

She ignored the censure in Henry's voice. "Is dinner ready?"

"Does it look ready? I was waiting for you to get home. Do you want to cook or wrangle Monty?"

Zoe walked in, her face set in a scowl. "Geez, kid. What's with all the noise? Steph jabbing you with a knife?"

"Zo! Zo!" Monty reached for her, but Zoe ducked around the counter. Monty's screams hit an agonizing pitch.

As Steph's ears rang she bit back "Selfish bitch!", lifted the thrashing and writhing Monty out of Henry's arms and maneuvered him into his highchair. She grabbed dip and crackers and, ignoring Henry's disbelieving look, gave them to their overtired and over-hungry son.

"Zo, do you want to set the table or cook the chicken in the wok?" Henry asked, not addressing the line about the knife.

Zoe recoiled from the counter. "Oh my God! I'm not touching raw chicken."

Henry didn't blink. "So that's a yes to setting the table."

"And I'm not eating chicken either. Do you know what its life was like? Stuck in a cage, having its eyes pecked out. I refuse to have anything to do with the inhumane treatment of animals."

"I think most Australian farmers go to great lengths to give their stock a contented life and a humane death," Henry said. "We certainly have the space for that. Perhaps this could be your passion project? You know, hearing both sides of the story rather than depending on the internet. The good thing is, we're surrounded by dairy and sheep farmers you can interview."

Zoe shook her head. "I'm never eating meat again!"

Steph wished she'd stayed at the surf club and drunk the second glass of wine Addy had suggested. "There's one slight problem with this plan, Zoe. You're not a big fan of vegetables."

"I eat potatoes," Zoe said sulkily.

"I was vegetarian once," Henry mused. "It takes a bit of planning to make sure you get the iron and protein your growing body needs.

Milk and eggs are good." He grinned. "And cheese. Lucky you love cheese."

Zoe's jaw jutted. "I'm not eating milk or honey or eggs ever again either!"

Steph wondered what the hell she'd done in a past life to deserve this. "So you're vegan?"

"Someone has to save the world you're destroying!" Zoe yelled.

"That's rich coming from someone who dumped her empty shampoo bottle in the trash instead of the recycling," Steph said.

"More!" Monty demanded.

Steph handed him a cracker covered in hummus, then offered the dip to Zoe. "Hummus is vegan."

The girl screwed up her nose. "You know I don't like it."

"So you want me to add tofu to the shopping list?" Steph said.

"What's that?" Zoe asked suspiciously.

"Curdled soy milk."

"Yuck! No way I'm eating that!"

Henry frowned at Steph and gave his head a slight shake that implied "be quiet."

"Over the weekend, Zo, we can research veganism together," he said. "Find out the full story and all the health impacts."

"There's nothing to find out," Zoe said mutinously. "I'm only eating stuff that comes from plants, and plants are healthy."

"The thing is, we're not plants and we need—"

"You're not talking me out of this, Dad! Mum understands!"

"So you've discussed going vegan with your mother?" Steph asked.

Zoe's eyes flashed. "It's my body and my choice!"

Of course Joanna would be encouraging Zoe to be vegan. It was yet another way to make Henry's—and by default Steph's—life harder. At thirteen, Zoe wasn't mature enough to eat all the food that was necessary for a balanced vegan diet and she risked making herself sick. But since the miscarriage, Steph didn't have the stamina, the inclination or the care and affection that was needed for the task.

A thought pierced her fog of sadness—was veganism the issue that would make Zoe demand to return to live with her mother?

"Wee! Wee!" Monty said.

Steph lifted him out of the highchair. "Fine, Zoe, I'll buy vegan food and you and your father can cook it."

She left the room before either Henry or Zoe said a word.

CHAPTER EIGHTEEN

IN-BETWEEN HER TEACHING LOAD, Addy was slowly visiting each department. Her aim was to chat to the teaching staff and help them pinpoint any glaring holes in their program so they could fill them before the audit. She'd started with Ravi. Even though she knew Grant wanted her for the 2IC position, she was sure Ravi would have applied. As she ran through his course work with him, she was pleased to see he lacked the experience to be a threat.

Next was the training farm. She'd arrived without considering her footwear, and Tim had been gracious and found her a pair of rubber boots before he walked her over the property. His knowledge of livestock and rotational grazing was impressive, and his students all had positive things to say about him. Back in his office, things were curlier.

"I'm more interested in the hands-on stuff," he conceded.

Addy nodded. "It's why we teach." She clicked through a series of incomplete reports and read some of the phrasing. Her heart sank. Was Tim dyslexic?

"Have reports always been a struggle for you?" she asked.

Tim looked at his hands. For a moment Addy held her breath,

worried she'd offended him. He sighed. "Pretty much. When I had the farm, the wife did all the paperwork and she helped me with my Cert IV. When I got this job, Craig—he was the boss before Grant—well, he said not to worry about reports."

Addy repressed a flinch. "And Grant?"

Tim's cheeks pinked. "He asks everyone to upload them, but he's never chased me for them."

Considering how on top of the budget Grant appeared to be, this surprised Addy.

"Unfortunately, reports play a role in the audit," she said. "To justify our funding we have to tick all the boxes."

Tim's flush suddenly paled and he licked his lips. "Are you saying I have to do two years' worth of reports?"

"Not on your own." She tapped the desk, trying to come up with an idea that would help Tim and not sink her under an even bigger workload. But her first thought wasn't about the problem, just an awareness that her fingers were playing "Badinerie" from Bach's *Suite in B minor*. Horrified, she clenched her fist. "Could your wife help you get the basics down? Then I'll edit them into vocational education speak. Do you think that will help?"

"Thank you!" Tim was suddenly pumping her hand. "That would be stellar."

She soaked in his appreciation. "We do have a deadline though. Are you sure your wife has the time?"

"We'll make it work."

Tim had sent her on her way with fresh milk and honey, and a promise to email the first report in forty-eight hours.

Three days later, the Automotive department was proving to be less welcoming. After failing to receive a response to her email asking Jett for a time that suited him, she'd called and he'd begrudgingly agreed to mid-morning.

As she stepped into the back entrance of the workshop, her first shock was the temperature. She was used to a warm office and the chill in the metal building ate into her. She berated herself for not grabbing her jacket.

The second shock was a calendar stuck on an old fridge showing a scantily dressed woman draped provocatively over a car. What year was this again? The calendar would have to go—there was no way it would pass the audit.

She found Jett's office empty, so she walked into the main workshop.

A teen girl in blue overalls and holding tools passed Addy, her head down.

"Hi, can you help me, please?" Addy asked.

The girl's head rose slightly and she gave Addy a sideways and extremely cautious look—like an animal sensing danger.

Addy smiled, hoping it would reassure her. "I'm looking for Mr. Longeron. Do you know where he is?"

Worry streaked across the girl's face. "Who?" she asked softly.

"She's looking for Jett," a male voice said.

The girl ducked her head again, her previous hesitancy replaced by embarrassment.

Something inside Addy ached. "There's no need to be sor—" But the girl was scurrying away like a mouse seeking shelter.

A male student was now looking straight at Addy, his gaze long and appraising. Despite a flash of discomfort, Addy forced herself to meet his eyes. "Do you know where Jett is?"

"He's probably," he glanced at the big clock on the wall, "nicked out for coffee."

Addy couldn't decide if Jett not being there was passive aggressive or a genuine coincidence. Meanwhile, she felt the curious glances from the other students in the workshop and instinctively knew she needed to be strong in this very male domain.

Stepping around an oil spill, she walked over to the student who'd spoken to her. "What are you working on?"

"What every woman with a car should be intimate with."

Only knowing the bare basics of car maintenance, Addy was intrigued. "And what's that?"

His eyes raked her lazily. "Head."

In that split second her gut cramped and she felt like the female student—exposed—but then he was saying, "gasket." She glanced around, looking for a reaction to prove he'd just sexually harassed her, but none of the other students had laughed or looked embarrassed— sure signs they knew what he was doing. Perhaps the slight hesitation was his speech cadence? Had he hesitated the first time he spoke? Or had this been deliberate?

Show no fear.

"Head gasket means the engine's useless, right?" she asked.

"It's not good. Do you ... want me to show you?"

She heard the hesitation a second time and relaxed. "Okay." She peered from where she stood.

"You won't ... see it from there."

"Addy!" Jett walked into the workshop and raised a coffee cup in salute. "Thanks for looking after Miz Topic, Reese."

The student grinned. "I'm showing ... her the engine."

"You'll need to get closer than that, Addy." Jett pointed to a raised platform. "Step up there."

Her high heels and pencil skirt were far more suited to the office and didn't lend themselves to easily scaling a platform. She needed to hitch her skirt to mid-thigh to take the step.

"So what am I looking at?" she asked.

Reese indicated a point on the opposite side of the engine, closer to where Jett was standing. Why hadn't he suggested she use the platform on the other side? Tamping down her frustration, she leaned over to see it and honor his enthusiasm for his area of study.

As Reese was talking, Jett was fiddling with his cell phone and she heard him mutter, "Bloody Lyn."

She couldn't help smiling, and he shot back a cheeky grin that gave her a snapshot of what he would have looked like as a kid. It was the first moment of simpatico they'd ever shared and she hoped it meant he'd be cooperative with the audit preparation.

"Righto, Reese, I reckon you've bored Miz Topic for long enough," Jett said. "Come on, Addy, let's do this meeting."

Fifteen minutes later Addy had relaxed. The meeting had gone far more smoothly than she'd anticipated and without any of the antagonism Jett usually directed at her in faculty meetings. His reports were excellent and the student surveys positive.

"There's a push to get women entering the trades," she said. "How many female students do you have?"

Jett leaned back in his chair and sighed. "The government might want that, but the reality is the work's dirty, heavy and dangerous."

Addy thought about the modern engines that always looked so clean and the hydraulic lifts that moved vehicles with seeming ease. "And?"

He skated his chair forward and opened up a spreadsheet. "And girls enroll, last a few weeks, then drop out."

"Can I see their survey responses?" Addy asked.

"We only survey students at the end of the year."

She opened the self-assessment document to page seventeen. "We need to show feedback to demonstrate the effectiveness of our practice. If female students are dropping out at a higher rate than males, we need to know why."

Jett leaned back and crossed his arms. "I just told you why."

Addy decided to ignore his combative body language and the slight edge in his voice. She nodded and smiled. "And ASQA will want to hear your opinion as well as feedback from the students on why they left the course early. Moving forward, when a student drops out, please ask them to complete an exit survey."

He swore, then grimaced. "Sorry, Addy. That wasn't directed at you, just the government in general. I got into teaching to give kids like Reese who've done it tough an opportunity. I didn't do it to push paper around to please the bureaucrats."

"I know it's a pain," Addy said. "But honestly, you've got this. Other departments aren't as on top of things as you are."

"Yeah?" Jett grinned at her. "Make my day and tell me I'm doing better than Bettina in Hair and Beauty."

She laughed. "No names, no pack drill." Wanting to finish on a positive note, she said, "By the way, great photo on the staff portal the other day."

"Thanks. I got one of the students to load it up. They have their uses."

She slung her satchel onto her shoulder. "Thanks for your time."

"No problem. I have to say, it was a lot less painful than I expected."

"Excellent! I'll take that as one of my three gratitudes for the day."

As Jett walked her across the workshop, she heard the respect his students had for him in their banter. At the door, he said, "Catch up soon, Miz Topic."

"See you at the next faculty meeting."

Feeling light and happy, she found herself humming on the walk back to the lecture theatre. It took her a moment before she realized it was the tune from "This Is Me." She bit her lip and tried to replace it with something else. It wasn't that she had anything against the tune, but the lyrics broke her out in a sweat every single time. She'd taken to having a couple of drinks before each choir rehearsal and a few immediately after just to survive the agonizing ninety minutes.

It was clear from the other choir members' enthusiasm for the Community Choir Crush that she was the only person bothered by the song. When word had gotten around town that the choir had a gig, more people had joined. Fourteen voices made it a choir, which was great news. As soon as the concert was over, Addy could quit without letting anyone down. She was counting the sleeps.

She was also counting the sleeps until the end of semester, when her teaching load finished and she officially started her new job. Grant had told her he'd pressed HR to interview her while she was down in

Hobart, but as Scott Matheson had spearheaded the conference he'd been too busy.

"Heather and Scott are syncing their calendars," Grant had said. "Hopefully it will happen in the next couple of weeks."

Addy stopped walking and checked the date, surprised it was twenty-two days since the conference. She and Grant had one of their dinner meetings scheduled tonight—she was briefing him on the internal assessment for the audit—so she'd ask him about the state of play then.

Not for the first time since the conference, a warm feeling of relief washed through her. Grant had been true to his word—what happens at conference stays at conference. Sure, they'd shared the occasional joke about the side effects of whisky and they stuck to cider at their working dinners, but as Addy's memories of the night were sketchy at best and Grant remained his professional and supportive self, she found it easy to leave behind any hint of indignity about blacking out.

There'd been a couple of occasions that could be interpreted as continuing interest from Grant, and Addy wasn't against the idea, but nothing could happen until she was officially 2IC. The last thing she needed were accusations she was sleeping with the boss to get the job.

She suddenly laughed. Having sex with him to get 2IC would be a hell of a lot easier than the two and a half jobs she was doing.

"Laughing alone in the parking lot is a direct line to insanity," a female voice said.

Addy turned and saw one of her older-adult social media students coming toward her. "You're probably right, Lana."

Together they walked into the lecture room. Despite Addy's stress at having to devise the course from scratch, the social media students were a fun bunch and a joy to teach compared with the challenges of her pre-college students.

Addy was halfway through the class on building social engagement and giving examples of "savable" content when she heard whispers and noticed bowed heads over cell phones. The bowed heads were normal—she encouraged the class to look at particular social media accounts as she discussed different strategies—but the whispering was unusual.

"Has someone found an example of savable content worthy of sharing?" she asked.

"Is this what you mean?" Lana offered her phone. "I've been experimenting with micro photos of the beach near our B & B."

Addy studied the photos—one of a man's and a woman's palms covered in white sand, another of sea stars clustered on a rock, and a lone beach chair on an empty expanse of sand. "This is fabulous."

She typed in Lana's Instagram name and brought the account up on the big screen. "Everyone, this is a perfect example of savable content. With these images, Lana is selling the idea of time to sit on an empty beach and relax. Time to soak up what nature has to offer. Time to step out of a busy life and chill in a beautiful and peaceful place. How are your bookings?"

Lana smiled. "They're up since I stopped focusing exclusively on photos of the inside of the house."

"But customers can find those easily?" Addy checked.

"Yes, I have the link to the B & B in my bio."

"Great work, Lana." She glanced expectantly at the rest of the class. "Who wants to share another example?"

By the time the class finished and she'd fielded questions on the assignment, Addy was late getting back to her office. She was checking her electronic calendar when an Instagram notification appeared. She'd started an account purely to understand the interface for the class. She had few followers and rarely posted, although she was a sucker for the many moods of the Rookery Cove beach and the penguins. She was surprised to see she'd been tagged in a post so she clicked through.

It was a close-up photo of a woman from the neck down leaning over a car engine. Although her breasts were hidden behind a scoop top, the angle showed them pressed together with a deep cleavage that hinted at generous and pillow-soft double-Ds. There was the perfect outline of erect nipples. The woman may as well have been naked.

Addy's mouth dried as she recognized the green silk top. *Oh God!* It was her! The cold of the workshop and the angle from which the photo had been taken made a perfectly sedate work outfit look like she was a sex worker touting for business.

She noticed a gray dot under the photo and forced herself to swipe left. The second picture showed her skirt pulled tight across her behind, exposing a large expanse of thigh and hinting at possibly no underwear. She shoved the phone face down on her desk and gulped in deep breaths.

Who'd taken the photos? Who'd uploaded them?

A wave of nausea hit her. Was this what her class had been tittering about? Had the photos gone around campus and everyone knew it was her?

She grabbed the phone and checked the account name—Hotties on Hoods—and scrolled through. There were lots of photos of scantily dressed and naked young women draped over cars. Most were posing, looking straight at the camera with pouty lips and sultry looks. But some, like the photos of her, had obviously been taken without permission, reducing the woman to body parts.

She wanted to curl up and hide. God, she needed a drink. Why the hell didn't she keep a bottle in her office or carry a hip-flask?

Different images suddenly flashed in her head—images she'd locked away a long, long time ago so they couldn't hurt her again. Suddenly the heat of anger burned through her shame. God damn it, she was 2IC and this was image-based abuse.

She rang Grant. "Are you free? I really need to talk to you."

"You sound upset. Are you in your office? I'll come to you."

His sincerity and concern wrapped around her like a soft blanket and tears threatened. "Thank you."

"Too easy. Hang tight. I'll be there in a tick."

CHAPTER NINETEEN

ADDY PACED until Grant walked in holding a college promotional bag with the slogan *Reach for your Future* printed on the front. He closed the door, lifted out a bottle of whisky and a shot glass, and poured.

"Get that into you. It'll take the edge off."

She almost hugged him, and downed two shots in quick succession. The fire burned through her fast before settling into comforting warmth, reassuring her that everything would be okay.

He pulled his chair in, his knees close to hers. "What's up?"

"I visited the Automotive workshop this morning as part of the internal assessment for the audit." With a shaking hand, she passed him her phone. "This turned up on Instagram."

He made a low moan. "Shit."

"Exactly!" His dismay buoyed her. "It's such an invasion of privacy, not to mention illegal and a nightmare for the campus if local media get hold of it."

"It's not great." He gave her a reassuring smile. "But on the positive side of an awful situation, no one can see your face and you're wearing a great bra."

She heard herself laugh and wondered why. Nothing about any of this was funny.

She showed him the second photo. "They were taken while a student was talking to me about the engine."

"Damn." He took a moment, his gaze fixed on her. "So two students whipped out their cell phones? I was hoping it was a lone ranger."

Addy sucked in a deep breath and forced herself to speak. "The entire time I was standing there, Jett was opposite me and using his cell phone."

Grant frowned. "Addy, are you implying Jett took one of the photos?"

She tensed, trying to stall the trembles in her toes from overtaking her body. "I think it's very possible."

Grant sat back in his chair. "I know you're upset and hell, you have every right to be, but this is Jett we're talking about. He's well regarded and he's run that department for years."

So? "I'm not sure how that's connected?"

"It's connected because there's never been a problem like this before."

"Never? You've only been here a year," she said.

"Sure. But if it had been happening before that, even if no one ever reported him, stuff like this has a way of getting out and becoming an open secret." Grant gave a quiet chuckle. "Besides, we both know Jett is clueless on technology. He can't even upload a photo to the staff portal, let alone Instagram."

I got one of the students to load it up. Jett's words shot back loud and clear. Had they been a shot across the bow?

Grant was still talking. "Anyway, how could Jett have taken a photo of you without you noticing?"

In an attempt to slow her racing heart and to help her think, she interlaced her fingers, pressing them together so tightly they hurt. "I was giving my full attention to the student, not Jett. But this photo's a close-up so who else could have taken it?"

"Probably any number of students." Grant sighed. "I'll talk to Jett. He knows his students so he might have an idea of the culprits."

"I think it's a bigger problem than just photos," Addy said.

"What do you mean?"

She told him about the calendar in the workshop, the attrition rate of female students, and what Reese had said to her. "There's a misogynistic culture."

Grant sighed. "You've had a nasty shock and it's completely understandable you're rattled. But a misogynistic culture? Let's not go jumping the gun."

"I don't think I am! The numbers don't lie. The trades are bleeding female students, and if it keeps happening we'll lose our funding, which impacts the budget."

He grimaced. "Are the dropout rates really that high?"

"Yes."

He rubbed his face with his palms and when he looked at her again, resignation ringed him. "I'll set up a meeting with Jett for a serious chat."

Jett was an oily snake so she wasn't certain "a chat" would be enough.

"Grant, I want the photos taken down. I want an apology. I want every student enrolled in Automotive to do training on why this sort of behavior's not only inappropriate, but illegal."

"I promise you I'll do everything we can to find the culprit and stop it from happening again," he said. "And we'll investigate if there are deeper issues regarding the female students' dropout rates."

"Thank you." Relief flowed through her like a river and she sank back in her chair, exhausted. "I just want the photos gone."

"Understood." His knees touched hers and he leaned in, his gaze searching and intent. "Are you feeling better?"

She smiled. "A bit."

"Good. Anything else I can help you with?"

"Would you mind if we rescheduled our dinner meeting to another night?" she asked. "I'm feeling wrung out. I think I'll take an early mark."

"No problem."

"Thanks. By the way, any news on an interview date yet?"

"Hopefully they'll confirm at our Zoom meeting, but pencil in Friday week." He checked his watch and shot to his feet. "Sorry, Addy, the meeting starts in two minutes. You okay if I go?"

"Of course." She stood too, her legs still a little shaky. "Thanks for the support."

He gave her shoulder a squeeze. "Anytime. Keep the bottle. You might just need another shot while you're tackling Instagram."

Her mind churned and came up blank. "Sorry?"

He gave her a sad smile. "As much as I want to sort this mess out for you, Hotties on Hoods isn't a college account."

"Not an official one anyway," she muttered.

He laughed. "I'm glad your sense of humor's intact. The problem is, as the photos are illegal pictures of you, you're the only person who can request they be taken down. Good luck and let me know how you go."

He walked out of the door before her stunned mind could muster a reply.

So much for an early mark! It turned out that trying to get a photo removed from an unknown account was a nightmare. She'd untagged herself and changed her privacy settings, but that didn't remove the photo from the internet. And surprise, surprise, there'd been no response from Hotties on Hoods to her request for it to be taken down. Although she'd reported it, the wheels turned slowly—after all, the only person its removal was important to was Addy.

The whole episode threw her back into the pond of powerlessness she'd floundered in as a teen, when adults dictated her life. She'd fought long and hard to keep her head above water and had finally hauled herself up, out and far away. Blinking hard, she forced back tears. She wouldn't cry—she'd come too far to let the bastards win. But dear God, why did it have to be so hard?

By the time she drove into the cove, the numbing effects of the whisky had well and truly worn off and she desperately needed a drink. But instead of turning into her street, she made a split-second decision to let the car roll down the hill to the beach. Perhaps Steph was there with Monty? But the sun was dropping fast and, apart from a dog, the beach was empty. She looked beyond the sand and saw a lone surfer out in the churning mess a northerly always blew up. They were either foolhardy or an adrenaline junky.

Addy craved drinking company and since Steph's miscarriage, her friend was usually up for a nice, cold bevvy. The good thing about Steph was that she could talk underwater with a mouthful of marbles, so Addy could enjoy her company without saying much.

Fancy a whine and wine? She typed on her cell phone.

Her finger moved to hit the send arrow when she realized the day and the time. Henry would be at band practice, meaning Steph couldn't just drop everything. She'd probably invite Addy to Four Winds instead. Even if Addy had a desire to see the renovations Steph constantly chatted about—and she didn't—she could already picture Steph distracted by the kids. Plus the flapping ears of a teen girl meant they couldn't talk about the Instagram issue.

New plan—she'd go home, reheat last night's pizza and crack open the bottle of sauv blanc the guy at the liquor store had recommended when she'd handed over her loyalty card.

Addy deleted the text and slid her phone back in her bag. As she withdrew her hand, her fingers were caressed by the soft leather cover of her bullet journal. After being without it in Hobart, she'd put it in her handbag so it was always close. Not that it had increased her use of it.

She tugged it from her bag, needing to read *I own this year*, but it fell open to *I will only party on the weekends* and her ever-increasing list of migratory tasks. An overwhelming urge to snap it shut tensed her fingers, but she refused to be hostage to a tool that was supposed to be helping her, not shaming her. Hell! Having a drink after work wasn't partying! Having a drink after a crap day like today wasn't partying either—it was absolutely necessary. As for the length of the migratory list, it existed purely because she was currently working two and a half jobs.

She rummaged for a pen, flicked the pages forward until she found the day she was looking for and scrawled *job interview TBA*.

"See? I do own this year."

She snapped the journal shut, but as she was shoving it back in her bag, she dropped it. It landed on the floor, open on the goals page— *I will get fit and lose weight*.

"I walk with Steph on Fridays!"

The journal mocked her.

"Fine! I'll walk now." Her indignation had her kicking off her shoes and propelling her out of the car.

"Fa-ar out!" The wind buffeted her and she was tempted to get back into the car, but she grabbed her puffer instead. She'd walk the length of the beach and then she'd go home for the drink she deserved without being harassed by the bloody black book. Walking on sand took double the energy of walking on hard surfaces and it burned fifty percent more calories.

The border collie on the beach ignored her, keeping its gaze fixed firmly on the surfer. No wonder people invested in dogs rather than relationships—that sort of undying loyalty didn't steal money from you, block you and cost you even more money trying to retrieve the original debt. *Bloody Jasper*. The small-claims process was yet another item on her migratory list. She either paid someone to serve the papers on him or she took a trip back to Victoria and did it herself.

Stop it! Be mindful. Breathe! You're on a beautiful beach.

A beautiful beach where the wind was doing a solid job of blowing her backwards. She screamed her frustrations into the air and let the gale carry them away.

Her straight skirt prevented her from striding out so she walked quickly to compensate and to get her heart rate pounding. By the time she reached the black volcanic rocks, her calves were screaming and a river of sweat was dripping down her back. The internet was wrong—walking on sand was three times more difficult than hard surfaces. Despite the windchill, she took off her puffer and spun around and around, welcoming the cool air on her steaming skin.

On the return walk she noticed the lone surfer. He'd been hanging out just beyond the break to avoid the foaming soup, but now he was kneeling and paddling. She stopped and watched him tackle the first decent wave. He rose, the action smooth and clean, and made the drop with grace and ease.

The dog barked, rose from its huddled position and charged into the shallows as the surfer rode the wave to shore and stepped off his board. The dog ran halfway around him before doubling back, leaping and barking as if he hadn't seen the surfer in days.

The bloke rubbed the dog's head before whipping off his ankle strap and tucking the board under his arm. He strode onto the shore and then both man and dog shook themselves, sending water flying.

Addy laughed and without thinking said, "Are you part dog or is he part human?"

The surfer gave a sheepish grin. "A bit of both."

She heard the burr in his voice. "Is that an Irish accent?"

"It is." He waved his arm to encompass the bay. "This part of the coast reminds me a bit of home."

There was something so warm and sexy about his brogue, it made Addy want to keep him talking. "Can you surf in Ireland?"

"To be sure. The Atlantic offers nugs—waves twenty feet or more."

"Wow! I've never considered Ireland a surfing destination. It's not one I remember reading about in surfing magazines."

He laughed. "Well, you do need a quality wetsuit, hood, booties, gloves and a certain amount of insanity."

"So that's why you're out today and none of the locals are."

His eyes—an arresting blue—twinkled at her and a dimple turned in his cheek. "Don't let the accent deceive you. I'm a local."

"You live in Rookery Cove?" She heard the disbelief in her voice.

"I do." He shot out a damp hand. "Kieran O'Flaherty."

As she took his cold hand, she remembered the choir conversation and laughed. "*You're* Kieran?"

"You seem amused by that?"

Embarrassment heated her from top to toe. "I'm sorry. It's just your name came up at choir. No one knew you so of course there was speculation about who you were. I had a different picture in my head."

His smile lit up his eyes. "Hopefully I've exceeded expectations."

"That depends on whether or not you can sing," she teased.

He opened his mouth and sang, "Oh, Danny boy, the pipes, the pipes are calling ..."

His rich baritone caught on the wind, eddying around her and shivers raced up and down her spine. "You might just pass the audition," she deadpanned.

"That's grand, Marilyn. I'm sorry I haven't managed to get there yet. Work's been nuts, but I'm still interested if you'll have me."

Addy's embarrassment surged again. She'd been so distracted by his accent and twinkling eyes, she was yet to introduce herself.

"Actually, I'm Addy. Addy Topic. Raised in Rookery Cove and recently returned after more than a decade away."

"Ah!" He gave her a commiserating look. "So everyone thinks they know you."

She laughed to numb the ache. "How did you know?"

"I grew up in a village too. If you're ever in Strandhill in County Sligo, Mrs. Byrne won't hesitate to tell you I'm a hooligan who can't be trusted."

The border collie dropped a stick between Addy's feet, but she was too preoccupied with the flirty way Kieran had said the words. She raised her brows. "So, you're a bad boy?"

"If accidentally breaking a window to rescue her cat when I was ten fits, then to be sure I am."

"I may have done worse than that." *Shut up!*

He winked at her. "I'm not saying I didn't."

She laughed again, enjoying the conversation despite the

increasing chill now the last vestiges of the sun's rays were fading. She suddenly felt something cold and wet on her inner thigh and automatically jumped back to avoid it. But her straight skirt acted like a lasso and the next minute she was sitting on the damp sand.

"Fergus! Sit!" Kieran pointed to the sand.

Fergus obeyed, casting a doleful look at his master and at Addy.

"Are you okay?" Kieran offered his hand and pulled her to her feet. "I apologize for my dog's appalling lack of manners. His love of chasing anything and everything means he gets pushy wanting you to throw a ball or a stick."

"I'm fine." Addy brushed sand off her skirt. "And I'm totally wearing the wrong clothes for the beach. I should have changed, but on the way home I had a hankering to see the water."

That's not quite how I remember it. You were looking for Steph and a glass of wine.

"I know what you mean." Kieran started walking toward the parking lot. "Being here means the workday's done and it's time to kick back."

Her radar picked up a signal of a possible drinking buddy. "I thought Guinness did that."

He laughed. "For sure, it does for some."

"Some?" Disappointment rippled through her. "Not for you?"

"I've been known to enjoy a glass."

Relief scuttled dismay.

When they reached his truck, Addy read the stenciling on the side. North West Carpentry and Construction. New builds and heritage homes. She suddenly got an idea. "Do you repair decks or is that too small a job?"

"No job's too small when you've paid thousands of dollars to move across the world."

"Could you come over and give me a quote? In return, I'll give you a drink."

"Sure!" He handed her his phone. "Put your address in there and

I'll pop round on Saturday morning at ten. I can measure her up and have a cuppa."

Stupid! Of course the man couldn't look at her deck in the dark. She forced a smile to cover her disappointment. "I'll make sure I've got Irish breakfast."

As she got into her car and watched his tail-lights disappear around the bend, the drama of the day rushed back, fast followed by a dumping wave of loneliness. The cove sucked for company and she regretted not staying for the work dinner with Grant.

Switching on the ignition, she backed out of the parking lot and headed toward home. At least she could depend on the company of the bottle of sauv blanc—it wouldn't let her down.

CHAPTER TWENTY

AFTER WEEKS of Steph's pleading phone calls, the childcare center in the next town finally rang with an offer of one day a week. It fell short of the three days she needed, but she accepted it as fast as a drowning woman grips a rescuing hand. But unlike his visits to the day care center in the cove, where Monty sauntered into the hall as if he owned it, each time she dropped him off at Kids Care the childcare worker had to peel him off her. He cried and her gut cramped as she walked out of the building. She then spent an agonizing ten minutes before calling the center to check that Monty was okay. According to the staff he was always "playing happily." She worked hard to believe them, although it didn't fully ease her mother guilt that she was inflicting misery on him every Tuesday.

But the reality was she couldn't start a business without childfree time and it was such a precious commodity she couldn't afford to squander any of it. As it was, she went straight to the shed each night at 8:00 and made toys for four hours before falling into bed. Working at night wasn't ideal. The metal shed lacked insulation and was basically the same temperature as the outside air, making it an ice-box.

To prevent her fingers from stiffening she used a fan heater and wore fingerless gloves.

To say Henry wasn't happy that she disappeared to the shed straight after dinner was an understatement. But tough! During the day, he could barely manage to give her one Monty-free hour, so other than nap time or dumping Monty in front of his TV favorite show, *Bluey*, she never got a clear run at either making toys or setting up the website.

This morning, after dropping a sullen and likely hungry Zoe off at the bus stop—the vegan had refused breakfast—and delivering Monty to day care, Steph swung by Sven's. She planned to buy a scallop pie for dinner and check her orders using the café's always reliable wi-fi. Unlike at Four Winds, there was no valley or mountain range between the shop and the cell phone tower.

Sven delivered her chai latte and saw the photo of the little circus men and women stacked in a pyramid on her computer screen. "They look like fun."

"Thanks. I made them."

"You did?"

She swallowed her sigh that people found it unusual that a woman made wooden toys. "Yes. It's my new business." She brought up some other photos.

Sven peered more closely at the screen. "Wow, I haven't seen one of those squeeze acrobat toys in years. I had one when I was a kid except it was a bear."

"My grandfather made bears, but as I'm living in the cove, I thought the penguin could be my logo for Steph's Retro Toys."

"Good idea." Sven straightened up. "My granddaughter would love one. How much?"

"Since I'm using your internet most days, I'll gift you one."

"That's not the way to run a business, Steph. Besides, you and Henry buy plenty from me and we're happy for you to use the iffy wiffy until you get yours sorted. So how much?"

"For you, thirty dollars." She smiled at the generous man. "Thank you."

He brushed away her thanks with a shake of his head. "Are you getting many orders?"

"I'm about to find out. Cross everything." She clicked through to her orders, saw the notifications and squealed. "Oh my God!"

"Good news or bad?" Sven asked.

"Good! I have eight orders. Five circus people and three acrobat penguins."

"Congratulations!" Sven pumped her hand. "You're off and running."

"Thank you. This is so exciting. I thought I'd be lucky to sell one item a week, not eight three days after the website went live."

Her computer pinged with another order for the circus people and suddenly logistics pierced her bubble of excitement. She'd just sold out of her preparatory inventory. As amazing as that was, it meant she needed to make more stock.

What was the most efficient use of her time? Go home and package up the orders and take them to the post office? Or work and do the post office run on her way to pick up Monty? It was never easy to predict how long it might take at the post office as it was inside the general store. People arrived to pick up their mail and grab some supplies as well as their weekly dose of gossip. If she was held up and then late picking up Monty, the childcare center fined her. Gah!

"You okay?" Sven asked.

She sighed. "I either need three of me or a wife."

"That's what Gloria's been saying for years so I bought her one of those smart wife things that connects to the internet."

"Oh, yeah?" Steph wondered what Gloria would have made of the gift.

"Yeah." Sven shot her a wry smile. "She threw it at me. I didn't dare use it after that. What sort of help do you need? I'm sure Zoe could do some odd jobs for pocket money."

Steph didn't bother explaining that even if she was desperate she'd never ask Zoe for anything. "I'd only be looking for some part time help now and then. You don't know any retired blokes who like to potter about with wood, do you?"

"You could try the community Men's Shed. Someone might be interested."

"Thank you!" She jumped up and hugged him. "I'll go straight over."

The Men's Shed was a green corrugated-iron building up on the main road, not far from the general store. She walked in and was immediately greeted with the clean and distinctive scent of freshly cut wood.

Three men who looked to be in their seventies glanced up from various machines, surprise clear on their faces that a woman was in their midst.

"Can I help you, love?" one of them asked.

"I hope so." She smiled. "I'm Steph Gallagher."

"Ted Benson."

She shook his hand. "Nice to meet you, Ted. I live in the cove and I have a small business making wooden toys. I've just had a rush of orders and I was wondering if anyone would be interested in some piecework?"

"The gig economy, eh?" Ted said. "I suppose you could put something up on the noticeboard and see if anyone bites."

Steph looked beyond Ted to the other men. "Are any of you interested?"

"We're retired, love," Ted said. "We don't need the pressure of a deadline, right, fellas?"

One of the other men nodded, but the third man said, "I'm Bill. What sort of toys?"

Steph fished her phone from her handbag and showed him the

photos. "I was thinking eight sets." She calculated packaging and postage, the cost of wood, her time, their time, factored in the profit margin and named a price.

Bill's bushy gray eyebrows rose. "Fiddly stuff, love. Takes a bit of time."

She knew all too well. "It's just the cutting. I'll do the painting."

"You might want to think about stickers to speed up the process and keep costs down," the other man said.

"That's a great suggestion, um …? Sorry, I didn't catch your name," she said.

"Jim," he replied.

"Thank you, Jim." Her mind sparked with ideas. She could offer a hand painted boutique collection and a cheaper one using stickers.

"So are you interested?"

"How often would you be needing a job done?" Bill asked.

"I honestly don't know. It depends on demand."

"Thing is, love, Men's Sheds aren't here to support private business," Ted said. "We're here to support the unemployed, men with disabilities and depression, and blokes who need a bit of time out from the wife and vice versa. So unless a bloke has the tools at home, he couldn't make them here and be paid for it."

Steph glanced around at the large variety of tools that could easily accommodate her needs. "What if I made a donation to the shed?"

Ted tugged at his beard. "That could work. We're always chasing funding."

"What about quality control?" she asked.

"People do their best," Bill said. "Some have more of a knack than others."

Steph had visions of losing an order to bad cutting, but at this fledgling stage she was between a rock and a hard place. "So my options are I put up a poster and hope someone can do it in their own shed, or I make a donation and hope one of you good men supervise someone to cut well?"

"Pretty much," Ted said.

"Tell you what," Bill said. "If you paint me a set of those circus pyramid people for my grandson, I'll teach young Alan how to cut and I'll supervise him doing it. Since he lost his job and Brianna took the kids, he's been at a bit of a loose end."

Steph didn't know why she trusted Bill—perhaps it was the way he was carving a piece of myrtle into a tiny jewelry bowl—but she got a gut feeling her little circus people would be in good hands.

A man walked through a door at the other end of the shed. His thin frame was stooped and she was surprised when he got closer to see he was probably only in his early thirties. His face was tanned but haggard, and she saw the yellow residue of nicotine on his fingers before she smelled the stale smoke. The man emanated weariness and defeat.

"Al, come and meet Steph," Bill said. "She makes kids' toys."

Adrenaline jolted her. This was the man Bill was suggesting would cut her circus people? She had an overwhelming urge to withdraw her offer.

Al peered at her from behind a lock of hair, which made it hard to see his eyes—what was he hiding? But his handshake was surprisingly firm and Steph's collywobbles slowed.

"Nice to meet you," she said.

Al nodded but didn't speak.

The collywobbles jerked back to life while Bill explained the proposal to Al. He listened intently, then looked at the video on Steph's phone.

A smile broke the tension on his face. "I r-reckon I c-could give it a c-crack."

Bill clapped him on the shoulder. "Good man."

"W-when do I s-start?" Al asked.

"Well, I'm free today and tomorrow, but then I'm away for a couple of days," Bill said.

"I can be back with the wood and the templates in twenty minutes," Steph said.

"Along with the donation," Ted said.

"I can arrange a direct debit right now, unless you want cash," she offered.

"Direct debit's fine. I'll give you the details and watch you make the transfer."

She sucked in a breath and matched Ted's negotiating skills. "And I need you all to sign an agreement that you won't use or replicate the templates for your own purposes."

Ted stuck out his hand. "Done."

"So nine sets. Eight for me and one set for Bill's grandson." Steph jotted the details down on her phone.

"Actually, I reckon Al's kids would like a set, right, Al?" Bill said.

Feeling hustled, Steph saw her profit margin dwindling fast. She opened her mouth to object when she saw Al's previous tension shoot back, circling him as tightly as a steel band.

Al stared at his feet. "I dunno w-when I'll s-see them."

Brianna took the kids. The memory of Bill's words pierced Steph's heart like the sharp end of a pin. Her own grief joined his. Was a partner taking your children away from you a form of death? Knowing your kids were alive but not being able to see them?

"I'll box up a set for your kids," she said. "Then you'll have them ready for when you see them."

"You m-might w-want to w-wait and s-see how I do."

Al's tone couldn't be confused with wry or self-deprecating humor —it was brutal self-criticism. Steph thought she understood. After all, her body had failed her in the most devastating way. Suddenly she was desperate for this man she barely knew to experience a win.

"I'm sure with Bill's guidance you'll do a great job. But experience has taught me that while I'm finding my rhythm the first three are usually crap."

Al lifted his hand and pushed back his hair. Tired brown eyes met hers, appreciation in their depths. "I'll p-protect your w-wood and practice on some s-scraps to get my eye in."

"Thank you." She glanced at Ted, Jim and Bill. "I'll be back soon."

"It's almost morning tea time," Ted said.

Jim added, "Anything from the bakery is acceptable."

Steph half-groaned and half-laughed. "The soft and cuddly grandpa look is just a ruse, isn't it?"

Ted laughed. "Pleasure doing business with you, Steph."

CHAPTER TWENTY-ONE

After Steph had delivered the templates, the timber and a sponge cake from the bakery to the Men's Shed, she returned to Four Winds, excited to tell Henry her good news. He was on the phone so she headed to her workshop and packaged up the orders.

When she returned at one o'clock, she hoped Henry would have lunch ready as she did for him on her non-working days. But judging by the yelling drifting down the hall he was on a call to their ISP. It didn't sound like the nightmare of their patchy internet was any closer to being resolved.

She threw together a salad and left Henry's plated in the fridge. Once she would have stuck a love-heart sticky note on it, but increasingly those endearments were harder to muster considering her ever-increasing frustration at Henry and her life in general. She took her lunch to the shed and it was a relief to turn on the scroll saw.

The intense concentration required to cut out penguins temporarily stalled her disappointment and blocked her grief. All too soon she was out of wood. She did an audit of all her other supplies and decided to drive to Ulverstone. She'd stock up on wood and paint, and then use the library wi-fi to research sticker companies before picking up Monty.

She momentarily toyed with going back inside and telling Henry her plans, but if he knew she was leaving, he'd give her a list of jobs. She didn't have time to collect the dry-cleaning or go to the wine store —she barely had enough time to achieve her own list. Justifying that when she'd worked in an office she didn't report her every move to Henry—hell, he often took off for a walk without telling her—she avoided the house, got into the car and turned up the music. As long as she was home with Monty by 5:00 as expected, Henry wouldn't even notice she was gone.

There was a particular bliss in being alone. Without the demands of a toddler, she was able to take her time researching sticker companies and narrowed the choice to three. After sending query emails, she walked to the post office and joined the line.

She was clutching her bubble-wrapped parcels when her phone vibrated. Henry's name lit up the screen.

"Hi," she said.

"Hey." Henry sounded distracted. "Where are you?"

"Ulverstone."

"Did I know you were going?"

She could picture him rubbing the back of his neck. "I would have told you at lunch, but you were still on the phone when I left," she flubbed and focused instead on her good news. "It's so exciting, Henry. I'm posting orders!"

There was silence, but unlike in their early days together when Steph had interpreted Henry's way of hearing, decoding and responding to news as lack of interest, she was now familiar with his slower responses and happily waited, anticipating his congratulations.

"Right," he finally said.

Right? She was about to say "A bit of enthusiasm would be nice" when he added, "We've got a bit of a problem. Can you pick up Zoe?"

Disappointment laced with irritation churned her stomach. "Is she sick?"

"No."

"Then why can't she get the bus as usual?"

A sigh rumbled in her ear. "She was rude to a teacher and has refused to apologize. I asked the principal if she could do detention, but apparently the school rules are she has to come home and reflect on her behavior."

She's not my child! Steph could just imagine the excruciating conversation with the principal and the silent drive home with a mutinous Zoe. "Can't you pick her up?"

"I've finally got Perth, LA and Tokyo on board for the conference call."

"And I've got to buy timber to fulfill new orders and pick up Monty. Reschedule the call."

He groaned. "If I pull out now it'll be weeks before I can coordinate everyone again. You know how hard I've worked to set this up. You're more flexible. You can buy the timber tomorrow."

His use of the word flexible met her irritation, and anger built inside her like the pressure of steam. "I have Monty tomorrow."

"Even better. He loves a trip to the hardware store."

Are you freaking kidding me, Henry?

"Why do I have to juggle my job with parenthood, but you never do?" she ground out in a low voice, aware people in the line were casting long looks at her.

"What?" He sounded perplexed. "Steph, you know I wouldn't ask unless it was important."

Did she know that? "Your daughter's important!"

"Of course our daughter's important, but it doesn't matter which of us picks her up as long as it's one of us. You're the closest so it makes sense it's you."

Steph had opened her mouth to say "You need to give me a Monty-free hour tomorrow" when Henry said, "Thanks, honey. I need to run. The call starts in a few minutes and I want to check my notes. Love you!"

The line went dead.

As Steph shoved her cell phone into her handbag with more force than necessary, the woman next to her caught her eye. "You okay, love?"

She nodded, not trusting herself to speak in case she screamed her frustrations or burst into tears in the middle of the post office. The last thing she needed was someone filming her meltdown and posting it online for all the world to see.

"Mrs. Sun. Christopher Gibbons." The school principal extended his hand.

Steph shook it. "Actually, it's Gallagher."

"Sorry?" His brow furrowed.

"I'm Stephanie Gallagher."

"Right. But you're Zoe Sun's mother?"

"No!" exploded out of her mouth—emphatic and devoid of any possibility of misinterpretation. "I'm married to her father."

"I'm sorry." Fatigue lines dug in around his eyes. "It's been one of those days. Please take a seat."

Steph remained standing.

The principal leaned against the corner of his desk. "As I explained to your husband over the phone, Zoe clashed with her homeroom teacher—"

"I'm aware, and my husband will discuss it with Zoe." Steph didn't want to know the ins and outs of the situation—it was Henry's problem. The less she knew the better.

"Yes, he assured me of that over the phone. We do understand that settling into a new school has its challenges, and please don't be alarmed—Zoe's not alone in her behavior.' He gave a wry smile. "We've been putting out spot fires all week with the seventh grade girls, but we're confident we've got everything under control now."

"That's good to know." Steph saw the time on the large clock on the wall. "I'm sorry, I don't mean to be rude, but I have to pick up my son from day care and I'm running late. If I could just have Zoe?"

"Of course." He ushered her into another room.

Steph instantly recognized Olivia and Courtney Burton. Courtney jumped to her feet.

"Zoe, your moth— Stephanie's here to take you home," the principal said. "Tomorrow's a brand new day and we look forward to seeing you."

Zoe kept her head down and mumbled, "Yes."

"Chris—" Courtney said.

"Just give me two minutes," he said apologetically, "and I'll be right with you." The principal disappeared into his office.

"Hello, Courtney," Steph said.

Courtney speared her with a look so loaded with loathing Steph took a step back. "That child of yours needs to be taught some manners."

"Mum!" Olivia pulled at Courtney's sleeve. "It wasn't Zoe's fault!"

"Be quiet!" Courtney shook off her daughter's hand. "After what you've done, you don't get to talk."

Crestfallen, Olivia sank back into the chair, blinking rapidly.

"Until Olivia met your stepdaughter, she'd never been in trouble," Courtney said tightly. "You might be familiar with being summoned to the school but I'm not! I blame Zoe entirely for this mess."

Steph thought it highly likely that Zoe was to blame for whatever had happened, but she wouldn't share that thought with Courtney if she was the last person on earth. "As both girls are being sent home to reflect on their behavior, I think it indicates they're equally to blame."

Courtney's eyes flashed. "You and Henry need to get your act together and discipline Zoe before she's completely out of control!"

"How Henry and I parent has nothing to do with you," Steph ground out.

"It has everything to do with me when her actions impact on my daughter!" Courtney said.

Desperate to get out of the room, Steph turned her back on Courtney. "Zoe, pick up your bag. We're late for Monty."

Zoe rolled her eyes. "Can't have that, can we."

"See you tomorrow, Zoe," Olivia said.

"Not if I have anything to do with it," Courtney said. "I'll be talking to Christopher about transferring Olivia to a different class."

Steph's body clenched, but instead of responding she ushered Zoe outside.

"What the hell have you done that's made Courtney have a cow?" she asked when they got to the car.

"Nothing." Zoe threw her bag into the back and stomped to the passenger seat, slamming the door shut behind her.

Steph slid in behind the steering wheel and fastened her seatbelt before starting the engine. "It's obviously not nothing."

"Courtney has a cow about everything," Zoe said.

Steph didn't want to agree with Zoe, but there was some truth in the statement. "What exactly did you and Olivia do?"

"Do you care?" Zoe stared at her for a long moment, her eyes swirling with who knew what emotions. Then she turned her head and silently stared out the window.

Steph threw the car into reverse, navigated her way out of the parking lot and drove down the hill to the Bass Highway. Neither of them shared another word until they pulled into the driveway at Four Winds.

"Go and talk to your father."

Zoe glared at her but she got out of the car, trudged up the front steps and walked inside.

"Me too!" Monty demanded from his car seat.

Steph had no intention of going inside and having Monty distracting Henry from talking to Zoe, or being co-opted into the conversation. This was one hundred percent Henry's problem. She slid the car into gear and continued along the circular driveway and back onto the road.

"Daddy." Monty twisted in his car seat. "Want Daddy!"

"It's ice-cream time."

"Daddy!"

"Ice-cream and a play on the swings. Won't that be fun?"

Monty's big brown eyes met hers in the rear-view mirror—he was clearly torn between the treat and his father. His thumb snuck into his mouth and Steph's chest cramped.

She shook off the mother guilt. It was nothing to do with her and everything to do with Zoe.

CHAPTER TWENTY-TWO

IN AN ATTEMPT TO settle the anxiety scuttling in her veins, Brenda was menu-planning for the family lunch. It had been pushed out by a couple of weeks due to Colin getting sick. "Man flu," Lucinda had said. But Brenda's nerves couldn't take another delay so this morning she'd sent out a reminder text to her children. Everyone had sent back a thumbs-up, so she had good news for Marilyn when she returned from work.

Now, she was distracting herself by planning a meal that featured a favorite food of everyone in attendance. The grandchildren were easy—a packet of chips as part of the nibbles—along with some blue cheese for Colin. Roast pork with crisp salted crackling and roasted apples for Richard, chocolate mousse for Courtney, and a prawn salad entrée for Marilyn.

As Brenda reviewed the menu, she experienced a rare moment of hope—this lunch was absolutely the right way to go about telling the family about the importance of Marilyn in her life. She added two bottles of her and Marilyn's favorite sparkling wine to the shopping list. After all, with Richard and Aaron's news along with hers and Marilyn's, there was plenty to celebrate.

The doorbell rang and she startled at the sound. Most visitors used the back door, and package deliveries went to the post office at the general store. Curious, she rose and opened the door.

Brian Jolly stood on the front mat. He was wearing his town clothes and clutching a bunch of wilting purple and white lisianthus.

Brenda's stomach dropped to her feet and she tried to hide her dismay behind good manners. "Brian. What a surprise."

He smiled widely. "Thought it was time I called around with a house-warming gift." He shoved the flowers at her.

"Right. Um, thank you."

"Barbara always liked the lissies."

He took a step forward and Brenda automatically took one back.

Brian read it as an invitation to enter the house, and the next minute he was standing in the hall peering at the artwork.

"Well!" he said. "This is pretty modern. Bit of a change from the farm."

"It's a new house, Brian."

He walked into the living room like a kid in a candy store. "Looks like all new furniture too. You have had a lovely time."

He may as well have said "you've had a lovely time spending Glen's money."

"Glen and I always planned to build here," she said.

"I can't imagine him on that sofa.' A curt comment rose to her lips but then Brian added, "I don't think I ever saw him without some oil on him."

Brenda realized Brian missed his friend and her irritation softened. "Cup of tea?"

He grinned. "Thought you'd never ask."

She served tea in the garden and Brian made an enthusiastic assault on the jam and coconut cookies.

"Glen was a lucky man," he said. When she didn't respond he added, "Barbara had many good qualities too, bless her, but cooking wasn't one of them."

Brenda didn't mention that as Barbara had enjoyed being married she hadn't needed to escape into baking. "She tried hard though. Who can forget the duck à l'orange?"

Brian laughed. "After that culinary disaster we switched to entertaining with barbecues and salad." He was quiet for a moment, lost in memories, then he cleared his throat and looked straight at her. "When Barb was dying, she told me I should marry someone who could cook."

Apprehension raised the hairs on Brenda's arms. She toyed with saying "Did she?" but rejected it as an invitation for further comment. Saying "Good luck with that" was rude, so she stuck with "Hmm."

"Would you have dinner with me one night, Bren?" Brian asked. "We could go to the club. They do a mean steak on a Wednesday."

"That's kind, Brian, but ..." She trailed off, uncertain as to the best way to jump.

He leaned forward, his face earnest. "I think it makes sense. We've both lost someone we love and we've known each other forever. There's a lot to be said for companionship and shared interests."

For the life of her, Brenda couldn't think what he thought they shared other than they'd known each other's spouses.

"I'm not passionate about tractor restoration," she said.

He laughed. "Good one, Bren. We've always shared a sense of humor."

Had they? This conversation was exactly how she imagined a parallel universe. Not knowing what else to say or do, she sipped her tea.

His gaze was suddenly wary. "Unless of course there's someone else?"

Yes! But she couldn't tell Brian that, even in the vaguest terms, because he'd ask who. If she fudged the answer by saying she'd met someone online, Brian was just as likely to mention it to Courtney or Colin and that would be a disaster.

Reassuring herself that she only needed to lie for a few more days, she said, "You've had longer on your own, Brian. I'm not quite ready yet."

He nodded, understanding clear on his face, and reached out and patted her hand. "I'm here when you're ready." Then he leaned back and refilled his tea, looking like he was settling in for a long visit. "This is nice, isn't it? You've done a lovely job with the garden."

"Thank you." Inspiration finally struck. "Actually, the nursery rang just before you arrived asking me to pick up my bare-rooted roses."

Brian thankfully took the hint and stood. "I better let you get on."

As she walked him to the gate he said, "Choir's an interesting bunch. I sometimes think Marilyn forgets we're not her students."

Brenda tried not to bristle. "She's the choir conductor. It's her job to keep us in line."

"As long as she's not bossing you around in your own home. Glen would be horrified you've taken in a lodger. Colin should—"

"No need to worry about me, Brian," Brenda said firmly. "Sharing with Marilyn's working well. I enjoy the company."

He looked skeptical. "I'm good company too. Remember what I said, Bren. I'm here, and we rub along pretty well."

He unexpectedly leaned in and kissed her quickly, his lips sliding across hers.

Stunned, Brenda watched him put on his hat, walk out the gate and disappear from view. It took the sight of Clyde diving for the gap to rouse her.

"Oh, no, you don't." She pushed the gate hard, and as it slammed shut she saw Courtney's face.

"Hello to you too, Mum."

"Sorry, darling. Brian left the gate open and Clyde's an escape artist."

"Is Brian losing it?"

Brenda had no idea what Courtney was talking about. "What do you mean?"

"When an old farmer doesn't shut a gate—"

"Enough of the old, thank you very much. He's the same age as your father."

Courtney's eyes dimmed, then narrowed. "Why was he here?"

Brenda thought of the limp lisianthus. "He dropped off something for Marilyn."

"What?"

"What?"

"What did he drop off for Marilyn?" Courtney persisted.

"I don't know. I didn't ask.' Brenda was fast regretting the lie.

"I've seen the way he looks at you at choir, Mum. I'm pretty sure he came to see you."

"Pfft! I'm not interested in Brian Jolly."

"Sure, Mum."

Brenda realized Courtney thought she was joking. "Brian Jolly's not my type."

Courtney laughed. "Mum, Dad was your first boyfriend and you married him. Brian's a lot like Dad, making him very much your type."

"Perhaps I want a new type."

But Courtney wasn't listening. She'd walked inside and was staring at the flowers. "I knew it! Brian came to see you."

"He's lonely is all," Brenda said.

"Aren't you?" Courtney filled the kettle.

"Between you and your brothers, the grandies, choir and helping out at school, I'm too busy to be lonely. Besides, Marilyn's good company."

"Oh, Marilyn's great," Courtney said. "But she's not going to keep you warm at night."

Was this a sign? Should she tell Courtney now? No. Marilyn needed to be part of the conversation and so did the boys. Still, was it a chance to feel the lie of the land? Was Courtney finally open to the idea of Brenda moving on?

"How would you feel about me seeing someone?" she asked.

"I'd be okay with Brian. There's something familiar about him that keeps Dad close."

Brenda swallowed a sigh.

"Has he asked you out?" Courtney said.

"Yes, but I told him I wasn't ready."

"There's no rush, Mum." Courtney uncharacteristically gave Brenda's hand a squeeze. "Dad's shoes are hard to fill."

Brenda busied herself putting the berries Courtney had brought into the fridge. "Are you looking forward to seeing Richard on Sunday?"

"You bet! It will make up for the crap week I've had."

There was always some sort of drama happening with Courtney, although they often had different definitions of what was a crisis and what Courtney had inflated to be one in her own head.

"Didn't the jam set?" Brenda asked.

Courtney waved her hand. "It's not the jam. We've pretty much nailed it now."

The jam lesson with the Burtons and Marilyn had turned out to be a fun afternoon. Marilyn's presence had a calming effect on everyone. Not that Ben ever needed calming. He was as easygoing as Courtney was highly strung and exacting, but together they'd made a very flavorsome jam by combining strawberries, blackberries and raspberries. The only extra thing Brenda would have liked to have come out of the afternoon was a thank you from Courtney.

"What's the problem then?"

Courtney grimaced. "I'm absolutely furious with Steph Gallagher. That Zoe Sun is a nightmare. She got Livvy into so much trouble they were suspended for an afternoon."

"Heavens!" Suspension and Livvy didn't go together. "What happened?" Brenda asked.

"I'm yet to get to the bottom of it, but it involved a group of girls. Lovely girls that Livvy should be spending time with instead of hanging around Zoe Sun! I'm used to meeting with Christopher about local school council issues, but this was the most embarrassing and excruciating ten minutes of my life. Olivia's grounded from all activities for the rest of the week and she's lost screen privileges. She's not allowed to be alone in the house."

It was the most severe punishment Courtney had ever meted out. "What's Livvy's take on what happened?"

Courtney huffed. "She says she was sticking up for Zoe."

Brenda frowned. "Isn't sticking up for someone a good thing?"

"Not when it gets you suspended! I've talked to Christopher about putting Olivia into the other seventh grade class, far away from Zoe's malevolent influence."

Brenda bristled. "Just because she dresses in black and wears eye make-up hardly makes her malevolent. I don't know the full story about Zoe, but Steph hinted it was a very sudden move for her to come and live with them. There's bound to be teething problems as she settles in."

"Mum!" Courtney's face flushed pink. "Livvy was suspended! Why are you defending Zoe? Why can't you be on my side for once? Marilyn understood!"

Every nerve ending tingled in shock. "How does Marilyn know about this?"

"The day it happened, I was so furious with Olivia that I left her with Ben and drove to the beach for a calming walk. I ran into Marilyn walking Clyde and we had a drink together at the surf club."

A couple of nights ago, Marilyn had walked in so late that Brenda had her car keys in her hand ready to go and look for her. "Oh, thank goodness," she'd said. "I was starting to worry."

Marilyn had kissed her. "Sorry. You know the cove. I ran into Fern and she cornered me about some choir issues. For all her energy and light, she's got a controlling streak a mile wide."

They'd shared a laugh at the accurate description. Then Brenda had served dinner and the conversation had gone in a different direction.

Now, betrayal streaked through her hot and sharp, accompanied by a bright flash of jealousy. Marilyn had offered Courtney advice, then lied to her by omission.

Marilyn understood. It was implicit in Courtney's statement that, as usual, Brenda did not understand.

Her mind remained stuck on this long after Courtney's frosty departure.

. . .

Brenda was determined not to say anything to Marilyn about her meeting with Courtney until she'd unwound from her workday. But all her intentions flew out the window the moment Marilyn walked in the back door.

"Why didn't you tell me you had a drink with Courtney the other night?" she demanded.

Marilyn blinked, sighed and put her bags on the table. "Because I was trying to avoid this."

"*This* wouldn't be happening if you'd told me."

"Yes, it would."

"No!" A flush of heat burned across Brenda's skin. "The only reason I'm asking is because you lied to me."

"Let's have a cup of tea," Marilyn said. "Or better yet a glass of wine. It's almost 5:00."

Marilyn's reasonable tone accelerated Brenda's anger as fast as lighter fluid. "I don't want a drink. I want to know why you lied to me."

Marilyn opened the fridge, poured two glasses of wine and sat at the table. "Because I knew if I told you, you'd get upset."

Brenda refused to touch the wine. "I think you've got that back to front. I'm upset because you didn't tell me."

"I was protecting you from being hurt," Marilyn said gently. "When it comes to Courtney, you're not always your level-headed self."

Brenda's anger vibrated the air around her and she glared at Marilyn through a vermilion haze. "As a courtesy to me, you should have told me you'd met her. Instead, I had to find out from her that the sun shines from your ass and once again I'm in the shit."

"Courtney's an adult so she gets to decide who she confides in. As much as you want to be that person, it's not my fault that on this occasion it was me." Marilyn leaned forward and put her hands on Brenda's. "Me being friends with Courtney is a good thing. It can only help things along on Sunday."

An ill-fitting coat of conflicting emotions tightened over Brenda as it always did when she thought about the lunch. Some were warm and comforting. Others jabbed as sharply as a barbed needle.

She sighed. "What advice did you give Courtney?"

Marilyn frowned. "I didn't give her any advice."

Brenda's hands rose and fell. "No wonder she likes you. Courtney never wants any advice, but that doesn't mean she doesn't need it!"

"I felt she needed to debrief so I listened." Marilyn took a long sip of her wine. "It's all pretty straightforward really. Livvy's a sheltered kid and to her, Zoe Sun seems exotic."

"Zoe's hardly exotic," Brenda said tersely. "She's the new kid at school trying to find her feet."

"It's a tricky age for girls," Marilyn mused. "Fortunately, she's not our problem."

Brenda scoffed. "You're living in a small town now. With Courtney and Steph in the choir, it becomes our problem."

"They're adults," Marilyn said easily, as if that solved everything.

"They're mothers."

"Same difference."

How could Marilyn be a school teacher and miss this distinction?

"Put it this way," Brenda said. "I'm glad the Choir Crush is on Saturday. Courtney and Steph should be able to hold it together for one more rehearsal and the performance."

"Stop catastrophizing." Marilyn studied the menu and shopping list Brenda had been working on when Brian arrived. "Wow! Are you sure you can manage all of this on top of Saturday?"

"You're the one with Saturday stress. I just have to turn up and play the piano."

"Which stresses you. If Addy didn't have such an amazing voice I'd ask her to play."

Brenda laughed. "Good to know where your priorities lie."

Excitement flashed like starbursts in Marilyn's eyes. "With Addy's voice, we have a real shot at a place. It will be a great way to announce the eisteddfod plans."

Brenda loved watching Marilyn, but it was even more joyous when enthusiasm lit her up from the inside. "I'm just happy you're happy."

"It's going to be a great weekend all round."

"A great weekend," Brenda said, as if repeating the words guaranteed it.

CHAPTER TWENTY-THREE

IT TOOK ALMOST three weeks before the Instagram photo of Addy was taken down and by then all her students and co-workers had seen it. She'd spent days fielding comments ranging from "you poor thing" to "I'd swipe right on that."

But it was Lyn's reaction that gutted her. "Honestly, Addy, what did you expect when you dress like that?"

The words had rained down on her like needles, piercing her skin and rushing pain into every part of her. She'd stood motion-less, unable to think and definitely unable to speak. Lyn took her silence as tacit agreement and had started sending her buy-links to high-neck tops and trousers.

It wasn't until much later in the day, when Addy was at home on the sofa, keeping company with some sauv blanc, that all the appropriate and cutting replies she should have said to Lyn had tumbled into her head. By then, it was too late to fire them.

Thank goodness for Grant—he'd done everything by the book. He'd interviewed the students and concluded there wasn't enough proof to pin the act on anyone specific, but he'd overridden Jett's objections and was insisting on sexual harassment training for the department.

But Addy wasn't thinking about any of that today. Her focus was one hundred percent on preparing for the afternoon's interview. She was working on an answer to a possible question about a workplace mistake and how she'd recovered from it when she heard a knock on the glass wall of her office.

Grant stood in the doorway. "Addy, you got a minute?"

"Of course." As he stepped inside and closed the door, she jumped up and cleared a stack of files off the chair. "Is it about the information for the best company to run the sexual harassment training?"

Grant laughed and lowered himself onto the edge of her desk. "There's got to be a better way of describing it. They already know how to harass."

"Don't I know it." She sat down and tapped on her computer. "I just emailed it to you."

"Thanks." He glanced down at her. "You interview prepping?"

She nodded. "I want to give it my A-game."

"You give everything your A-game. Which is why I don't want to give you this news."

Apprehension scuttled along her gut. "What news?"

"Unfortunately, Heather's just rung. She's sick so the interview's postponed."

Nooooooooo. Addy forcibly held in her scream of frustration, trying to hide her disappointment. It took every reserve of calm to say, "Oh, well, these things happen. I hope she's feeling better soon."

"Thanks for being so understanding," Grant said.

"I don't feel very understanding."

He gave a wry smile. "I know it's frustrating and disappointing. You're amazing the way you're dealing with the most protracted interview process in history."

Grant's plaudit cast her in a warm glow of appreciation and she seized the opportunity.

"Considering this new delay and my audit work, is there any

chance Ravi can teach the last three weeks of the social media course? It's all about website design, which is his area of expertise."

"It's possible," Grant said slowly.

Addy couldn't tell if his reply was a clear yes or no. "I'm sensing a but ...?"

He sighed. "Sure, it can be done."

"Great!"

He grimaced. "It's just ... I'm not sure if it's in your best interests. If it was week five of the semester it would be a no-brainer. But it's the pointy end and exams and final assignments are looming. You know how antsy the students get. They'll feel you're abandoning them even though you're not. After all your stellar efforts, I don't want you bearing the brunt of their frustration and getting a poor exit survey. Can you hang in there just a few more weeks?"

Addy fought tears. "Grant, I'm exhausted."

"I get that, I truly do. But you're so close, Addy. You'll be home free soon."

Except between now and the vacation there were still a few teaching weeks, followed by exams and grading, plus the audit prep. But Grant had a point. With the audit focus now very firmly on the students, she didn't deserve a bad exit survey—not when she'd worked her guts out for them and the other teachers.

She slumped in her chair and a long sigh rolled out of her. "Promise me I'll be interviewed soon."

He gave her shoulder a reassuring squeeze. "I'm sorry it's been a series of unfortunate events, but I'm on the case. It will happen."

"Thanks."

"Too easy." He stood. "Any weekend plans to take the sting out of this disappointment?"

She toyed with telling him about the Choir Crush, but knowing Grant, he'd not only come along to support her, he'd encourage the staff to attend as well. The thought struck fear deep in her solar plexus.

"Just kicking back," she said.

He grinned. "Sounds perfect."

. . .

Saturday dawned a crisp and clear-sky day with sparkling calm seas and emerald views of Table Cape. It was a day that inspired and motivated great things—perfect for the Choir Crush. But instead of embracing what the sunshine offered, all Addy wanted to do was crawl back into bed. Singing in front of a crowd was one thing. Singing those lyrics in front of a crowd was like standing on the stage naked.

A heavy feeling pressed on her chest. She consciously breathed deeply, lifting her diaphragm to try and banish the weight, knowing if she didn't shift it, she'd give in to it and let it sink her.

At the final choir rehearsal, Marilyn had informed them they were the first choir on the bill. Then she'd outlined the plan for the day—arrive in Penguin at 5:00, warm up and sing the song once or twice, before a quick stroll along the waterfront to relax and center, ready for 6:00. Fern had suggested they all meet at a raw food café, but even if Addy had been vegan there was no way she'd be able to keep anything in her stomach. As it was, breakfast sat like a stone and the thought of lunch made her gag.

At least she didn't have to drive. Steph had offered to pick her up and Addy had accepted, knowing she could sit in the passenger seat and let Steph's excited chatter wash over her while she battled to protect her kernel of calm.

She glanced at the clock. God! She still had hours before Steph arrived. Justifying that protecting her kernel of calm started now, she opened the fridge and poured herself a small medicinal glass of wine. She downed half of it in one gulp, welcoming the glow that rushed into her with long warm fingers, massaging and loosening her muscles. The thumping weight in her chest immediately lightened. She murmured thank you to the remains in the glass, then drank it.

With calm restored, she knew she should reinforce it by going for a walk. She reached the front door, then realized a walk meant she'd meet people who'd want to talk about the Choir Crush. They'd say unhelpful things like "Bet you're excited" and "You're our ace in the hole." Tension bubbled back, stealing the therapeutic effects of the wine.

Changing her mind, she returned to the living room and switched on her laptop. She'd lose herself in work by reading Tim's final two reports and then make a start on essay grading.

She was halfway through the first report when she heard a knock on the door. Her heart raced. *Please don't let Steph have changed her mind about joining Fern and going to Penguin early.*

Opening the door, she did a double take. Grant stood on her porch, holding a Southern Wild Distillery bag in one hand and a shopping bag in the other. She glimpsed a baguette and a wheel of cheese.

She smiled. "This is a surprise."

"I hope it's a good one." He waved the bags. "I come bearing gifts."

"So I see. Come in." She stepped back from the door.

"You sure? I should have called first, but it was a spur-of-the-moment decision." He pushed a bottle of sloe gin into her hands. "You've had a crap few weeks and I just wanted to check you're okay."

She didn't know if she wanted to smile or cry at his thoughtfulness. "Thank you. You didn't need to do this."

He shrugged as if it was no big deal. "You looked so downhearted when you left yesterday I thought you needed cheering up. Believe me, Addy, your stars will align."

"Thanks." She cradled the squat bottle. "Let's give this baby a test run."

"Only if I'm not in the way."

She thought about the Choir Crush and the urge to crack open the gin intensified. "I've got a few hours before I'm needed elsewhere."

"Excellent." He followed her inside.

By the time Addy had sorted out glasses and ice, Grant had arranged a platter of cheeses, dips and bread that he'd brought with him. Addy poured them each a generous slug of the sloe gin, loving the audible crack of the ice as the viscous ruby liquid flowed around it.

She raised her glass. "*Živjeli.*"

"What's that?"

"Croatian for cheers." She tipped the glass back and as the ice touched her teeth the gin filtered through, cold, fresh and sweet.

"Oh my God! This is amazing."

"Right?" Grant grinned. "Cordial with a kick."

Addy gestured to her laptop. "I was just checking Tim's reports. As soon as they're uploaded to the portal, the Ag program is fully compliant."

"That's great, but the point of me dropping by is to take your mind off work." He refilled their glasses. "To the joys of Saturdays."

They clinked and drank.

Addy refilled them. "To thoughtful friends."

"Nice." Grant's smile warmed her along with the alcohol. "We should probably eat something."

As Grant cut bread and cheese, Addy watched him through a blurry haze, embracing the floating feeling that was deliciously drifting her far away from all her anxieties.

He passed her a plate. "God, we're so lucky to live here. Fresh air and the best food."

"Not to mention spirits." She refilled their glasses. "To Tassie."

They ate between brilliant ideas for toasts. Just as Addy was luxuriating in the blessed disconnect drinking gave her, the mournful tune of "Für Elise" played on the radio. With it came unwanted memories—hours of practice, the cloying air around the piano, being torn between playing it correctly or deliberately making mistakes because the consequences differed by a hair's breadth.

Her body flinched violently, scattering her joie de vivre like leaves in a wind squall. In her haste to shut off the sound, she tripped over paint cans and almost fell onto the radio.

As she flicked it to a rock station, Grant said, "I've always liked that tune."

"Too bad." She hated the wobble in her voice so she tried for sassy. "You said you wanted to cheer me up. That means no Mozart, no Beethoven and no Chopin."

He laughed. "So it's all about you, is it?"

"You bet."

Her lovely cocoon of warmth and wellbeing had drained away, exposing the slime and grunge she worked so hard to keep hidden.

They loved you. They fled a war for you and you let them down. You broke their hearts.

The all-knowing voices of doubt and despair roared in her head, before echoing back toxic and demanding. With a trembling hand, she poured more gin and drank it fast.

An Ariana Grande song came on and she turned it up so loud the windows rattled. Anything to drown out the eviscerating statements in her head.

"Dance with me." She pulled Grant to his feet and shimmied around him, sliding her hands over herself and rubbing her spine along his.

He laughed. "Addy, you make anywhere a party."

"Life's a party," she lied. "Work hard, play hard's my motto. Hey, that's a toast." She reached for the bottle and disappointment slammed her hard. "S'empty. Lucky! I've got wine."

She turned quickly and the world spun. She flailed her arms to steady herself and her hands grabbed Grant's shirt as she slid down his chest. "Oops!"

The next moment she was laughing and tumbling backwards, but the landing was unexpectedly soft. It took her a few seconds to realize she'd fallen on the sofa, bringing Grant with her.

Her limbs relaxed into the cushions. "Lying down's lovely."

Grant murmured "hmm" as his lips gently nuzzled her neck.

She closed her eyes, luxuriating in the feeling she was weightless and hovering just above the sofa, disconnected from everything that anchored her to her life. Her mind was finally, blessedly, silent. Peace surrounded her. She'd do anything to stay here.

She was vaguely aware of Grant's hands on her. Of cool air on her skin. Of his ragged breathing. But she was outside herself, floating above it all, lost in that safe place she'd sought refuge in, never wanting to leave.

. . .

Addy woke later to a quiet house, a sticky residue between her legs and a note stuck to her bra. She pulled it off and squinted, trying to focus on the scrawled words.

You added acrobatic to adventurous, you sex fiend. Figured you deserved to sleep. Grant.

Acrobatic? Her head throbbed and her mouth was drier than the Nullarbor Plain. She sat up and pain shot through her temples before spiraling on a jagged helix. With superhuman effort she staggered to the kitchen and poured herself a glass of wine.

Her phone buzzed and she squinted at the text.

Running ten minutes late. Steph

She reread it three times before she remembered. *Shit!* The choir.

All she wanted was to take the wine bottle back to bed, but Rita's voice was in her head. It had been easier to ignore and disobey Rita when she was an adolescent, but since returning to the cove she was finding it increasingly difficult.

Think before you say yes, Aida. Once you commit, you must see it through.

"God, Mama!"

She drained the glass and stumbled into the shower.

CHAPTER TWENTY-FOUR

STEPH EXPECTED Addy to be waiting on the wide grassy verge outside her house—it was the reason she'd texted so they could avoid any extra delays. Steph still couldn't believe she was late when she'd been excited and ready all day.

Things had gone crazy soon after she'd put on her choir costume—black pants and a white T-shirt. After gathering her phone, wallet and keys, she was about to kiss Henry goodbye when he'd announced, "There's no point taking two cars. We'll come with you."

No! "But I have to be there early to rehearse. You'll be hanging around for an hour."

"Monty and Zoe love the penguins on the waterfront and we can have fish and chips on the beach."

Steph thought Zoe enjoying the outing was more than a stretch and the last thing she needed was the teen's downer vibe in the car. Truth be told, she didn't want Monty or Henry in the car either. She wanted four hours away from being Henry's partner and Monty's mother so she could just be "Steph in the choir."

"It's only polite that I stay and hear the other choirs sing, and after that we might go out for drinks," she said. "Monty will be well past it by then."

"Someone will be able to give you a ride home," Henry said easily.

"I've already offered to drive Addy so that puts her out as well. Let's stick to the original plan."

Sadness touched Henry's face. "I just thought it would be nice to do something as a family."

Steph bit back the words "fractured family." "I agree, but this isn't a family outing. I have to go or I'll be late."

Henry had sighed and kissed her goodbye. "Break a leg!"

Now Steph honked a second time. "Come on, Addy!"

But the front door didn't open and Addy didn't appear from around the side of the house either.

Leaving the engine running, Steph jumped out of the car and jogged up the front steps. She banged on the door before peering through the rippled glass, trying to glimpse signs of movement inside. She couldn't see anything other than paint tins, boxes and the outline of a ladder. How could Addy stand to live like this?

Her heart rate suddenly picked up. Had Addy tripped over, hurt herself and wasn't able to come to the door? Or use her phone?

Steph was running down the stairs, intending to try the back door, when she heard, "Where's the fire?"

She turned and blinked. Addy, who was always impeccably dressed with her hair straightened and make-up perfect, stood in a pair of ratty jeans that bulged over her belly. She'd teamed them with a multicolored T-shirt that stretched so tightly over her breasts it was almost transparent. Her feet were bare, her hair wet and tangled, and mascara bled under her eyes.

"What are you staring at?" Addy demanded belligerently.

"I ... We're supposed to wear black and white."

Addy tapped a large tote bag. "All sorted."

Steph had no idea why Addy wanted to get dressed in a public bathroom and wondered if there'd even be time. Marilyn's running sheet had been very precise.

"Is everything okay, Addy?"

"Everything's great! You're late." Addy giggled. "Hey, that rhymes. Come on, let's get this show on the road!" She got into the car.

Steph pushed away the niggling feeling that Addy seemed different and put it down to nerves. By the time she swung into the driver's seat, Addy was pulling so hard on the seatbelt it locked. The more she tugged, the more it refused to move. She finally managed to pull it across her body, but then her fingers fumbled and she kept missing the latch. "Fuck!"

The invective sliced through Steph with tingling shock.

"Let me help." She leaned over, but instead of breathing in Addy's usual signature scent, she was hit by the fruity fermentation of alcohol. Anxiety hollowed her stomach as she matched the odor with Addy's bedraggled appearance and lack of coordination.

Driving up the winding road toward the highway, Steph decided not to ask Addy outright if she'd been drinking, but to hint around it.

"Are you nervous?" she said.

"Are you?"

"I've been jittery all day."

Addy's unfocused gaze swung toward her and she pulled a hip flask out of her tote. "Have some of this. It settles your nerves."

The offer shocked her. "I'm driving!"

"Suit yourself." Addy took a swig. "I mean, you've got way more reason to be nervous than me."

Confused, Steph took her eyes off the road for a second and gave Addy a quick glance. "Why?"

"Because you can't sing in tune to save yourself."

The words stamped themselves painfully on Steph's mind before diving deep and branding her heart.

"That's a very hurtful thing to say," she finally managed, the words stiff and wounded.

"Oh, yeah," Addy said. "The truth's a bitch."

She took another swig from the flask, then closed her eyes. A minute later she was snoring loudly.

♫

While the choir members arrived in dribs and drabs, Brenda's fingers flexed over the piano keys, warming up with scales. Out of the corner of her eye she noticed Marilyn doing a mental head count and the frown that followed.

Then Marilyn checked her cell phone, slid it into her back pocket and clapped her hands. "Right, everyone! Let's start warming up."

"But we're not all here," Fern said.

"Sing and they will come," Marilyn said lightly.

Brenda stopped playing and saw the tension in Marilyn's shoulders.

"Let's start with some deep breathing," Marilyn said. "Fern, can you lead that? I need to make a call."

Fern happily took charge and Marilyn put her phone to her ear and walked over to Brenda.

"Addy's phone's going straight to voice mail," she said softly.

"Try Steph?" Brenda suggested.

"That's the plan."

The door opened and Steph rushed in. Her cheeks glowed pink from the cold and her eyes darted around the room as if she was looking for someone in particular.

"We've started our deep breathing," Fern said. "Join in. You look like you need it."

Steph ignored her and walked straight to Marilyn and Brenda.

Some of the choir members opened an eye to follow her.

"Focus," Fern said sternly. "We only want positive energy."

"I think we have a problem," Steph whispered.

"What do you mean?" Brenda asked.

"It's Addy." Steph shot the choir members a furtive glance, then leaned in closer, her head almost touching Marilyn's. "I'm pretty sure she's drunk."

Marilyn shook her head. "No. She wouldn't ... would she?"

"She was swigging from a hip flask in the car and now she's asleep," Steph said.

"The drive's not long enough for her to get drunk," Brenda said.

"I think she's been drinking for a lot longer than that. She said some things ..." Steph bit her lip.

"What sort of things?" Marilyn asked.

"Things we might think but we'd never say unless we're drunk and we've lost our filter."

Brenda read the distress on Steph's face and gave her hand a squeeze. "Go and join the others and find some calm. Marilyn and I will deal with this."

Steph gave her an uncertain look, but Brenda nodded her encouragement and gave her a gentle push toward the group.

"Shit," Marilyn said once Steph was out of earshot. "What if Addy can't sing?"

Brenda ushered Marilyn to just outside the door so they could talk privately. "Let's not jump the gun. Addy works long hours so it's likely she fell asleep because she's tired. You stay here and if anyone asks, just say Addy's on her way. I'll go and check on her. It's probably as simple as her drinking a quart of water and taking a walk."

Marilyn gave a wan smile. "I love how calm you are in a crisis."

"Years of experience," Brenda joked.

Marilyn hugged her tightly. As she pulled away, she kissed her on the lips.

"There you are!" Addy's voice slurred loudly behind Brenda.

Hot and cold flashes collided, tingling pain across Brenda's skin.

She swung round and watched Addy weaving her way toward them. Her concern that Addy had seen the kiss vanished under the weight of the other woman's obvious intoxication. Water and a walk wouldn't do a damn thing.

"Plan B," she mumbled.

"What the hell is plan B?" Marilyn hissed.

"I'll take her to the bathroom. You talk to the choir."

"Oo-oo! Secret wo-men's business." Addy giggled. "You can tell me. I'm a wo-man."

The sound of "Bumblebee" drifted out of the rehearsal room. Fern must have finished the breathing exercises and decided to start the vocal warm-ups. Before Brenda realized what was happening, Addy had sailed past her and into the room.

"Hello, choir. Ready to crush it?" Addy laughed. "Crush it like ..." She frowned, then laughed and waved her hands. "Doesn't matter. You get it."

"You're late!" Fern said.

"I'm here. We're all here." She bowed low to the group and lost her balance. "Oops!"

"You're drunk." Brian's tone dripped disgust.

"Am I?" Addy stared at him as if the statement was a revelation. "Lucky! 'Cos drunk's the only way I can sing that song."

Marilyn blanched. "I thought you—"

"Oh God," Steph wailed. "Who'll sing the lead?"

"Definitely not you, sunshine," Addy said.

"Aida Topic, your mother would be very disappointed," Vera said in a tone that reminded everyone she'd once been a Sunday School teacher.

"Very disappointed," Addy parroted, then reached for her hip flask. "But sometimes, V, we need to tell the truth. Today's the day. Steph can't hold a tune to save her life and Brian thinks yelling's singing."

"She's got a point," Courtney said.

"I really don't think this is a useful conversation for the choir to be having," Brenda said sharply.

"The truth will set you free," Fern said.

Addy snorted. "Free yourself with this, Fern. For all your New Age bullshit, you're super judgy and controlling."

Fern's eyes blazed with anger. "At least I'm not a drunk!"

Addy shrugged. "Like I said. Judgy."

"People," Marilyn said, "let's focus."

"You can't let Addy sing in that state," Fern said. "She's a loose cannon."

Addy stuck out her tongue. "I love you too, Fernie."

"The last thing we need is Penguin, Burnie, Stanley and Devonport holding this over us," Morgan said. "We'd never live it down. And it'll tank any plans we have to host the eisteddfod."

"Heidi, do you want to sing the solo?" Marilyn asked.

The woman blanched. "Not really."

"To Courtney!" Addy raised an imaginary glass. "Courtney saves the day again."

"I'll get her some water," Heidi said.

"What's Addy talking about?" Morgan asked.

"I was her understudy in a high school production. One night she was sick and I had to sing," Courtney said. "I know the words so I guess I could do it again."

"Perhaps we should just withdraw," Brian said.

"We are not going to withdraw," Marilyn said firmly.

"I hate to say it, but Brian might have a point," Steph said.

Brian gave Steph a grateful smile. "I don't want to make a fool of myself."

"Too late for that!" Addy said.

"Addy!" Marilyn barked. "Shut up!"

After Addy's truth bombs, Brenda felt the need to reassure both Brian and Steph. "If you sing like you did on Thursday, there's no chance of anyone feeling foolish. You can do this. All of you can do this."

Brian beamed at her. "Thanks, Bren. You're a good woman."

"Aww, sweet," Addy slurred. "But mate, you're shit out of luck there."

Brenda caught Addy firmly by the arm and marched her toward the door. "Let's get you some coffee."

"Good idea," Brian said. "Get her out of here before she upsets anyone else."

"Bri, s'not personal," Addy called over her shoulder. "Nothing you can do about it. Is what it is."

Confusion creased Brian's gray-stubbled cheeks. "What is?"

They were so close to the door, but Addy stopped dead and Brenda tripped. Then Addy swung wildly and faced Brian.

"Bren'a and Mar'lyn being lesbians and in lurve," she said solemnly.

Just like the arrival of a fire front, all the air was sucked fast from the rehearsal room. Brenda struggled to draw in breath, let alone form any words.

She heard Brian say, "For God's sake, Addy. Go and sleep it off."

Sheer relief kickstarted her breathing. Brian didn't believe Addy. No one would believe her. They'd chalk it up to drunk ravings. She was home free.

Courtney's voice suddenly cut through the ripple of chatter in the room. "Mum? Is this true?"

Brenda's heart hurled itself against her ribs as dread, thick as treacle, ran through her veins. Her head screamed "Not now, not this way", but her tongue was swollen, her throat choked and her lips numb. No words came.

She was vaguely aware of Marilyn moving to her side and then she heard her say, "Yes." One tiny word that reverberated like a sonic boom, shaking the walls to their foundations.

Noooooooooooooo!

"I'm not asking you, Marilyn," Courtney spat. "I'm asking *my mother*."

"Courtney ..." Brenda finally managed to push her daughter's name across her lips. "We'll talk about this privately after the performance."

"Privately?" Courtney shrieked. "That horse has well and truly bolted. Addy knows all about you and Marilyn, and now everyone in this room does too. But you didn't have the decency to tell your family. To tell me!"

"I was going to tell you tomorrow." Brenda wrung her hands. "At lunch. With the boys."

"I can't believe you've humiliated me like this!"

Brian gave Courtney's shoulder a pat. "You're not on your Pat Malone there, love."

"Believe me, Courtney, I never wanted you to find out this way," Brenda offered, hearing the words fall like stones.

"Gee, thanks! Too bad it didn't happen." Courtney picked up her bag. "I'm not staying for any more of this BS."

"Good idea," Brian said. "Let's go."

"So that's it?" Steph's anguished voice rose above the chatter.

"I can't believe we're not singing because of two selfish people."

"Exactly," Courtney said tightly. "Did you hear that, Mum? So freaking selfish."

"I meant Addy and *you*," Steph said tartly.

Courtney's cheeks burned red. "Oh, that's rich coming—"

"Courtney, we're gutted you found out this way and of course you're in shock, but if you leave now we can't answer any of your questions," Marilyn said smoothly as if the bottom hadn't just dropped out of Brenda's world.

"So we're not singing?" a new member asked.

"Please, Courtney," Brenda begged, "stay and sing. As soon as the performance is over I promise you we'll find somewhere quiet to talk."

"I can't believe you expect me to sing after this betrayal." Courtney's arms sliced the air. "Why should I do anything for two lying bitches?"

"Language, Courtney," Vera said mildly. "Remember, you're not singing for your mother and Marilyn. You're singing for the choir, the hall roof and the cove's reputation."

"There's no argument that Addy's let us down big time and you're hurting," Morgan said. "But can you find a way to sing? I know it's a big ask but we need you."

Addy's snorty snores rumbled across the tense quiet.

Brenda watched the internal battle play out on Courtney's face.

The desire to stalk out with dramatic flair versus the heady attraction of being begged to stay, sing and save the day. Of the likely accolades that would follow.

"Fine," Courtney said. "I'll sing, *but* I'm only doing it for the choir and for the cove." She speared Brenda with a look of pure loathing. "I'm not doing it for you or her. Not when you've destroyed our family."

Marilyn turned so only Brenda could see her and smiled, but Brenda couldn't return it. She couldn't agree that this was just Courtney being a drama queen playing to an audience and that tomorrow she'd act as if nothing had happened. Brenda knew her daughter was capable of holding a grudge with the strength of a limpet on a wave-pounded reef.

All the gains she'd made with Courtney since Glen's death—repairing and shoring up their mother-daughter relationship—had just been wiped out by a simple yes.

CHAPTER TWENTY-FIVE

BRENDA HAD NEVER BEEN HAPPIER to walk into the sanctuary of home, close the door and shut out the world. Somehow, through a fog of shock and despair, she'd managed to play the piano for the choir, acting as if her private life hadn't just been exposed to her daughter, the choir and most of the north-west coast.

Misery and exhaustion pulled her onto the sofa and she finally gave in to tears.

Marilyn hugged her and stroked her hair. "It's okay."

"It's not okay. I can't believe Addy did that."

"Me neither," Marilyn agreed. "I'm absolutely furious with her. I mean, she risked everything for the choir—"

"Not the choir!" Brenda pulled back fast, stunned by Marilyn's obtuseness. "I can't believe she outed us. No one knew! And now ..."

Marilyn squeezed her hand. "It wasn't ideal—"

"Ideal?!" Brenda grabbed tissues and wiped her eyes roughly so she could see Marilyn clearly instead of through a veil of tears. "That's the understatement of the year."

"True." Marilyn sighed. "But at least we're finally out. In a way, it's freeing."

Freeing? How?

"It's not bloody freeing! Addy stole our control." The anger she'd tried to contain broke its restraint, crashing inside her like white-capped waves. "And so did you!"

"What?" Confusion creased Marilyn's brow. "No, I didn't."

"You did. When Courtney asked me 'Is this true?,' you answered for me."

Marilyn stiffened. "I answered for us."

"No, you answered for you!" Anguish surged, riding the coat-tails of anger. "For months you've pushed and pressured me to come out on your timeline, not mine. We had a plan, and all you had to do was stay silent for a few more hours and everything would have happened quietly and calmly at family lunch. But you couldn't even wait eighteen more hours. You saw a chance and you took it!"

Marilyn's skin flushed pink. "That's *not* what happened! When Courtney asked her question, you looked like you'd seen a ghost. You were mute and I stepped in to support you. To support *us*!"

"No." Brenda shook her head as if that would stop the words from landing. "When Addy said we were a couple, there was doubt on the choir's faces. You heard Brian telling her to go and sleep it off. We could have easily sloughed away Addy's comments and put the focus back on her being drunk and the choir crisis. *That* would have been supportive."

Incredulity widened Marilyn's eyes. "So your plan was to say to Courtney 'No, it's not true' and then tell her tomorrow, 'Actually, about that, Marilyn and I have been together for years.' Brenda, that's crazy thinking!"

Thoughts and words ricocheted in her mind, and her body ached as if stampeded on by a herd of cattle. "I have the right to control my own story!"

"But it's not just your story, is it?" Marilyn accused. "It's mine too and you've been controlling it since I moved here."

Resentment poured oil on her anger. "Well, it's well and truly out now. Happy?"

"As a matter of fact, I am."

Brenda stiffened, unable to detect if the words were sarcastic or true. "You're happy my daughter isn't talking to me?"

"Oh, for heaven's sake!" Marilyn breathed out a long and exasperated sigh. "Of course I'm not happy about that. But tomorrow's another day and we'll sort it out over lunch."

"How the hell can we do that? Courtney's not talking to me!"

"She never said that."

"She accused us of destroying the family. It amounts to the same thing."

"You don't know that. One of my cousins threw a similar hissy fit and the next day she was fine. Courtney will feel differently after a good night's sleep. You'll see," Marilyn said confidently.

Brenda's back teeth locked. "She won't."

"Being negative won't help."

Brenda had a sudden urge to shake her. "I'm not being negative. I'm being realistic."

Marilyn's mouth screwed up. "Honestly, Brenda, you complain that Courtney makes mountains out of molehills, but perhaps she gets that from you. This isn't a disaster. No one at choir said anything negative—"

"I'm not making a mountain out of a molehill," she ground out. "Remember Brian?"

Marilyn gave a dismissive shrug. "His opinion doesn't count. And if he leaves the choir that can only be a good thing. We want allies around us, not bigots."

Brenda thought of her family and her stomach hollowed out.

"I know things didn't go exactly to plan, but let's focus on the positives," Marilyn said, sitting a little straighter. "We're finally out. We can live our lives on our terms. When your family sees your strength and determination and your love for me, they'll have no choice but to respect your right to live the way you choose. Be proud, Brenda. It was my pride that won over my family."

Marilyn had eschewed marriage and children long before she'd come out as gay. She'd wanted more freedom in her life than her mother, who'd been locked in a traditional marriage and then trapped in financially strapped widowhood. "When I finally came out to Mum," Marilyn had told Brenda years earlier, "she said, 'I did wonder, dear. More cake?'"

And once again they were back to the circular argument that had dogged their relationship from the start—their very different lives and families. Brenda still struggled—not with her love for Marilyn; that was a given—but in identifying with the community.

At various times across the years she'd tried reading some of the literature, but none of it seemed to apply to late-in-life lesbians. And the language kept changing, meaning different things to different people. These days many young women were reclaiming gay and dropping lesbian, because the word had attracted some trans-excluding connotations. Others embraced the word queer. Brenda involuntarily shuddered. She couldn't even think about "queer" without flinching, let alone say it. Growing up she'd heard it hurled at anyone who was slightly less blokey and outdoorsy than the hunting, fishing and football community of the cove.

Just the other day Marilyn had told her that being different was the exact reason the word was making a resurgence. All Brenda knew was that her love for Marilyn didn't need labelling or defining. It did, however, need protecting. But now the news was not only out, it had been delivered in the worst possible way.

Marilyn always drew on her own experience of familial tolerance, but her mother had long suspected Marilyn loved women, making acceptance a natural progression. Brenda's children had no idea their mother loved, and had loved, Marilyn for a long time so there was nothing to cushion the shock.

"You know our families are chalk and cheese," Brenda said, not for the first time. "Yours is tolerant, mine's ..." She sucked in her lips against the threat of tears. "I don't know what mine is. God, I'm their mother! I raised them. I should know. But there's a disconnect—a distance between us that I can't seem to navigate."

"It's because you've been living a lie," Marilyn said.

Brenda glared at her. "It's not that simple."

Marilyn sighed again, as if weary of the topic. "It is that simple. Now you can finally be your true self with them. Believe me, it will change everything. It will bring you closer together."

Brenda tried to shut out Courtney's screaming words and hang on tightly to Marilyn's long-held belief. She was under no illusions that being out would change everything. It was exactly how that terrified her.

♬

The next day, Brenda was up early and staring out the kitchen window, but she was blind to the striking autumnal show of the Japanese maple lit by the apricot morning light. Unlike Marilyn, who'd slept soundly, Brenda had spent the night staring at the ceiling. Each time she'd got close to falling under sleep's spell, her mind lit up like an IMAX screen with Addy saying "lesbian" and Marilyn saying "yes," fast followed by the look of shock and horror on Courtney's face.

A loud knock rapped on the mudroom door, startling Brenda so much she almost spilled her tea. Colin strode in, dropping his hat on the table.

"Mum, what's going on?" he asked in a way that was reminiscent of his father—the lack of a social preamble. "Courtney woke me at 6:00 with some cock-and-bull story that you're a lesbo. I told her she'd lost her mind."

Brenda sucked in a fortifying breath. "But you came to check anyway?"

A sheepish look crossed his face. "Lucinda suggested it. You know, find out what's going on so we can avoid a tricky lunch."

That sounded like Lucinda.

"I doubt your sister's coming to lunch." Brenda crossed the room and rose on her toes to kiss him on the cheek. "Cuppa? Breakfast?"

"Nah. All good." He pulled out a chair. "Sit down, Mum."

She didn't want to sit down. Didn't want to face an inquisition without Marilyn in the room, but determination was written across Colin's sun-weathered face.

For a moment she was flung back in time to an afternoon in the farmhouse kitchen. Glen was insisting she sit and explain why, when he'd tried to contact her and tell her Courtney had broken her arm, the conference hotel hadn't been able to find her.

"Of course I was there!" She'd blamed the ineptitude of the hotel staff, when in reality she'd been in Longford with Marilyn.

Colin pulled a chair in next to her. "It's loopy-loo, right?"

"What is?"

"Courtney's saying your boarder's your lesbian lover."

Brenda's heart hammered and she forced herself to look at her eldest child. Was this the last time he'd sit in her kitchen and chat to her? Would he join Courtney in her disgust?

"I love Marilyn."

Colin frowned. "As best friends, right? Like Luce and Jessica?"

"No." She laced her fingers so tightly her knuckles glowed white. "It's a far deeper love than that."

Colin swallowed. "But you've got separate bedrooms."

She shook her head slowly. "We share a bed."

His face paled. "Shit, Mum! You're nearly sixty."

Brenda didn't know whether to laugh or take offence. "What's that got to do with anything? Sex isn't just for the under-forties."

"Yeah, but ..." Colin shook his head, clearly unable to find the words.

She reached out and patted his hand. "I hope you're as much in love and enjoying sex as I am when you're my age."

Colin made a choking noise. "Mum! Too much information."

"Sorry, darling." She rose and poured him a cup from the pot she'd brewed not long before he'd arrived. She added sugar. "Are you okay?"

He rubbed his eyes with the heel of his hand as if trying to change an image. "No one wants to imagine their parents having sex, let alone

..." He downed the tea. "Lucinda thinks you're lonely and depressed since Dad died and that's why ... you know."

For years Brenda had battled depression, and if the children had suspected they'd taken Glen's lead and ignored it. Now, for the first time in years, she was happy and they thought she must be depressed. The irony hit her like a slap.

"I'm not depressed. I'm certainly not lonely. How can I be when I've got Marilyn in my life?"

"But it's not normal, is it?" he asked earnestly. "I mean, who wakes up one day and says 'I'm gay now'?"

She mustered a faint smile. "That's not quite how it happened."

"How did it happen then?"

She snagged her bottom lip and used the discomfort to keep herself strong. "I know you've got lots of questions, and your brother and sister will have them too, but when I answer them, Marilyn needs to be in the room. Can you talk to Courtney for me? Persuade her to come to lunch?"

Colin gave a low whistle. "I'm not a miracle-worker. And to be honest, Mum, I don't know how I feel about all this. I didn't believe Courtney, so it's a bit of a shock. I'm not ready to sit down for lunch with your boarder."

"Marilyn," Brenda said firmly. "Her name's Marilyn."

"Yeah, okay. Marilyn." He ran his hands through his hair. "I need to talk to Luce about it. She might not want the boys to come now."

A raging wall of flames leaped inside her. "I can't imagine why the boys can't come. After all, they've been here every Monday afternoon all year and *nothing* has changed."

He rubbed his jaw. "Everything's changed."

"Nonsense! Marilyn's been living here for months. Tell me. What have the boys talked to you about on Monday nights?"

Bewilderment ringed him. "I dunno."

"Well, if it was 'Mémé sleeps in the same bed as Marilyn' you'd remember that. But it hasn't been that, has it?"

He sighed. "Mostly we hear about Clyde."

"Exactly. As far as they're concerned, Marilyn's a teacher at school and my friend. Both are the truth."

"But it's way more than that." He pushed slowly to his feet and jammed his hat on his head. "I better head off."

Brenda stood, her arms folded as much in frustration as to keep herself upright. "Will you be back for lunch?"

"I dunno. I need to talk to Lucinda."

She thought about the child Colin had been—a little boy whose world had revolved around her. A child who'd enthusiastically hugged her and told her he loved her. But it had been years since he'd hugged her and now his love and loyalty was to his wife, which was as it should be. And yet ...

"I'm still your mother," she said tersely. "I'm the same person I've always been."

Colin's face scrunched up as if in pain. "Are you?"

Brenda wrenched open the pantry door and grabbed the packet of chips and a box of water crackers, before pulling the wheel of Colin's favorite blue vein cheese out of the fridge. She shoved them at his chest.

"I bought these for you and the kids. Take them. Give my love to Rusty and Jake."

"Mum ..." Colin shook his head. "Don't be like this. It's a lot to take in."

"I understand that. What I don't understand is why you won't sit down with me for lunch."

"It's too soon."

The mudroom door closed with a soft click and he was gone.

Anger and resignation dueled inside her as bloodied hope lay splattered against her heart. Of her three children's likely reactions, Colin had been the unknown. She'd desperately hoped he'd fall on the side of acceptance along with his younger brother, leaving Courtney alone in her feelings. It would have provided a path for their sister to walk down and join them. At this point, Brenda would settle for Courtney tolerating her, but even that seemed a bridge too far.

Marilyn appeared in the kitchen, showered, dressed and ready to face the day. Clyde trotted over for some love and attention.

"Who was that?" she asked.

"Colin."

"At this hour?"

"Courtney called him."

"Why didn't you come and get me?" Marilyn asked, an edge to her voice.

Brenda sighed. "Because he isn't ready to meet you."

"Don't be ridiculous. He's met me many times at school and at the market."

"Yes, but that was as Rusty's teacher, not as the woman I love. Apparently, that changes everything."

"It doesn't."

"That's what I said, but in his mind it does. He left saying he needed to talk to Lucinda."

Marilyn smiled and put their oatmeal porridge into the microwave to cook. "Then you're worrying over nothing. Lucinda's one of the most down-to-earth women in the cove."

"Down-to-earth doesn't mean not homophobic! The cove isn't Hobart. It's a small country town in a conservative, churchgoing district. As it stands, Colin's not coming to lunch and he isn't certain the boys will be here tomorrow after school."

Marilyn pulled the bowls from the microwave and stirred in nuts and seeds before adding brown sugar. She placed one bowl in front of Brenda, then sat opposite her and ate her breakfast with enthusiasm.

Brenda picked up her spoon, but her appetite had vanished, so she used it to stir the contents around and around the bowl.

"Have you called Courtney?" Marilyn asked.

"No."

"I could call her."

"No, thank you."

"Brenda, I want to help. The sooner we resolve this the better."

Brenda railed against the pressure. "And if we push her, we risk making it worse."

"What about talking to Ben? Would that help?"

"I think the best person to talk to her is Richard." Her phone beeped and she picked it up, reading the notification. "Speak of the devil." She swiped to read the full message.

Hi, Mum, I'm really, really sorry, but I can't make today. The Premier's announcing a snap election at ten and you know what that means. The crazy's started and will continue for the next six weeks. Sorry again. Give my love to everyone. Rich xxx

Richard had been her one hope. The one member of the family guaranteed to be in her corner. The one person Courtney listened to.

The need to be on her own propelled Brenda to her feet. "They say things happen in threes, don't they," she said dully. "Richard's not coming."

She walked outside before Marilyn could say a word.

CHAPTER TWENTY-SIX

SUNSHINE BORED into Addy's room with the intensity of lasers. She rolled over, trying to hide from the light. Her head thumped, her mouth was dry and she had no memory of changing into pajamas or hopping into bed. As she pushed herself up to sitting position, pain gripped her wrist. She peered at it, surprised to see a purple bruise blooming on the heel of her hand. How had that happened?

Gingerly, she turned her head and by squinting made out a plastic bucket, two full water bottles and some paracetamol. Had Grant done that?

Something niggled in the depths of the fug that was her mind. No, that wasn't right. Grant had brought gin and lunch. They'd danced. She was almost certain they'd had sex and then he'd left. What had she done after that?

She ransacked her hazy memories. She heard the music of *The Greatest Showman* in her head and felt the words slicing through her like blades, but no matter which part of her mind she searched, she couldn't find a picture of herself singing on a stage. She'd obviously blocked the memory by wiping herself out after the concert.

A barrage of memories suddenly downloaded. Steph's look of dismay when Addy had answered the door and her snippy refusal of a drink. The choir members dressed in their neat black and white and their questioning faces. Fern's curled lip. Vera saying "Your mother would be very disappointed," as if that was a completely new concept.

A wave of guilt hit her. Had she been drunk before the concert and not sung?

She instantly dismissed the thought. She prided herself that she only drank when she was off the clock and free of responsibilities. Her drinking never interfered with work.

It kinda did at Wrest Point when you were late for your presentation.

One time! And I was barely late.

Of course she'd sung at the Choir Crush and then she'd celebrated a difficult performance. But how had she gotten home? Steph had driven her there so it made sense she'd brought her home, although she had a vague memory of Brenda saying "Let's get you some coffee."

Whoever it was had put her in her pajamas and tucked her up in bed. Shame prickled under her skin. It was fine to crash with a drinking buddy who was equally out of it, but something about the line-up of water bottles, the blister pack and the vomit bucket told her whoever it was had been sober. They would have seen her at her worst. She cringed at the thought of having to thank them.

Oh God! Embarrassment reinforced her shame—she had no idea who to thank.

Forcing down a rising combination of alcohol and stomach acid that burned the back of her throat, she rummaged around, patting under her pillow and on the nightstand until she found her phone. She scrolled quickly, looking for a message from Steph, Brenda or Marilyn that implied they'd brought her home, but the last text was the one from Steph telling her she was running late.

Addy squeezed her eyes shut as if that would conjure up a memory, but everything from lunchtime onwards was a pixelated mess.

She'd have to start by thanking Steph and hope she was right, otherwise she'd look a right fool. Perhaps she could just ignore the whole incident and hope they did too?

Her heart fluttered uncomfortably in her chest, and rafts of agitation pulsed along her veins. She had a love-hate relationship with the blackouts. She loved the free fall into them—their blissful welcoming silence—but she hated the associated memory loss. It stole her control and left in its place festering loathing and humiliation that poked, prodded and blamed. It made her feel—her mind shied away sharply. God, she needed a drink.

You don't day-drink before noon and it's not even 9:00 on a Sunday morning.

One glass! Hair of the dog! And there's hours to get sober for work on Monday.

She threw off the covers and immediately cried out as a white flash of pain ricocheted through her from head to toe. Shivering, she walked carefully down the hall, trying to glide and not jolt her head.

When she opened the fridge, she was surprised to discover there were no long-necked green bottles standing in the door or lying seductively on the interior shelves. Not to worry; it had been a chilly night so one straight from the case would be cold enough.

Avoiding turning on lights that would exacerbate her headache, she peered into the semi-lit room. Shadows from the ladder and paint tins formed a silhouette of a city skyline on the wall, which was far more agreeable than their daylight taunting presence.

She heard the crunch of plastic breaking at the same time something sharp dug into her foot. She jumped back. "Bloody hell!"

She picked up the broken television remote and went to put it back in its usual position on the wine case. It was missing. Had she moved it? She couldn't remember doing that or think of a reason why she would.

She turned slowly, taking in the room. The wine had vanished.

The sun was up now, and the usually soft autumn light felt harsh and uncompromising. She noticed her handbag lying on the floor, pulled out her sunglasses and slid them on. After a second sweep of the room—still no wine—she searched the other rooms without success. Had she drunk it all yesterday?

Her chest cramped in horror then relaxed. If she'd drunk sixteen bottles of wine she'd be dead. No, she'd been burgled. *Bastards!*

With her head pounding like a jackhammer, she immediately searched for her laptop. It was sitting on the dining table where she'd been using it before Grant arrived. Relief softened her legs.

She sat down hard and did a visual inventory of the room. The TV sat in its place on the sideways bookshelf, and everything else—from the china figurines to the photo of Dubrovnik and the metronome on the piano—was in its rightful place. There was really nothing worth stealing. It must have been kids.

Luckily online shopping didn't care what time of the day she ordered booze. She got halfway through the process then remembered it was Sunday and no one would deliver to the cove until Monday. New plan! She'd drive to Wynyard at 10:00.

After taking a shower, swallowing two paracetamol and drinking a bottle of water—making coffee was currently beyond her—she was padding down the hall when the doorbell chimed. Addy flinched and pressed on her thumping temples. Technically she was vertical, but she wasn't ready to face anyone until her armor was in place. That meant being fully dressed and with a layer of foundation and powder on her face, blusher on her cheekbones, eye shadow and eyeliner carefully applied, and all finished with a bow of ruby-red lipstick.

The bell rang again. "Addy!" Steph's voice drifted under the door. "It's me. Steph."

As much as she liked Steph and appreciated her easy and undemanding friendship, the thought of the woman's happy chatter clattering on her headache like rain on a tin roof was enough to convince her not to answer the door. She turned into the bedroom and crawled under the covers.

Thirty-seconds later her cell phone rang, the screen lighting up with Steph's number. *Go away. Go away.* She flicked the phone to mute and the loud pealing noise thankfully ceased.

She closed her eyes. She just needed an hour. Sixty blessed minutes to allow the water and paracetamol to do their jobs, and then she'd be ready to face the day and talk to Steph.

The staccato rapping of a key on glass sounded above her head. Her eyes snapped open, meeting Steph's gaze through the window. Addy quickly shut them, but it was too late. The connection had been made and Steph knew she was awake. Why the hell hadn't she closed the blind last night?

Because you have no memory of getting into bed, let alone an evening routine.

"I've brought coffee." Steph's voice carried through the slightly open window.

Addy lay perfectly still and focused on the softening edges of her mind.

"Addy, please open the door."

Sleep pulled at her and she dived thankfully into its cozy warmth, welcoming the inky darkness. It freed her from the thudding pain behind her eyes, from the piercing needles of anxiety and the visceral pulsating ache of years of self-loathing. She floated away into the silent calm.

Addy. Aida. Ads. Jumbled images joined the voices tumbling through her head. Playing piano and singing. Her parents' proud smiles. Her teacher's praise. Tumbling off her surfboard into the foam and giving herself up to the wave's hypnotic pull.

You'll never amount to anything without me.

Shut up! Leave me alone.

Jasper standing in a pile of money.

Grant's mouth on her breast.

Steph's tears.

Ice-cold jagged fingers dug in and gripped her. She gasped and surfaced fast from the nightmare, coughing violently. Completely discombobulated, it took her a moment to realize her covers had slipped to the floor.

As she girded herself to lean down and grab it, something moved, startling her. Her hand flew to her chest and she screamed before she realized it was Steph standing at the end of the bed.

"What the hell?" Addy panted. "Are you trying to kill me by frightening me to death?"

"Of course not." Steph shook the covers over her. "I was just checking you're okay. I brought you coffee."

"Thanks, but I'm pretty sure breaking and entering is an offence."

Steph gave a dismissive shrug. "I didn't break anything. You really should do something about the lack of window locks."

Addy fell back on the pillows. "I know. Kids broke in last night and stole all my wine."

Steph grimaced. "Actually, that was me."

Indignation tangled with surprise. If their friendship had a mathematical equation, Steph had done ninety-eight percent of the work to establish it. She'd offered help, suggested get-togethers and generally fallen over herself to please Addy. There'd only been one exception—the forgotten phone call when Steph was having her miscarriage. But that had been forgiven, so Steph taking her wine made no sense.

"I don't understand. Why would you take my wine?"

Steph pushed a pile of clothes off a chair and sat primly, her hands clasped in her lap. "Because I think you're an alcoholic."

The words fell like boulders, slamming into Addy and pinning her hard. She clawed to get out from under them.

"Last time I looked you weren't Doctor Steph," she said tartly. "You're way off the mark."

"Maybe alcoholic is too scary a word. Would it be more accurate if I said you have a problem with alcohol?"

"Not remotely accurate." Addy took a fortifying sip of Sven's coffee. "I enjoy a drink the same as everyone. The same as you."

"I wasn't the one falling down drunk yesterday afternoon," Steph said softly.

"Neither was I! If I had been, I couldn't have gotten into the car with you. Look," she said conspiratorially, knowing Steph had almost salivated the few times Addy had shared something about herself. "I know I partied after the performance, but tying one on occasionally is hardly a sin."

"The thing is, Addy ..." Steph hesitated, then straightened her shoulders. "It's not that long ago that you tied one on in Hobart, is it?"

Cold dread trickled through Addy. She'd told Steph that the casino had been loud and that was the reason she'd misunderstood the phone call. She'd never said she'd been drunk. No one other than Grant knew what had happened in Hobart and it was their secret.

She forced a laugh and gave a dismissive wave of her hand. "Letting your hair down is kind of expected at a work conference."

Steph's mouth tightened and Addy moved fast to mend fences and deflect her friend away from any other questions.

"Thanks for bringing me home last night. And for the coffee. That was above and beyond, but as you can see, I'm fine. All good."

"Oh my God!" Steph's hand flew to her mouth, her blue eyes disappearing behind inky pupils dilated with shock. "You don't remember anything, do you?"

Addy stilled like a cornered animal, her gaze frantically flicking over Steph's face seeking clues. "Of course I remember. I'm just a teeny bit hazy on the post-performance drinks."

"Oh, Addy." Pity rose off Steph like a bad smell. "You didn't perform. You were too drunk to stand, let alone sing."

She didn't sing?

"I ..." Anxiety cramped her gut with the knuckle-crunching pain of a punch. "I ..." The urgent need to obfuscate dominated all thought. "It's just I ..." But for some reason she couldn't push the lie "I got bad news" over her lips.

Her shoulders slumped as the full weight of what was required hit her. "I'll apologize to everyone."

"That would be a start." Steph's tone was surprisingly firm.

Addy couldn't look at Steph and as her fingers worried the piping on the covers she noticed a tear in the spun cotton. "Did the ..." She cleared her throat and tried again. "Did the choir still compete?"

"We did. Courtney sang the lead, and even with my voice in the mix, we came third."

"That's so great!"

The choir had a ribbon and a lead singer in Courtney so they'd forgive Addy. Even if they didn't, it was no biggie. She'd never wanted to join in the first place. As relief buoyed her, she had a sudden urge to reassure Steph, who had a tendency to sing flat.

"And don't be so hard on yourself. You have a lovely voice and singing's all about practice, so keep at it. I've been saying from the start that Courtney would do a better job than me. I know she can be a pain sometimes and she rubs you up the wrong way, but how great for Brenda. I bet she was stoked hearing—"

"Letting down the choir wasn't the worst thing you did," Steph said sharply.

The euphoric rush drained out of her. "Did I throw up in your car?"

"You wish."

Something about the way Steph said it catapulted Addy's heart into her mouth. She slid down the pillows, giving in to the strong desire to disappear under the covers.

Steph kept talking. "You had no filter and you dropped a lot of truth bombs. You told me I couldn't sing in key if my life depended on it."

"Oh God. I'm so sorry." She put her hand on Steph's arm, but Steph threw it off.

"And you told Brian much the same thing. You pretty much voiced an opinion on everyone."

"I'm sorry. I'd had a couple of drinks to steady my nerves and—"

"You were flat out drunk."

"No—"

"But the worst thing you did was outing Brenda and Marilyn."

Chagrin surged. "I would *never* do something like that."

"Well, you did and I have proof. It seems that someone connected to another choir or one of the tech people must have been in the rehearsal room. Whoever it was filmed you and uploaded it to the Choir Crush's Facebook page."

Steph pulled out her cell phone and suddenly Addy saw a grainy photo of herself and heard her voice, thick and slurring, saying on repeat "Bren'a and Mar'lyn being lesbians and in lurve."

She pushed at the phone. "Turn it off!"

The noise stopped. Addy buried her face in her hands and rocked as palpitations thudded in her chest.

"It stunned everyone," Steph said quietly. "No one in the choir knew they were gay, let alone a couple. Not even Courtney."

"Oh God." Addy rocked harder as if it would turn back time and change everything. "How did Courtney take it?"

Steph's brows rose. "How do you think? Take her usual over-the-top reaction to most things and quadruple it. But it's not Courtney I'm worried about. It's Brenda and Marilyn being publicly outed and humiliated. If I was them, I'd never speak to you again."

"Not helpful!"

The need to do something, anything, overtook Addy. She scrambled out of bed, then stopped, uncertain what to do.

A thought broke through her panic. "We need to get the video taken down."

"You need to apologize to Brenda and Courtney."

Just the thought of doing that made her gag. "Who made you the moral police?"

Steph sighed. "It's nothing to do with morals and everything to do with taking responsibility for your actions." She sounded like a parenting manual.

"Okay, fine!" Addy stormed to her closet and pulled out some fine-corduroy pants and shoved her legs into them. They dragged at her skin and stuck on her hips. She tugged hard but they wouldn't budge. Nor would they button up. "Fuck!"

She tried kicking them off. Her feet got tangled in the tight material and she fell, her hip hitting the wooden floor with a bone-crunching thud.

"Here." Steph stood and stretched out her hand to help Addy to her feet.

Still smarting from the "take responsibility" jibe, Addy ignored her. She didn't need judgmental people in her life. She heard enough judgment in her own head every day of the week. Was hearing it now.

She shucked off the pants, pushed herself to her feet and ran to the kitchen, looking for something to silence the critical inner voice that was now stridently berating her. She opened every cabinet, desperately searching for a drink.

When Steph walked into the kitchen, Addy was holding vanilla extract in one hand and Chinese cooking wine in the other. Addy was about to yell "You bitch! Give me back my wine!" when she saw the look on Steph's face.

Steph didn't speak. She didn't have to. Her face said it all—horror and pity overlaid with bewilderment, sadness and solicitude.

In that moment, Addy saw herself reflected in Steph's gaze—wild-eyed and so desperate for alcohol she was considering downing salty and bitter rice wine. She wasn't this person. She was well-educated, good at her job, and being promoted. Sure, she enjoyed a drink, but she was in control.

You're flipping a coin between drinking vanilla extract and rice wine.

You have no idea what Grant means by a sex fiend, but it makes you feel dirty.

You were so drunk yesterday you can't remember violating Brenda and Marilyn's privacy.

The horror that came with that reality hitched her breathing to a rapid pant, spinning her head. How had her life gotten to this point?

Her hands shook so hard her fingers released the bottles and they clattered onto the counter.

"Steph?"

"Yes."

"I need help."

"Oh, thank God." Steph wrapped her arms around her and burst into tears.

CHAPTER TWENTY-SEVEN

Rain heralded June, dominating the weak sunshine of the Australian winter and clouding the cove in a low, wet and all-consuming fog. Cold and flu viruses lingered in the air, targeting those with weak chests. Monty barked like a sea lion. He was back using the Ventolin nebulizer after scaring Steph and Henry with his struggle to breathe. They'd had a fraught and terrifying midnight drive to the Burnie hospital.

"We moved here for the clean air," Steph had told the emergency doctor, seeking reassurance they'd done the right thing. "He's been so well."

The doctor lifted the stethoscope off Monty's heaving chest. "Damp winters are tough for asthmatics. Queensland might have been a better choice."

Monty was slowly improving, but he still wasn't sleeping through the night, nor was he well enough to return to day care. He was also super-clingy and ended up in their bed most nights. Steph dreamed of not having a child permanently glued to her.

Alan, from the Men's Shed, had kindly dropped off the pyramid circus people. "I l-liked c-cutting them," he said. "It was g-good to just th-think about one thing."

Steph remembered Bill saying that Brianna had taken the kids, and she understood. "I find it soothing too. For a while I forget everything that's going on in my life."

And the "everything" list was long. The loss of her baby and the lack of another pregnancy; Monty's hard-fought breaths; Addy's cry for help; the choir; work and the bloody internet; her rising frustration with Henry ...

What about Zoe?

Zoe's Henry's problem.

Steph blinked. Alan was still standing on the veranda, staring at the box in her hand.

"You b-better ch-check I cut them like you w-wanted," he said.

"Come in," she offered. "I'll put the kettle on."

He shook his head. "I'll wait here."

Something about his demeanor said he didn't believe he deserved to come inside and that added to her sadness. She stepped out onto the veranda and placed the box on the table. As she lifted the lid, the fresh and pungent smell of cut wood rose to meet her and she smiled.

Lined up in neat rows were identical little circus people with squat feet and short arms pushed high in the air, all ready to be balanced, built into pyramids, lined up like dominoes or a hundred other things creative kids might do with them. Steph stood four on top of one another, checking how well they stacked, and was pleased. She imagined what they'd look like with the stickers that would gift them clothes and grinning faces.

"Oh, Alan, they're perfect." She smiled at him. "Thank you."

"T-took a b-bit of p-practice." He shoved his hands in his pockets and looked at his feet. "I c-can do m-more if you w-want."

"That's great, but I'll have to renegotiate with Ted at the shed. Unless ..." She studied Alan. His clothes were worn but clean. Bill had thought him capable of the job and that belief had been borne out.

Alan had also taken the initiative and delivered the order to Four Winds. "What was your last job, Alan?"

"F-furniture mover. C-company closed. N-not a lot of w-work about."

"Sounds tough."

"Yeah."

"I'll have to check with our insurance company, but while you're looking for a real job, would you like to be my cutter? It totally depends on orders, but I'll pay cash and throw in lunch. I can't promise anything as fancy as the Men's Shed, but mine's got a heater and a view."

Alan met her gaze. "Sounds good."

It was the first time he'd looked straight at her. The first time he hadn't stuttered.

"Great! Of course, any job interview you get takes precedence."

"Mum-meee!" Monty's hoarse voice drifted out onto the veranda.

Steph tapped the box. "As of yesterday, these only put me three orders ahead. We've got internet issues, so when I finally get to Sven's or up to the intersection today, I'll check my website and let you know. Can you pop your number into my phone?"

"Mum-mee!" Monty coughed, a wet phlegmy sound.

Alan handed her back her phone. "S-someone sick?"

"My son. He got the double whammy of asthma and croup. He's getting better now so hopefully I can get your kids' set of circus people painted by the end of the week."

"N-no hurry," Alan said firmly. "No fun with s-sick kids. It can wait."

"Thank you." She almost asked him about his kids, but Monty yelled again so she said goodbye and hurried inside.

Monty was ignoring the playdough, the figure-eight train set she'd built complete with a tunnel, bridge and a rail crossing with cars waiting to cross, and the coloring book that she'd set up to keep him occupied while she worked. He was sitting in the middle of the long table with Pen firmly clamped under his arm and happily painting acrobatic penguin pieces in bright red.

"Monty! No!" She swooped and lifted him off the table.

Startled, he squawked in protest and fright, before lurching sideways, trying to reach the table. "My penguins!"

"They're not your penguins," she said, breathing deeply and trying to access a well of calm despite the fact that he'd ruined them. "Pen is your penguin."

"Want my penguins!" Monty cried, then coughed, his little body shaking with the effort of trying to breathe.

"Oh, mate." Sagging with despair, she sat down and rocked him gently, kissing his curls. Trying to settle him so he stopped coughing and could breathe more easily.

Henry appeared, his face lined with concern. "Has he had a relapse?"

"I was answering the door and he got into my paints and wrecked four orders. I yelled and he got upset."

Henry lifted Monty out of her arms and gently patted his back. "The doctor said to keep him calm and quiet."

Henry's accusatory tone struck a nerve. "I was. I've set up activities for him to do while I work."

Henry sighed. "Should you even be working when he's been so sick?"

The double standard struck her so hard she gasped. "You're working."

"That's different and you know it."

"No, it's not different, Henry," she said, exasperated by his lack of understanding. "I've got orders!"

He grimaced. "It's hardly life and death if someone gets a toy a week late."

"It's upsetting if someone orders it for a special occasion and it arrives late."

"So email them and explain. They'll understand."

"No, they won't. They're customers and they don't care about our lives." She turned her back on him and started clearing up the mess, but anger made her movements jerky. "All they care about is that the product they bought is late. They won't order from me again and they'll leave cutting one-star reviews." Her hands paused on the wrapped newspaper. "You know what? It sounds like you don't want me to succeed."

"Don't be ridiculous," Henry said behind her. "Of course I want you to succeed. I'm just saying that while Monty's sick—"

"We should share the care."

"We do that anyway," Henry said.

She whirled around to face him. "No. We don't. Despite what you promised when we moved down here, I do the lion's share."

"That's not true! You've been disappearing into the shed every night for weeks, and now you're visiting Addy before work and leaving me holding the fort," he said, clearly aggrieved.

"Don't be so selfish. You know she needs my support." Henry mumbled something, but Steph refused to be sidetracked. "I work at night because I can't get a clear run at anything during the day. And exactly what fort are you holding? Monty's in bed before I leave, and half the time when I come in you haven't even done the dishes!"

His jaw jutted. "We do have another child who needs our time."

"Pfft! Zoe hardly comes out of her room."

"And shouldn't we be worried by that?" Henry asked. "You seem more concerned about Addy than you do about Zoe."

Steph threw off the guilt Henry's words tried to cast over her. "Addy's in the early days of sobriety, whereas Zoe's in her room because that's what girls her age do when they want space from their parents and annoying half-brothers. And it's not like she can easily access the internet and you limit her data. She'll be drawing, listening to music and writing dreadful angst-filled poetry."

Henry didn't look convinced. "She's not eating properly."

"That's hardly my fault. I buy her plenty of vegan food."

"I know you do," Henry said carefully. "But expecting a thirteen-year-old to cook for herself ..."

"I don't expect that," Steph said firmly. "I have no problem with her being vegan, but I'm not adding cooking three meals each night to my already overloaded life."

"You cook different food for Monty," Henry said. "Why is this different?"

"Monty's barely three! Zoe's being willfully difficult, but if you're worried she isn't eating properly then you take over the cooking. That's fine by me. It's one less interruption in a day already filled with them!"

Henry snorted. "Here we go! Why do you think you have the monopoly on being interrupted? If the internet isn't screwing up my plans, I've got clients or head office ringing me every ten minutes. It's reached breaking point. We have to bite the bullet and spend eleven thousand dollars to get fiber optic installed to the house so we have fast and reliable internet."

Before now, Henry had only ever said "the big bucks." She stared at him. "Eleven thousand dollars?" It hurt to say it. "That's a huge chunk of our savings."

"I know, but what choice do we have? We've tried everything and the technicians are out of suggestions on how to make it reliable, let alone improving the speed. It's completely insane that we're driving into town or to the highway to access reception. You're trying to start a business and head office is fed up with my unreliability with video conferencing. Believe me, it will cost us a lot more if I have to travel back to the mainland once a week."

Steph stared out the window toward the majestic mountain that was the cause of their internet woes. How had they arrived at this point, so very far from the life they'd conjured for themselves that day on the beach? A volcano of emotions erupted, swamping her in frustration and fury.

"This isn't what you promised, Henry! Winter's only just started and Monty's sick. There's no freakin' childcare. Joanna dumped Zoe on us and now she's ghosting you. I lost the baby and what if I can't get pregnant again? You said living here would be stress free, but look at us!"

Monty, who'd settled quietly on Henry's shoulder, burst into tears at her shouting.

"Shh, buddy, it's okay," Henry said, giving Steph a perplexed look. "Mummy's just a bit tired and overwrought."

"I'm not bloody overwrought!"

Henry didn't say a word—he didn't have to. She'd heard her shrewish yell and felt the agony of hopelessness boring through her. Battling tears, she swiped at her eyes with the backs of her hands and tried not to completely fall apart.

Henry stepped in close and hugged her, sandwiching Monty between them. Her little boy's soft and warm body steadied her.

"How about you go down to Sven's, grab a coffee and spend an hour in the shed cutting out penguins?" Henry said. "I'll mind Monty."

She knew she should stand her ground and make him understand how far they'd strayed from their utopia. Call him out that as Monty's father, he was co-parenting, not minding him. Point out that very attitude was the source of so much of her discontent. However, she recognized the look in Henry's eyes and knew that until she'd calmed down he'd refuse to engage. But mostly, it was the thought of an hour on her own that called like a siren song.

Her phone beeped with a reminder. There was no time for coffee or work. "Oh, hell! We've completely forgotten our appointment with the gynecologist."

"I don't think Monty should be dragged to Burnie. If you leave now you'll make it. Doctors always run late." Henry handed her the car keys and kissed her on the cheek. "Drive carefully."

When Steph arrived at the specialists' rooms at the private hospital, the receptionist explained that Doctor Sharma was delivering a baby.

"There's tea and coffee and iced water." She indicated a drink station. "Help yourself then take a seat."

Steph used the time to check and answer emails. The good news was there were more orders for circus people and penguins. Exactly how she was going to manage to deliver on the promised timeline and sleep was a problem for another day. Instead, she focused on solving other issues—completing an online chat with her insurance company, ordering more timber and calling Alan.

The most surprising communication was a text from Ben Burton— he wanted more tractors. Didn't he know that she and Courtney weren't talking?

She suddenly knew exactly how to get more time to make toys.

Hi, Ben, I'm so glad the tractors are selling for you. Let me know if you want any wooden fruits as well. I can make all the berries. I have to work all weekend, which is boring for everyone, so I was wondering if I could take you up on the offer to show Henry and the kids around the farm?

She signed off and hit send. *Suck on that, Courtney.*

"Stephanie. Sorry to have kept you waiting."

She glanced up from her phone and saw Nira Sharma beckoning her.

"Was it a boy or a girl?" Steph forced herself to ask as she followed the doctor into the consulting room.

"A little boy." Nira sat behind her desk. "How are you?"

Steph laced her hands. "Oh, you know. Up and down."

The doctor nodded. "The weeks and months after a miscarriage are not easy."

"Any idea when the empty feeling might go away?" Steph asked, even though she knew there wasn't a definitive answer. That there were no rules. No timeline. Oh, how she wished there was.

Sympathy crossed the doctor's face. "Are you and Henry still wanting to conceive?"

"Very much. We want Monty to have a sibling."

Nira glanced at her computer screen. "He has an older sister, yes?"

"A half-sister," Steph corrected. A half-sister who ignores him. "We want him to have a sibling closer to his own age."

"Of course," Nira said smoothly as she clicked some keys. "You mentioned at your last visit that it had taken you over a year to conceive your last pregnancy."

"That's right. You suggested I have some blood tests."

"I did and I have the results."

Something about the way the doctor said the words made Steph sit up a little straighter. "And?"

"I'm afraid the hormones responsible for ovulation are a bit hit and miss. This may be part of the reason why it took you so long to conceive last time. It can happen when we get older."

Indignation rippled. "I'm hardly old."

Nira smiled. "I'm talking in reproductive terms. Fertility starts to decline in your mid-thirties. Looking at these results, I'm not convinced you would have ovulated this month."

The words pushed unease through her. She knew enough that not ovulating meant not getting pregnant. "You said part of the problem. What else is a problem?"

"It takes two to make a baby so before we treat you, we need to rule out Henry having any issues too. We'll do a sperm count and if that comes back within normal limits, we'll look at assisting your ovulation with medication."

Steph's heart rate picked up. "And if Henry has a problem?"

"Considering your age, I'd refer you to the IVF clinic."

IVF? Pregnancy in a Petri dish. Steph sat back, stunned. Back in Melbourne, she'd ridden the tram past an IVF clinic each day to and from work. She'd watched the women with strain on their faces get off at the stop with a certain degree of smugness, secure in the knowledge that all her bits worked. Not once, not even when she was pregnant and those women had cast their eyes away from her, had she stopped to consider pregnancy and babies from their perspective. And now she might be one of them. Infertile.

She swallowed past a lump in her throat. "Does Burnie have an IVF clinic?"

"No. It's in Launceston."

Launceston was a ninety-minute drive away.

"Every time the media mentions IVF it sounds expensive."

Nira's shoulders lifted slightly. "There's some government rebate, but yes, the out-of-pocket expenses are in the thousands."

Steph thought of the eleven thousand dollars to get fast and reliable internet connected and pictured hundred-dollar bills from their nest egg blowing in the wind, far, far away from her. It was another reason her online business needed to be nurtured so it could grow and refill their bank account.

"But let's not get ahead of ourselves," Nira continued. "Hopefully it will be as simple as you taking some clomiphene to nudge your ovaries along. Tell Henry to pop in next time he's in town to do the sperm test. We have a private room and we can get the specimen to the lab quickly."

"Why do the guys get to have all the fun?" Steph joked lamely.

"I'll call you when I have the results and we'll go from there."

Nira rose to her feet. Clearly the appointment was over.

Steph rose too, smiled and said "thank you" and "goodbye." She chatted to the receptionist about the weather, paid her bill, and slid the trifolds about sperm testing and ovulation induction into her handbag as if they were glossy tourist information brochures about places she wanted to visit.

She reassured herself that Henry's swimmers would be fit and fast. The tablets would shake an egg from her ovaries and they'd make a baby. Everything was going to be fine.

She drove home through a veil of tears.

CHAPTER TWENTY-EIGHT

I<small>T HAD BEEN A ROUGH WEEK</small>. Rougher than Addy had expected, despite the sage advice from the online support group she'd joined— Sober Country Women, known as SCW. Steph had suggested Addy join Alcoholics Anonymous, but AA in the country wasn't the anonymous event it was in a large city. Addy preferred a single-sex group so together they'd searched the internet and found SCW. It had been a huge relief when a member had contacted her twenty minutes after she sent a tentative message.

Addy had wanted to visit Brenda and Marilyn immediately, but SCW advised her not to rush.

You're still hungover. Also, it takes up to a week for the alcohol to be totally out of your system and your body will fight its absence. Don't add more stress on top of that. Wait until you're in a better mental place

Addy hated the thought of waiting, but on that life-altering Sunday she knew she wasn't up to facing anyone. After Steph had pre-prepared her lunch and dinner and returned to Four Winds with promises to call three times that day, Addy had contacted the worthless prick who'd uploaded the video on Facebook. She'd donated five hundred dollars to his favorite charity—himself—to take it down. But she wasn't stupid; she knew there was a chance he'd upload it again in the future and try to blackmail her, so she'd created a file of all their correspondence and backed it up on a thumb drive. If there was a next time, she'd involve the police.

She'd also ignored some of the SCW advice, justifying to herself that Brenda and Marilyn needed to know she was now aware of what she'd done and how she ached with regret. She'd emailed them but hadn't received a reply.

On Monday, she'd gone to work as normal and proceeded to put in five fourteen-hour days, keen to be out of the cove from 7:00 in the morning until 9:00 at night. Thankfully Grant was in Hobart for the week so she was able to file "drunk sex with your boss again" under "stupid" and "deal with it later." By some miracle, no student or colleague appeared to have seen the Facebook video.

The days were long and she was challenged not only by sobriety but by exhaustion. Each night it took her forever to fall asleep, and then sleep abandoned her at four every morning. She'd taken to power-walking in the dark, trying to quell the skittering agitation that was a permanent companion. By 2:00 in the afternoon, when she needed to be alert for her students, all she wanted to do was curl up and nap. The temptation to drink a double espresso or down a caffeine-loaded energy drink was almost as hard to resist as wine, but drinking caffeine in the afternoon only exacerbated her sleep problems.

On the Wednesday as she struggled to fall asleep, she experienced a horrifying moment of clarity—exactly when was the last time she'd fallen asleep sober? She couldn't remember.

To stay sober and to get around her low energy levels she settled on sugar—she was stuffing confectionary snakes in her mouth every afternoon and evening. Another addiction? Possibly, but she'd worry about dealing with it when she was sleeping better. The SCW were correct—there was only so much she could cope with in early sobriety without sinking completely. It was enough just to make it through each day. *One day at a time* was her mantra and she clung to it as tightly as Dorothy clutching Toto in the twister.

On Friday night, after a ten-hour workday and a long walk in the bush, Addy finally managed to fall asleep at 9:00 and blessedly slept until 6:00.

She wouldn't say she felt like a new woman—far from it. It turned out being well-rested was a double-edged sword. The mind fog and the mud-sucking fatigue that came with a daily hangover had vanished, but her new clarity of thought brought into focus many of the reasons she drank. Without alcohol to numb them, they danced and spun continuously, unnerving her.

"What about talking to a professional?" Steph had suggested on one of her nightly visits.

"At the moment staying sober's my priority," Addy said firmly.

"Yes, but ..." Steph's brows pulled into a sharp V. "Isn't it all connected?"

It was too difficult to explain that until she learned how to stay sober, she couldn't risk delving into dark places.

Now, ten days alcohol-free, she could hardly claim she was long-term sober, but she was clear-headed—the first requirement of an honest apology. Addy sat in her car studying a mixed bunch of hyacinths—blue, pink and white. According to the internet, hyacinths were apology flowers and represented an intention of making peace. Addy needed every symbol of remorse at her disposal when she faced Brenda and Marilyn.

Steph had offered to accompany her, but Addy knew she needed to do this on her own. She had, however, accepted Steph's offer to stand with her later tonight to provide silent support when Addy faced the fire-breathing dragon that would be the choir.

The urge to have one drink, just to take the edge off her stress, hammered hard in her veins.

One glass. You know you want it.

"Lah, lah!" she sang to the windshield.

She picked up her cell phone, brought up the SCW app and typed.

I'm outside the house of the people whose personal situation I shared without permission when I was fall-down drunk. Right now I'm sober and everything's vivid and hugely real. More real than it's been in a long time. I want to apologize to them. I need to do this, but my body's screaming for a drink. Help!

The words *someone's typing* appeared, followed by: *One step at a time, Addy. Walk to the door and ring the bell. We're with you*

Addy picked up the flowers and got out of the car. She'd agonized over whether she should have made an appointment to see Brenda and Marilyn or just rock up. Eventually she'd decided that there was no good time, so with a "rip the band-aid off" attitude, she'd left work early to do all the face-to-face apologies on the same day. Now it seemed like a reckless decision.

Quit choir. You were always going to anyway and I'm far more fun, her craving taunted.

She reached the front door and rang the bell, rehearsing what she'd say while she waited. When Brenda opened the door, Addy's mouth and her words dried. She thrust the flowers forward.

"Addy." Brenda neither smiled nor accepted the hyacinths. "You look tired."

"So do you."

Brenda gave a wry smile. "I suppose you'd better come in." She turned and walked down the hall.

Addy followed her into a light and airy kitchen and tried again with the flowers. "These are for you and Marilyn. Is she here?"

"I'm here," a voice said behind her.

She turned and Marilyn gave her a nod, but she didn't accept the flowers either. Addy placed them on the table.

"Thank you for inviting me in. I wasn't sure—"

"Tea or coffee?" Brenda asked.

She didn't want to be difficult and ask for caffeine-free tea so she said, "A glass of water would be lovely."

"Take a seat."

Brenda poured three glasses of water while Marilyn sliced a

lemon. Addy's heart pounded hard and fast, thumping in her ears like the beat of a drum.

"I'm sorry," she blurted out the moment the glasses were set down on maple coasters. "There's no excuse for what I did."

"No," Marilyn said. "There really isn't. You hurt a lot of people."

Addy couldn't tell if Marilyn was talking about her and Brenda's family or the choir. Probably both.

"I know I let the choir down and I'll apologize to them tonight. But I feel what I did to you and Brenda was so much worse. I wanted to apologize to you both first. Privately ... for saying what I said." She swallowed hard and forced out the words. "Unfortunately, I can't remember exactly what I said, but Steph—"

"'Brenda and Marilyn being lesbians,'" Brenda said quietly.

"We prefer the term queer," Marilyn said.

Brenda made a strangled sound and Marilyn sighed. "It's more inclusive."

The correction seemed out of context and it threw Addy. "Um, right. Okay. But just so you know, I don't ever plan to tell anyone again."

"There's really no one else left to tell," Brenda said wearily.

"The video pretty much did the job," Marilyn added.

"I got it taken down," Addy said.

"Well, it was pretty damning for you," Marilyn said.

"No, I ..." Being sober wasn't helping Addy work out what was going on. There was a layer of tension in the room she was certain had nothing to do with her, and Marilyn's comments were muddying what she'd thought would be a straightforward apology.

Addy gazed at Brenda's drawn face. "I got the video taken down for you. To make amends. You've always been kind to me, to Mum ..." She blinked rapidly, unable to discuss her mother on top of everything else. "I'm so, so sorry. I didn't set out to intentionally hurt you, your family, Courtney ..." Her throat thickened and she cleared it. "If I could turn back time I would."

A silence descended on the kitchen, broken only by the ticking of the clock and the hum of the fridge.

Tick hum, tick tick hum, you are scum, you are scum.

That person wasn't me, Addy countered, but the taunting clock and fridge refused to be silenced.

"But we all know that turning back time's not possible. What about you not getting ..." Brenda hesitated, clearly uncomfortable.

Shame burned through Addy, curling her insides. "Pissed, sloshed, blotto, tanked, wasted, hammered, bombed, smashed or completely f'd up?" she said, saving Brenda from voicing the ugly words.

"Let's just say drunk," Brenda said simply. "What about not getting drunk?"

Addy pulled her eyes away from the gray whorls on the maple coaster and looked at Brenda. "I haven't had a drink since."

Brenda leaned forward. "How hard has it been?"

She knows. Humiliation joined the shame parade. Addy almost said "Not hard at all," but there was something about the look in Brenda's eyes—quiet desperation? Sensibility? No, neither of those, but whatever it was, it demanded she tell the truth.

"Horrifyingly hard. So much harder than I expected." Her left hand gripped the fingers of her right so tightly they pulsed. "I didn't realize things had ... I thought I controlled my drinking. That I chose when to drink, when to start and when to stop. I can see now that drinking controls me. I hate that it does. I hate that it makes me a person who lets people down. Betrays them. And I know for my own safety I have to stop drinking."

"I'm glad you've come to that decision," Brenda said.

Addy mustered a wry smile. "That's what Steph said. She's been amazing. Brutal honesty meets support. I'm not sure I deserve friendship like that."

"Nonsense!" Brenda said. "If you broke your leg or were sick, your friends would help you."

Addy fidgeted with the coaster. "I'm not sure this is quite the same thing. Right from the start I've been the reluctant friend, the reluctant choir member. And breaking a leg doesn't hurt people's feelings. I can't imagine the choir will want me back."

"Anyone who refuses to sing with a recovering alcoholic or a same-sex couple doesn't belong in our choir," Marilyn said.

"Do you want to come back?" Brenda asked.

Addy had spent a lot of time pondering this over the last week and a half. Despite the fact that she'd felt railroaded into joining and singing the solo, and although she wasn't a fan of everyone in the group, she liked more members than she disliked. And singing as one voice among many was enjoyable. As long as she could do that, she'd be fine. And SCW had pointed out how choir gave her some much-needed structure to her week. Structure she'd need more than ever as she traversed her new way of living.

"I do want to come back," Addy said.

"Good," Brenda and Marilyn said simultaneously.

The unexpected care in the words quickly unraveled the stitches that loosely knitted together her self-control. She'd hurt Brenda and Marilyn with careless words, trampled on their privacy and, knowing Courtney, probably caused ructions in the family.

"I don't deserve your understanding."

Brenda shook her head. "Of course you do. I'm no stranger to unhappiness, but I'm devastated that a talented young woman I care for is so deeply unhappy she's drinking herself sick. But that understanding exists completely separately from you outing us."

"I'm so—"

Brenda's hand shot up like a stop sign. "Don't say it."

"But—"

"I know you're sorry, Addy. I heard it in the words. I see it on your face and I read it in the email you sent. But I don't need or want to hear you say 'sorry' again, because words won't change the fallout."

"I'll apologize to Courtney," Addy offered, desperate to fix the mess she'd created.

"Again, just words," Brenda said firmly. "They might make you feel better, but they won't change how angry she is with me. Nothing you can say will change that."

"I hate that it won't," Addy whispered. "I hate that I don't even remember causing the pain. I don't even know why—"

"Shh." Brenda slid her hands into hers. "What's done is done and can't be undone. You need to focus on protecting the future."

The future. The vastness of the concept terrified her.

It meant a life devoid of that moment in the day when the first glass of wine streamed through her, relaxing her and reassuring her she was happy, worthy and kicking goals.

What goals? It's a life without balance. You're unfit, overweight, still living in an unrenovated house and working crazy hours. The only goal you hit was an unintended record spend at the wine store. Great going. Let's celebrate that.

The urge to drink hit with the force of a bat to the head.

I went to choir every week, she told the craving. *I will continue to go to choir every week. Suck on that goal.*

You hate singing and besides, I'd rather suck on—

"Let's go to choir," Addy said loudly. "Sorry," she added, hearing the abruptness in her voice and seeing Marilyn's and Brenda's confused faces. "I'm nervous."

"Come on then." Marilyn picked up her keys. "Let's go and get your apology over and done with so we can focus on the eisteddfod. After all, the hall isn't going to roof itself."

"It's chilly out," Brenda said. "I'll just grab my puffer."

As she walked away, Addy looked at Marilyn and sought clarification. "I can't work out if you're upset with me or not?"

"On the night, I was incandescent with fury."

Addy accepted the hit. "That's fair. Sober me would have been too."

Marilyn nodded. "You cost us. If you'd sung, we'd have won first prize."

Addy stared at her, utterly flummoxed that the "us" was the choir. "What about me betraying your relationship with Brenda?"

Marilyn sighed and spoke softly. "If I'm honest, Addy, it's a relief to finally have it out in the open."

Addy considered Brenda's reaction and had no idea how to match it to what Marilyn was saying. Or what to do with the information.

"Are you sure you still want me in the choir?"

Marilyn gave a reassuring smile. "Of course. And it's not just for selfish reasons." Her face settled into serious lines and Addy glimpsed the classroom teacher establishing expectations. "But just so you know, you'll have to prove yourself to me before I trust you with a lead role again."

"Of course," Addy said.

Marilyn had no idea that her reprimand-cum-encouragement reassured her for all the wrong reasons.

♫

Brenda sat on her bed with her puffer jacket in her hands, giving herself a few moments to recover from Addy's apology. She'd been taking these recovery moments more and more over the last week and a half—reconstituting herself in the hope it would fortify her for the next encounter.

Her thoughts drifted to Richard. After receiving his text about the election on that fateful weekend, she hadn't bothered calling him. She knew from years of experience that when the Premier's office was in crisis or election mode, Richard screened calls. Any texts, calls or voice messages not connected with the election campaign would be declined and ignored. So when her phone had lit up with Richard's name the same night, she'd snatched it up in a combination of shock, delight and relief.

"Richard!"

"Hi, Mum." Fatigue strained his voice. "I've just listened to two garbled voice messages from Courtney that don't make much sense."

Brenda swallowed a sigh, wondering why she was surprised that Courtney had called Richard too. Perhaps it was because Courtney always treated Richard like a baby brother who needed protecting, but she supposed it made sense that her daughter was seeking support from both her brothers.

"She told you I'm in love with Marilyn?"

"Are you?"

"Yes. Very much." It was such a relief to say it to someone she knew would understand.

A couple of beats of silence echoed down the line, making Brenda stiffen instinctively. Surely Richard wasn't going to side with his siblings?

There was a muffled noise and then Richard was saying, "I'm just glad you've met someone."

"Thank you." She hugged his reassurance close. "I wanted to tell the three of you together at lunch, but ..." She didn't want to go through it all again. "We were outed by a drunk choir member. It wasn't ideal."

"Yeah." The word rolled out on a sigh. "I can imagine. It must be a nightmare for you."

His soothing words released a flood of her own. "Oh, Richard, it's everything I feared. It's just awful and Courtney isn't taking it well."

"I heard that in the voice message."

"And Colin ... Well, I'm waiting to hear from Lucinda. I can't predict her reaction."

"Right."

She waited for Richard to say something else. When he didn't she asked, "Have you spoken to Courtney?"

"No."

"But you're going to." She deliberately didn't frame it as a question. *Please tell me you're going to talk to her.*

He sighed. "You know how crazy things get during the campaign. Right now, I don't have the energy to deal with Courtney's drama. I'll talk to her when she's calmed down."

The words stung like a slap. Richard was supposed to be in her corner, providing love and support. The weight of her children's betrayal pressed heavily, making it hard to move a muscle.

"Calmed down?" she said tartly. "And when do you imagine that might be?"

"I'll come up after the election."

"That's six weeks away!" It would be even longer if the government was re-elected.

"Look, Mum, I'm sorry she's being like this—"

"If you tell her about Aaron, it will put things into perspective for her." The words were out before she could stop them.

The silence on the line buzzed and crackled loudly in her ear.

"When I told you about Aaron, Mum, you said very clearly it was my news and it was up to me to decide who I tell and when." His tone was icy.

"And that's a luxury you still have and I've lost. I need your support, Richard!"

"You've got my support. I'm happy you're happy, but believe me, telling Courtney about Aaron when she's all het up about you won't help anyone." He sighed. "You know what she's like. Give her time to calm down."

Brenda was sick of people glibly saying that, especially without any real evidence it worked. The only person who was made to feel better by the words was their speaker.

Suddenly there were loud voices in the background and Richard was saying, "Sorry, Mum. I have to go. Love you." The line went dead.

Brenda had tossed the phone on the sofa, not wanting the hurt that oozed from the call to wound her even more.

She'd spent the next week walking into a variety of cove haunts, hearing conversations abruptly die and seeing the "caught out" looks of people who'd almost certainly been discussing her and Marilyn.

"I was just saying to Paula, if this cold snap's anything to go by we're in for a long winter," Laurie Jeffrey had said hastily as he handed Brenda her package.

Peter Jarvis had leered and pushed a business card at her. "Two women on their own will eventually need a handyman. Call me anytime."

"There's a reason your business is struggling," she'd said, vibrating with fury. "And it's not limited to shoddy workmanship!"

Lisa Culkin, a woman with whom Brenda had long shared a show-baking rivalry—Brenda outgunned her on jam, scones and sponge cakes, but Lisa's yo-yos and fruit cake always took the blue ribbon—had kindly patted her hand. "I told Courtney the shock will pass."

The unexpected understanding had left Brenda blinking back tears. "Thank you."

Lisa had nodded and indicated the other women drinking coffee at Sven's. "And when it does and you're back to your old self, we won't mention your little lapse. It will be water under the bridge."

It had taken a moment for the words to register. Did people assume she'd lost her mind with grief because Glen was dead?

"You'll be waiting a long time, Lisa," she'd said. "My old self was miserable and I don't intend ever going back."

The conversations were disconcerting, horrible and alienating. Brenda kept asking herself why so many young people willingly pushed themselves into the limelight on social media or reality television if it meant the world considered your private life to be public property and open for discussion. People she'd known all her life scrutinized her more intently than they had when she'd been a newlywed and they were seeking signs of pregnancy. Now they looked for the *something* they'd missed—the one thing that told them she loved Marilyn. But all Brenda saw in their eyes and on their faces were questions and confusion, because since the news had broken, nothing overt had changed. She still wore the same clothes and carried the same tote bag.

The irony was that she'd changed months earlier when she'd moved into the new house, and again when Marilyn had joined her. For the first time in years, happiness flowed in her veins without ceasing, lightening a lifetime of sadness. Although, recent events had cracked open the door to an old and familiar despondency. It had dashed in like Clyde through an open gate, but people were blind to that too.

"Choir's different," Marilyn had said firmly when Brenda suggested she skip rehearsal as she needed a rest from the cove's reaction. "Half the choir didn't even know you when you were with Glen."

Brenda didn't bother pointing out that Courtney had known her as Glen's wife for thirty-four years. There was no point. There was a bigger chance of winning the lottery than Courtney ever attending choir again. Anyway, their conversation had been cut short by Addy knocking on the door.

Since Addy's return to the cove, Brenda had taken her at face value—beautifully dressed and accessorized, career-focused and driven with a tendency toward being a workaholic. But having experienced her so drunk she could barely stand, Brenda now realized the clothes, hair and make-up were armor. Today she'd looked beyond their smoke-and-mirrors razzle-dazzle and glimpsed a fragility in Addy that reminded her of Rita. Was Addy heading down the same path, fighting the demons of mental illness? Brenda's heart twisted in a complicated mix of love and loss for her friend and sympathy for her daughter who was clearly struggling.

Addy had lost her mother the first time when she was a teen and Rita's OCD had hospitalized her. After the first crisis, there'd been moments when Rita seemed like her old self, but Brenda had always sensed a part of her had been swallowed by the illness, never to return to them. Then Addy had lost both Ivan and Rita to early deaths.

Now, Addy was very much alone and living in a house that leached memories, reminding her of her absent parents. It couldn't be easy, and right then Brenda knew she couldn't let Addy go to choir on her own.

With a sigh, she hauled herself to her feet, slipped on her puffer and met Marilyn and Addy in the hall.

CHAPTER TWENTY-NINE

TEN MINUTES LATER, as Brenda followed Marilyn and Addy up the hall steps, Marilyn said, "Isn't that Courtney's car?"

Brenda turned in the direction she was pointing and saw a familiar muddy four-wheel drive. Hope took a giant leap. "She's come to choir? I can't believe it."

Marilyn squeezed her hand. "I said all she needed was time."

The hall was abuzz with chatter and people gathered around the refreshments table. A few weeks earlier Brenda had started a roster to share the set-up duties and tonight was Vera's turn. It looked like she'd brought along her famous chocolate and raspberry bars.

From the doorway, Brenda's eyes hungrily sought out Courtney. She was talking to Morgan and glanced up as the frigid night air followed them inside. For a second their eyes met and Brenda, who hadn't prayed in years, heard herself whisper, "Please." Courtney's mouth tightened, then she turned away.

Hurt stung like a thousand bees and Brenda berated herself for daring to hope.

No one else seemed to notice Courtney's rejection of her mother.

It was the thud of Addy's heels against the bare boards that rolled a hush into the hall as thick and pervasive as sea fog. Some people's faces hardened, others softened, but all held questions.

Addy's feet stalled.

"Hi," Steph called out. "Addy, come and try Vera's bars. They're amazing."

Heidi's eyes lit up. "Can we eat before we sing now?"

"I'd prefer it if you didn't." Marilyn dropped her puffer over the back of a chair. "Remember Brian's coughing fit?"

"We don't have to worry about that anymore," Morgan said.

"Brian quit."

Brenda wasn't surprised. When he'd come face-to-face with her in the general store, he'd immediately put down his basket of groceries and left.

Rob Ricardo's face fell. Marilyn had convinced the burly farmer and hall committee member to join the choir by reassuring him he wasn't the only male.

Vera, who'd taught Rob when he was in short pants, prodded him with her walking stick. "Looks like it's up to you now, Robbie, to bring in a few more blokes."

Rob rubbed his thigh where the stick had connected and mumbled something that could have been "okay" or "no way."

Fern looked straight at Addy. "Are you sober?"

"Fern!" Steph cautioned. "What happened to choir being open and inclusive?"

But Fern was unrepentant. "Addy may choose to poison herself, but that doesn't give her permission to bring negative energies into our safe space."

"I'm sober." Addy dragged her gaze up from the floor and met Fern's. "Which means, any negative energies you're feeling must be coming from a different source."

Fern's eyes narrowed as she clearly tried to determine if Addy had just taken a shot at her.

"I want to apologize," Addy said, more loudly this time. "To each and every one of you. I'm incredibly sorry for letting you down and for placing you all in a difficult and uncomfortable position. And for the hurtful things I said—"

"Things you don't even remember saying." Fern huffed and crossed her arms. "And aren't you forgetting something? What about apologizing to Marilyn and Brenda for betraying them in the worst possible way."

"I wouldn't be too concerned for them," Courtney said sharply. "They've done their fair share of betraying." She flicked a look of pure hostility at Brenda.

Marilyn reached for Brenda's hand but she kept it fisted, not wanting to add fuel to the fire.

"Your mother deserves your understanding," Fern said.

"Oh my God, Fern!" Steph said. "You're such a hypocrite."

"Can everyone please be quiet and let Addy finish her apology," Brenda said firmly.

Courtney's brows flew to her hairline. "Can we expect an apology from you anytime soon?"

"Courtney, I'm sorry I caused you and your family pain." Addy's words rushed out, then she took a deep breath. "I'll always regret it. After I betrayed what should have been a private family matter, you had every reason to walk away, but you didn't. You put aside your own feelings and chose to stay and take my place for the choir and the cove. You did my job, but without the benefit of my level of preparation. I'm humbled by your generosity. Thank you for holding the choir together. It can't have been easy for you."

"Believe me, it was easier to deal with than the other things that went down that night," Courtney said tightly. "And in a twisted way, I think you did me a favor. I can't describe the buzz I got for pulling it off and I treasure the kind words of the judge." Her face unexpectedly softened. "But for all that, I'd rather the reason I had to step in had been different. I hope you'll stop writing yourself off like that."

Addy blinked rapidly.

"Are you getting some help?" Heidi asked.

Addy laced her hands together tightly as if seeking strength. "I am."

"And you'll keep coming to choir," Steph said, more as a statement than a question.

Addy looked at everyone. "If you'll have me."

"Good. Apology accepted." Morgan glanced at the group as if to say "Come on you lot, say something supportive."

There were general murmurings and a shuffling of feet. Fern's usual warmth, harmony and acceptance vibe was clearly struggling.

Brenda gave Addy's shoulder a reassuring pat. "That's the hard part over."

But the moment the words slipped out she regretted them. The hard part was only the beginning. Addy needed to learn to live her life in a completely new way.

What about you?

Brenda brushed away the thought and its prickle of unease, declaring it to be ridiculous. The cove might have just heard the news about her and Marilyn, but they were far away from the beginning of their relationship.

Marilyn clapped her hands. "Thanks, Addy. Welcome back to choir. Everyone take a seat. Before we sing, we've got some admin to—"

The hinges on the door squeaked and everyone turned to watch a man walk in. He hesitated, then pulled off his woolen hat. Salt and pepper curls—both distinctive and disconcerting in someone so young —bounced wildly, free of their confines. "Is this the choir?"

"Thank God," Rob said, clearly relieved to see another bloke.

A few women sighed at the Irish accent and Morgan jumped to her feet. "It is. Come in."

"Marilyn, is it?" He walked forward, his hand extended.

"No, I'm Morgan." She blushed and sat down, pointing to Marilyn.

"With that accent, you must be Kieran," Marilyn said. "Glad you could finally make it."

"Yeah. Sorry. Work's been full-on."

"Well, your arrival's perfectly timed. We're just planning the eisteddfod and our next piece. Grab a seat."

"Ta." He sat down next to Steph and gave Addy a nod of recognition. She managed a wan smile.

"Of course with the Irish, music runs in their blood," Vera said to no one in particular.

"I use a beautiful Irish pan flute recording in my studio," Fern said breathily, sounding more like her usual self. "It's so soothing and relaxing for clients."

"I thought the Welsh sang and the Irish played the music. When I was in Ireland, every pub had a band with a fiddle and an accordion. Right, Kieran?" Rob looked at him, seeking confirmation.

Brenda couldn't tell if the Irishman was taken aback by the conversation or trying not to laugh.

"Go on, Kieran. Put them out of their misery," Addy said.

Steph shot her a quizzical look.

"Well, me brother plays the fiddle," Kieran said, "and me da plays the squeezebox, but I could never sit still long enough to learn either. I much prefer to do this." He broke into song, his voice rising and falling with ease. The unfamiliar Gaelic words filled with heartache and tears lingered on the air and when the last note faded, the hall was a silent gasp.

He gave a sheepish grin. "Did I answer your question about the singing?"

Steph gaped at him. "That's not intimidating at all."

He laughed. "Good. It wasn't meant to be. Every voice has a place in a choir."

"You're absolutely right, Kieran. Welcome to the cove choir."

Marilyn exchanged a look with Brenda, her eyes shining with competitive glee.

Look out, Devonport. Brenda smiled and her heart expanded.

"Let's get down to business," Marilyn said. "We cut our teeth on the Choir Crush and our third place gives us enough kudos to reinstate the eisteddfod. Although we need everyone to be involved, there are a few key positions. Brenda and I are happy to be president and treasurer, but we need a secretary and someone with the IT skills to look after ticketing.' Marilyn looked at Heidi, who glanced at her feet.

"I just have to get through the last few weeks of the semester and I could do the ticketing," Addy offered.

"You're already dealing with a lot," Brenda said hurriedly, torn between accepting Addy's offer and worrying it might sink her.

Perhaps this was an opportunity to involve Courtney? It might be the path to their reconciliation. The fact that Courtney was continuing on with choir must mean something.

"Courtney, you do all the farm accounts and you know your way around a computer," she said tentatively. "Perhaps you could take on ticketing?"

Courtney ignored her and spoke to Addy. "My mother's always found it easier to worry about people outside her own family."

Addy winced. Steph rolled her eyes.

"Actually, Addy, in the spirit of sharing roles, I was hoping you might be our rehearsal pianist," Marilyn said, ignoring the exchange.

Addy suddenly reached for her hair, winding it tightly around her fingers. "I can't play any classical music."

Brenda knew this was a lie, but she also knew all about keeping secrets. "I don't think we have any plans to sing the 'Hallelujah Chorus,'" she said lightly.

"Oh!" Heidi's face lit up. "What about Leonard Cohen's 'Hallelujah?' That would be an awesome piece to close the eisteddfod."

"Or the one from *Shrek*," said Lily, a recent member. "When I was a kid, I drove Mum nuts watching that movie."

"It's the same song," Morgan said.

Addy's hand fell from her hair. "I can play that no problem. And any other Disney songs."

"*Shrek* opens with the boy fishing off the moon," Lily said. "Pretty sure that's DreamWorks."

"We are *not* doing Disney!" Fern said.

"Why not?" Courtney demanded. "There are so many great songs about strong women."

"We have two men in the choir now, dear," Vera pointed out.

"Actually, I've given a lot of thought to our next song," Fern said, as if no one else would have bothered. "I think we should sing something inclusive, like 'Born This Way' by Lady Gaga."

"I'm not singing a gay pride song!" Courtney said.

"Actually that song's about being true to yourself," Steph said, obviously torn between agreeing with Fern and setting Courtney straight. "I think that's something everyone can relate to."

"Or we could go with our strengths and do an Irish ballad," Morgan said, smiling at Kieran.

"What does the choir conductor suggest?" he asked, looking straight at Marilyn.

Brenda sent up a silent vote of thanks that one choir member had some diplomacy.

Marilyn unrolled a sheet of butcher paper, uncapped a marker pen and in her clear school-teacher script added the suggestions from the choir to her own list.

"Do you feel comfortable raising your hand for each song or would you prefer voting on paper?" she asked.

There were shrugs and nods, sighs and huffs. Brenda wished she could think of an easier way to raise funds for the hall roof than trying to mold this prickly collection of individuals into a cohesive choir. Although she had to concede they did a better job of pulling together when they sang.

"Perhaps we should sing now and vote at the break?" she said, hoping it would generate some *esprit de corps*.

Marilyn shot her an irritated look, but enough people rose to their feet indicating their support of the suggestion.

Minutes later, the usual laughter at missing stomps and claps echoed around the hall—the tension slowly dissipating. As the sopranos sang their major scales, Brenda's eyes rested on Courtney, soaking in her fierce concentration.

Gradually, the other voices faded until only Addy and Courtney were singing. Addy suddenly stopped, her chest heaving.

"You let me win." Courtney sounded piqued.

Addy shook her head, gulping in air. "No, I ran out of breath. You won fair and square."

Courtney's cheeks pinked. "I've been doing breathing exercises."

"Good for you."

Brenda realized her daughter's mouth—too often reminiscent of Glen's mother—had softened with happiness. Courtney loved to sing and thankfully she wanted to be at choir more than she wanted to avoid her mother. Some of the dents in Brenda's hope smoothed out.

After Marilyn had reshuffled people's positions so Steph was in front of Kieran—on the alto side of Addy and next to Lily for pitch support—they sang "California Dreamin'" followed by "Blackbird." Then for some fun, Abba's "Take A Chance On Me."

Brenda noticed that Courtney wasn't looking at Marilyn's conducting, but watching Addy for cues. Once she was late coming in, but Marilyn didn't mention it or anyone else's mistakes. Tonight was about bonding through song.

"Great job, everyone," Marilyn said. "Grab a drink and some of Vera's baking, and please remember to vote."

As people drifted to the refreshments table, Brenda was pleased to see Steph was sticking close to Addy. This meant she could keep a close eye on Courtney and hopefully find an opportunity when her daughter was on her own. Eventually Courtney went to the bathroom and Brenda followed, waiting outside the door in the short corridor.

When Courtney reappeared, she immediately moved to walk past Brenda without pausing.

Brenda moved, making it harder for her to pass, and said hurriedly, "I was worried you might not come to choir. I'm so glad you did."

"I wasn't going to, but then Ben pointed out I'd be giving up something I enjoy and I'm good at," Courtney said stiffly.

Brenda nodded. "He's right."

"I don't see why I should suffer that indignity as well."

"Can we please talk?"

Courtney's nostrils flared. "There's nothing to talk about."

"Darling, there's everything to talk about. Obviously not here, but at the house—"

"I'm never coming to your love shack." Courtney spat the words, darkening their meaning.

Brenda worked on keeping her voice calm. "We can come to the farm."

"No! You and Marilyn are not welcome at the farm."

She swallowed, trying to slow her racing heart. "Somewhere else then."

"You don't get it, Mum! I'm not sitting down with you and Marilyn anywhere and pretending everything's normal when it's not. God!" Courtney's arms flew into the air. "How could you do this to Dad?"

Frustration flared like a flame—the way it so often did when Courtney canonized Glen.

"I haven't done anything to your father! I protected him when he was alive, just like I protected you and the boys by staying with him even though I wanted to be with Marilyn."

"But you didn't know Marilyn—" Courtney's eyes dilated fast as her face drained of color. "Oh my God. How long have you known her?"

Choking regret tightened Brenda's throat, but it was too late. Anger had released the incriminating words and they hung around them, illuminated with bright lights.

"Mum?"

It was like falling into quicksand. No step, no word was safe. "A while."

"What the hell is 'a while'?"

Despite the cold night, sweat beaded on Brenda's hairline. Suddenly it was too hard not to tell the truth.

"We met at a Women in Agriculture conference. She was asked to speak about the importance of math education for women in farming."

Courtney stared at her as if she had two heads. "Math?"

"Yes."

"Didn't we have a huge fight about math?" Courtney frowned as if she was trying hard to remember. "I wanted to drop it and Dad said it was up to me, but you kept at me, insisting I do it in senior—No!" She breathed out the word, then shook her head so violently her hair slapped her cheeks. "Tell me you didn't meet her when I was still at school."

"I'm sorry." The words came out as a whisper.

Courtney made a sound reminiscent of a dog in distress. Brenda's heart tore and she moved to hug her.

"Don't. Touch. Me." Antipathy dripped from the words. "You've lost that right."

"You're my daughter." Brenda opened her hands palms-up. "I love you."

Courtney held up her hands to ward her off. "You've got a funny way of showing it. I can never forgive you for this."

Desperation clutched at her like it had when Addy had outed her, only this time it was amplified with chords of finality. "You forgave Addy. Why can't you forgive me?"

Courtney stared at Brenda as if she didn't recognize her. "Addy stuffed up because she's sick. You've lied to me for almost half my life! That's a freakin' big difference."

"I did it to protect you," Brenda pleaded.

"Really?" Courtney scoffed. "I think that's a lie too. I think you did it to protect yourself."

"That's not—"

"In fact I don't believe anything you say anymore."

Brenda locked her knees as if that would be enough to reinforce her resolve. "The only lies I told were about the monthly weekend agriculture meetings."

Courtney's face darkened with realization. "So you were with *her* when I broke my arm? The night I understudied for Addy ..."

Truth bounced off guilt. "To be fair, I saw you in the play the night before. Not even you expected to be singing the lead on—"

"There's no 'fair' here, Mum! But there's a long list of times when big things happened in my life and you weren't there for me."

So often you didn't want me there.

Brenda straightened her shoulders. "I was there far more times than I was absent."

"Your body might have been there, but believe me, you weren't. And now I know why. I don't know why you even bothered to stay with us when you obviously loved her more."

"That's not true. I was ..." But even if Courtney had been listening, standing in a corridor in a public space wasn't the place for this conversation. "I love you, darling. You and the boys and Ben and Lucinda and the kids. You're my family. You're the reason I didn't go to Hobart. Why Marilyn came to the cove."

"And what? I'm supposed to be grateful for that?"

Maybe.

"No. I ..." She took a breath and tried again. "I know Marilyn and me being together is a lot to take in. I don't expect things to go back to the way they were overnight, but perhaps tomorrow when you pick up Livvy and Jesse—"

"They won't be coming."

Her head screamed and she reminded herself that at least once a month they missed their usual Monday night. "I know they missed last week because of the dentist—"

"And they're missing this week and every other week because of you, your lies and your betrayal of us all."

Courtney's critical intransigence was a perfect and devastating replica of Elaine's. Bitter experience had taught Brenda that nothing changed her mother-in-law's opinion. But with Courtney, she had to keep trying.

"Darling, please ..."

But Courtney was already walking away, spine ramrod straight and proud as only a Lambeck's could be. The hope that had buoyed

Brenda since she'd seen Courtney's car outside the hall shriveled and died.

The truth will set you free? She bit her knuckle to stop herself from crying out. She'd just lost her daughter and her beloved grandchildren. How did the truth reconcile that?

CHAPTER THIRTY

STEPH WAS TAKING a quick break from packing orders. While she waited for the kettle to boil, she checked the bank balance on their joint account, then refreshed her phone screen as if that might change the numbers.

She was just wondering what HK Distrib was—and why Henry had spent two hundred and fifty dollars with them—when he walked in, pink-cheeked from the cold and with Monty on his shoulders. They'd been out watching the workmen on the road and in the garden as they inched the fiber closer and closer to the house, bringing with it the promise of a fast and reliable internet connection.

"Mummy!" Monty's little body trembled with excitement. "There's a Bob the Builder with a yellow hat!"

Monty ran off to find all his construction toys and Henry slid his arm around Steph's waist, danced her around the kitchen, then kissed her full on the mouth.

"This time tomorrow, *everything* will be easier," he said.

Steph wasn't certain fiber to the house solved infertility, her never-ending to-do list or the oppressive presence of a sullen teen.

"Great," she said, but heard the lack of conviction in her voice. She pulled away and poured two cups of tea. "What did you buy from HK Distrib?"

"Who?"

She handed her phone to Henry, who frowned, clearly trying to remember the purchase. His face cleared. "Zoe's make-up kit."

"What?!"

Henry startled. "You said you didn't want her using your good stuff."

"So you bought her good stuff? She's thirteen!"

"It's not high quality, but it came with fifty colors of eye shadow and a heap of brushes. Think of it as a painting kit. Anyway, she knows she can't wear it out of the house until she's older, but she can experiment with it as her art. It'll keep her going for ages."

I'm sure there were plenty that were cheaper. "I just wish you'd discussed it with me first."

"I would have, but just lately you've been ..."

"What?" she said coolly, feeling the unwanted but all-too-familiar irritation rise. "I've been what?"

He swallowed, clearly choosing his words carefully. "Distracted. Sad. Short with Zoe. And I get it," he said hurriedly. "We're all sad about the baby. The only reason I didn't tell you was because I didn't want to bother you with something I could do myself."

Her scalp suddenly itched with ferocious intensity and she clenched her fists so she didn't rip at her hair. Henry bothered her all the time— *Have you seen my ...? Do we have any more of ...?* —as if she alone was responsible for carrying the mental load of the mind-numbing minutiae of their domestic life. Yet he spent two hundred and fifty dollars on Zoe without telling her?

"We're bleeding money, Henry, and now with IVF ..." She blinked back the tears always so close to the surface.

"The doctor said not *all* my swimmers are duds," Henry said defensively. "And with the tablets, we probably won't need it."

Steph tried keeping her voice steady when what she really wanted to do was yell and shake some sense into him. "Before you asked Dr.

Sharma four different ways if it was worth trying the clomiphene first, she'd already said we *both* have reduced fertility. She strongly recommends IVF."

He stroked her hair and grinned. "Yeah, but after the last two nights of fun, it might be moot."

She ducked away from him again and pulled open the dishwasher. How could Henry have enjoyed that sex? In keeping with their life at the moment, of course the ovulation stick had produced a smiley face when she was exhausted from working long into the night and being woken by Monty at three most mornings. Added to that, the drug heightened her emotions, swinging them from hopeful and happy to miserable and discouraged, and back again without warning. It was counter-intuitive that a drug that was supposed to make her pregnant turned her off sex. But she wanted a baby so she'd faked her enjoyment and gone through the motions helped out by a generous amount of lube. The moment Henry had orgasmed, she'd rolled onto her back, put a pillow under her hips and pushed her legs into the air.

Now, clinking glasses into a cabinet, she said, "My period might come in twelve days. I don't think we should be wasting any more time."

"With our recent expenses, we need six months to shore up our savings," Henry said. "If we're not pregnant by then, I promise we can do IVF."

Steph didn't want to wait six months. Hell, she didn't want to wait a month. She wanted the guarantee the IVF Petri dish offered—no obstacles between the sperm arriving at the egg and some added assistance entering it. She'd always admired Henry's fiscal prudence, but right now she hated it.

"Talking about money," she said tartly, "stop spending ridiculous amounts of it on non-essential items for Zoe!"

He frowned. "It isn't non-essential when it's something she's interested in."

But Steph didn't want a reply. "And why are we paying for everything for her? That's not fair either. You have to talk to Joanna."

"It's a bit hard when she won't answer calls or respond to emails and texts," Henry said bitterly.

"Then ask Zoe to tell you the next time she's on the cell phone and talk to Joanna then."

"I'm not going to do that," Henry said with an edge to his usually even tone. "It's not fair to Zoe. You know I've always kept her out of my issues with Joanna."

"But your parents aren't here to intercede anymore." A thought hit her, throwing up a question as to why Joanna may have sent Zoe to them. "She's not sick, is she?"

"Joanna? I doubt it. She was tagged in a photo at the university reunion I couldn't get to and she was actually smiling. To be honest, I've never seen her look so good."

"So she's alive then?" A green streak of jealousy lit up inside Steph. Of course Joanna was looking good. She wasn't dealing with an obstreperous teen. "Henry, she's taking advantage of you and I've had enough. Go to Melbourne and bang on her door until she talks to you."

Henry's eyes rounded. "That's aggressive, isn't it?"

"And what's her ghosting you?" Steph threw her hands in the air. "Honestly, Henry. Stop letting her walk all over you. Apply for child support."

He shook his head. "You know she doesn't earn much."

"She bought Zoe an iPhone!"

"An old iPhone," he reminded her. "Look, Joanna's Joanna. She's either between jobs or on a short-term funding grant. It's just not worth the rigmarole or the angst trying to pursue child support."

His passivity riled her. "That's not the point! For years Joanna's hassled you for money even when you've always paid more than the Child Support Agency calculated. She can't suddenly dump Zoe on us and not contribute anything. Either Joanna kicks in some regular money or—"

"Or what?" Zoe dropped her school backpack on the kitchen floor and gave Steph a flinty look.

She takes you out of my house.

Steph turned, took a deep breath and banged the dishwasher shut.

"Zo! You're home early," Henry said overly cheerfully. He put down his mug and tried to hug her. Zoe stiffened like a board.

Steph noticed Zoe's kohl-rimmed eyes. So much for Henry's rule of no make-up outside of the house.

She sighed. "Please tell me you haven't been suspended again."

"Duh," Zoe said. "If I had, you'd have had to come and get me."

Henry widened his eyes at Steph, semaphoring "go gently."

Steph glared back. Why should she go gently with this girl whose selfishness infiltrated every corner of their lives? But as the thought landed, she realized she really didn't care enough to go hard or gently.

"So to what do we owe this pleasure?" Henry asked Zoe's back as she opened the fridge.

"It's a half day. I told you."

"Right. Of course," Henry said. "I should have put it on the calendar."

Steph snorted. Henry stiffened.

"But I've been saved by my lucky socks," he said lightly. "Both Steph and I are free to help you with your passion project."

"I'm packing orders." Steph indicated the pile of prepaid-postage envelopes, bubble wrap, packing tape and scissors on the table.

"Which is perfect for brainstorming," Henry continued doggedly.

"Whatevs." Zoe sat down with a glass of apple juice and an enormous piece of the vegan caramel cake Henry had made. "It totally sucks. Mrs. Delacour said I can't do make-up because it doesn't involve the community."

"I suppose she might have a point," Henry said, trying to align himself in neutral territory.

"Yeah, then why call it a passion project if you can't do your passion?" Zoe asked.

Since Zoe had dropped netball and now spent most of her time in her room, Steph found it hard to imagine she had any passions.

"What about making a vegan cookbook with nutritionally

balanced meals?" she said, ripping packing tape off the dispenser as she lobbed the salvo. "You could cook and take photos."

Zoe's glare said "I see straight through you." "That's not community."

"It is if you feed people," Henry said. "It's actually a great idea. You can invite your friends and—"

"No," Zoe said. "It's a dumb idea."

"You have to choose something, Zo," he said gently. He brought up the cove's Facebook page and scrolled through it. "Too bad it's not market seas— Hang on! What about joining the choir?"

No! Steph's finger slipped and the serrated edge of the tape dispenser broke the skin. She sucked it and the metallic taste filled her mouth.

"It's a community activity and it says on the page 'all ages welcome,' right, Steph?"

"There's no one under thirty," Steph warned. "Zoe would be bored stiff."

Zoe stacked circus people. "No, I wouldn't."

Steph couldn't tell if the girl had spoken the truth or just said it to contradict her—although she'd bet more on the latter.

"What would she actually do for the project, Henry? She has to have something to show on presentation night."

"Zo, you could video interview all the members and ask them why they joined the choir," Henry enthused. "And maybe you could do their make-up for a performance. That's community—Mrs. Delacour can't object to that. Maybe the choir might even sing on presentation night."

Zoe scrunched her face as if the idea was painful.

Steph relaxed. The last thing she needed was Zoe coming to choir and casting her pall of ennui over the one thing Steph did for herself.

"Why not make and decorate a set of circus people and record all the different ways they can be used?" Steph suggested as casually as she could. "If the video's good enough, I'll use it on the website and give you credit."

The last thing Steph wanted was to be in the close confines of the shed with Zoe—or be alone with Zoe period—but she'd suffer it if it kept Zoe out of the choir.

Zoe swiped the pyramid of circus people with her hand, sending them tumbling across the table. "That's boring."

"So's choir," Steph said doggedly.

Zoe flicked her a combative look. "I'll risk it."

"Both my girls in the choir." Henry grinned at them. "This is going to be great."

Neither Steph nor Zoe said a word.

CHAPTER THIRTY-ONE

ADDY DID her third and final pass through the exam paper for her pathway students, checking for any pesky typos that had snuck through. Satisfied, she uploaded it onto the portal and emailed Lyn to notify her it was ready. Then she opened her bullet journal, flinching at the beautiful calligraphy and the empty aphorisms she'd believed proved her life was on track. In her sobriety, it was easy to tell which entries had been made under the influence of alcohol—most of them.

She grabbed a small gold clip from her office drawer and slid it over the older pages so the journal opened to June. It looked very different from the first half of the year. It was ruled up, free of embellishments and with a column for each day of the week spread over two pages. Her eyes strayed to the number at the bottom of the previous day's column—her days sober. She scribed it each night just before bed as both a reward and a reminder that she'd gotten through another day without a drink. Some nights it was knowing she could write a digit one number higher than the previous day's that got her through the long evenings. That and playing show tunes on the piano.

She'd downloaded a book of contemporary Disney sheet music and one of Rodgers and Hammerstein, and played until she dripped in sweat and her arms ached. At first, her long-out-of-practice fingers had stumbled over the keys, unable to obey her quick mind that read the music easily. Frustrated, she'd stuck to chords on her left hand, but now her hands were stretching and flexing and it was all coming back.

Courtney was right: Disney had a lot of songs about strong women. Addy belted them out, finding strength in the words and the breath they took. She played songs from movies she'd not seen and took out a streaming subscription to catch up. She particularly liked "I See the Light" from *Tangled*, although it wasn't because she'd met a Flynn Rider like Rapunzel, but because sobriety had lifted her own personal fog and everything looked and felt different. Across a day, those differences could either terrify or reassure her.

She wished she had a way of predicting her reaction to situations, but as with grief, sometimes it was the tiny things that undid her. Like when the piano tuner came. She'd left work early to meet him at 5:00 and after an hour of plink plink plunk and tortuously pulling the fifty-year-old piano back into tune, Greg had played a final set of scales followed by "Twinkle, Twinkle, Little Star."

He finished with a flourish and grinned. "That's as close as I come to playing."

Addy had burst into tears.

"Oh, jeez." Greg had shoved a clean handkerchief into her hands and patted her on the back. "Didn't think my playing was that bad," he'd joked weakly. "Then again my granddaughter's my only fan."

Addy had pulled herself together with a long and shuddering sniff. "Sorry. My mother loved to play *Twelve Variations on 'Ah, vous dirai-je, Maman.'*"

Greg gave her a blank look.

"Mozart used the tune of 'Twinkle, Twinkle, Little Star.'"

"Right." He gave her shoulder another pat. "Sorry. Didn't mean to upset you."

"Please don't apologize. I wasn't expecting to be upset."

When Greg left, she'd approached the piano cautiously. Now it was tuned and dusted, it suddenly seemed far more like Rita's piano.

I can play one piece.

She breathed in and out three times. "Okay, Mama. This one's for you and then it's back to show tunes."

But she'd only gotten halfway through "Für Elise" before her fingers stalled and the cravings to drink made her race outside and gulp in deep breaths of salty air. She'd half-walked, half-run to the beach and then sat in the dark on the windswept rocks, listening to the hoarse whoops and throbbing growls of the little penguins. Eventually, the past retreated like the waves at low tide.

She'd almost rung Steph, but it was arsenic hour. Besides, this particular meltdown was far too complicated for Steph.

She'd eyed the surf club and the lit-up beer sign that flashed like a beacon. *Come on, baby, you and me can rock this town.*

She needed someone who understood the cravings and didn't judge her. She messaged SCW.

I'm scared I'm going to walk into a club and buy a drink

Instantly, messages of understanding lit up her phone.

It's hard, Addy, but drinking makes life even harder

Go for a walk or a run. Read a book. Watch Netflix. Yoga?

Stay here and chat with us

You've got this. We've got your back

Half an hour later, with the past shoved back where it belonged and her heart rate ticking along in the normal zone, she'd walked home. Once inside, she turned up a noughties playlist on Spotify and, as she sang along to Beyonce and Rihanna, she cooked herself a nutritious meal and got through the evening. Then she'd recorded another day sober and had fallen wearily into bed.

Most nights, she stayed at work late, preferring the quiet of her office to the quiet of home. Now, as she put an X through the dot next to *proof and upload exam*, she scanned the column for another task. There were none. It was time to go home.

The first ripples of anxiety rolled through her and her body tensed. But before the voices in her head chimed in with unhelpful suggestions, she closed her eyes and breathed deeply. In ... out. In ...

out. In ... out ... The ripples stilled and the voices snoozed. A picture drifted into her head of brightly colored yarns and herself hooking a blanket in rows of pacific blues, turquoise greens, palm-tree greens and golden sand.

The idea to craft something had come to her at choir. She'd noticed whenever they weren't singing, Vera was knitting. It made sense to Addy that busy hands were less tempted to pick up a drink so she'd jumped online looking for a project. The choice had almost overwhelmed her and it had taken force to ignore the critical voices in her head— *Surely you're not choosing that one? You're not even staying in the cove.* She'd settled on a blanket in coastal hues—it reminded her of the cove beach. Since sobriety, the beach was an important tool in her sober toolkit.

"You okay?"

Her eyes flashed open at Grant's voice and she smiled. She'd hardly seen him since the sloe gin afternoon.

Under normal circumstances, she'd probably have driven herself mad agonizing about the events of that afternoon. Did it mean there was a definite shift in their relationship from colleagues to something more? Or was it just a fun afternoon? Did his thank-you note infer things had shifted between them? Did his usual *appreciate your work* now have a second meaning?

But her first week of sobriety had been so excruciatingly tough, there'd been no spare bandwidth in her brain to worry about whether weekend sex with her boss had changed things. By the following Friday, when she'd been hanging by a thread and they'd seen one another at the faculty meeting, she'd just been relieved and grateful Grant had greeted her in exactly the same way he always did. Everything else in her life might be a complicated mess, but she could depend on Grant keeping things at work on an even keel.

"Everything's good," she said to him. "I was just taking a moment to be mindful."

He laughed and walked into her office carrying a green reusable bag. The aroma of coriander and lemongrass came with him. "I thought you type A personalities found mindfulness difficult."

She grimaced. "It takes some practice that's for sure. You're here late."

"There's a bit of a stuff-up with semester two enrollments. Sometimes it's easier to stay late and fix it than have it greet you on a new day."

"I know exactly what you mean."

He grinned. "I knew you would, which is why I ordered extra from Binh's. Join me?"

"Sure. It beats reheated leftovers."

"Lemongrass and chili chicken or satay beef?" he asked.

"The chicken, please."

He dug into the bag and handed her a very hot plastic container, bamboo chopsticks and some paper napkins.

"Thanks." As she turned to the shelf behind her for her water bottle, she heard the distinctive whoosh of a can being opened. She stiffened. Her cravings sat up straight, salivating. *Oh, yeah, baby.* Chances it was soda were pretty much zero.

Blowing out a long breath, she turned back and smiled at the proffered can. "You enjoy that," she said lightly. "I'll stick to water."

He laughed. "Yeah, right. We both know you never say no to a drink."

"Actually, I haven't had a drink since the sloe gin afternoon."

"Crikey! Lucky for you I'm here tonight to rescue you from that horrifying state of affairs." He opened a second can of cider and pushed it toward her.

She returned the can to him. "I'm serious, Grant. I did things that day that—"

"Were incredibly hot." He smiled at her, his eyes darkening with lust. "And you loved every minute of it."

Did I? Shame poured through her. "I don't remember all of it."

"I'm more than happy to remind you." He leaned in close, his breath on her cheek, his hand caressing her breast.

She flinched and her heart thudded in her throat. She slowly moved his hand back to the desk. "The thing is, Grant, that person isn't me."

He laughed. "Yeah, right. We both know it's very much you. Life-of-the-party Addy."

Her cravings eyed the open can. *He's right.*

No, he's not bloody right.

"That's the alcohol, not me," she said.

"Nah. You've buried a natural porn star under all that A-type perfection and every now and then she needs to be unleashed. I understand. You won't get any judgment from me. In fact, I was hoping that one day soon we could live out your fantasy of you riding me on your desk."

Her mouth dried as her head spun, seeking a memory, a flash of something—anything—but all she found were blank spaces. Too many blank and black spaces.

"M-my fantasy?"

He nodded, his face lit with enthusiasm. "You've mentioned it both times we've had sex, but we've never been anywhere near the office. But we're here now. Alone." He winked and pushed the open can toward her before taking a gulp of his own.

Her sobriety teetered violently. Oh God—she needed a drink. Hell, she needed five so she could numb the disgust and humiliation that was crashing over her like storm waves. She didn't know or recognize this person Grant was describing.

He's not judging you, so why are you being so harsh? It's been a couple of weeks. You've proven you can stop drinking so live a little. You can stop again anytime you want.

She eyed the can anticipating its sweetness and high alcohol content, and the delicious buzz that would streak through her veins. How she could swim in its glorious and freeing high and escape from herself.

And then what? her hard-won sober-self demanded. *Have sex with*

Grant here at work and add yet another excruciating moment you may or may not remember to an already long list?

You won't get any judgment from me.

Surely that worked both ways?

She wrested her gaze from the can and told him the truth. "My drinking got to the point where it was controlling me rather than the other way round. I'm taking a break."

Disappointment flashed across his face. "You're serious?"

She nodded and picked up her chopsticks. "Lucky it doesn't stop us from enjoying this delicious food."

He shot her a wry smile. "I'm guessing that means no sex on the desk tonight then?"

"Thanks for understanding."

"Too easy." He ran a fork down the bamboo skewer, deftly removing the cubes of chicken. "Just promise me something."

"What's that?"

"Don't turn into a sober bore."

Her noodles fell off her chopsticks and onto her blouse with a wet splat.

CHAPTER THIRTY-TWO

ADDY WOKE up on Saturday morning with the words "sober bore" still playing on a loop in her head.

"It was a joke," she said loudly, shutting down the voice that was always happy to suggest a drink. She knew it was a joke, because at the end of the meal Grant had gathered up the containers and said, "Next time I'll bring non-alcoholic cider."

Weak winter sunshine streamed into the bedroom and she lay there, warm and cozy, headache-free and soaking it in. Delaying getting up. Weekend days were so much longer than they used to be now she had sixteen cognizant hours to fill, but she was stunned—and a little bit excited—at how productive those hours were. She hadn't realized how much time alcohol stole from her.

She suddenly remembered that Steph was coming over this morning to help paint the kitchen. With a burst of enthusiasm she threw off the covers and padded down the hall for a quick breakfast before setting up the drop cloths. Just as the microwave beeped telling her the oatmeal porridge was ready, her phone buzzed.

Really sorry, Addy. Monty had another asthma attack last night. He's fine now but clingy and exhausted. Will have to take a raincheck on painting unless you want a sulky teen to help? I could send her over —a scream emoji followed. *Kidding. I wouldn't inflict Zoe on anyone I like xx*

Disappointment trickled through Addy. Painting alone was mind-numbingly boring and she'd learned quickly that boredom wasn't a safe emotion for her. What could she do instead that was fun and challenging?

It's not all about you! Steph's exhausted. Make her a meal and take it over.

Unease peppered her gut like shot on a road sign. Wanting it to settle, she reached for her phone and called Sven's.

"Hi, Gloria. It's Addy. Can you charge me for a family size lasagna, garlic bread and salad, and deliver it to Four Winds?"

"Sure, honey, but not until after the lunch rush. Say two? If you need it earlier, you'll need to take it yourself."

Addy bit her lip against another round of agitation. "Two's fine, thanks, Gloria."

As she finished the call, she justified that her delivering the meal risked getting in the Suns' way. Besides, lasagna for dinner was a better idea than for lunch.

She opened her bullet journal, drew and colored in a dot, then wrote *Monty sick, lasagna for Steph* and immediately put an X through the dot, getting a buzz from having achieved a task. Then she put a line through *painting* and sighed.

The only thing remaining in the Saturday column was housework. She couldn't do any college work, because the combination of the exam period and three weeks of being sober meant she'd totally caught up. She fist-pumped the air. There wasn't even any prep work for next semester because she wouldn't be teaching.

There was, however, housework.

Do the boring jobs first, Aida.

With a sigh, she pressed earbuds in her ears and found a podcast to keep her entertained. Then she hauled out the cleaning bucket and mop, the all-purpose cleaner and cloths and started in the kitchen.

Later, when she walked out of the bathroom, she noticed dust motes dancing in a stream of sunlight. She watched them and their accompanying rainbow of colors before lifting her gaze to the source. Crossing the hall, she stood at her childhood bedroom window. So often in winter the sea was a writhing gray beast, but today it was turquoise green and picture-postcard perfect with white-tipped waves rolling in as evenly as the beat of a metronome.

An image of her younger self running to the beach with her board under her arm made her set down the bucket she was holding and scrabble through the embarrassing number of unopened boxes—purchases made during drunken online shopping sprees. She found the box badged with waves and ripped it open, lifting out a one-piece bathing suit, a rash top and a full-length sea green wetsuit with decorative blue panels on the sleeves and legs. She laughed in relief that her fashion sense had weathered the alcoholic maelstrom and come out on top. But had she ordered the right size or the size she wished she was? There was only one way to find out.

Shucking her clothes, she put on the swimsuit and the rash suit before hauling the wetsuit up her legs and jumping up and down to shift it over her hips. By the time she'd shoved and tugged the neoprene over her arms she was panting hard. She grasped the zipper cord. Would it close? She heaved, felt the teeth mesh and then the cord was at her neck. She squealed in delight.

Avoiding the mirror that would only show her fat bulging in all the wrong places, she dug out some beach shoes and ran to the back shed. Would her board still be there or had her parents thrown it out?

Her fingers struggled with the ancient padlock but she finally managed to open it, then drag the wonky metal door over the uneven concrete. Cobwebs greeted her, as did her old board. It still leaned against the wall in the place Ivan had assigned it when he'd eventually, and reluctantly, bought it for her.

"But you can't sing when you're in the waves, *dragi*," he'd said sadly.

She hadn't told him that was the very reason she surfed. Instead she'd hugged him hard and said, "Thanks, Papa."

Addy blew a kiss to her father's memory and, ignoring the clash of negative voices in her head— *the board's too old, it needs waxing, you're too heavy*—she grabbed a brush, wiped away the worst of the dust and checked for spiders before tucking it under her arm. As she made her way down the grass-lined path, past hydrangea bushes taller than her and ducking under the banksias, it felt like both a pilgrimage and a homecoming.

The skin of her feet wrinkled at the touch of cool sand and there was a stiff breeze dropping the temperature. Most people were enjoying the view from inside the heated café, leaving the beach blessedly empty.

She was bending over and attaching the leg rope to her ankle, wondering if the Velcro was too old to hold, when doggie breath and a wet nose touched her face.

"Fergus!" She ruffled his ears and felt the first flutters of anxiety. If the border collie was here then Kieran was close by. For a moment her determination wavered. Taking a nosedive today was a given, but did she want to do it in front of anyone she knew?

You hardly know him. They'd never had the cup of Irish breakfast tea and a conversation about her deck. She'd woken up that Saturday too hungover to entertain anyone at 10:00 in the morning and had texted him to cancel. Apart from the occasional acknowledging wave from the beach to him in the surf, the next time they'd met was at choir where there was little time to chat.

"I can do this," she said to Fergus.

She waded into the water, ignoring the painful ache of her ankles when the icy waves hit them. Fergus accompanied her until it was too deep for him to stand and then he gave her a doleful look: *What? You're abandoning me too?*

She pushed the board in front of her, delaying the moment she had to bite the bullet and lie on it.

You'll sink.

Shut. Up!

She lay on the board, instantly remembering to line her chin up with the decal that had come with it. She started paddling, pushing her arms toward the back of the board with a familiar freestyle stroke. Her muscles screamed in protest. Would she even make it out to the break? She could see three other surfers now, including Kieran, waiting out the back behind the waves.

The lip of an approaching wave with its sparkling silver lining broke earlier than she'd expected and white foam spilled over her. She squealed as a droplet of icy water managed to sneak in under her snug wetsuit and trickle down her neck.

What are you doing?

Salt stung her eyes and her arms burned, but old memories of freedom and exhilaration poured through her. She remembered this— the excitement of being out on the water and the sense of accomplishment when she'd ridden a wave to shore.

Dream on, sweetheart. You were twenty pounds lighter then.

She gritted her teeth, studied the oncoming set wave and paddled herself into position. When the ocean's pulsing energy nudged the back of the board and lurched her forward, its power made her paddling redundant. With her elbows up, she pressed her hands on the deck of the board and brought her right knee forward. She pushed up, keeping most of her weight on her back leg.

I'm bloody up! She couldn't believe it.

The board nosedived and she was pitching forwards into the foam, feeling the sharp tug of the leggie on her ankle. Lightness followed. When she surfaced and wiped the hair out of her eyes, she saw her board yards in front of her. Apparently fifteen-year-old Velcro was unreliable after all. She bodysurfed into shore, retrieved the board and paddled out again, breathing deeply and ignoring the burn in her arms.

This time when she pushed to her feet, she avoided self-congratulations and concentrated on staying on the board. The power of a swell generated hundreds of miles away lifted her and with it came the indescribable feeling she'd always loved—lurching down the line with air rushing past her face. Pure weightlessness. Oneness.

She rode the wall and even managed to turn back toward the pocket, before digging a rail and wiping out. This time when she retrieved her board she met Kieran in the shallows.

"Addy? I thought me eyes were deceiving me," he said, his accent making "thought" sound like "taught."

She gave an embarrassed shrug. "No, it's me."

He was grinning at her as if he'd just been given an unexpected gift. "I didn't know ye surfed."

She indicated the sand and seaweed on her wetsuit. "As you can see, it's been a long time."

He didn't show any signs he agreed with her. "Today's waves are perfect for getting right back in."

Her fingers and toes now held a bluish tinge. "I suppose in Irish terms, today's positively balmy."

But he'd turned away to grab her board and didn't appear to have heard her. When he returned with the board, his dark brows were pulled down in concentration. "I'm thinking perhaps this board isn't the best for you. I've got a spare in the truck that might suit. Want to give it a go?"

Addy's out-of-shape body groaned and pleaded for her to rest, but a memory of her younger self heaving herself back on her board over and over until she'd mastered turning came back to her. She'd never know if she could still surf if she passed up Kieran's offer.

"Why not?" she said. "I can't do any worse."

"You could do plenty worse, but you won't. Back in a tick. Fergus, stay with Addy."

He jogged up the beach and returned with a fish design board with twin fins that was beautifully decorated in blues and orange. It looked like a magic carpet and she fell a little bit in love with it.

She reached out and stroked it. "And you just happened to have this beautiful board in your truck?"

"I do and it needs using." He shrugged at her raised brows. "A mate bought it for his girlfriend, hoping she'd come surfing with him. But before he gave it to her, she dumped him for spending too much time on the water."

"Ouch."

"Yeah." Kieran shook his head ruefully. "He misjudged that one. He was pretty cut up there for a bit and just wanted the board out of the house. So I put it in the truck and waited for him to ask for it back. He never did and then he moved to the mainland, leaving it with me."

Addy stroked the board again. "Surely he could have sold it?"

"I think he just wanted shot of it." Kieran handed it to her. "She's a nice board. The fish shape gives two points of control so you can hold onto the wave and glide through the fatter sections without falling off the back. Plus the width means moving from rail to rail with more control."

She smiled, enjoying his earnest description. "I'd forgotten surfing has its own vocabulary."

He grinned. "You'll be carving and hitting the lip in no time."

She laughed at his optimism. "I'd be happy to stay on my feet longer than just making the drop."

As they both paddled out, Fergus barked indignantly. Addy expected Kieran to return out the back, but he stayed with her. When they were near the break, she gave thanks there was a lull so she could catch her breath and rest her arms.

"They're back." Kieran pointed to the swell a minute later. "Let's do this." He started paddling.

Addy did the same, loving the feel of the board skimming through the water, and then she was pushing up, keeping her knees bent and riding the drop. It was tempting to stay there but she'd quickly run out of momentum and the fun was back on the wall of the wave.

I can do this.

Focusing on her weight she turned the board, riding along the bottom of the wave. Out of the corner of her eye she caught Kieran executing a cutback and returning to the shoulder. Motivated, she turned again, only this time the rails didn't dig in. The next moment she was tumbling into the foam.

Kieran paddled over to her. "Legs are looking good, but turns are about the whole body. Throw your shoulders into it too."

"It's that easy, right?"

He grinned. "And that hard. You're doing great."

Half an hour later she was waterlogged but flying on endorphins. She collapsed onto the sand and laughed. "That was awesome, but I'm absolutely knackered."

Kieran lowered himself down next to her. "It was all starting to come together for you on those last two waves. Muscle memory's an incredible thing."

"I think I've wiped their memory with fatigue," she said. "Every muscle in my body will hate me tomorrow."

"Some gentle squats and lunges will help."

She dried her face with a towel and pushed her hair behind her ears. "So will increasing my general fitness. I've talked about exercising all year but ..." She trailed off, not wanting to say "I was too hungover in the mornings," but uncomfortable hiding totally behind work. "Until recently, I've struggled to find the motivation." She raised her hand toward the sea. "I think I just found it."

"I think the seed was sown earlier."

Her gut clenched and her breakfast rose to the back of her throat. Did he know she'd disgraced herself at the Choir Crush? Of course he knew. He lived in the cove. It had been on Facebook. Fern had probably gleefully informed him at the choir refreshments table. Addy wanted to curl up into a tight ball and roll far, far away.

"To be sure you sounded gracious when Courtney hit the higher note," Kieran continued, "but I saw the shock on your face."

He wasn't talking about the video! Her body slumped in relief, then her brain registered he was keenly observant. She couldn't decide if this was a good trait or not.

"Courtney's always had a lovely voice," she said.

"She does. Still, I'm sensing a but."

Right then Addy decided that Kieran being observant wasn't ideal. She scooped up a palmful of sand and let it trickle through her fingers —giving herself time to work out how much to say.

"Courtney and I were at school together and she loved to sing, but she wasn't given many opportunities to shine. I, on the other hand, found myself stuck in a situation where it didn't matter if I wanted to sing backing vocals or the lead, the teacher gave me the solo every single time. Even when I objected and insisted others have the opportunity, it made no difference. Courtney should have hated me."

I hated me.

"The teacher ... my parents ..." She sighed. "There were expectations. I reached a point where I'd do just about anything to avoid singing. And music. I escaped into surfing, and then I escaped period. But the moment I returned to the cove, I was shanghaied into the new choir."

She watched the sunlight dancing on the lip of a wave. "I was a very reluctant member until ..." She swallowed. "Until recently. So the other night when Courtney out sang me, it shocked me, especially since all through high school I'd wanted the spotlight for Courtney."

For anyone but me. Although no one deserved what came with that particular spotlight.

Her breath caught on the past and she coughed. Then she cleared her throat and left the past where it belonged.

"When Courtney hit that note the other day and I couldn't, I honestly didn't expect to experience any emotion other than happiness for her. And I was happy, but at the same time I got this overwhelming sense of sadness." She sighed and gave him a sideways look. "That's pretty messed up, right?"

"Oh, I dunno," he said reflectively. "Life's a confusing conundrum most of the time."

She laughed. "That's reassuring."

"I'm glad." He grinned at her and then his face sobered. "It sounds like back in the day there was a lot of pressure on you to sing. Maybe the sadness you felt has more to do with not singing for so long rather than Courtney hitting the high note."

Once, just thinking about singing made Addy reach for a drink. But today, with a clarity of thought she'd lacked in a long, long time, she turned Kieran's words over in her mind. They jostled uncomfortably, their intensity prickling and jabbing, and her first impulse was to find a way to banish them.

I'll do it for you, her craving offered. *And you know I'll do it so well that not only won't you remember those feelings, you won't remember a thing.*

But whether it was her current state of satisfaction and achievement from surfing or her lucidity from being sober and a few weeks free of hangovers, or a combination of both, for the first time since she'd stopped drinking the urge to resist her craving didn't come with a monumental challenge. This time she wasn't depending solely on a fast-dwindling supply of willpower. This time she had a modicum of insight.

You won't help. You'll make it worse.

A line from the online course she was doing with SCW drifted into her head: *Sit with your feelings. Acknowledge them and accept them with compassion.*

Her craving snorted. *Hah! As if.*

Bugger off!

Slowly, Kieran's words "maybe the sadness you felt has more to do with not singing for so long rather than Courtney hitting the high note" settled with a heavy sigh. A complicated mix of pain and shame infused her. Breathing deeply, she focused on the rhythm of the breaking waves and tried to understand what the words were really saying.

"When I walked away from singing years ago—well, music really— I honestly thought I didn't miss it. Perhaps I've been wrong."

"There's an easy way to tell," he said simply.

Addy didn't think anything to do with her and music was simple. "Oh? And what's that?"

"Do you feel happier after you've belted out a tune? I know I do."

Happy was a stretch. Relief? Release? It depended on the song. Playing show tunes in the privacy of her home was definitely part of her sober toolkit.

"I feel calmer," she said.

"Calmer's good. It's why I love surfing after work. People think working with wood must be soothing. But some days I struggle to get me hands on the wood because I'm stuck on the phone wrangling customers and suppliers. Surfing and singing puts life back into perspective for me."

The sun disappeared behind a cloud and Addy suddenly felt the chill of winter. "My work's been insane since February, but thankfully that's about to change. So much so that when there's an easterly, I might be able to take an early mark and come surfing." She looked at him then. "Can I buy this board?"

He shook his head. "No need for that. Use it for as long as you want."

"I can't just keep it," she said, unsure of why she was objecting. It wasn't like she had money to spare—Jasper remained intransigent about the five thousand dollars and she was going to have to pay someone to serve the papers on him. Although, since she'd stopped drinking and drunk online shopping, the good news was that her bank balance was rising steadily.

She studied Kieran's face, knowing when it came to men her judgment was hit and miss. Too many relationships had started and ended with drunken sex. Was he being kind like Grant or was this a gift that came with strings attached?

A flash of Grant at her door holding a bottle of sloe gin rocked into her, immediately followed by him on top of her. Had that gift been kind and thoughtful or had he come with the intention of sex? It can be both, she reminded herself. After all, she hadn't objected to the sex. But had she consented? Had he asked?

God! What's wrong with you? Grant had asked her the other night if she'd wanted to have sex in the office and he'd accepted her refusal. Of course he'd asked on that Saturday afternoon.

"Addy," Kieran said firmly, rocking to his feet, "I don't want any money for the board. I just want to see it used. But I can see the lack of a business transaction is making you uncomfortable. How about you donate the money you'd have given me to your favorite charity?"

All her agitation instantly settled. "Deal."

"Good." He proffered his hand and she shook it. "You're looking as blue as your wetsuit," he said. "Can I give your boards and your weary bones a ride home?"

"Thank you." She let him pull her to her feet, her bones, muscles and sinews all aching.

"I could take a look at that deck too, if you're still interested," he said.

She remembered why she'd originally invited him to look at the deck—she'd wanted a drinking buddy. The shame tried to settle over her, but she wouldn't allow it. She was no longer that person and the deck definitely needed some work.

"I'm still interested and I'll make you that cup of Irish breakfast tea I promised."

"It's long past breakfast now," he said, his blue eyes twinkling.

"The sun's over the yardarm and I could definitely be doing with something a little stronger."

Her stomach sank, taking the starbursts of the morning with it. She enjoyed Kieran's easy company, but she didn't want to dent things by telling him that she currently found it hard to be around alcohol. However, it looked like she had no choice.

"Do you have coffee?" he asked. "Or do we grab some from Sven's first?"

She was still processing the relief he wasn't suggesting an alcoholic drink when she heard a male voice call Kieran's name.

"G'day," Kieran said.

She turned and was surprised to be greeted by a wetsuit-clad Henry Sun. "Addy! Are you taking up surfing?"

"More like breaking a twelve-year drought," she said. "I heard you had a rough night with Monty."

He sighed. "Steph took the brunt of it. It's tough because when Monty's sick, he only wants her."

"Poor Steph. Are they okay now?"

"Nothing a bit of sleep won't fix. Unfortunately, the steroids Monty's on at the moment make him a bit hyper." He indicated the girl standing behind him. "Zoe and I are taking a break."

What about Steph? But then Addy remembered Steph's comment about sulky teens. Perhaps Henry taking Zoe out of the house for a while was giving Steph a break.

Zoe was wearing track-pants and a hoodie—not exactly surfing gear—and she looked less enthusiastic about being out in the sunshine than a vampire. Addy couldn't imagine how sitting on the beach watching her father surf was going to improve her mood.

"Hi, Zoe, I'm Addy. A friend of your ..." She'd never actually heard Steph use the term step mum. "Of Steph's." She pointed to her original surfboard. "Do you want to use my old board? It's friendly. I learned to surf on it, but I've outgrown it now."

"Might be fun," Henry encouraged.

Zoe glanced between Addy, the board, Kieran, her father, and back to the board. "Maybe."

Addy wondered what was in the big bag on the sand. If Zoe didn't have a wetsuit then taking the board out would end in hypothermia. "Have you got a wetsuit?"

Zoe gave a reluctant nod.

"Great! I'll just change the leg rope so you don't have to chase her down and you'll be good to go."

"I'm two steps ahead of you." Kieran had already removed the old leg rope and was lacing on a new one, his fingers deftly untying and tying knots. "Are you a regular-footer or a goofy-footer?" he asked Zoe.

She looked to her father as if Kieran had spoken a foreign language.

Henry laughed. "It's like being left or right-handed. You're a goofy-footer like me."

Addy couldn't tell from Zoe's face if she considered this a good or a bad thing.

"Thanks for the use of the board, Addy." Henry tilted his head and widened his eyes at Zoe. Zoe stared at her feet. Henry sighed.

"I'll drop it back to you later this afternoon."

"Hey, Zoe," Addy said, feeling the need to pay the use of surfboards forward. "If you and the board bond, keep it. It doesn't deserve to be abandoned in a shed any longer."

Zoe looked at her then, her eyes dark and full of unreadable thoughts. "Whatevs."

Addy was instantly tumbled back to her own adolescence and her constant state of confusion. How the world offered so many opportunities with one hand and took so many away with the other. How it flung her between terrifying and exciting and back again, leaving her floundering and uncertain. Lost and alone.

Had anything changed?

CHAPTER THIRTY-THREE

BRENDA'S AFTERNOONS, which had previously been filled with minding grandchildren and ferrying them to after-school activities, were now achingly empty. The hours between 3:30 and 6:00 stretched out in front of her, throwing her back to the days when she was the mother of young children and ten minutes of pushing a swing felt like thirty. Just as she had during those long and lonely days on the farm, she'd returned to baking. It kept her hands busy, but it didn't stop her mind churning. She revisited conversations with Richard, Colin and Courtney, hearing the words drop like stones over and over—hard, uncompromising and unforgiving.

She paused in her kneading, dusted her hands and reread a text conversation from Olivia that had arrived at lunchtime.

Mémé, I miss you!!!!!

I miss you too, darling

Can I come & c u after school?

Brenda's fingers had wanted to type *yes!* but had settled on *Ask your mum.*

Olivia had sent back a crying face emoji. *I'll catch the bus then she can't do anything!!*

Brenda's chest had cramped. As much as she wanted to see Olivia, the last thing she needed was Courtney accusing her of encouraging Olivia to disobey her and adding yet another log to the bonfire of reasons why Courtney hated her.

Your mum will panic if she arrives at school to pick you up and you aren't there, she'd texted.

The phone rang in her hand, making her jump. She answered it before she'd taken in the number. "Hello."

"Hi, Mum," a woman's voice said.

Her heart leaped. "Courtney?"

"Ah, no," the voice said, sounding confused. "It's Lucinda."

Brenda leaned her forehead against the wall and closed her eyes. *Stupid!* Of course it wasn't Courtney. For reasons never discussed, Lucinda had started calling her "Mum" soon after she'd given birth to Rusty. Brenda had taken it as a sign of growing affection from her practical, no-nonsense daughter-in-law.

"Sorry, Lucinda." Brenda tried to steady her breathing and keep a lid on the hurt and disappointment that her daughter-in-law had kept Rusty and Jake away from her. "How are you?"

"Better now."

"Better?"

"Yeah." Lucinda gave a wry laugh. "Rusty brought stomach flu home from scout camp and kindly gave it to us. We're okay now and no longer infectious."

Brenda's hand gripped the phone. "If I'd known, I would have brought over some chicken soup."

"I found some in the freezer, which was lucky because we didn't want to risk you and Marilyn getting it."

You and Marilyn. "Thank you." *I think.*

"I'm sorry it's taken this long to call, but honestly Col and I haven't been that sick in years. Are you okay picking the boys up from school tomorrow?" Lucinda asked.

Brenda thought about Colin saying "everything's changed." "And Colin knows and is okay with that?" she checked.

Lucinda sighed. "Col got a shock and it's taken him a while to wrap his head around the fact his mother's gay. But in-between throwing up, we've had plenty of time to talk. He got himself stuck on the sex part of things, so I asked him if he ever thought about you and Glen having sex. For a minute there, I couldn't tell if it was the stomach flu or the thought of his parents doing the deed that was making him green."

Lucinda's laugh tinkled and then she cleared her throat. "I'm pretty sure he's coping by telling himself that you and Marilyn are best friends. But if that gets him inside your door and sitting at your table again, will you be okay with that?"

Brenda's throat tightened at the unexpected support. "It sounds like a good start. Thank you."

"No problem." There was a brief hesitation. "Mum, I've had more luck with Col than with Courtney. She's ..." Lucinda sighed.

"Angry, hurt, furious ..."

"And then some. I doubt even Saint Ben can get through to her."

As they finished the call, Brenda thought about her easygoing son-in-law who rarely objected to anything Courtney did. Did he side with his wife?

The timer beeped, interrupting her thoughts. She donned an insulated glove and pulled hot scones from the oven and tumbled them onto a rack to cool.

"Hi." Marilyn walked in from work, put down her satchel, kissed Brenda on the cheek and eyed the pile of scones. "I thought Lily was on choir refreshments tonight?"

"She is, but you know she'll just buy a packet of Tim Tams at the supermarket."

"And that will be fine," Marilyn said. "Everyone loves Tim Tams and choir's about singing, not the food."

Brenda ignored the comment and indicated two plastic containers filled with chocolate and peppermint bars. "They're for you to take to school tomorrow for the faculty."

Marilyn frowned. "Have you been cooking all day again?"

Irritation dug in. "No. Just this afternoon."

"I thought you would have been out in the garden," Marilyn said. "It's so glorious it's enough to trick us into forgetting it's winter." She slid her arm around Brenda's waist. "Come to the beach with Clyde and me and we'll revel like nymphs in the sunshine."

Brenda snorted. "This nymph has to cook dinner."

Marilyn rolled her eyes. "There's enough food in this house to feed half the cove. Have a night off and we'll heat up some quiche."

"Lucinda just rang." Brenda wiped the counter, her movements jerky. "The boys are coming after school tomorrow, so I'm going to make chocolate chip cookies."

"The boys will be fine with the bars." Marilyn put her hand over hers. "Please come for a walk with me."

Brenda moved her hand away. "I need to stay here."

"Why?"

"Because ..." She scrubbed at a lump of hardened chocolate that was stuck to the counter. "Because Lucinda rang, which means Courtney might call or drop in and I need to be here."

"Oh, sweetheart." Marilyn sighed. "Stop putting your life on hold for her."

Indignation roared in Brenda's veins. "I'm not."

"You are," Marilyn said with an increasingly familiar edge to her voice.

"I'm her mother! Being available is part of the job description."

Except for years Brenda hadn't been emotionally available. First, it had been because she was struggling with motherhood and the loneliness of her marriage. Then her life had become punctuated by moments of intense excitement when she was to meet Marilyn, followed by melancholic days after their weekend together and counting the weeks until they met again.

"Brenda, ever since I arrived in the cove you've been living your life around Courtney, not to mention the grandchildren and the town," Marilyn said firmly. "The whole point of coming out is so you can live your life authentically and be happy. We've waited a long time for this.

We deserve it. Stop letting other people's opinions hijack our happiness."

Happiness? Brenda flicked on the hot water faucet and squirted dishwashing liquid under the flow. Lemon scent rose in a whoosh, reminding her of gin and tonics on the veranda of their cottage in Longford and here in the garden when their glorious bubble of happiness was still intact.

"That's easy for you to say. You didn't lose anyone by coming out."

Marilyn folded her arms as if she was dealing with a recalcitrant child. "Is it really losing someone when that person can't love you for who you are?"

The words rolled into Brenda like massive boulders, flattening her under their weight. "What you don't seem to understand is that these *someones* are my family."

"You said Rusty and Jake are coming tomorrow, which means Colin and Lucinda must be talking to you again. So really, it's just Courtney."

"*Just* Courtney?" Brenda had a momentary desire to slap Marilyn. "It's Olivia and Jesse too. And Ben."

"I get that you're upset about Courtney," Marilyn said in a tone that hinted perhaps she didn't fully understand. "But you're so busy obsessing about her, you seem to forget that I'm here and in your corner."

The rush of anger almost buckled her knees. "You pressured me to come out!"

Marilyn's forefinger jabbed holes in the air. "You begged me to move up here when I wanted you to come to Hobart. You promised me you'd come out and then you did *nothing* for months. In the end, you didn't even do it. It was Addy!"

"That's not my fault! You knew I was going to do it. You knew how worried I was and you kept pushing and pushing." Brenda heard herself yelling but she couldn't rein it in. "Now everything I feared would happen has, but you're so tied up with the selfishness of doing whatever makes you happy irrespective of anyone else's feelings, you can't see that."

Marilyn flinched and her open and friendly face shut down fast.

A sharp pain jabbed Brenda and her fingers tightened around the stainless-steel rim of the sink. In all their years together they'd never really argued, let alone hurled hurtful words at each other. She desperately wanted to turn back time to those long and languid years when they'd shut out the world and its opinions and basked in their devotion to each other.

"I'll take Clyde for a walk and meet you at choir," Marilyn said stiffly to Brenda's back. "I assume as Courtney will be there, you're prepared to leave the house for her even though you won't leave it for me."

The back door slammed.

Brenda jumped, then dropped her head in her hands and cried.

CHAPTER THIRTY-FOUR

"I'm leaving for choir," Steph told Henry, desperately hoping Zoe had changed her mind.

Henry frowned. "That's early, isn't it?"

"I'm picking up Addy."

"I've never understood why you do that. She lives so close she could walk."

"It's dark and it's wet." Steph pointed to the rain that was hammering the bay window. "But even if it wasn't, walking into the hall with her is my way of showing support."

"Oh, right, and helping her paint, walking with her twice a week, popping around to see her most nights and texting her ten times a day isn't?" Henry grumbled.

Steph paused her bag check for tissues, hand sanitizer and her wallet. "She's our friend and she's doing it tough at the moment."

"She's your friend and she's been sober for weeks."

Henry sounded jealous and Steph was gripped by a sudden desire to argue with him. They'd fight and then she could storm off to choir without Zoe.

"You should be pleased she's stopped writing herself off instead of saying the word sober like it's an accusation. And she's *our* friend, Henry. She sent round lasagna after that awful night with Monty. God, she gave Zoe her old surfboard."

Henry grimaced. "And that was kind of her."

"But? I know there's a but."

"Zoe," Henry called out. "Choir taxi's leaving."

"But what, Henry?" Steph demanded. "Spit it out."

His mouth tightened. "If she was *our* friend, she'd visit, take an interest in us and the kids. Instead, she has you running to her all the time."

"She does not," Steph said hotly, ducking the jabbing memories of Addy rejecting her numerous invitations to Four Winds.

"So are we going?" Zoe asked. "Or are you two just gonna keep arguing?"

"We're not arguing," Henry said.

Zoe gave a disdainful eye-roll. Steph instantly noticed the girl had perfected the winged liquid-eyeliner technique, drawing two perfect cat's eyes that elongated her already beautiful eyes.

"Have a great time," Henry said, kissing them both on the cheek.

Steph stared at him. Was he really letting Zoe leave the house looking twenty? Did she care? She did if asking Zoe to remove it meant she chucked a fit and stayed home.

"You're not going to choir wearing eyeliner. Right, Henry?"

He blinked and looked at Zoe. "Oh, right. You know the rules, Zo."

Wait for it. Steph was already marshaling the words "It's your choice," for when Zoe objected.

"Fine." Zoe pulled a make-up wipe out of her bag as if she'd anticipated the request.

Steph got a double-edged stab of regret—first for the loss of the perfectly applied eyeliner and second for the fact that Zoe was coming to choir.

. . .

The hall was warm and welcoming and Steph, Zoe and Addy propped their sopping umbrellas by the door to join the others in a parade of colors.

Voices called out, "Hi," "Wet one tonight," and Steph noticed Kieran glance up from his conversation with Morgan and smile at them.

"The surfer dude's in choir?" Zoe sounded animated for the first time in forever.

Addy laughed. "Does that give the choir some cred, Zoe?"

When Addy had gotten into the car and Zoe—who was sitting in the back seat with earbuds firmly in her ears—hadn't even looked up, Steph had mouthed "Sorry." A flash of something undecipherable had crossed Addy's face and she'd turned in her seat, tapped Zoe on the knee and waved, before turning back seemingly unperturbed that Zoe had barely acknowledged her.

Kieran gave Steph, Addy and Zoe a wave. "Good to see you again."

Zoe stood a little straighter.

"I thought the choir was only for adults." Courtney's voice rose above the general chatter. "If minors are coming, we'll all need to apply for background checks." She gave an exaggerated sigh. "Such a pain."

If any other child had walked into the hall, Courtney wouldn't be making a fuss. Steph's hands clenched unexpectedly. What was that about? She should be pleased Courtney was objecting.

"Most people here would already have one." Morgan glanced around. "Except maybe Vera?"

"I've got one," Vera said indignantly. "I help out with classroom reading on Wednesdays. What about you, Kieran? I doubt you meet many kids as a carpenter."

"I had to get one when I volunteered at the learn to surf program, but I'm thinking it's a good idea just to have one these days."

Courtney threw Steph and Zoe death stares.

"Actually, Zoe's here as part of a school assignment," Steph said pointedly.

"You're joking. The passion project?" Courtney shook her head as if she couldn't believe Steph had brought Zoe to choir.

"Yes, the passion project." Steph was working hard to stay civil.

"You do understand there's a reason the word passion's in the title? It needs to be something they're interested in. You'd know that if you'd come to the information evening," Courtney said scathingly. "Mind you, being interested in something could be an issue for Zoe."

"Courtney," Addy said with a smile, although there was caution in her tone. "Remember when we were thirteen and we couldn't decide if we wanted to be lead singers in a rock band or play netball for Australia? I know my parents didn't count either of those things as worthy passions."

Marilyn appeared from the kitchen with a smile, but there was something different about her. It was as if she'd been caught in the rain and it had washed away her usual sparkle.

"Hello, Zoe. This is a surprise."

Steph scowled at Zoe. "You were supposed to text Marilyn and ask if you could come," she said through gritted teeth.

Zoe gave a "whatever" shrug.

Steph thought she heard Courtney snort and her antagonism toward both Zoe and Courtney intensified. She hated that Zoe had put her in this embarrassing position. Hated that the girl and her sullen negativity were oozing into her joyful two hours of "me" time. Hated that it gave Courtney a reason to lord it over her.

"I'm sorry, Marilyn," Steph said.

"Don't be silly," Marilyn said.

Zoe threw Steph a "gotcha" look.

"You may not feel that way when she tells you about the school project she has to do," Steph countered, forgetting Marilyn was a teacher.

"What project's that?" Marilyn asked Zoe, her face alight with interest.

Zoe fiddled with a loose thread on her sleeve. "Passion project."

"And choir's your passion?"

Zoe waved her hand as if to encompass everyone in the hall. "It's their passion. Mine's make-up."

"And you can see a connection?" Marilyn asked.

Zoe's chin rose. "Maybe. Yeah."

"Well, to fully understand their passion, you need to sing too," Marilyn said firmly.

Steph thought she heard Courtney mutter, "This will be interesting," but as much as she wanted to hurl something caustic back at her, there was some truth to it. Steph expected Zoe to sneer, but her face remained impassive and she stayed silent.

Marilyn must not have been expecting a reply as she'd already shifted her attention to Addy. A frown creased her round face. "You remembered the music?"

Addy tapped her tablet. "It's right here, along with lots of other options."

"Good," Marilyn said briskly. "Let's go over to the piano and discuss the order."

"Sure." Addy gave Steph a bemused look—Marilyn was usually far more laidback than this.

Addy followed Marilyn to the piano, leaving Steph with Zoe who was back to staring at her feet. Steph was torn between letting her stand alone with her unfriendly aura of "do not approach me," or suggesting they go and chat with people, aware both suggestions would be met with derision. A rush of fury flared at Henry. Come tomorrow, he could take Zoe with him on his surfing afternoon.

Brenda usually called everyone to order by playing a few piano chords, but tonight she seemed to be taking a back seat. It was Addy who played, but there was no crash of chords—instead a rousing verse of Benny Goodman's "Sing, Sing, Sing."

Almost everyone's jaws dropped. Steph struggled to align the woman who talked about audits, policy and procedures and pedagogy with the pianist whose fingers were flying over the keys.

Since the morning Addy had asked Steph for help, she'd been slightly more open about her life. She'd told her about Jasper the

Bastard and the money he owed her, her long struggle with work-life balance and relationships, along with the occasional childhood memory, although those were usually prompted by something Courtney had said or done. But not once had Addy mentioned playing the piano. When Steph had asked her about the instrument in her living room, Addy had said "It was my mother's." Now Steph recalled the first choir rehearsal when Addy had told Brenda she hadn't played in years. But she'd obviously played as a kid and played well, because no one who'd learned as an adult had those skills.

People toe-tapped their way into position. Kieran bowed to Vera and extended his hand. She accepted and he pulled her into a dance position and wide-stepped her across the floorboards like Fred Astaire, before setting her in position next to Lily.

Slightly breathless and with pink cheeks, Vera called him "a wicked flirt" and demanded her stick. Kieran gave her a wink and soft-shoe shuffled back across the hall, returning with her cane.

The warm-up exercises started on the remains of the feelgood buzz, and when they were singing "Bumblebee" Marilyn said, "Zoe, you've got great pitch."

Zoe actually smiled.

A green flash lit up behind Steph's eyes.

Vera leaned over and said softly, "She's very pretty when she smiles."

Steph swallowed "she's a nightmare" and dug deep, managing a wan smile.

Marilyn split the singers into rehearsal groups. When Zoe followed the choir conductor into the kitchen, Steph was relieved they were in different groups.

After a few minutes of waiting around, Addy finally said, "Brenda, do you want to make a start?"

"You can do it," Brenda said.

"I only signed up for the piano playing," Addy joked, although her face had puckered into a frown.

"We don't always get a choice," Brenda said, uncharacteristically caustic.

Addy flinched.

Steph wished she understood enough about music to help. "Is everything okay, Brenda?"

"I'm sorry, Addy," Brenda said. "That was unfair. It's been a difficult few weeks."

Addy reached out and touched Brenda's hand. "And that's my fault."

Brenda sighed. "Not all of it. Never think that."

"If neither of you are feeling up to it, I'll give it a crack." Kieran looked around the rest of the group. "Unless of course someone else wants to?"

There were shakes of heads and murmurs of "No, you do it" and "Sounds good to me."

Addy and Brenda gave him grateful smiles.

"Right, Addy, can you give us an E," Kieran said. Addy hit the key and everyone sang "lah." "Great. Now you've got your note, I'll count you in."

They ran through the three songs twice each. In-between, Steph noticed that Kieran always stopped and talked to Addy, his attention fully focused on her. Steph remembered how Henry used to look at her like that—as if no one else in the world existed.

Addy seemed oblivious to Kieran's interest. Should Steph mention it to her? Or was Addy aware but not interested? Judging by the few things Addy had said about her past relationships it sounded like she'd been attracted to the sort of bloke who'd hurt her. Or had that been tied up with her drinking? Either way, Kieran wasn't a dick and Steph thought that alone was worth mentioning to her friend.

When the sopranos spilled out of the kitchen Steph was unsurprised that Zoe was lagging behind. She crossed her fingers that one night of choir was enough to put her off coming again. Heidi suddenly turned back and said something to Zoe. The girl nodded then accompanied her o the refreshments table.

But it wasn't just Zoe being at choir that felt wrong. With Addy on piano duty, Steph missed standing next to her and exchanging knowing looks and comments. After the moment with Brenda, Steph was keen to check that Addy was okay, but Addy and Kieran were deep in conversation with Marilyn about an issue with one of the songs. Steph stood stirring her tea and feeling lonely in a crowd.

The hall doors opened unexpectedly and Ben Burton walked in, accompanied by his daughter. Olivia made a beeline for Zoe. What was she doing here? Since the Seventh Grade girls' meltdown, Zoe hadn't mentioned Olivia, but then again, Zoe didn't say much about school and Steph didn't inquire. No doubt Courtney had persuaded the principal to split the girls into different classes, but perhaps that hadn't broken the friendship. A certain smugness warmed her—Courtney was about to have a pink fit.

"And Ben makes three," Rob said heartily. "Good to see you, mate."

Courtney, who had her back to the door, swung around on hearing her husband's name. Her face paled and she ran to him. "Oh God, what's happened? Is it Jesse?"

"He's fine," Ben said calmly. "It's all good. Please don't stress."

Courtney sagged against him for a moment and Steph felt a dart of sympathy for her. She could understand why Courtney had gone straight to the disaster scenario—she'd have done the same thing if Henry had walked into the hall completely out of context.

"Then why are you here giving me a heart attack?" Courtney's adrenaline-fueled voice cut across the hall.

Ben's brows pulled down and he looked suddenly wary. "Livvy said she needed to come for her school project."

Courtney's mouth thinned and she whirled around just as Olivia was hugging Brenda and doing some sort of complicated hand maneuver with Zoe.

"Olivia!" Courtney ground out as if she was using every gram of restraint not to launch herself at the girl. "Come here."

The girl stilled and took in a deep breath. "Um, I'd um, like you to come to me, please."

"Young lady, you do *not* get to call the shots when you've disobeyed me and conned your father," Courtney said.

"What?" Ben gave his daughter a look Steph was certain Olivia rarely saw from him. "Did you lie to me?"

"No! Dad, I didn't." She threw him a beseeching look and gripped her grandmother's hand. "I promise you, there really is a school thing. It's the passion project and Zoe and I—"

"No," Courtney said through gritted teeth. "You are not doing that ridiculous idea."

A surge of loyalty for Henry made Steph say, "Actually, it's quite a good idea."

"Of course you'd say that," Courtney snapped. "You indulge that child and let her run wild without any boundaries or consequences. Ben and I don't parent that way and Olivia knows it. She respects our boundaries and us." She turned her attention back to her daughter. "We agreed your passion project was designing jam labels for the farm."

"That's your and Dad's passion!" Olivia cried. "Not mine!"

So much for boundaries. Steph enjoyed a delicious moment of schadenfreude.

Ben scrubbed his face with his palms. "Livvy, what project do you want to do?"

"The choir! We're going to interview everyone and ask them why they sing," Olivia said, her eyes bright with enthusiasm. "And I'm going to design a costume and Zoe's going to design the make-up so when the choir performs they'll have a ..." Olivia looked at Zoe. "What did you call it?"

"Integrated look," Zoe said quietly.

Steph glanced at Zoe in surprise. Had she actually put some thought into this?

"That sounds wonderful," Vera said.

"It would have been an idea to ask the choir first," Marilyn said wryly.

"Ask us now," Heidi said, raising her hand. "All those in fav—"

"It's up to her parents!" Courtney glared at Marilyn and Brenda.

"And we say no, don't we, Ben?"

Ben squirmed. "Let's talk about this at home, eh?"

"No!" Olivia and Courtney said simultaneously.

"You really want to do this here?" Ben said, an edge creeping into his voice. "Fine! This passion project is the sort of thing kids are expected to do on their own but can't without a ridiculous amount of help and it ends up sinking the parents. Why make it worse by forcing Livvy to do something she isn't interested in?"

A look of betrayal crossed Courtney's face. "You know my feelings about this. There has to be something else."

"There's not!" Olivia said dramatically. "And if you make me do jam labels, I'll fail due to a lack of passion."

"That'll do, Liv," Ben said firmly. "You promised to design the labels and I expect you to keep your word. But if you don't want to research berries and make jam for the project, that's okay. It probably seems more of the same old thing to you."

"Thanks, Dad."

Courtney made a strangled sound and brushed Ben's hand off her shoulder.

"Marilyn, are you okay with the girls doing this choir thing?" Ben asked.

"As long as everyone agrees and is onboard. I also expect the girls to sing in the choir and help with the eisteddfod," Marilyn said. "We could do with some extra hands."

Olivia grinned and said something to Zoe, who grimaced but nodded.

"We can do that," Olivia said. "It will be fun!"

Zoe rolled her eyes.

"All those in favor?" Heidi shot her hand back up and nodded encouragingly to the others.

Steph and Courtney were the only ones who didn't raise their hands. Steph's eyes slid away from Addy's questioning stare.

"Great. Well, now that's settled, let's get back to singing," Marilyn said. "Olivia, stand next to your grandmother for now, although if you sing like your mother, I'll move you next to Zoe, okay?"

Olivia, who was still holding Brenda's hand, said, "That's epic."

Steph risked a look at a stony-faced, tight-mouthed Courtney and wondered if she looked much the same. Neither of them wanted the girls involved in choir and Zoe was the common denominator.

CHAPTER THIRTY-FIVE

EXAM PERIOD GAVE with one hand and took with the other. There were fewer students on campus and those who were in attendance were circled by an air of quiet desperation. The faculty on the other hand were almost jaunty. The place had the feel of a vacation camp, and with no lectures to prepare or teach there were some long lunches at the pub. Addy had successfully avoided them, not only because of the alcohol but also because they meant being around Jett. Since the Instagram incident she was avoiding him as much as possible.

At the Monday faculty meeting, Jett had taken advantage of Grant being in Launceston to launch into a tirade against the sexual harassment training, which was essentially a tirade against her. Addy was disappointed that Lyn, Bettina and Jodi had stayed silent, especially as Lyn had told her earlier in the year "this place is pretty blokey."

Ravi had surprised Addy by supporting her, but Jett had silenced him with a raft of derogatory comments, the least offensive of which was "You're a girl now, are you?"

Grant had told Addy he wouldn't leave his Launceston meeting without an interview date and time for her, and she was counting down the days until she had the official power of 2IC to instigate a series of warnings to Jett. He could either choose to change or be sacked. Addy was hoping for the latter.

Although her workdays were less frantic, there was still lots of grading and the audit work. The Hair and Beauty department was her current concern. Unlike Jett, Bettina was fully onboard and had agreed with everything Addy had suggested. But her promised changes were yet to be implemented and the ASQA grace period ended soon. When that happened, an audit could occur without notice and Addy didn't want one department pulling the others down. She'd tried three times this week to meet with Bettina, but the woman had been on sick leave one day and "catching up" the next.

When Addy had gone down to Hair and Beauty on Tuesday at the time suggested by Bettina, she'd found Jodi from Health and Community Services seated in a chair with foils in her hair and flicking through a magazine. Bettina was nowhere to be seen.

"Is Bettina here?" Addy asked.

"She's just ducked out to grab us some coffee," Jodi said. "I can text her if you want one?"

"Um, that's okay. Did she mention anything about an audit meeting?"

Jodi gave Addy a pitying smile. "Oh, Addy. You need to learn our traditions."

Addy, who just wanted the documents Bettina had promised three weeks earlier, forced her mouth into an enquiring smile. "And what traditions are those?"

"Well, for starters, we don't do any extra work over exam period. It's a much-needed breather for everyone."

"I thought that's what vacations are for?" Addy said without thinking.

Jodi's mouth pursed. "I've got a tip for you, Addy. If you want to fit in here, you need to chill. Pull up a chair, put on a facial mask and let's chat."

A facial meant sitting for twenty minutes and that was the equivalent of being trapped in a cage.

"As lovely as that sounds, I'm sorry but I have to take a raincheck. I've got an audit meeting with Grant."

Jodi raised her brows. "Of course you do."

Something about the way the woman said it made Addy wonder if she was implying something other than work, but she immediately sloughed it off. It was far more likely to be connected to Addy's work ethic.

"But after that, I promise I'll try and chill," she said.

"That's the spirit," Jodi said.

That night when Addy was recording her days sober in her bullet journal, she wrote *Make nail appointment with Bettina.* If that was what it took to get the documents, so be it.

On Wednesday morning, Addy woke early and her muscles twitched, urging her out of bed. She was still getting used to waking up rested and ready to face the day instead of groaning at the light and diving back under the covers. Not wanting to waste the energy thrumming in every cell, she pulled on her wetsuit and snuck in a surf before work.

The beach was surprisingly empty of dog walkers and the sea of surfers. The winter dawn streaked the sky with vivid fingers of peach and periwinkle, coloring the water a dark violet. Not only did the waves sense her capabilities, they didn't offer up anything she couldn't handle and without the need to worry about other surfers, she luxuriated in long, wide rides.

But when she got home, she realized she'd wildly underestimated the time. She scrawled *Buy surfing watch* in her journal and raced for the shower. Once out, she applied her make-up, but had to forgo blow-drying her hair into its smooth sleek bob so she finger-styled it instead.

When she walked into the administration building forty minutes later, her hair was still slightly damp.

Lyn's brows rose. "Did a Hobart again, did we?"

Although she had no idea what the woman was talking about, the hairs on Addy's arms rose. "Excuse me?"

Lyn laughed. "No need to be coy. Everyone knows you got plastered at the training and arrived late for your presentation with no make-up and wearing crushed clothes."

Panic fluttered and a muscle twitched rapidly at the base of Addy's throat. God, Hobart had been months ago. And yes her clothes had been crushed, but she hadn't been late. Well, she had been late, but as everyone had still been drinking coffee, scarfing their breakfast Danish and chatting when she'd arrived, she'd actually been there for a good seventy-seconds before Heather had finished her conversation with Jessie, put down her cup and said, "Right, everyone, let's make a start. Addy, I believe you're first." The presentation had been well received and Grant had been true to his word and not told a soul about their night together. So how did Lyn know and why was she raising it now?

It doesn't matter! Deny! Obfuscate!

Addy deliberately looked down at her pale green silk blouse, which she noticed hung far more loosely over her breasts than it used to, then took in her tailored pants with knife pleats. She raised her head and gave Lyn what she hoped was a cool and disinterested glance.

"Neither of those things happened in Hobart. And today I'm not wearing crushed clothes nor am I late so I've no idea what you're talking about."

"It's the bird's-nest hair," Lyn said, snark infusing every word.

"Wherever you woke up this morning, it was a long way from your hairdryer."

The double standard invoked by a woman made Addy's head spin.

If a male faculty member turned up with wet hair and in clothes that resembled gardening clothes more than work attire, no one blinked, let alone commented or implied that they'd slept elsewhere.

Addy forced a laugh out of a tight throat and touched the damp tips of her hair, striving for nonchalance. "This is post-surf hair. It was so glorious this morning, I stayed out a bit too long and something had to give in the morning routine. I just popped in to pick up the exam papers and see if you'd had time to process the expenses I submitted?"

"I can't approve them," Lyn said.

Really? "But they're identical to the receipts you've reimbursed me for all semester."

Lyn shrugged. "Things change."

"Without notice?" When Lyn didn't offer an explanation, Addy said, "I'll talk to Grant."

Lyn smirked. "You do that."

"Morning, ladies." Bettina walked into the office and gave Addy a beautician's critical head-to-toe sweep. "What on earth didn't you do to your hair?"

"I went for a surf this morning—"

"That's code for Addy tying one on last night," Lyn said.

"No, it's not!"

"Ohh, do tell," Bettina said eagerly.

"As if," Lyn said. "Addy's far too lah-de-dah to tell us anything."

"That's not—"Addy started.

"Actually, we're all a bit hurt you never come to Thursday-night drinks," Bettina said.

Tell them you're no longer drinking.

No. So not a safe crowd.

"It's nothing personal." Addy shrugged, aiming for a "what can I do" gesture. "I teach on Thursday nights. Bettina, I was wondering if I could—"

The woman's phone rang and Addy mouthed "Talk later" and left the office, having no desire to be alone with Lyn. Exam week might be when the faculty took a breather, but considering the difficult faculty meeting, Jodi telling her to chill and this most recent incident, it seemed it was also the week they all went a bit feral.

She was halfway to her office when her cell phone rang and she was surprised to see Jett's name on the screen. Her stomach sank. She had no desire to talk to him, especially after what he'd said on Monday.

"Hi, Jett."

"Hey, Ad-dy." He elongated her name in a sardonic tone.

She waited for him to say something else and when he didn't, she said with boss-like crispness, "What can I do for you?"

"A blow job would be good."

Her entire body tingled with shock. "The ... that's ..." She scrambled for composure. "That's an incredibly inappropriate comment."

"Nah. It's perfect for a bossy slut like you."

The words broke her protective reserve. "You not only took that photo, you posted it onto Instagram, didn't you?"

"I don't know what you're talking about." But the glee in his voice was undeniable.

"You'll understand perfectly when you've completed the sexual harassment training."

There was a short pause. "Yeah, about that ... I've looked at all the dates and none of them work for me."

Her hand tightened on her phone. "This isn't an opt-out situation, Jett. Your employment will be on the line if you don't undertake the training."

A shot of perverse pleasure darted through her. Jett hated being mandated to do anything.

"I doubt that," he said.

"I don't. When you add the attrition rate of female students to my complaint about the photo, your department's screaming for an external review. When that happens, there's nowhere to hide."

"Go fuck yourself, Addy. Better yet, come down here and I'll do it for you. You know you want it."

The line went dead. Addy was shaking so hard she almost dropped the phone.

Forcing some tension into her unsteady legs, she made it back to her office, closed the door behind her, locked it and sank to the floor.

He's not going to rape you in the office.

But Jett's threatening words boomed in her head, gaining volume.

She crawled to her desk and scrambled through the drawer looking for chocolate. Her trembling fingers finally located a small block at the back. She shoved it in her mouth and focused intently on its thick creaminess, its sweet taste and how it coated her mouth and tongue.

The noise in her head reduced from a loud roar to a constant hum. She was desperate to be outside and walking in the fresh air. To center all of her attention on the shape of the leaves on the trees, the wind scudding clouds across the sky and the butcherbird's melodic song until calm came to her and restored her equilibrium. But she was stuck inside with an exam to supervise.

A shot will steady you. Just one. It's medicinal. Grant has whisky in his office, remember.

She did remember. She pushed to her feet and dusted floor lint from her pants. Grabbing her make-up bag, she uncapped her lipstick and looked in the mirror. A riot of spiral curls framed her face—her hair's natural state and one she hadn't allowed in a very long time.

Your face is thinner.

She leaned back, then forward, rechecking her reflection, not fully recognizing herself. Her face, which had been puffy for months, was now shaped by the high planes of her cheekbones. Her eyes, so often lined with tiny red capillaries, were as clear as her skin, which was no longer blotchy. Despite the surge of anxiety racing her heart so it pumped unease all over her, she looked well and rested. She hadn't looked like this in a very long time.

Her reflection reassured her. *Short-term relief equals long-term disaster. Grant's whisky is not just a bad idea, it's not required.*

"But I need to tell Grant what happened," she said out loud.

And she would, as soon as the exam was over.

When the exam finished, Addy got caught up with a conscientious pre-college student who'd convinced herself she'd failed, which was unlikely. Finally, after ushering a calmer Aimee out the door, she picked up the exam booklets. She planned to lock them in her office, then find Grant.

Balancing the booklets along with her travel mug, phone and keys, she opened the door and gasped. "Rylie!"

The travel mug slid sideways and Rylie caught it. He stayed standing in the doorway, holding onto the cup, his breadth and height filling the space.

Over the semester, Rylie's work ethic had continued to blow hot and cold—he did really well in the topics that interested him and poorly in the rest. They'd fallen into a routine of him complaining that the system was holding him back and Addy offering him the chance to meet with the student welfare officer. He always refused, saying he preferred to talk to Addy, but she wasn't a counselor, nor did she want to be, so she made sure their conversations stayed focused on course content.

But for all the times Rylie had stayed back after class, he'd never once stood in the doorway as he was now, without any sign of stepping back to let her pass or entering the room to chat. Something about the set of his mouth—a definite smirk—and the way he continued to hold her cup disconcerted her.

"What can I do for you, Rylie?" she asked.

The words echoed in her head, immediately followed by Jett's reply to the same question. Her hands tightened around the exam booklets.

Rylie jutted his chin. "You failed my last essay."

"To be fair, you failed your last essay," she said evenly. "I've seen much better work from you this semester."

He flattened his palms against the architrave. "Yeah, well, I was busy. I needed more time."

"You could have applied for an extension."

"Like I said, I was busy." He took a step into her personal space, towering over her. "I have to pass this exam, Addy," he said, his breath hot on her face. "You understand that, right?"

She instinctively took a protective step back. "You'll know the results by Monday."

"Working hard all weekend, are you?"

He asked the question conversationally without any hint of the intimidation Addy thought she'd heard before. She gave herself a mental slap.

"Grading's all part of a teacher's lot," she said.

He nodded and stepped in again. "That's a drag. Especially when you live somewhere as pretty as Rookery Cove."

Her mouth dried. How did he know where she lived? She'd never told her students that information and no one had ever asked. Was he threatening her? The thought cramped her chest so hard she lost air and coughed, while her mind skittered and slid over words, unable to choose which ones to say.

"I was thinking," Rylie added. "I could come down and keep you company while you mark the papers. You know, so I can explain what I meant by my answers."

"That's not necessary. In fact it's—"

"And we could have some fun at the same time. I've heard from the blokes in Automotive that you're fun."

He thumb-tapped his phone's screen and there was the bloody Instagram photo again. He tapped a second time and there was a grainy photo of a woman with a blouse clinging to her like a second skin and holding up a glass. Was it her?

She grabbed for the phone, but Rylie pulled his arm away and tipped her travel mug. Milky brown liquid bloomed across the silk of her blouse and into the lace of her bra, making everything transparent.

He grinned before taking a photo. "Nice. Now I've got two. You'd totally win a wet T-shirt competition, Addy."

Outrage poured through her. "I'm reporting you! You won't just fail, you'll be expelled."

"Yeah, but if you do that, all these photos will end up on the internet."

"That's illegal."

"No revenge-porn laws in Tassie." He leered at her. "But no need to upset yourself. Just give me top grades and I'll delete the photos. Too easy."

Deleting the photos didn't delete the fact that he knew where she lived.

She tried to move past him but he wouldn't budge and the only way to exit was for her body to rub against his. She refused to give him the satisfaction.

"I'm calling campus security."

"Ohh!" Rylie laughed. "You mean Wozza? What is he, seventy?"

"Would you prefer the police?"

Rylie immediately held his arms up and stepped back. "Jeez, Addy. No need to go all dramatic. I'm leaving."

But he didn't walk away.

Addy's heart was beating so hard her chest vibrated. Every part of her screamed, *Risk it. Go now! Leave.*

She was halfway through the door when Rylie stepped in close.

"I might still see you on the weekend though. Have a good one."

CHAPTER THIRTY-SIX

WHEN ADDY LEFT THE MAGISTRATES' court three hours later, she was wrung out. She'd gone to the police station first to ask about getting a restraining order against Rylie, but the desk officer had advised that since there'd only been one incident with no witnesses, the magistrate was unlikely to issue it.

"He might not even know where in the cove you live," the officer had suggested.

"It's not that big a town!"

She'd gone to the court anyway and calmly lodged five copies of the form along with the filing fee while she raged inside. First Jasper had forced her into legal action to reclaim her money and now Rylie. What sort of system was it when the victim had to pay for her own safety?

She called Steph from the court steps. "You will never believe what just happened ..."

"Oh my God, that's awful," Steph said. "Are you okay? I mean, obviously you're not okay. I'm worried this will trigger you."

"Actually, I'm too furious to drink." It was the startling truth.

Anger ran along her veins with the purity of cocaine, making her mind razor sharp and decisive. "Besides, now I have to go and report it all to my boss."

"Will he understand?"

"Oh, yeah. He's one of the good ones. Rylie Kendall is toast." She was about to hang up when she added, "Thanks, Steph. I appreciate having someone to call."

"Me too! Anytime." Monty squealed in the background. "Monty, no! Use your own paints. Sorry, Addy, gotta go."

When Steph hung up, Addy called Grant but she got an auto message about the person being unavailable. She texted instead: *Hi, there's been a couple of incidents. I need to see you urgently to discuss*

Grant's usual prompt reply failed to arrive and she was driving into the work parking lot when her cell phone finally beeped. *Can see you at 6*

She stared at the text. 6:00? That was two hours away. Every other time she'd had a problem, Grant had made himself instantly available. Was he tied up in meetings? Even if he was, meetings would finish by 5:00.

She checked the team's app—no meetings—and Skype listed him as "in his office and available." She supposed he could have gotten caught up and not thought to change his status.

Ask Lyn.

But Lyn's reference to Hobart this morning and her aggressive stance on the reimbursements had raised red flags—she wouldn't offer to help.

If Addy had thought the start of the week had been strange, it had nothing on the nightmare of today. She tried channeling the freedom she'd experienced that morning in the surf, but it seemed like a lifetime ago.

Back in her office, she attempted grading papers but Jett's and Rylie's voices were never far away, stealing her concentration. Needing to stay calm so anxiety didn't pop the lid on her craving for alcohol, she signed herself out and went for a walk in the reserve, soaking in the scent of eucalyptus, the calming mist from the waterfall and the lyrical birdsong of the currawongs. By the time she returned, the parking lot was virtually empty and the campus quiet.

She collected her thoughts so she could tell Grant coolly and concisely what had happened with Jett and Rylie. When she was happy with the order of events, she walked to his office.

He was on the phone and waved her to a chair that was covered in boxes. She pulled at the first box, trying to slide her fingers under the edges. She could barely move it enough to allow for that, let alone lift it. After two attempts she gave up, not wanting to risk her back. Grant would move them when he was off the phone.

She stood waiting, feeling uncomfortable that she was hearing one side of a conversation, so she walked to the window. It was almost dark and she could see the receding lights of a ship as it headed north.

She heard Grant saying goodbye and she turned back from the window, expecting him to rise and move the boxes for her. He remained seated.

He tilted his head and studied her. "What's that look all about?"

She indicated the laden chair and said wryly, "I just got a flashback to high school and being made to stand in front of the principal."

He shook his head slowly. "Addy, Addy, Addy. What are we going to do with you?"

His supercilious tone was unexpected and for the first time Addy felt distinctly uncomfortable.

"I need to sit down and fill you in on what happened today," she said.

Grant leaned forward, but didn't rise. Instead he tapped his keyboard and the printer whirred into life. He picked up the A4 sheet and pushed it toward her. "I need to talk to you about this."

Addy read the name at the top of the email and her gut cramped.

"This is from Rylie Kendall?"

"Yes. He's making some very serious accusations."

"What?" She scanned the email and strong pressure built behind her eyes so quickly she thought her head might explode.

Grant steepled his fingers. "He says you've singled him out all semester. That you ask him to stay back after class after everyone's left, and you failed his essay because he refused to go out with you."

The rage started in the soles of her feet before burning through her with the speed of a wildfire. "It's all lies! Time and time again he sought me out after class, not the other way around. And I failed his essay because it was three paragraphs of nonsense. I can show it to you."

Grant's gaze locked with hers. Unlike previous times, there were no signs of sympathy or understanding in their depths. Addy's discomfort ratcheted up to unease.

"Did you threaten to fail Rylie in the exam?" he asked.

"No!" The word exploded out of her on a wave of incredulous indignation. "He threatened me! He returned to the exam room after everyone had left and stood in the doorway preventing me from leaving and—" she tapped the brown stain on her chest, "—poured coffee on me. I've spent the afternoon at the police station and the court applying for a restraining order."

"Jesus, Addy." Grant's hands slapped the desk. "You went to the police before telling me?"

"Sorry." The apology slipped out before she thought to stop it.

"I wasn't thinking straight. I was so rattled about him saying he'd come to my house. I just wanted to feel safe."

"Well, it's a pretty provocative move after his accusations," Grant said. "You do realize you've put me in an impossible position."

The floor under her feet shifted like sand and she swayed, fighting for balance. She'd expected understanding, not blame. From day one Grant had always been supportive of her, a cheerleader—hadn't he?

"As head of campus, it's impossible for me to publicly support a faculty member who's used her position of authority to intimidate and bully a student."

His words rained down on her, making it hard to breathe.

"Rylie's lying! We have proof he's been difficult since day one, and you know me better than you know him. You know I wouldn't threaten a student."

His mouth pulled down, giving him a sad look. "You've had issues with some of the faculty."

"What issues?" She had no idea what he was talking about.

"Accusing Jett of posting that photo could be construed as bullying. And to be honest, you've hardly gone out of your way to be friendly with the team. That sort of thing's important."

Incredulity buffeted her. "You told me to steer clear of them! You said it would make my 2IC job more difficult."

"I think you've done that all on your own. Anyway, the job's a moot point now. Even before this complaint, Heather and Scott had concerns about your drinking."

Addy stilled, intently wary. "Why would they have that sort of concern?"

"Come on, Addy." Grant shook his head wearily. "You know you turned up late and hungover for your presentation in Hobart."

"My presentation was perfect and other campuses are using the plan. I still get compliments about it. Hell, you led the applause."

He shrugged. "I'm not Heather and Scott. But it's not just Hobart. A cleaner put in a report about finding empty alcohol cans in your office. That was the straw that broke their support of you. Now with Rylie's accusations ..."

Addy's mind spun on his words, seeking clarity, but none offered any insight. Why would the interview committee be privy to a cleaner's report from this campus? She scanned her memories of the times she'd drunk in her office and came up with just one occasion. The Instagram incident when Grant had brought her the bottle of whisky. But she'd returned the bottle before she'd left for the day.

Grant drank cider in your office two weeks ago.

"They were your cans, not mine! You have to tell them that."

Addy hated the desperation in her voice.

"I doubt it will make any difference," he said gravely.

"Why not?"

"Because your probation's almost up and they won't renew your contract."

"But ..." Her thoughts jumbled and words struggled to come.

"But isn't that your decision? From the start you've said the probation's a standard clause. That the 2IC job is a given."

"That was before you fucked up everything."

She flinched at the unfairness of the criticism. "I haven't done anything wrong! And I need this job, Grant. I deserve it. Hell, I've been doing it for months without the pay grade. There's got to be a way out of this nightmare."

He didn't say a word.

"Grant?"

"It's a mess, that's for sure." He sighed and pushed himself to his feet, opened a cabinet and pulled out a bottle of whisky. He poured two glasses and carried them around the desk until he was standing next to her. "Here."

Every part of her tensed. "No, thank you."

"Addy." He tilted his head and gave her the sort of indulgent look a parent gives a tired toddler. "You know it takes the edge off and makes it easier to think. And God knows, we need some out-of-the-box thinking to get you out of this mess with your reputation intact."

She eyed the deep tawny fluid, but instead of experiencing a rush of anticipation, all she got were warning barbs of suspicion.

"I think far more clearly without alcohol," she said firmly, knowing it was the truth.

"Yeah, right," he scoffed. "Look where being sober's gotten you."

Memories rose. Grant in her office with the whisky—"Get this into you." Grant at her house with the sloe gin—"I thought you needed cheering up."

The truth hit her with such shocking clarity it was like being horsewhipped. From the first time she'd sought Grant's advice—which ironically had been about Rylie Kendall—he'd offered her a listening ear, understanding and alcohol. The first time hadn't led to sex, but had that been his intention all along? Had he been gaslighting her this whole time and she'd missed every sign because her affair was with the drink, not the man?

"I want to help you, Addy," Grant was saying. "But I can't work with you when you're irrational and difficult like this." He stepped in close, his body skimming hers. "No one can, but there's an easy solution."

Don't turn into a sober bore.

Her mind lit up like a stage. "Oh my God! Are you saying you'll only help me if I get drunk with you?"

He smiled. "Why sound so horrified? It's not like it hasn't happened before."

She pulled at her hair. "Yes, but both times it had absolutely nothing to do with work!"

He gave her a look that said he disagreed. "And we had a great thing going in and out of work until you made a very stupid decision to stop drinking. You're such a slut when you're drunk, Addy. You'll do anything and I mean *anything*."

Self-loathing washed into every part of her like a river in flood. Silver spots swam in front of her eyes and her head spun so fast she could feel herself being pulled into its familiar vortex. The past confirmed her stupidity: *You're not fifteen anymore. You deserve all of this.*

Her legs softened and more than anything she wanted to follow them to the floor and curl up and rock. As she started to succumb to the inky depths of ignominy, her hard-fought sobriety suddenly brought its accompanying lucidity. The truth screened in her head in a series of vignettes. Grant's insistence she start the audit work before the job was official. His confidential chats about the other staff. His reasons for not letting Ravi help her. So many little things she'd been blind to. He'd danced her on a string like a puppeteer, controlling her, and she'd been too consumed by her love affair with alcohol to recognize it. But now everything was crystal clear.

Rage poured through her, trumping shame. "There was never a 2IC job, was there?" she said.

Grant sighed as if she was being obtuse. "Of course there's a job. God, you've seen the job description on the portal and I hired you because you appeared perfect for the position. We're alike you and me, and we work well together." He grimaced. "Well, we did until recently."

The events of the past week that had seemed so random and disconnected suddenly snapped together like pieces of a puzzle.

"Oh my God! When I refused to have sex with you in my office, you told Lyn I'd gotten drunk in Hobart and disgraced myself, because you knew she'd tell everyone. You've never had any intention of running the sexual harassment training, have you? God, you and Jett must have laughed about that, or did you put him up to taking the photo so I'd run to you for help?"

Grant snorted. "Come off it, Addy. Now you're just being paranoid."

"No. I'm perfectly lucid." Her breath was coming as fast as if she'd sprinted. "Now I can see you've stage-managed everything. You ate and drank with me under a guise of friendship and loaded me with so much work I barely had time to sleep let alone make other friends. And you actively discouraged me from getting to know anyone so if I needed help, I came to you."

She gasped as the memory of Rylie telling her to have a good weekend boomed in her head. "Oh my God! You gave Rylie Kendall my address."

Grant's face was granite. "If you think I orchestrated a student to make a sexual harassment complaint about you then you've totally lost the plot and you need help."

"I wouldn't put it past you!"

His mouth twisted. "Acting the innocent doesn't suit you, Addy. You knew right from the start what you had to do to secure my support and protection, and then you stopped playing the game."

"Game?" Her arms flew into the air. "I didn't know it was a game!"

"Game's the wrong word. It's more along the lines of mutual support. Anyway, the way I see it, you have two choices. Leave here in disgrace with allegations of sexual harassment and bullying hanging over your head. Or you can trust me to sort everything out for you so no mud sticks."

The strings he'd been pulling for months jerked tight. He'd stitched her up from every angle—no allies, the gossip about her drinking, the whole Instagram photo set-up and now an official student complaint. Even if she proved her innocence, which would take time and money, she'd be considered a troublemaker. Her career on the island was toast. Possibly interstate too.

She forced herself to ask, "And exactly what do you need from me in the way of support?"

"Don't look so worried. It's no big deal." He ran his finger softly down her cheek. "I just want fun and fuckable Addy back."

She stepped back as her stomach lurched, splashing acid up to burn the back of her throat. The past screamed in her head.

Addy, I'm the only one who understands just how tough things are for you at home, especially with your mother. Your parents mean well, but they can't help you like I can. This is our secret. Trust me. I know how to make you shine.

Suddenly, this was no longer just about her job and her reputation. This was about her moral right to live her life her way. If she agreed to Grant's request of sex in exchange for her job she'd spiral into that dark, dark place she'd visited on and off for too many years. Only this time it wouldn't be a visit, it would be permanent with no way out. This time it would kill her.

"The thing is, Grant, *that* Addy's gone and she's never coming back." She walked to the door.

"If you go, prepare to be slut-shamed out there in the big wide world."

She raised the middle finger of her left hand. "Working here's given me plenty of practice dealing with misogynists."

"Just think this little feminist tantrum through," Grant said calmly. "You're out of a job and unlikely to get another, and you know you live to work. That alone will have you drinking within the hour. If you stay and play, you keep your job. Walking away from me will be your biggest and most stupid mistake yet."

"No," she ground out. "My biggest and most stupid mistake would be staying."

Living sober and in the light was hard. And if today had taught her anything, it was about to get a lot harder. If she was to survive and thrive, she'd have to face her past head-on. Getting help to deal with that had to be better than drowning in shame and degradation. Didn't it?

Only she couldn't answer the question with any degree of certainty.

CHAPTER THIRTY-SEVEN

STEPH'S MORNING was rolling out in its usual disrupted way. Zoe was home from school, supposedly sick. Steph was willing to risk money there was nothing wrong with the girl and she just wanted a day off so she could stay in bed and watch TikTok videos.

"Henry, she needs to go to school."

"She's complaining of a stomach-ache. What if she's getting her first period?"

"You bought her period pants and pads so she's got what she needs. We are not setting up an expectation that she gets a day off school every month!"

"We're not. I'll make her some of Mama's immune-boosting soup so she'll be good for school tomorrow," Henry said.

"Ring the school then so we don't get another 'where is she?' call."

Zoe had skipped school for a few hours last week and refused to say where she'd been. Now she was on an attendance contract, which was yet another issue to deal with. The last thing Steph needed was Zoe being kicked out of school.

"And make her do some homework too," she said, struggling to get

Monty out the door to childcare while she was mentally checking she had her keys, phone and wallet.

Henry had his head in the pantry. "Can you grab some shiitake mushrooms on your way home?"

"Sure, why not! Anything else you need?"

Henry smiled, once again missing her sarcasm. He handed her the shopping list she'd expected him to take care of on his way home from Devonport later in the day. "Remember to take the reusable bags."

Resentment rose so fast she needed to clamp her mouth shut so she didn't start an argument she didn't have time for. To be honest, these days she was often beyond arguing with Henry—it changed nothing. Instead, she nursed her discontent and hustled Monty out the door.

When she returned from her errands, Alan was in the kitchen, clutching a mug of tea as if it was his only source of heat. Steph took it as a major breakthrough that he'd come inside at all.

He put down the mug and gave her a worried glance as he helped her with the shopping bags. "I st-started at 8:00."

She smiled at him, hating the way he always looked as if he was anticipating criticism. "You're doing better than me then. You've been running the heater, right?"

He shook his head.

"Alan, cold hands make mistakes. Turn it on, please."

"Okay."

"Any job nibbles?"

"Nah." He hauled his gaze from the floor. "S-saw the k-kids on the w-weekend. They l-loved the c-circus people. Thank you."

"That's great news on both fronts." Steph was treading a fine line with the Brianna situation—trying to show an interest in the children without intruding on his marriage breakdown. "Are you seeing them again soon?"

"Saturday."

"Oh, Alan, that's great."

"Yeah." His mouth curved into a quiet smile. "B-Bri's trying to be f-fair. This job's h-helped heaps. Thanks."

Steph wished Joanna understood about "fair." "Believe me, Al, you're a vital part of keeping this fledgling business afloat."

He grinned then and his face lost ten years and its haunted look.

"Win-win then."

Steph didn't miss that the stutter had gone too. A warm glow rippled through her and she knew she needed to add something else to her business plan. Retro Toys wasn't just about giving kids joy, assuaging parents' concerns about plastic and generating income. Perhaps it could also be about helping people get a foot back into the job market and finding their self-esteem along the way.

Henry walked in and frowned. "Oh, hi, Alan. Didn't realize you were here today."

Alan rinsed his mug. "I b-better get b-back."

"Henry's making soup for lunch if you want a bowl," Steph said, trying to take the sting out of Henry's unfriendly remark.

Alan nodded and disappeared out the back door.

"The soup's for Zoe," Henry said. "And I'm not keen about Alan just letting himself in, especially with Zoe home. I mean, we don't know anything about him."

"He's a bloke who's had his confidence kicked out of him." Steph slammed the kettle onto its base. "He's also a reliable employee who's doing me a favor by working part time."

"Can't you buy him a kettle and put tea and coffee and cookies in the shed?"

"No! God, Henry, would you do that to the people you work with?"

"They have a break room."

"And when I get to the point of having a factory, my employees will have a break room too. Until then it's the kitchen."

"Employees plural?" Henry blinked at her. "Are you hiring more people?"

"Down the track. Maybe sooner if this volume of orders stays constant."

"But I thought the plan was for a small kitchen-table business so you can work around the kids."

The ache for her lost baby stirred and immediately tangled with Henry's attitude that the wooden toys were more of a hobby than a serious business. "Some very successful companies started out on a kitchen table."

"And they had a business plan," he said quietly, but the criticism was loud.

"I have a business plan." *It's just you've never asked about it.* "Most wooden toys are made in China, but I've found a niche in the market for toys made in Australia from locally sourced products. Parents want a guarantee of non-toxic and safe, and they'll pay a premium for it. My next step is themed children's party plans."

Bewilderment played across his face. "But what about getting pregnant?"

"What about it?" The anger that was never far from the surface these days flared. "You're the one delaying IVF!"

"I'm the one being sensible."

"Sensible?" Every part of her body tensed. "You're the one who turned our lives upside down by moving here."

Henry threw out his arms. "You wanted to come!"

"Nothing about this is the life I agreed to!"

He blew out a long breath. "I know losing the baby's been hard, but the last thing we need is to add more stress to our lives by going into debt to have a baby. And then there's the drugs. I haven't read one positive thing on any of the forums about them. It sounds like they're going to string you out even more than being on clomiphene. And lately you've barely been coping with two kids. Can you really manage three?"

His words bombarded her, ramping up her anger to the point where she wanted to hit something hard. Really hard and feel a release.

"You want to reduce my stress?" she bit out, deciding not to deconstruct the mess of issues he'd just raised.

He nodded. "Of course. Last time you got pregnant was when you were relaxed, so to avoid IVF we need to make our lives as stress-free as possible. That's why now's not the best time for you to be expanding the business."

The business was the only thing she had any control over. An icy calm rolled in.

"If you really want to reduce my stress, send Zoe back to Joanna."

His eyes widened as if he'd just been stunned by a blow to the head. "You don't mean that."

I do.

Henry's phone rang. These days he no longer said "Sorry, I have to take this call"; he just turned and walked back to his office.

Steph swore.

"Language," Zoe said, walking into the kitchen with her phone in her hand—these days it was permanently attached to her.

She sat down at the kitchen table, her thumbs moving across the screen as the device buzzed with notifications.

"If you'd gone to school you could be talking to your friends face-to-face," Steph said. "What a concept."

Zoe didn't look up. "All my friends are in Melbourne."

Steph wondered where that left Olivia. The girl was as enthusiastic and positive as Zoe was apathetic and negative.

"You must miss them," she said. "Why don't you talk to your mother about going home to visit them during the vacation?"

"They're all going skiing or to Queensland."

Damn. "Right. Well, if you're well enough to be up and chatting with friends, you can unpack the shopping. I need to paint circus people."

"Why are you pandering to stereotypes?"

A line of tension ran up Steph's spine. "Excuse me? I have both male and female circus people."

"You should do a set of just women," Zoe said. "A doctor, a lawyer, a tradesperson, a footballer, stuff like that. And you should do a gay pride set."

"I can barely keep up with the orders I have." But despite herself, Steph pushed some wooden shapes in front of Zoe, intrigued by her idea. "Paint me a demo set and I'll consider it."

Zoe lifted her head, her gaze combative. "Will you pay me?"

The question uncapped all the resentment she harbored toward the girl. "I feed and clothe you."

"No, you don't!" Zoe's eyes flashed. "I have to make my own food."

"Your father cooks for you using the vegan food I buy for you."

"Everyone else's mothers cook for their kids!"

"But as you point out at least twice a day, I'm not your mother and you don't want me to be." Steph crossed her arms, no longer prepared to play this game. "And talking about Joanna, I want to call her on your phone."

Zoe's eyes narrowed. "Why?"

"So she sees your number, thinks it's you and answers the phone. She's not returning Henry's calls and, unlike your father, I've had enough." She held out her hand for the phone.

Zoe clutched it tightly. "As if."

"I'm not interested in what's on your phone," Steph said. "I just want to talk to Joanna."

"So you can bitch about me? No way." Zoe flounced out of the room.

Steph closed her eyes, breathing deeply until her racing heart slowed. How the hell was she going to get pregnant while the negative force field that was Zoe was in her house?

An hour later, Steph's phone rang. "Addy! Better day today?"

"Hard to know for sure," Addy said. "I quit my job a few days ago."

"Oh my God! Why? Are you okay?" The questions tumbled over each other as Steph's worry ramped up.

"I'm ... it's a long story." Addy sighed. "I was wondering if you could come over for lunch?"

Steph heard the hint of a plea in Addy's voice and almost said "Of course." But a stack of orders needed packing and posting, not to mention the orders requiring thermal printing. Monty was in childcare until 4:00 today and she couldn't squander that precious time.

Henry's comment about how Addy had Steph running to her all the time came back to her. "Why don't you come to Four Winds for lunch?" she said. "That way, I can keep working while we chat."

There was a brief pause and then Addy said, "You sound busy. Don't worry about it."

But quitting a job was a big deal for anyone, let alone someone who was in the early months of sobriety. Steph wanted to see Addy and check she was okay. At the same time, she wanted her friend to accept her hospitality for once.

"Please come. I've wanted to show you the house for ages."

"It's probably best I take a raincheck," Addy said quickly.

Steph's current short fuse sparked. "That makes no sense. You called wanting to do lunch. If you're really determined to be the hostess, then bring the food here."

There was a long silence. "What about a quick picnic in the garden?"

It was about goosebump weather outside, but Steph agreed just to get Addy to Four Winds. She'd overrule the garden idea the moment her friend arrived.

CHAPTER THIRTY-EIGHT

ADDY STOOD at the gate to Four Winds, gripping the handle of Rita's old picnic basket so tightly her hands ached. On either side of the gate, the ancient and gnarly rhododendrons still grew wide and tall, forming a welcome arch. The once dilapidated fence had been replaced with cream pickets and steel gray uprights, but Steph and Henry had replicated the original gate—a ninety-five-degree arc of pickets that looked like a rising sun.

Over the preceding months, Steph had talked long and often about the renovations and Addy tried telling herself that this was a completely different Four Winds from the house she'd last visited. But it didn't help that the massive magnolia with its high buttress roots still dominated one side of the front garden. She caught sight of a white garden chair by the tree and the years vanished in a gut-wrenching whoosh.

It was her first paid performance—a garden society event with people attending not only from the district but as far away as Launceston. Even though Addy would have preferred to perform something more modern, she was excited and smug. While her friends were earning money stacking shelves or cooking burgers, she was earning cash for doing something she loved.

Her parents, so proud and happy, sat in the front row of a sea of white chairs. On a rare good day, Rita was relaxed and wearing a frothy summer dress she'd made for the occasion. Ivan, whose brow was now almost permanently furrowed in worry for his wife, beamed at Addy from under the brim of a Panama hat, his smile full of love and anticipation.

Moments before she was to play, she spontaneously hugged them both, thanking her mother yet again for her perfect garden party frock. She adored its white lace, sheer sleeves and waterfall hemline. Not only was it the most beautiful thing she'd ever worn, she couldn't resist twirling, loving the way the skirt rose and fell like a wave. She'd added a circle of summer roses to her hair to suit the garden setting and the piece—Percy Grainger's light, pretty and wholesome "Country Gardens." Ironic really, after what had happened later in the day.

After her performance, when the applause had died down and people had wandered away to the afternoon-tea tables groaning with cucumber sandwiches and light fluffy scones, her piano teacher had whispered in her ear, "You were brilliant."

She'd studied his face. "Really?"

"Always."

She bit her lip, needing to believe him so she could banish the eviscerating words he'd spoken to her the day before at the final rehearsal. To ease the hurt at his coolness when she'd arrived today.

"Thank you."

He nodded. "I've gotten a present for you."

Excitement skittered in her belly and she looked around eagerly for the gift, scanning the pockets of his tweed jacket for any bulges.

"Where is it?"

He smiled at her, his eyes taking in her garland, the fall of her frock and all the way down to her bare feet. "Patience, my little woodland nymph. I'll give it to you after everyone's left."

Had she known the effect a white lace dress would have on him, she'd have insisted on wearing sackcloth.

A violent shudder ripped through Addy and she pulled her mind away from the past, gripping the gatepost to steady her shaking legs. Why had she thought she'd cope better in the garden instead of inside the house?

But during their phone call, she'd heard the edge in Steph's voice—the change from general disappointment to aggravation. Back in March, it had been easy to refuse Steph's invitations to Four Winds, but not now. Friendship came with responsibilities, and sober Addy wanted to be a good friend. She owed Steph that and she hoped she could pull it off without falling apart. The last thing she wanted was to taint Steph's love of her home.

Hell, she didn't want to be tagged as the difficult friend with *all* the problems. The basket-case. She just wanted to be happy and healthy. Normal—whatever the hell that was.

The counselor she was seeing had suggested she try visiting Four Winds when she felt better. "You're in a much stronger place now."

Addy wondered if the woman was clueless. "I just lost my job."

"No, you quit your job. That's an important distinction. You quit because you were sober and able to recognize the abuse. Based on how you've lived your life for years, this is a massive breakthrough, Addy. Be proud of yourself."

Now Addy closed her eyes and breathed deeply. "I can do this," she said out loud.

"It's a s-simple l-latch."

Her eyes flew open and a man she didn't know stood next to the now open gate. "Oh!" She laughed nervously. "Thank you."

"S-sorry to s-startle you." He stretched out his hands. "C-can I h-help?"

Surprised and struggling with her roiling emotions, Addy automatically parted with the basket. The moment it left her hands she realized her mistake. The man immediately turned and his long-legged stride took him quickly to the sandstone steps, where he didn't pause.

He bounded up them two at a time, crossed the veranda and opened the front door.

She had no choice but to follow.

"Addy!" Steph waved from the end of the hall. "Come in. You too, Alan."

Alan walked away from her toward the kitchen, but Addy's feet seemed nailed to the hall floorboards. The first thing that struck her was the light. Despite the winter's day it spilled into the hall, casting its glow everywhere, vanquishing all the dark corners she'd come to fear.

Steph reached her at the front door and hugged her. "You okay? You look a bit stunned."

Addy forced a smile. "I'm fine. I just got a surprise at all this light."

"Oh, of course! You would have learned music here." Steph grabbed the high handle on the living-room door. "You won't recognize the—"

"Don't!" It came out soft and strangled, barely forced past a tight throat.

But Steph had already opened the door. "Ta-dah!"

For a moment Addy heard Beethoven's *Sonata in G* and flinched.

Listen! What can you really hear?

She forced herself to stay in the present and heard the trilling song of a gray shrike-thrush.

"Addy? What do you think?" Steph's face was lit with the expectation of a positive response.

Addy stayed where she was, swallowed hard, and dragged her gaze into the room. Cream walls were hung with beautiful artwork. Pretty cushions lay scattered on the sofa and the chairs, bringing the garden into the room. The Arts and Crafts bay window with its tapestry bolster had been liberated from heavy curtains. All in all the room was unrecognizable, but even so she blinked a few times just to check.

"There's no piano," she said finally.

Steph laughed. "If Monty shows any interest we might get one. I was tempted to hang curtains over the bay so he can have an indoor playhouse."

"No!" Addy realized she'd spoken far too loudly and covered with, "You don't want to hide that beautiful window."

"That's what Henry said. We can picnic in here if you like. It's warmer than the garden."

Addy shook her head. "Let's not make a mess." It was one thing to understand that the renovation had repurposed this room, but it didn't mean she needed to spend any time in it. "Besides, I was thinking I could help with your packaging and that's in the kitchen, right?"

"Really?" Steph asked, already hurrying out of the room. "That would be great."

Addy paused for a moment, alone in the room, and stared it down. Although the memories of all that had happened here would never fully leave her, she was no longer hostage to them. No longer trying to drink them away.

Now, just like in Grant's office, instead of being doused in shame, humiliation and embarrassment to the point of needing to numb herself with alcohol, she only felt rage. Molten fury streaked through her on behalf of her younger self—a girl who should have been safe here to pursue her dreams of a life filled with music. Instead, her dreams had been stolen from her and from her parents. Addy had run from here and the cove, thinking she had no other choice. She'd been running for a very long time.

Thankfully she'd stopped now and she was reclaiming her life. Sobriety had made way for the truth to be heard. For the first time, she knew in her head and in her heart that she'd never done anything wrong in this house. It was him. All him.

"Denton, I hope you're being tormented in hell, you manipulative, sick bastard." She gave him the bird before firmly shutting the door behind her.

Taking a restorative breath, Addy walked into the kitchen. Neither Alan nor Steph was there, but Zoe was standing at the stove stirring the contents of a glossy red soup pot.

Addy smiled at her. "Hey, Zoe. Nice to see you."

The girl's eyes narrowed like a cat's and her antagonism whipped out, circling Addy like a lasso. Addy remembered doing exactly the same thing when she was a few years older than Zoe—closing out any extraneous images to fully check if the person was being sincere or lying to get what they wanted. Keeping herself safe—or at least attempting to. A shiver ran up her spine. Did Zoe feel unsafe?

"That smells great," Addy said. "What's in it?"

Zoe shrugged. "Dunno. Dad made it. There's some sort of Chinese mushroom and stuff. It's my Yin Yin's recipe and it's supposed to warm my yang."

"I'm guessing that's good?"

Zoe shrugged again. "I really like your hair. I wish I had curls."

"And I've straightened my hair for years, thinking people would take me more seriously, but ..." Addy gave Zoe a similar shrug.

Since she'd quit her job, she'd also quit using her hair straightener.

"Now I have more time in my day to do the fun stuff, like surfing. Have you been out lately?"

Zoe's cell phone buzzed and her gaze slid from Addy to the screen. Her pretty face twisted and she blinked rapidly before shoving the phone in her pocket.

Addy got an overwhelming desire to ask her if she was okay, but before she could Steph returned.

"Alan wouldn't stay for lunch," she said, explaining her absence.

She picked two plates off the counter—one filled with salad and the other with a section of the long baguette Addy had made—and handed them to Zoe. "On your way back to bed, take the baguette to your father."

Zoe continued stirring. "I'm having soup."

"Then serve yourself a bowl and take it with you." Steph opened a drawer and picked up a bowl. "Addy needs to talk to me."

Addy was sure the kitchen had been designed to be the heartbeat of the house—warm, nurturing and inclusive—but right now it was anything but. Tension hung so thick and heavy it suffocated any goodwill. She remembered her own adolescence—confusion and shame had fused together into something wild and untamed. Rita and

Ivan had been bewildered by the loss of their happy-go-lucky daughter, and Addy had seen a similar look on Henry's face at the beach. But Steph didn't look bewildered by Zoe—she looked grim and implacable.

"I don't mind if—" Addy started, but Steph cut her off.

"Zoe's home today because she says she's sick. If she's not well enough to go to school then the rules are she stays in bed."

Something made Addy say, "I'm not working at the moment, Zoe, so when you're feeling better come and surf with me after school if you want."

Zoe flicked her a look that said "whatever" and left the room without a word—and without any food.

Steph scowled at Zoe's retreating back before picking up their lunch and carrying the plates over to the table. Addy poured them each a glass of sparkling water, added a slice of lemon and joined her at the end of the table that was free of puzzle stock and Australia Post bags.

"And now you know why I don't want Zoe at choir," Steph said. "I get enough of her bratty behavior at home." She bit into her baguette as if she was biting Zoe.

"Is she happy at school?" Addy asked.

"She's not happy anywhere," Steph said.

"Do you know why?"

"Because she's Zoe and her goal in life is to make mine difficult."

Addy fiddled with some green salad that protruded from the bread, trying to work out what she wanted to say.

"When I was fifteen, I went from happy to horrible and no one ever asked me why. They just jumped through hoops trying to make me happy."

"Well, I've given up even trying that with Zoe," Steph said briskly.

"Anyway, you didn't come over to talk about Henry's obstreperous daughter."

Addy bit her lip. She wasn't a parent and she'd never been a step-parent—her relationships with men may have been messy but a semblance of self-preservation had prevailed. On some level, she'd known she could barely take care of herself, let alone risk a child's mental health. As wearing as Zoe's behavior must be for Steph, her heart ached for the girl.

Addy took a close look at her friend. Fine lines creased around Steph's eyes and dark shadows inked the soft skin beneath them. Everything about her radiated unhappiness and resigned acceptance. Suddenly, the mess that was Grant and work, and whether Addy should risk everything and file a report against him or just walk away, took a back seat.

"You're looking down. Do you want to talk about it? I'm happy to listen."

Steph's gaze drifted to the workstation she'd set up and a long sigh shuddered out of her. "When Henry and I arrived in the cove we were so excited about our new life here. Fresh air, a chance for me to start my own business, no commuting, more time to be involved in the community ..."

"You're in choir," Addy said.

"And Henry's surfing, in the band and working as many hours as he was in Melbourne! He says he's supportive of me starting the business, but his job takes precedence every time. Plus we're supposed to be doing fifty-fifty parenting and domestic stuff, but it's more like eighty-twenty. When Monty's sick, I'm the one who has to drop everything. God, even with Zoe, I end up being pulled in.

"He promised me that once we got reliable internet everything would change. It hasn't," Steph said bitterly. "He's working even more. And when I try and point out how our lives are so far removed from what we committed to on that life-changing day on the beach, he asks me what he can do to help! Once I almost hit him with the whiteboard planner! He isn't supposed to help! He's supposed to do!

"But when I say that, he gets this hurt look on his face as if I'm the one being unreasonable. He blames the fertility drugs I'm taking and my grief about the miscarriage, but if neither of those things had happened, I'd still be pissed. It would still be unfair. It's like his time is finite and mine's infinite. I work too, but on top of that I'm carrying the mental load for everyone in this house. How did I become the default?" Her voice cracked. "I love him, Addy, I do, but lately I'm starting to hate him and that terrifies me."

Steph's frustration and grief rolled over Addy like a slow swell. She reached out and squeezed Steph's hand. "It sounds tough."

Steph gave a long and noisy sniff. "I just want him to value my work and my time as much as he values his."

Addy gave a wry smile. "I can't offer you any relationship advice. It turns out all my love affairs were actually with the bottle not the bloke, making me utterly blind to my poor choices in men. But I do have other skills and I'm a big one for quantitative data. Numbers don't lie and there's no emotion in data."

Steph wiped her eyes. "What do you mean?'

"Instead of telling Henry all the things you do in your day and have him competing with you about all the things he does so you both end up in a who's-the-busiest-person competition, show him what you do."

"For that to happen he'd have to shadow me all day and even that's not all I do. He can't see inside my head," Steph said.

Addy reached for the laptop on the table. "May I?"

"Sure." Steph rose and came around to sit next to her.

Addy opened Excel and created a document— *Stuff Steph Does*.

"Let's make a tab for everything you do, from the big and obvious things like arranging childcare and picking up kids, to the invisible stuff that you probably don't even think about."

"Like what?"

Addy thought about their walks together and how Steph, without pausing in conversation, would sunscreen Monty and jam a hat on his head. "If you and Henry are out, do you both make sure Monty's sun-protected?"

"Either I sunscreen him or I ask Henry to ... Oh! I get it." Steph groaned. "What do we put sunscreen under?"

"What about healthcare slash medical?"

Steph laughed. "Put administering Monty's asthma meds in there too, along with making sure the sports icepack is always in the freezer and ready to go if someone injures themselves."

Addy smiled. "Now you're getting the hang of it. I reckon you'll end up thinking of at least two new tabs or more every day. Don't tell Henry about it until you've done it long enough to get the full picture. Probably at least a month for the everyday stuff. Longer if you factor in everyone's birthdays, vacations and Christmas. When you feel it reflects all your visible and invisible work, email it to him and ask him to read it. I'll take the kids out that day so you can sit down together and discuss it."

Steph hugged her, then burst into tears.

Addy hugged her back. She might not have a job and she had no idea what she was going to do to earn any money, but in this moment, the most important thing was she'd reached a place where she could give back to her friend whose straight talking had started her on the road to recovery. That was gold.

CHAPTER THIRTY-NINE

When Ben had dropped Olivia off after lunch, Brenda had found herself peering beyond him to the truck, seeking the outline of Courtney. The cabin was empty, and she hated the disappointment that had socked her, layering on top of a growing heap.

"Mémé! The tension's all wrong!"

Now, Brenda watched her usually sunny granddaughter throw the practice piece of material onto the table in a display of frustration. The action reminded her that Olivia was a teen and growing up fast.

Brenda picked it up and studied the lines of puckered sewing.

"This silky material's tricky. Do you want me to have a go?"

"I'm supposed to do it on my own," Olivia wailed.

Brenda gave Olivia's shoulder a squeeze. "Everyone needs a bit of help now and then. Besides, this machine and I have been arguing with each other for years and I know its quirks. How about you iron on the interfacing and I'll fix the tension?"

Olivia sighed and switched on the iron. "Where's Marilyn?"

Brenda forced a smile. "She's gone to Hobart for the school vacation."

"I love Hobart," Olivia said dreamily. "Why didn't you go too?"

I wasn't invited.

Since their argument, a frost had entered the house, coating everything with its icy chill and freezing a wide river between her and Marilyn, stranding them on either side. Marilyn slept in the guest room and conversations were limited to domestic tasks and the choir. There'd been some horrifying moments when Brenda thought she'd been thrown back into her marriage, only this was so much worse. She ached for Marilyn's understanding, but the traits she'd always admired so much—a solid sense of self and a strong will—were now causing her the most heartache.

Three days earlier Marilyn had wheeled a suitcase into the kitchen and said, "I'm going to Hobart."

Brenda's heart had leaped into her throat and she'd dropped the bread knife. "Just for the weekend?" she'd made herself ask. *Please.*

Marilyn shook her head. "No."

Fear clenched her gut and she gripped the kitchen counter to stay standing. "How long for?"

"I need a break. I'm spending the vacation down there."

Anger had quickly plundered fear, scattering it far and wide. "So without discussing it with me, you're putting yourself first again and going to Hobart for the entire school vacation? What about the eisteddfod planning meeting? And choir? The choir you insisted on starting!"

Marilyn sighed. "Unlike some people, I value myself and I delegate. I've hardly left you in the lurch. Addy and Kieran are onboard to support you while I'm gone."

"You told Addy and Kieran you were going to Hobart, but you couldn't tell me?" Brenda's voice rose in disbelief.

"Was there a point?" Marilyn asked wearily. "If I'd invited you, would you have come?"

"Invited me? Surely we make vacation decisions together! We *both* have responsibilities in the cove! But only one of us is running from them."

Marilyn's face hardened. "Only one of us is a martyr and living their life to the tune of others."

And there it was. The ever-widening gap between them that was starting to feel unbridgeable. What one of them considered selfish the other considered thoughtless. Had their long-term affair of precious and magical moments snatched out of their real lives masked this difference? Real life was a hell of a lot more complicated.

Marilyn had texted *Arrived* and Brenda had replied with a thumbs-up emoji, but neither of them had made contact since. The only thing giving her any hope that Marilyn would return was the fact that she hadn't taken all of her clothes and she had a teaching contract to the end of the year. But neither of those things were enough to stop vestiges of old panic from flickering and flaring like a flame in a breeze.

It brought back the anxieties she thought she'd put to bed when Glen died. Once again they circled her like barbed wire, pricking and prodding.

What's wrong with me? Can I only be loved if I please people?

She'd pleased people all her life. She'd honored her marriage vows and stayed with Glen so he didn't suffer the indignity of being the cuckold husband of a lesbian in a small town with a long memory. She'd stayed so the children grew up with two parents and hadn't suffered taunting at school that their mother was a lesbo. More recently, she'd given in to Marilyn's pressure to come out so Marilyn could live the life she wanted in the cove and she'd lost Courtney in the process.

Did you ever have Courtney?

She wanted to believe that in the last couple of years they'd become closer, but if that were true—and she wasn't convinced it was—they were estranged now. Courtney refused to answer the phone or return voicemails, texts or emails. But Brenda valiantly continued, mixing up the order of communication styles, but sending similar content on all four mediums. It was exhausting.

She pulled her mind back to the task and to Olivia, trying to jolly herself along. "If I'd gone to Hobart with Marilyn, I wouldn't have been able to help you."

Olivia frowned. "But I could have come another time."

"When exactly? You're going to Queensland next week."

"Yeah, but I feel bad you stayed home for me," she said.

Brenda felt tears stinging the backs of her eyes and quickly twiddled the tension dials on the old sewing machine. "It's not a hardship, darling. I love spending time with you. Besides, I need to be here for choir and the eisteddfod meeting."

And Courtney.

Only one of us is a martyr.

Brenda suddenly realized that Olivia was studying her. "What?"

"I don't get why Mum says you're being selfish when you gave up a vacation in Hobart for me."

Brenda mustered a wan smile. "Your mum thinks I've been selfish for a long time. In some ways she's right. When she was growing up I was often distracted by ... by other things."

"You mean Marilyn?"

Brenda startled at Olivia's directness. "Marilyn was only part of it. For a long time, I wasn't very happy."

Olivia nodded as if she understood perfectly. "We got told at school that if you're gay, you're more likely to have depression and anxiety." She wrapped her arms around Brenda. "I'm sorry you were sad, Mémé, but it's so great you're not sad anymore."

"Thank you, darling." Brenda hugged her back, amazed by her granddaughter's easy acceptance and understanding. "But I'm very sad your mum won't talk to me."

Olivia pulled a face. "I keep telling her she needs to chill and not just about you, but about *everything*. She stresses about the dumbest stuff. She's in my face *all* the time about what's happening at school. She wants me to be friends with the girls from netball. OMG, she even invited two of them for a sleepover without asking me! Can you believe it? I had to be nice to them and they're never nice. Mum might be peeved off with you because you were ... what did you say?"

"Distracted?" Brenda said.

"Yeah, that, but I'd literally kill for distracted! She has to know *everything*."

"She loves you." But even as Brenda said the words she knew that love wasn't always enough. Her love had never been enough for Courtney. "Let's focus on the good things. She's still coming to choir."

"Yeah." Olivia looked thoughtful. "But I don't get that either. She rants about you and Zoe the whole way there and back. I used to fight her about having to sit in the back of the car 'cos I'm not a kid, but not anymore. I use my earbuds so I don't have to listen to her."

Oh, Courtney, can't you see what you're doing?

"Your mum's never been one to bottle things up," Brenda said wryly. "Counselors say that's healthy."

"Maybe," Olivia mused. "When Mum invited Gemma and Mia to stay, I went to the greenhouses and screamed. Dad told me to go to the hay-shed so I didn't upset the berries."

Brenda tried not to laugh. "The fact she's letting you visit gives me hope."

Olivia's face twisted. "Mémé, I'm only here 'cos of Dad. He told Mum it wasn't fair that she'd made him and me and Jesse part of her fight with you. I've never seen him get so mad with her before. I even felt sorry for her."

Was Ben her ally? Brenda had never understood Ben and Courtney's relationship, but then again, no one could ever tell what went on behind closed doors. Her own marriage had been a perfect case in point. From the outside looking in, Ben appeared to follow Courtney's lead on most things, yet Courtney did the farm accounts and had learned how to make jam to support his plans for the store. Was that proof Courtney respected his opinions? Would Ben stay with her if she didn't?

You stayed with Glen for years.

She shook the thought away—she was a different generation, raised to put husband and family first. Guilt and shame had trapped her in a marriage that society and her family expected her to reside in forever, but it hadn't been easy. There'd been dark periods when she'd wondered if she might lose herself completely. But she'd clung tenaciously to her bone-deep belief that waiting until the children were adults so they could weather the emotional storm and understand her truth was absolutely the right thing to do. Had she just delayed the inevitable? Her daughter wasn't speaking to anyone in the family. Was Courtney determined to die on this hill of hating Brenda and fighting with those who loved her?

Was that what Brenda was doing with Marilyn? Risking everything for a daughter who might never forgive her?

The uncomfortable thought dug in deep and stayed put.

After Olivia left, Brenda couldn't settle to anything. The mess of thoughts in her head hammered their opinions, each vying to be heard and acted on, so she left the house. After a brisk walk in the hinterland her head wasn't exactly quiet, but for the first time in weeks she knew exactly what she needed to do.

She walked to her desk and pulled out the box of stationery she usually used for writing condolence letters. She fingered the heavy ecru writing paper, sighed and uncapped her fountain pen.

Dear Courtney,

I'm writing to you the old-fashioned way in the hope you'll read this letter. I know there's a risk you'll scrunch it up and throw it in the fire, but if you only read this paragraph, I want you to know this letter is nothing like the many emails, phone calls and texts I've sent begging to explain and asking you to meet and talk. I finally understand that you're not ready and perhaps you never will be. As hard as it is for me to accept that, this letter is my word that I do accept it.

Are you still reading? I love you, Courtney. I always have and I always will. I understand that me coming out has shocked and hurt you, and I own I've caused that pain, devastation, anger and fear despite never wanting to. Why come out now, I hear you ask, when I've hidden who I am for forty years? Well, forty years is the answer. I want to live my third-age life comfortable in my own skin.

I've never been brave, Courtney. When I was seventeen I had an all-consuming crush on a girl. I hated and feared the intensity of my feelings. I lived in a swirling state of chaos and panic. I stopped eating and sleeping. My parents took me to their pastor and begged me to tell him my problems. Remembering how a boy who'd declared his love for another boy in the congregation had been shamed and shunned by the church, along with his parents, I babbled out nonsense about school. I was petrified of stepping off the cliff and being abandoned by everyone I loved for feelings I wasn't certain were real.

I desperately wanted to live the life everyone expected of me.

When I met your father and he smiled at me as if I was the only person in the hall, it was such a relief to bury my guilt and shame. I told myself that what I felt for that girl was wrong, an aberration that would never happen again now I loved a man. I threw myself headfirst into the safety of normalcy. Glen offered me security and the chance of children so I married him and the happy-ever-after dream as fast as I could.

When I said "I do", I didn't realize the farm was a third person in our marriage and that she would always come first. I struggled to be heard, not just by your father, but by Grandma Elaine and Poppa Stan who had very traditional opinions about gender roles. I thought once I had a baby things would improve, but I found the early years isolating and overwhelming. I struggled to cope. That added even more shame and guilt onto a growing heap. I battled long periods of depression, and threw myself into the choir, the Country Women's Association, the Agricultural Society, anything and everything to keep busy so I didn't have any spare time to think. I couldn't understand why, when I had everything I'd told myself I ever wanted, I wasn't happy. Then I went to the Women in Agriculture conference and met Marilyn. It was like coming home. For the first time in my life I felt whole.

You said to me that I've lied to you for half your life. I've lied to myself for so much longer. I'm sorry. I was terrified of claiming what I wanted, fearing it would cost me too much and hurt you and the boys. I didn't realize it had already cost me far too much. By trying to protect everyone, I lost myself in the process.

It's taken me until now to understand that I'm deserving of happiness. For me that means loving and living with Marilyn. This is who I truly am and this is my life. I love you, Courtney. When you're ready to join me, I'm here.

Your loving and fallible mother, Brenda xxx

Brenda put down the pen and stretched her cramping fingers, before folding the paper and sliding it into an envelope. She wrote Courtney's name and address and took ten minutes to find a stamp.

Then she drove to the general store and stood in front of the mail box for a full minute before she forced her fingers to pull open the handle and drop the envelope. It hit the metal with a lonely thud that echoed in her chest. Would Courtney even read it?

CHAPTER FORTY

WHEN BRENDA RETURNED from the general store, she let herself into the quiet house and made a call.

"Hello." For someone on vacation, Marilyn sounded weary.

"It's me," Brenda said. "Are you okay? You sound flat."

"I haven't been sleeping very well," Marilyn said. "After the cove, Hobart's noisy."

Dread clawed in Brenda's veins. *Are you missing me?* After all, they'd spent years only seeing each other once a month so it wasn't like this past week was unusual. Except it was very different. There'd never been this angst-filled space between them vibrating with resentment and hurt.

"I'm not sleeping either," Brenda said. "I miss you. I even miss Clyde waking me up at 6:00 A.M." She chewed her bottom lip. "I'm coming to Hobart."

"To see Richard?"

"No. I mean, perhaps but ..." She hauled in a deep breath, needing to get the words right. "I'm coming to see you. That is, if you're not too busy."

"You want to leave the cove for a few days?" Marilyn asked.

"Yes. I just said I miss you. Why do you sound so suspicious?"

"Because Courtney's going to Queensland," Marilyn said curtly.

Brenda's chest tightened at the inference. Was her gesture of reconciliation going to be misconstrued? Considering what she'd said and done since being outed, she supposed it wasn't an unreasonable assumption.

"That's just a coincidence."

Marilyn made a huffing sound. "You've known for weeks that Courtney and Ben are taking the kids to the theme parks."

"I have." She sighed. "But until tonight I didn't know me."

When Marilyn didn't say anything, Brenda had a sudden need to tell her how she'd reached this new point in her life. "Can I explain?"

"I'm listening," Marilyn said.

"Thank you." Brenda took a sip of wine and wondered where to start.

"When Glen died, I wanted us to be together so much that I promised you I'd come out even though I'd have rather dealt with a cancer diagnosis. I'm sorry, Marilyn. It was incredibly unfair of me, because of course you believed me. You had no reason not to, just like I had no right to accuse you of pressuring me to come out. But in my conflicted head it felt like unrelenting pressure. I desperately wanted to control my coming out and you know how much planning I put into that lunch. By then, I'd convinced myself coming out would be quiet, calm and respectful. Today I realized that was magical thinking. Things between Courtney and me have rarely been calm."

She laughed, the sound weary. Marilyn stayed silent.

"And then Penguin happened," she continued. "Being outed was like being caught in a roaring fire front, and ever since I've been falling over myself hosing down spot fires only to turn around and find another one. It tied into every fear I've ever had about telling the kids. It ramped up my guilt about letting Courtney down yet again and it reinforced why I didn't want to come out in the first place. Then it all got worse."

The silence on the line spooked her. "Are you still there?"

"Yes," Marilyn said. "Go on. I'm hearing every word."

"Thank you. Where was I?"

"Everything got worse."

"Oh, yeah, it did," Brenda said, riding the emotions. "I resented being outed, and although the choir was caring, my kids ranged from barely supportive to hating me. I could see how happy you were that the secret was finally out, but I couldn't fathom how you could be happy when I was hurting so much. Instead of turning to the one person who loves me for who I am, I took out all my fears and anxieties on you. I wish I could take back much of what I've said. I'm sorry, darling. I'm so very, very sorry."

There was an even longer silence and Brenda regretted doing something this big and significant on the phone. She hadn't meant to—the plan had been to do it in Hobart—but it had all just tumbled out.

She heard a loud sniff. "Marilyn?"

The honk of a nose being blown followed and then Marilyn spoke, her voice unusually wobbly. "You're right, I was happy. Hell, I was relieved and excited we were finally out. But that night in Penguin when Courtney asked if it was true and I answered for you, I shouldn't have done it, sweetheart. I've regretted it ever since. Everyone's entitled to come out the way they want. Not only were you denied that, I made it worse. I'm sorry too."

Tears fell and Brenda didn't try to wipe them away. "Why did I do this on the phone? I just want to hug you."

"Me too," Marilyn agreed.

"I can be in Hobart in four hours," Brenda said.

"I love that you want to do this for me," Marilyn said, "but we can both be in Longford in 2:00."

Three hours later, Brenda lay on the familiar bed in the Longford B & B with Marilyn in her arms, Clyde at her feet and floating on relief. "I love you so much."

"I love you too." Marilyn turned to face her. "But I want to know how you got here."

Brenda laughed. "I took the Bass Highway."

Marilyn shook her head. "Not that. You said on the phone you understand yourself now. I want to know what's happened in one week."

"It started with a conversation with Livvy," Brenda said, still surprised a thirteen-year-old had put her on the path to acceptance of herself.

"What did she say?"

"She told me she was sorry I'd been sad for such a long time. That she was glad I had you and I wasn't sad anymore."

"That's lovely."

"It is." Brenda sighed. "And I know it's far too simplistic to ask that if my granddaughter can accept me no matter who I love, why can't my daughter? Especially when I hear Olivia's increasing frustration with her mother about things that could go on to fracture their relationship—"

"But?" Marilyn asked, keeping her on track.

"But it made me see my relationship with Courtney in a new light. I love the boys, but I've never had the same expectations of them in relation to me. Society tells us that boys grow up and leave their mothers, but every magazine article, Facebook post and Instagram photo promotes the special bond between mothers and daughters. I've never experienced anything close to that with Courtney. I blame myself. I was emotionally absent a lot of the time, struggling to be all things to all people in the family."

Marilyn frowned. "Do the boys feel you let them down?"

"If Colin does, I'm not sure he could find the words. And Richard —well, I think I come third after his partner and the Premier. Possibly fourth if you count Hooper."

"Jack Russells are pretty cute," Marilyn teased.

"By the way, he's gay," Brenda said.

"Hooper?"

"Ha ha. Richard."

A flash of hurt crossed Marilyn's face. "You never said."

"He told me on the run-up to the lunch and asked me not to tell anyone. At the time, things between you and me were a bit tense. The plan was Richard would bring Aaron to the coming-out lunch and they'd come out too."

Marilyn gave her a cautious look. "And you and Richard thought that was a good idea?"

Brenda shook her head as if she didn't quite believe how crazy her thinking had been. "To be fair, Richard didn't know I was planning on coming out. Today, I'd say it's a terrible idea, but back then I wanted safety in numbers. When the lunch didn't happen and Courtney went ballistic, Richard decided to delay."

She slammed her palm to her forehead. "Oh! There's another apology I need to make. In my blinkered Courtney obsession, I asked Richard to come out to her thinking it might help me."

"Perhaps if you tell him everything you told me today, he might understand," Marilyn said.

"I can hope."

Marilyn squeezed her hand. "I've sidetracked you by asking about the boys. Back to Courtney, please."

Brenda shifted on the bed. "You know how much Courtney adored her father. When he was alive I didn't really get noticed, and when he died, I decided now was the time to build bridges. I've tried everything I can think of to bring us closer and I believed I'd made progress. Perhaps I've been deluding myself. Perhaps I've only ever been a convenient babysitter, cook and dressmaker for her."

"But with a great relationship with your grandchildren," Marilyn said. "I know how much you love them and while we're being honest, I'm ashamed to say I think I've been a little bit jealous of your children and grandchildren."

Regret twisted beneath Brenda's sternum. "I think you feeling jealous is probably fair, and the boys would be entitled to feel the same way as I've been in such a tailspin about Courtney. I've been so desperate to have the perfect relationship with her and prove I wasn't a total failure as a mother that she got the bulk of my attention this year.

Despite my best intentions, all I've done is make everything about her and her feelings. I had no idea what I was risking."

"What were you risking?" Marilyn asked.

"Me. Us." A long breath rumbled out of her. "I've realized that for all my efforts and apologies to Courtney, they may count for nothing. She's so much like Elaine. She may never forgive me for what she believes to be an absolute betrayal of Glen, her brothers and herself. For a long time I believed that to have you in my life, I had to give up Courtney. Now I realize Courtney was never mine to give away. I regret lying to her and I've apologized for that, but ..."

"But what?"

She gave Marilyn a wry smile. "But I've raised my kids. I'm almost fifty-nine years old and the next thirty years is our time. I'm sorry I accused you of being selfish, but that was when I was stuck in the black mud of denial. How can my and your happiness be selfish when living a lie has made me so miserable for so long?"

"Oh, sweetheart." Marilyn wiped away a tear and hugged her tightly. "I'm sorry it's been so hard for you. Is so hard for you."

Brenda mustered a smile. "I can't promise there won't be times when my grief about Courtney rises, but I'm trying to embrace acceptance of what I can't control. I'm sorry it's taken me so long to get here. Anyone else would have given up on me a long time ago."

"You know I was happily part of our secret relationship," Marilyn said.

"Until you weren't." Brenda fought tears and lost. "I hate that I drove you to the point of leaving me. I'm sorry I was so slow to work it all out."

"I wasn't leaving you." Marilyn stroked Brenda's hair. "I went to Hobart because I needed a different perspective. I spoke to a counselor who helped me see past my frustrations and impatience. She pointed out that I came out as a single woman in her thirties and you coming out as a widow and mother was far more complicated. I don't have a maternal bone in my body so I'm sorry I wasn't more understanding.

The truth is, I've been so desperate for us to live our authentic life I've had tunnel vision."

"We can start our authentic life now."

"And I guess this is the perfect place," Marilyn said.

Brenda shook her head. "I don't think so."

"But we have so many special memories here."

"We do, but all of them are part of our secret life." Brenda tried to find the right words. "I think I've been clinging to those golden sunlit memories instead of embracing real life."

"Which isn't quite so golden," Marilyn said ruefully.

Brenda laughed. "I think it's fair to say a lot of the time it's tarnished and messy, but when we find the gold it's far more precious."

Marilyn laced her fingers between Brenda's. "I know things have been rocky recently, but if we take away the coming-out issue, we don't really argue much about other things."

Brenda took the opportunity their honest conversation was providing. "True, although I think sometimes my experiences as a mother put us on opposite sides of an issue. And I don't just mean about my kids and grandkids."

"You mean about Steph's miscarriage?" Marilyn asked. "I did hear you on that one."

"I know you did." Brenda kissed her. "Waking up next to you every day is so special. I never expected it to happen and I'm still pinching myself. For a long time, I wanted to keep you to myself, but now I want everyone to know how happy you make me and how you complete me. Let's go home so I can take you to the surf club and hold your hand all through dinner."

Marilyn's face creased in an all-consuming smile. "That sounds perfect, but seeing as we've paid for the room, wouldn't it be a shame not to use it and celebrate the start of the rest of our lives?"

Brenda laughed, floating on relief and wonder that this special woman was hers. She wrapped her in her arms and kissed her.

CHAPTER FORTY-ONE

ADDY WAS USING the art supplies she'd bought at the start of the year for her bullet journal to sketch a poster for the eisteddfod. A kernel of an idea had come to her after Olivia showed her the design for the choir shirt, but it had firmed up when she'd been hanging out the back on the water letting her mind wander. She'd raced home and outlined it in pencil while it was clear in her head. Now she was exploring it with color.

Kieran was outside replacing the deck. Although finances were tight, she was paying him with the money she'd saved by not drinking two or three bottles of wine every night or buying expensive glasses of whisky for absolute bastards. The beautiful planks of spotted gum were tangible evidence of her sobriety, as was her weight loss and the joy of waking hangover-free with a sharp and focused mind.

Between surfing, choir and the eisteddfod meetings, she'd been seeing quite a bit of Kieran. He was a calm presence in the choir and she enjoyed his non-threatening company. Now she was the rehearsal pianist, she'd taken to arriving at the hall half an hour early to focus and warm up. Since Brenda had handed over the alto coach role to Kieran, he was often early too and they chatted, discussing ways of helping the choir nail the melodies. It was companionable and easy and she looked forward to it.

The thok-thok-thok of the nail gun halted and Fergus, who was resting at Addy's feet, glanced up with hope in his eyes— *can I go out now?*

She laughed. "Don't try and guilt-trip me. You were the one who wanted to stay inside."

She put down her brush and opened the sliding door. Fergus shot out, then came to a screaming halt when he quickly ran out of deck.

Kieran was kneeling and when he glanced up she noticed a light smattering of sawdust on his face and in his curls. She got a definite zip of attraction and immediately batted it away. All the sober gurus recommended a year of sobriety and tackling the demons before embarking on a new relationship.

That news anchor met her husband three months in. They're married now with a kid.

Addy reminded herself that Kieran hadn't indicated any interest in her other than as a friend, which she found oddly reassuring. It was one less stress to deal with.

"Do you want a cup of tea and a scone?" she asked.

"That would be grand."

"I'll put the kettle on."

Fergus padded back inside behind his master and settled by the door. Addy heard Kieran washing his hands in the laundry and just as she'd set the table with jam and cream, he appeared in the kitchen. His face was free of dust and the tips of his salt-and-pepper curls sat damp on his forehead.

"Me apprentice says the college vacation is over and he's got class today," he said. "Is he having a lend of me?"

"You trying out some Aussie expressions?" she teased.

He grinned. "Thought I should so they give me citizenship. Did I get it right?"

"Yep." She poured their tea, remembering he liked his strong. "And your apprentice is telling the truth. Semester two's started."

"You didn't have to give up a day of work to make me cups of tea and scones." He shot her a cheeky grin. "Although I'll not be complaining."

She laughed. "Sorry to disappoint you and your ego, but I didn't take a day off."

"So your promotion came through with more flexible working hours?"

She looked into her tea as if she was fascinated by the stray leaves that had slipped through the strainer. "Actually, I quit my job a few weeks ago."

He choked on his tea and hurriedly put down his mug. "All those conversations in the swell and you never said?"

She shrugged. "The beach is my happy place. I didn't want to taint it."

He studied her for a long moment, his blue eyes swirling with unnamed emotions. "There's been other times when it's just been us." There was a hint of hurt in his voice not dissimilar to the early days of her friendship with Steph.

Us? Her gut squirmed but she wasn't certain if it was discomfort, annoyance or something else entirely.

"Not telling you isn't personal, Kieran. I love talking to you about things that have absolutely *nothing* to do with my hot mess of a life. For that, I have a counselor."

She watched him carefully, waiting for the recoil. Part of her hoping for it and part of her fearing it.

He bit into a scone and chewed thoughtfully. Her gaze drifted to the broad column of his throat, watching the muscles at play. She suddenly realized this wasn't like sneaking looks at him in the surf—he was only a table width away. She hastily hauled her gaze up.

"I'm glad you've got someone to talk to," he said.

"Thanks."

"And on one level, I know I don't have the right to expect you to confide in me but ..." He looked straight at her. "Addy, I really enjoy your company. We have a laugh, and I thought you knew I've been coming to choir early to catch you on your own." His hand moved close to hers, almost touching but not quite. "I think you're gorgeous, inside and out."

Her heart jumped. *He thinks you're gorgeous!*

He doesn't know the real you.

"I've wanted to ask you out for a while now," he said, "but you have this way of rushing off after a surf and after choir."

Date him and you'll lose a friend.

Her gut squirmed yet again. "I'm just not sure us dating's a great idea."

Disappointment settled in the laugh lines bracketing his mouth. "Is that because you've put me firmly in the friend zone?"

He was offering her an instant out, no explanations required. Considering everything she was dealing with at the moment, she should take it. But part of being sober was acknowledging her feelings and being true to herself—accepting who and where she was in this life. Lying would just complicate things, and right now she was swimming in a sea of complications without adding more.

She looked straight at him and her fingers brushed the tips of his. "Actually, I think you and your accent are pretty gorgeous too."

For a moment his eyes twinkled and his sexy dimple appeared. Then his eyes dimmed under a frown. "There's a but coming, right?"

She nodded and took in a deep breath. "I'm an alcoholic."

"I'm Irish."

"I'm serious," she said.

"So am I." His face fell into earnest lines. "I've got a bit of an understanding. Me da drank and he was a miserable drunk."

She pulled her hand away and placed it safely in her lap. "So you know all about it. You should be running from me, not wanting to date me."

He shook his head. "You're so much more than an addiction, Addy."

His words circled her, offering care and understanding, but she wasn't brave enough to accept them. "You don't know me well enough to say that."

"I think I do." He rubbed his jaw. "Me da taught me how bad the demons can be. I know defeating them takes incredible strength and a commitment to totally change your life. I can tell you for sure that no drunk is ever on the water at dawn, sober."

She needed him to understand. "I'm what they call a high-functioning alcoholic. I've been drinking since I was fifteen and in that time I've gained a degree, a master's and held down demanding jobs. Few people knew how much I drank."

His gaze held hers. "But could you have surfed at dawn?"

She thought about the increasing struggle to get out of bed in the mornings. "Once in my twenties I ran a six mile fun run at 8:00 in the morning and I was probably still drunk. But I couldn't have done it the last couple of years."

"So I'm right in saying you're not drinking now?"

"It's early days, Kieran. The cravings are definitely less and I don't want to break. I love waking up in the morning keen to face the day, but I can't lie. There have been moments when I've found myself thinking addictive thoughts like, one last bender and then I'm done for good."

He ran his fingers along the edge of the placemat. "Whether we have an addiction or not, we all have thoughts about things we shouldn't do. We're all tempted by things we know aren't good for us. It's how we deal with the temptations that counts. You didn't act on those thoughts. You rejected them as dangerous or magical thinking or whatever. So don't beat yourself up for the thought. Be proud you told them to eff off."

She found it hard to be proud when she'd spent so many years loathing herself. "I struggle with that concept as well. Basically I'm too hard to date."

His mouth wriggled as if he was chewing on something. "Can I at least have the chance to decide that meself?" When she didn't reply he said, "Addy, I'm not suggesting we move in together. I'm talking about doing the things we already do like choir and surfing, but adding in dinner together a couple of times a week. Taking a bushwalk, having a picnic. Things like that."

The normality of it called to her and the optimistic voice in her head that had been gaining volume since she'd stopped drinking said, *Go on, give it a shot!* The rest of her said, *No sane person throws themselves off a cliff into the unknown without a safety net.*

Take one day at a time, Addy.

"And sex?" she blurted out, not certain if she wanted to know his thoughts on the topic or if she was hoping to scare him away with her bluntness.

He blinked at her. "I ... um ... well ..." He rubbed his jaw again. "If you wanted to, I wouldn't say no."

She bit her lip. "Kieran, I doubt I've ever had sober sex. I don't think I even know how. Just the thought of it threatens a panic attack."

"There's no rush and no pressure." He smiled. "When you're ready, it would be an honor to be your first sober sex partner."

"And what if I'm never ready?" she challenged, needing to know exactly where he stood.

"How about we cross that bridge if and when we come to it."

"Okay, but FYI, it's your time you're wasting," she said.

"Spending any time with you isn't a waste, Addy." His eyes did that twinkling thing she loved. "And as you've already told me you think I'm gorgeous, I'm cautiously optimistic."

She laughed and was suddenly hit with an overwhelming desire to cry. "I appreciate you saying I'm more than my addiction, but if you're crazy enough to want to try dating me, you should know I drank for a reason. I liked myself better with a few drinks under my belt. I thought I was far more interesting and funny."

"I only really know sober you and I find you interesting and funny and fascinating. And you surf." He smiled again. "For me, that's the icing on the cake."

She wanted to sink into the warmth his words kindled, but she needed to tell him the full story and give him one more chance to run.

"Mostly I drank to block out the shame, humiliation and guilt about something that happened to me here when I was a kid."

His smile faded. "Does this have anything to do with that music teacher you said always gave you the solos? The reason you stopped your music and started surfing?"

She stared at him—shocked he'd remembered their conversation, horrified he'd made the connection, yet relieved that he had.

"Yes," she said softly. "It's only since getting sober that I've realized he was the adult, I was the child, and what happened to me was one hundred percent his fault."

A muscle twitched in his cheek and his fists clenched. "Are you going to report him?"

"He's dead."

His shoulders drooped as if pressed down by a great weight.

"Addy, I hate that happened to you."

She grimaced. "There's a certain irony that coming back to the place where I started drinking, the place that recently took me to rock bottom, is now helping me stay sober. Being given the solo in the choir pushed me over the edge, but now my involvement's helping me rediscover how much joy music gives me. That bastard stole that from me. Now I'm trying to take it back but it's not always easy."

"I can't imagine it would be," he said softly. "But good for you for trying."

"Who knew being sober makes you see all sorts of things in a new light," she tried to joke. "Even my job."

"Are you taking a mental-health breather or looking for another job?"

"My boss pretty much stitched me up so chances of another teaching job are slim to none." She toyed with the jam spoon. "But I'm not even sure I want to teach anymore or work in marketing."

Kieran was frowning at her. "What do you mean by stitched you up?"

Oh God! She hadn't meant to tell him the sordid work story, but Kieran had this way of making her feel comfortable, almost safe, and she'd dropped her guard. But as she'd already committed to honesty, there was no turning back.

She hauled in a deep breath. "The first few months I was back on the island I drank a lot. It meant I missed the signs it was a toxic workplace. Long story short, my boss was gaslighting me. I lived and breathed work all semester, doing two and a half jobs on the promise of the promotion I'd moved for. He appeared to work similar hours to me so he became my social life as well as my boss. When I stopped drinking, I was clear-headed enough to piece together many things. He wasn't happy I gave up the booze and he wanted things back the way they'd been. He set me up with a false sexual harassment claim from a student, then put an offer on the table. Either I kept my job and risked my sobriety, or I left and he trashed my reputation."

"Jesus. You're better off out of there." Kieran rubbed his face. "But ..."

She stiffened, uncertain she wanted to hear what he'd decided not to say. She lost the battle not to ask. "But what?"

"This bastard ..." Anger rippled along Kieran's usually relaxed cheeks. "Did you ever hear any rumors that he'd done something like this to anyone else?"

A shiver ran through her at the thought; it had never occurred to her.

"Before I arrived, he hadn't worked there very long. I know he was fast tracked into the position, but only one person appeared to have a problem with that. Most people like him. God, I liked him. He's a personable misogynist."

She stabbed the spoon into the raspberry jam, picturing Grant's smug face. "Personable, clever and absolutely evil. When there's a sexual harassment accusation by one staff member against another, often the investigation's basic at best. But when a student makes an accusation against a teacher it's taken extremely seriously and thoroughly investigated. Since I've been accused of meeting with the student alone, it's his word against mine. Even if by some miracle I managed to prove my innocence, I'd likely never get another teaching job. But what really sticks in my craw is I worked seventeen-hour days all semester doing two and a half jobs for him and almost killing myself in the process. I got his entire department audit-ready and made him look fabulous!"

Her arms rose and fell in a combination of frustration and disbelief. "Now I doubt that promised 2IC position even existed."

Kieran poured them both another mug of tea and sipped his slowly, gazing at the vase of daffodils she'd picked from the garden.

Addy couldn't even guess at what he was thinking, but for the first time since he'd asked her on a date she relaxed. Now he had all the facts laid out before him—her greatest shames and humiliations—he held a get-out-of-jail-free card. Of course he'd take it.

By the time he spoke, she'd already heard his voice clear in her head withdrawing his offer to date, so when he said, "Could you prove that?" she had no idea what he was talking about.

"Sorry, what?" she asked, her mind scrabbling.

"Can you prove the 2IC job didn't exist?"

"I don't follow." She wound a curl around her finger. "How would proving that help?"

"It's the first domino." He leaned forward, his deep blue gaze intense. "People knew you were doing those extra jobs, right?"

"Oh, yeah. I took a lot of shit from the other teachers about the audit."

She suddenly whacked her forehead with the heel of her hand. "I'm so stupid! That's why he got me to do the audit preparation, so they'd hate me not him. And along with the rumors he spread about me, it totally worked. By the time I left, there was no one in my corner."

Except perhaps Ravi?

Oh God, she'd listened to Grant ahead of Ravi. Was Grant bullying Ravi too?

Kieran's mouth had thinned into a hard line. "Addy, if you can prove his job offer was bogus, then it points to other shady dealings. People might listen to you."

Her mind churned through everything Kieran had said, then she revisited all of Grant's references to the job.

"He insisted on helping me with the job application, which I didn't really need. But now that I think about it, the upload link didn't work so I emailed my application to him. And there was always a reason why the interview got cancelled. Someone was sick, or there were car troubles, or department meetings. At the time they were all valid reasons, but looking back I'm sure he was gaslighting me. When I was pushing hard for the interview, he told me I no longer had the full support of the panel because of something that had happened in Hobart. At the time, it didn't make a lot of sense."

A thought landed, brilliant white in its simplicity.

"Kieran! I met the woman he said was on the interview panel when I was at the Hobart conference. I can ring her and if there truly was a job, she'll corroborate his story that I was deemed an unsuitable applicant. Or she won't have a clue what I'm talking about."

Kieran nodded encouragingly. "And if it's the latter, it's evidence. You know, if you decide to try and prove a case against him. But that's totally up to you. I can't imagine it will be easy or pleasant, but if you choose that way, you've got my support. I'm sure you'll have Steph's and the choir's too."

"Maybe not Fern," she joked and wondered why. Perhaps humor made the whole sordid situation just that bit easier to deal with.

Kieran sighed. "Vera told me Fern's ex-husband drank so alcohol's a touchy subject for her. But she's very pro women's rights so you might have an unexpected ally."

Addy already had that with Kieran. She turned his words "prove a case" over in her head and instead of wanting to run from them, she had a sudden urge to grab them and hold on tight.

"When I was fifteen, I didn't have the power or the experience to fight for myself. I didn't have it six months ago," she reflected. "But now I'm angry. All that guilt and self-loathing that's been weighing me down lies at the feet of two men who trampled my hopes and dreams and used me for their own needs. Denton's dead, and I don't want my job back, but I'd love to nail Grant Hindmarsh to the wall so he doesn't try it again with anyone else."

"Good for ye. Right then." Kieran rose to his feet. "This deck's not building itself so I better get back."

"And I should finish the poster." She started stacking mugs and plates.

"Addy, will you have dinner with me at the surf club tonight before choir?" Kieran asked.

Her hand stalled on the cream bowl. "I haven't been in a bar since I stopped drinking."

"Right. I hadn't thought of that." He rubbed his head. "I'm more than happy not to drink, Addy. I rarely do anyway because of Da, but if seeing other people drinking is an issue for you, I can whip us up a curry at mine."

She thought about the chat on SCW and how successful sobriety wasn't about willpower and resisting, but about changing her beliefs around alcohol. She knew she was well down that road already, because when the craving hit she now looked at the evidence—her sober life was healthier. Now she had a chance at happier. If she was going to date Kieran and give a real and respectful relationship a shot, was it fair to limit the places they could go? Maybe when it was in her best interest, but the advantage of starting at the surf club was that Rob from choir was the bartender and he had her back.

"If I ever want to eat out again, I have to start somewhere," she said.

"The surf club it is then." Kieran smiled. "But Addy, promise me if you get there and you change your mind, just say the word. We can always grab a burger from the general store. I don't mind where we eat. I just want to spend time with you."

Knowing the offer was on the table was enough.

CHAPTER FORTY-TWO

The special choir meeting was in full swing and the hall was a hive of activity. Addy realized with both a pang and some pride that earlier in the year there was no way she would have been feeling this alert and happy so early on a Saturday morning.

Brenda and Marilyn had laid out a huge amount of food, from a crockpot of curry and a platter of chicken sandwiches—Marilyn's contribution—to Brenda's passionfruit sponge cake and apple and walnut muffins, to feed the willing workers. Steph, Courtney, Vera and Brenda had set up their sewing machines and two long trestle tables were spread with fabric. Kieran and Heidi were carefully cutting out the patterns.

When Vera had teased Kieran, he'd laughed. "There's not much difference between using a jigsaw to cut around a template on wood and using shears on fabric. To be sure, wood's a lot easier to manage than this slippery stuff."

"Sorry," Olivia said. "I fell in love with the colors and the pattern." She bit her lip. "Maybe I should have listened to Mum."

Ben glanced up from cleaning the feed dogs on Vera's sewing machine. "Hey, Court, did you hear that?"

Courtney, who looked tired and worn, stayed silent and didn't return his smile.

"Sometimes the hardest things yield the best results," Addy said.

She was wearing Olivia's prototype blouse and she threw out her arms and spun around twice. "I love how it floats and falls like a gentle swell and an ascending and descending scale. It says cove choir perfectly."

"It does, dear, but you don't have to sew it," Vera said pragmatically. "Ben, have you finished? I want to get started."

Fern gave Addy a critical look.

"What?" Addy flinched and glanced down at herself. "Can you see my bra? My muffin top?"

Fern shook her head. "I was just thinking how fit you look. You've lost all that puffiness in your face. Being sober suits you."

Addy met Fern's gaze. "Thank you. I think being sober suits me too."

"If you think adding massage into your stress management program would be beneficial, I could squeeze you in," Fern offered.

"Addy, can we run through some music changes," Marilyn said.

"I've decided we're going to sing 'Under The Sea' at the girls' passion project presentation night."

Addy frowned. "But 'Hallelujah' is ready."

"Yes, but for the girls I want something upbeat that appeals to students and parents so everyone's tapping and singing along. Plus it ties in perfectly with Olivia's blouse and Zoe's make-up design."

Marilyn laughed like a young girl. "I'm quite excited about my mermaid look."

"Ohh! I've just had an idea." Addy's words tumbled out in an excited rush. "We could do an a cappella version and create the sounds of the steel drum, marimba and vibraphone ourselves."

Henry carried in a wingback chair. He was helping Zoe set up an interview space in a small room off the hall. "I can stay and help," he said to no one in particular.

Monty climbed onto a chair so he could reach the food.

"Monty, no!" Steph was out of her seat and grabbing him seconds before a plate of sandwiches landed on the floor. She glanced around, her face flushing pink. "Where the hell is Henry?"

Steph's frustration filled the hall. Addy felt for her friend but she busied herself at the piano, not wanting to be drawn into a domestic argument that had nothing to do with her. Even so, it was hard not to overhear the Suns' conversation.

"Isn't your job keeping us all safe from Monty?" Zoe asked her father.

Steph dumped Monty into Henry's arms. "Please take him and go."

"Actually, I thought I'd stay in case Zoe needs me."

Steph glared at them both.

Zoe rolled her eyes. "Yeah, Dad, like I don't know how to video."

Disappointment dimmed Henry's hopeful enthusiasm. "If you need anything, just text. Steph, where's Monty's backpack?"

"Shouldn't you know as you're the parent-in-charge today?" Steph said tightly.

"Jeez, since when is it a crime to ask?" Henry said.

"Since you ask me where it is before you've even looked!" Steph stalked back to her sewing machine.

"Looks like you're in the shit today, Henry," Rob said cheerfully.

"Nessa once locked me out of the house for an hour when I came home with the wrong ketchup." He shook his head as if the situation still baffled him. "If you're looking for a kid's *Bluey* backpack, there's one in the kitchen."

"Thanks, Rob." Henry leaned in to kiss Zoe, but she ducked away. "Have fun," he said.

Zoe crossed her arms. "It's not fun, Dad, it's work."

"It can be both," Henry said.

Zoe's phone buzzed. She hesitated, then glanced at it before shoving it in her pocket.

"That's a good idea," Henry said.

Zoe chewed her cuticle. "What?"

"Putting your cell phone on silent so you can focus on the choir."

Henry smiled at her. "You know Steph and I are very proud of you for doing this."

"Yeah, right. Please just go."

"Love you too, Zo." Henry blew her a kiss and walked away.

Zoe turned her back on them and headed toward the piano, stopped, turned, then doubled back. "Um, Addy?"

Addy's hands paused on the keys. "Hey, Zoe."

Unlike Olivia Burton's sweet and puppy-like enthusiasm, Zoe's aura was a confusing mix of bring-it-on and anxious. Addy remembered all too clearly that adolescent angst. Who was she kidding? There were many times she still lived it.

"Can I ... um ... interview you first?" Zoe asked.

No. I was planning on dodging the interview completely.

Perhaps Zoe sensed Addy's hesitance because she added, "I want to start with someone I know."

The logical answer was to start with Steph, but Addy had spent enough time with the two of them to know nothing easy or relaxed flowed between them. A slight movement behind her made Addy turn and she saw Kieran approaching. Had he sensed her unease?

For God's sake! This isn't a movie. You've had two dates. And you thought Grant understood you and how well did that go?

I was drunk a lot of the time!

Sober Addy recognized that Kieran was very different from Grant and Jasper, and the other men she'd dated.

"Is this girl talk or can I join in?" Kieran asked, giving them both a grin.

Addy wanted to hug him. "Zoe wants to start her interviews with a friendly face."

"Do I qualify?" Kieran asked.

Zoe blushed and glanced at her feet. "I s'pose."

"Grand. Or you could interview Addy and me together," Kieran suggested.

Zoe's phone buzzed and her hand moved to her pocket, hovered, then fell away. "Mrs. Delacour said people talk more if it's just them."

"Well, I wouldn't want Addy stealing any of my limelight." He gave Addy a wink.

She laughed. "You'll have to edit him, Zoe. He can talk underwater with a mouthful of marbles."

Kieran's hand hit his heart. "Harsh, but fair. Come on, Zoe, let's go to your movie set and I'll tell you how it's impossible not to sing if you're Irish."

Addy watched them walk away and blew out the breath she'd been holding. She was off the hook—for now. Of course she wasn't going to bare her soul to a thirteen-year-old girl's question of "why do you sing?" But for some reason she was having trouble making up a lie about why she'd joined the choir. The simple answer was her mother, but simple didn't mean uncomplicated. Addy didn't trust she wouldn't give that away with a wavering voice or worse, tears.

Unable to play the piano now because the noise would filter onto Zoe's videos, and with no sewing skills, Addy considered going home, but that wasn't in the spirit of the day. If Courtney could spend a day at the hall sewing when she still wasn't speaking to her mother and was clearly unhappy about Olivia's involvement in the project, then Addy could stay and find something to do besides dodging Zoe.

For the last couple of weeks, she'd been helping Steph with packing and tweaking the Retro Toys website, redoing the artwork and filming videos of the toys in action. With Monty's love of anything to do with penguins he was a natural star and had happily played with the full complement of toys and the new puzzles Steph was testing. Now Addy suggested to Steph that she pop into Four Winds, pick up the toy orders and bring them back to pack and chat.

"I can pick up coffee orders from Sven's too," she said.

"Oh my God!" Steph hugged her. "Thank you."

"I should be thanking you. Packing keeps me from fidgeting. Really I'm just jockeying so I'm first in line when you do your next hire," she joked.

"Yeah, right." Steph laughed, then gave her a long look. "Are you serious?"

Addy went to say no and heard herself saying, "Maybe. I'm working Fridays in the post office agency at the general store, but until I work out what I'm going to do when I grow up, having something to cover groceries and electricity would be nice."

"Have you heard back from that woman yet?" Steph asked. "The one at the college in Hobart?"

"No." Addy gave a wry smile. "I coughed up the courage to email her only to discover she's on two weeks family leave. I've written *Call Heather* in the BuJo on her second day back."

Steph squeezed her arm. "Remember, I'm in your corner."

"I know and I appreciate it." Addy pulled out her phone and brought up a note. "Latte or espresso?"

After taking everyone's drink orders and collecting the money, she was just pushing open the hall door when Brenda caught up with her. "I thought you might need a second pair of hands."

"Thanks, but aren't you needed at the sewing machine?"

"Olivia's taking a turn."

As they exited the building, the tang of salt and seaweed hit Addy's nostrils and the heavy thump of a big swell boomed around the cove.

"Your mum would have loved all this," Brenda said.

Addy deliberately steered the conversation away from the choir.

"She wasn't a huge fan of the beach and she constantly worried about the effect of the salt air on her piano. It always made me wonder why she and Dad chose to settle in the cove."

"Did you ever ask her?"

"No." Addy got lost in memories. "It came under the banner of the war and that was a definite no-go zone."

"Well, I think their choice to settle here makes a lot of sense," Brenda said. "On summer days when the water shimmers and changes from turquoise to bright blue, it reminded Rita of Dubrovnik. And knowing your mum, she would have worried about the salt and her piano there too, only you were too young to remember."

"I remember they missed Dubrovnik like an amputee misses a limb. The photo on the wall at home was treated with all the reverence of a shrine," Addy said.

Brenda nodded. "But they came to love the cove, and your mother loved the choir. I'm sure she's watching over us and thrilled you're back living here and singing again."

Aida, why are you breaking our hearts?

Addy zipped up her puffer with a jerk and picked up her pace.

"The thing is, I'm not singing, am I?"

Brenda gave her a sidelong glance. "If you want to sing, that's easy fixed. Marilyn will give you a solo in a heartbeat."

Addy stalled a shudder. "Did Mama ever talk to you about me?"

"When mothers gather, they invariably talk about their kids."

"I mean did she talk to you about me giving up music and taking up surfing?"

Brenda's look turned thoughtful, as if she was digging deep for a memory. "I know everyone in town was surprised you gave up music when you had such talent. You lit up when you sang and played. I remember saying to Vera, I didn't know who was more shocked by your decision—Rita and Ivan or the Dentons. After all, you'd been their poster child for their music school for years."

Brenda laughed. "I enrolled Courtney thinking their teaching skills might rub off some of the farm and find the pianist within, but that was wishful thinking. The farm won."

"Thank God for the farm," Addy said harshly. "I wish I'd had a lot less talent. I would have been a hell of a lot safer."

Brenda stopped walking and stared at her. "What do you mean?"

Addy made herself meet her gaze. "Denton taught me piano, singing and how to hate myself."

Brenda's mouth sagged and then she was wrapping her arms around Addy. "Oh, Addy, darling. I had no idea."

Addy allowed herself to sink into the caring depths of Brenda's arms. "No one knew, although I've often thought Lilian Denton may have been complicit. Either way, he started grooming me at twelve."

She suddenly realized that was the same age as Livvy and Zoe and her knees softened. Thankfully they'd reached the park bench seat the seven-day makeover committee had installed halfway between the hall and the shops for those who needed a rest or just wanted to admire the view.

"I had no idea," Brenda said again, clearly grappling with the news.

"Don't beat yourself up. No one knew about the grooming, not even me, and Mama and Papa adored the Dentons. They were one of only a few couples who were ever invited home to dinner. Mama told me constantly how lucky I was they'd accepted me as a piano student and with Denton's depth of experience I was well on the way to being ready for the Conservatory. A year later, he offered me a full scholarship for singing lessons, telling Papa I was destined for great things. They were both so proud of my talent so of course they believed him. Looking back, he groomed my parents too. They never hesitated to say yes when he offered to take me to the Symphony concerts in Hobart or Launceston. They thought he was offering me opportunities they couldn't give me."

Addy stared hard at the horizon and felt the reassuring warmth of Brenda's hand sliding into hers. "The singing lessons coincided with Mama's OCD taking over and Papa spending more and more time in his shed. After all the frenetic cleaning and piano playing at home, Four Winds felt like a calm oasis. I knew my parents loved me, but they were never physically or verbally demonstrative like him. He was full of effusive praise, which I lapped up like a puppy. It sounds so stupid, but none of it felt wrong. Not the end-of-class duets with his thigh pressed against mine. Not the shoulder massages after playing Chopin's *Ballade* or the congratulatory hugs and kisses. For me it was all about the music and pleasing him."

"It wasn't up to you to know if it was wrong or not, Addy," Brenda said firmly. "You were a child."

"It's taken me until recently to fully understand that." Addy huddled into her puffer and kept talking. "By Year Nine, Mama was checking every window and door over and over and taking fifteen minutes to leave the house. It drove me nuts. He said he was worried that if I complained about Mama's neediness to her, I might make her sicker and he encouraged me to vent to him. He listened to me with an intensity I'd never experienced from anyone, and when he told me over and over that he was the only person who truly understood me, I believed him.

"Once he'd reeled me in and I was his, things started to subtly change. Four Winds had always been a sanctuary, but suddenly there were random lessons when he didn't speak to me. Once he pulled my hands off the keys and sent me home, telling me he'd decide if and when I could return. I was hurt and confused and desperate to please him. All I wanted was for things to return to normal. Only with pedophiles, there is no normal.

"After that, Four Winds became both a refuge and a prison. It was the only place I was happy and it was the source of my greatest miseries." She shuddered. "The sex started after the first garden party recital. I wasn't quite sixteen. It happened at different times but always after a public performance. I assume he got off on being congratulated for my talent—who the hell knows, perhaps it was just another form of control—but suddenly he was the musical director at my high school and putting on shows."

Brenda gasped and oddly Addy found herself squeezing her hand, trying to reassure her. "It was a good thing. It ultimately saved me. Seeing how different he was with the other students, how he mostly ignored them, opened my eyes. Although any girl with big breasts complained he was a perve. Mostly his gaze was always on me. He either praised me or belittled me in front of everyone. I was his star and his shame.

"On the opening night of *Little Shop of Horrors* he made a big fuss and presented me with flowers. God knows why he did it. Perhaps because I was older then and he thought I would think it romantic."

She shrugged. "I remember Courtney saying how lucky I was, but I felt so far from lucky it didn't bear thinking about. I gave her the flowers."

Brenda startled. "I remember that. Poor Courtney. I kept asking her over and over if she was certain you'd given them to her."

Addy couldn't hold back a harsh laugh. "Someone must have told him I'd given them away, because when he arrived the next night he was angrier than I'd ever seen him. He dragged me into an office and berated me like he often did. When I was down on my knees sobbing and begging for his forgiveness, he—" She shook her head, refusing to verbalize the image.

"For years he'd told me my talent had blossomed and grown because of his love for me. How this special thing between us was a vital part of my talent and must remain our secret, because if people found out they wouldn't understand. They'd be jealous and I'd lose my chance at being the star I deserved to be. I believed him. I'd always believed him." Her voice cracked. "But that night away from Four Winds, down on the school's floor with my costume half off, I knew that if someone walked in and found us I'd lose everything. I completely freaked out. I guess terror gave me the physical strength to push him off me and I ran and hid in the girls' toilets. Courtney found me vomiting and she went and got Mum. She took me home, thinking I had stomach flu."

"Oh God." Brenda swiped at tears. "I hate that Courtney's golden moment of understudying was because of a horrifying moment of your own."

"A defining moment," Addy said firmly. "It was like the blinders fell away, revealing the truth. What I'd convinced myself was love and a soul-deep connection was warped and wrong. So very wrong. I gave up music. I took up surfing and drinking and disappointing my parents, but it kept me safe from him." Addy found a tissue in her pocket and blew her nose. "But I hate that I broke Mama's and Papa's hearts."

"You didn't—"

"I did. I saw it etched in the lines on their faces. Their confusion and pain every time they looked at me. A part of Mama disappeared after her first admission to the psychiatric hospital and Papa was begging me to go back to music to make her better. I promised them I'd audition for the Conservatory and hoped that lie was enough to appease them. I knew in my heart if I told Mama what the man she'd trusted me and my future to had done, I'd have dug her grave."

"I wonder at sixteen or seventeen if you'd even had the words?" Brenda mused. "I know I wasn't being abused, but I didn't have the words then to explain my confusing attraction to girls."

Gratitude swam into Addy, filling the painful spaces inside her.

"I didn't have the words. For a long time my brain's refused to visit the memories, and if my thoughts started to dive toward them, I drank to change the direction and lock them away. Only it didn't work. It's taken me all this time to acknowledge that the shame and humiliation he sowed in me has not only grown, but thrived like a hothouse plant. It's always told me I don't deserve to be treated well so I drank hard and played hard and put myself into dangerous situations over and over because I didn't matter."

"You do matter. You deserve all good things," Brenda said fervently. "You were a child and you did nothing wrong. He was the one committing a disgusting and heinous crime. Never you."

Addy blinked fast. "I appreciate your understanding and generosity, Brenda, I really do. Especially when my demons have made your life harder and Courtney's still not talking to you."

Brenda shifted her weight on the bench. "I've come to understand that even if I'd come out earlier or not been outed, Courtney would likely have reacted this way. She has some valid reasons to feel let down by me. Like Rita, I spent a lot of years in survival mode. Your mother was fighting memories of war and deprivation. I was fighting my sexuality."

"I wish they'd told me more about the war," Addy said, feeling old anger stir. "I might have understood them better."

"They wanted to protect you, and I'm sure they wanted to forget." Brenda's voice quivered with emotion. "I thought staying in my marriage was the best way to protect my children, but when so many days are a battle, there's not always enough energy left to be the mother you want to be. My sons coped better, but back then Courtney needed more of me than I could give. Now I'm finally in a place where I can, she can't forgive me. I have to live with that and hope one day she feels ready to talk."

"I can recommend a good therapist," Addy said.

"I'll keep that in mind." Brenda turned to look at her. "Most importantly, are they helping you?"

Addy thought about the difficult conversations in the room with the pale pastel walls, Swedish furniture and the large box of soft aloe vera tissues. "She's made me see how his toxic legacy's influenced and doomed my attempts at adult relationships. Work's the one place I believed I had control, but even that's been proved incorrect."

Exhaustion clawed at her. "My therapist tells me on average it takes twenty-three years before people are able to talk about their abuse."

Brenda squeezed her hand. "You've always been ahead of the curve."

Addy laughed, but her biggest regret swamped the moment of lightness. "But I was too slow. Mama and Papa died thinking I gave up music to hurt them."

"Oh, Addy, no!" Brenda shook her head so hard hair flicked into her eyes. "They didn't believe that. They never believed that. One thing we learn as parents is that as much as we might wish to live our own failed dreams through our children, we can't. Rita was disappointed for herself that you gave up music, but she loved you dearly."

Addy's fingers shredded the tissue. "I want to believe you so much."

"You can believe me, because it's the truth. After Ivan died and your mum moved into the care home, I visited her every couple of weeks. She always showed me photos of you and told me what you were doing. When you won that teaching award she almost burst with pride. When you got your master's, she ran a finger across your graduation photo and said, 'My Aida has found her own path.'"

Tears ran warm down Addy's cheeks. "Except I was pushed off my path and I've been wandering lost for years. God, I don't even have a career now, let alone a job!"

"You served me at the store the other day," Brenda said mildly. "You've stopped drinking, you're seeing a counselor and you're back playing the piano. Your compass is well and truly pointing you in the right direction. And when you're ready, I have a strong feeling you'll sing again."

"Only as a voice in a sea of many."

Addy couldn't picture herself singing a solo anywhere other than her shower and her living room.

CHAPTER FORTY-THREE

ON THE DAY of the passion project presentation, Steph found herself unexpectedly excited. With a couple of extra choir rehearsals, "Under The Sea" was sounding fabulous and Addy had devised some fun choralography. Even if she hadn't, it was impossible to sing the song without swaying like kelp beds.

At breakfast Zoe had chatted animatedly, telling Henry about her and Olivia's display in the school hall and how the videos would run continuously for people to watch. At 6:25 she and Olivia would give a brief talk on stage about how they designed the costumes and make-up and then they'd join the choir and perform.

"Monty can't come and you have to be there at 6:00," Zoe had instructed.

Henry had raised his hands in surrender. "The babysitter's all sorted."

The babysitter Steph had organized yesterday, when she realized it hadn't occurred to Henry to do it. She'd typed it into her ballooning spreadsheet under the tab of childcare.

"I wouldn't dare be late," Henry said.

Zoe threw Steph a look. For a second she thought she read "Can I believe him?" Steph instantly dismissed it.

"And I need you to pick me up at the bus with my make-up and costume so I can go straight to the hall and start painting faces," Zoe said.

Henry frowned. "I've got a conference call then."

"Dad!"

"What?" Henry looked bewildered. "I moved it so I'd be on time for the show."

"It's not a show!" Zoe's voice rose. "It's a presentation. I knew this was a dumb idea. I knew you'd let me down!"

"Hey!" Steph said, uncertain which Sun was irritating her the most. "Your father's not letting you down." *He's doing that to me.*

"You're conveniently forgetting the hours he spent this week helping you and Olivia edit the videos." Steph thought of Joanna and her indignation grew. "And when you asked him to fly your mother down, he booked and paid for her flight even though she didn't have the d—"

"Steph," Henry said sharply. "Can you meet the bus?"

"I don't have a choice, do I?"

"Don't put yourself out," Zoe muttered.

Steph ground her back teeth. "What time?"

Zoe didn't look up from her phone. "Four o'clock."

"I'll be working right up until I leave so put everything you need for tonight in the car now," Steph said.

Zoe glared at her. "Would you leave your make-up in a hot car all day?"

Hot was an unfulfilled dream as Monty wheezed through a wet and cold spring. "Fine. Leave it all by the door."

But Zoe hadn't been listening. Just like her father, her attention was fully on her phone. At 3:45, Steph looked at the pile of gear by the front door, including the laminated posters of Zoe's make-up designs. The make-up kit was missing.

"Zoe!"

Most of her wanted to pack only what was at the door, so Zoe experienced a natural consequence and took some responsibility for her phone obsession and not listening. But Steph could just picture the scenario: Zoe's tantrum in the car, followed by sullenness; the choir members' frustration at the delay; Courtney's smug look—what did you expect from Zoe? Not packing the make-up would have the biggest impact on Steph. With a sigh, she ran upstairs and into Zoe's room, a place she rarely ventured.

It was the usual teen chaos. Steph stepped over clothes to check the dressing table for the distinctive silver box, before going to the desk that was covered with drawings. The intricately decorated dragons and wizards were impressive in their detail, but it was the luminous fairy that stopped her.

Steph picked up the paper. Zoe had sketched a lush forest and placed the fairy in the center, wearing a flowing white and gold gown and with her hands cupped under her belly. With her wings extended, she looked like she was about to take flight, but black tears poured from her eyes, streaking down her face and to the ground. Nothing grew where they fell.

It was like being punched in the gut and Steph doubled over. Although the fairy didn't look anything like her, the drawing perfectly represented her feelings around losing the baby. About not being pregnant. About her life.

Fighting a wave of melancholy, she pushed the paper under the dragon and returned to her hunt for the silver make-up box. It wasn't on the desk so she checked underneath it.

The overflow from Zoe's wastepaper basket littered the floor and Steph picked up what looked like an upside-down photo. As she dropped it onto the desk, she saw Zoe's smiling face—a face not seen at Four Winds since the summer—but whoever she was standing next to had been scrubbed out with black marker pen. Steph narrowed her eyes, trying to recognize where the photo had been taken. Was it the beach? Was it her scrubbed out? Highly likely as Zoe reminded her most days she wasn't her mother.

Steph shoved the photo in her pocket, planning to show Henry proof that Zoe hated her. That Zoe needed to return to the mainland to live with Joanna.

Her phone buzzed, reminding her she needed to leave. Where the hell was the make-up box? She found it under the thrown-back bed cover, grabbed it and ran downstairs.

She arrived at the bus stop with a minute to spare and, with a jolt of surprise, noticed Courtney's four-wheel drive. According to Zoe, Olivia was only allowed to catch the bus once a week when she visited Brenda, otherwise Courtney picked her up from school.

The bus pulled up and a couple of boys got off, wearing their school uniform in that thrown-on way teen boys specialized in. The bus doors closed and the driver pulled back onto the highway.

What the hell? Steph blinked as if that would change the image, but no, the bus was disappearing around the bend. Occasionally Zoe missed the early bus and walked into Four Winds forty minutes later. But there was no time for that today.

Steph checked her phone. No missed calls or texts from Zoe. Had Steph misunderstood? She recalled the breakfast conversation—Zoe had definitely said four o'clock.

A knock on the window made her jump and she looked up to see Courtney frowning at her. She pressed the window button and the glass slid down.

"Where are they?" Courtney demanded.

"I don't know. There's no message from Zoe. Has Olivia called you?"

"Olivia doesn't have a phone."

"Really?" Considering how much of a helicopter parent Courtney was, Steph had assumed that not only would Olivia have a phone, but the location tracking service would be switched on and monitored at all times.

"Yes, really." Courtney glanced around as if the girls might have appeared. "God, I knew I should have picked her up! Call Zoe."

Steph bristled, having already hit the call button. "It's ringing."

As she held the phone to her ear she felt Courtney willing Zoe to answer. "It's rung out."

"I'm calling the school," Courtney said, her voice unsteady.

Steph watched her pace the length of the small grassy area as she spoke to someone, her free hand gesticulating wildly. Most of Steph wanted to believe Courtney was typically overreacting. After all, Zoe had been adamant no one could be late and surely that included herself? But a niggle of concern penetrated the scar tissue that had thickened over her tangled feelings for Zoe.

Courtney returned to the car and sat in the passenger seat, her face pale. "According to the teacher on bus duty, she remembers seeing them at the bus bay."

"So they either got on the bus or—" Steph facepalmed. "Shit."

"What?"

"Zoe's mother flew in today. Maybe she picked them up from school on her way past?"

Courtney stared at her wide-eyed. "Why wouldn't she tell you? What sort of mother does that to another?"

"Joanna," Steph said bitterly and turned on the ignition. "We'd better go to the hall or I'll get into trouble for being late with the make-up."

Courtney stayed where she was and pulled on her seatbelt. "Just so you know, when I meet this Joanna, I'm giving her a piece of my mind."

"Knock yourself out."

They walked into a buzz of noise.

Addy met them, curls bouncing and with a big smile. "Oh, good, you're here. Kieran's set up the lights Zoe wanted and I thought while the girls are doing the make-up, we could ..." Addy glanced over Steph's shoulder. "Where are they?"

Courtney's words tumbled over Addy's as she marched past them.

"Mum! Is Olivia here?"

Brenda turned from her conversation with Marilyn, scanned Courtney's face and walked straight to her. "Was I supposed to meet her at the bus? I can go now."

Courtney made a strangled sound. "She wasn't on the bus."

Brenda hugged her, then clapped her hands even though the hall was now silent.

"Has anyone seen Olivia?" she asked.

"And Zoe," Steph said.

There were shakings of heads and murmurs of no, and then Courtney seemed to recover.

"Steph, ring Zoe again. Mum, check the kitchen. Morgan and Heidi, can you go out the back, and I'll check the toilets."

"What's going on?" Addy asked Steph, her face lined with concern.

Steph's gut spasmed and her fingers trembled on Zoe's number.

"When the girls weren't on the bus, I thought Joanna must have picked them up and brought them here. Maybe they got lost? I'd better call Henry." She groaned. "Oh God. He's on a conference call and he won't pick up or check his messages."

"Kieran." Addy waved him over. "Henry's tied up on a work call. Can you go to Four Winds and bring him here?"

"I can and I will." Kieran gave Steph's hand a squeeze. "I bet by the time I get back, they'll have turned up."

Steph wanted to believe him. "I hope so."

"We'll call you the moment they get here," Addy said to Kieran. "Is your cell phone on ring?"

He pulled it out of his pocket and flicked the switch. "It is now."

Then he leaned in and gave Addy a quick kiss goodbye before striding out the door.

Steph stared at her. "I know I'm stressed, but did that just happen?"

Addy shrugged and gave a wry smile. "We're trying old-fashioned dating and that's as racy as it gets. Now give me Joanna's and Zoe's numbers. You never know, they might pick up from me."

Courtney rushed back into the hall. "They're nowhere!"

"They're somewhere," Brenda said calmly. "Let's think it through. Surely, if Zoe's mother had picked them up she'd have brought them straight here."

"There's no surely with Joanna," Steph said, stabbing Joanna's number for the fourth time. "Could anyone else have picked them up?"

"Ben's on the farm and he knew I was bringing Olivia here," Courtney said. "Her school friends all live walking distance from campus so none of their parents would have picked them up. Besides, they're a lovely well-mannered group and all very responsible. They'll be busy with their own preparations for tonight."

Steph ignored the inference that she, Henry and Zoe were neither well-mannered nor responsible and tried to stay focused.

"I've never heard Zoe mention these girls."

"I don't think Zoe's part of that group," Courtney said stiffly.

"But she's Olivia's friend. Maybe they went together? Can you call these girls' parents? They might know something."

Courtney looked unconvinced, but she walked away with her phone to her ear.

"I've texted Zoe," Addy said. "I told her I suck big time at make-up and I need her help. I even added a GIF for extra cred. Fingers crossed she texts me back."

"Oh God. I don't know if I want to kill her or ..."

"Hug her?" Addy suggested.

"She wouldn't want that," Steph said quickly. "We're not exactly close, and this year she's made herself pretty hard to like."

And what about you? Steph brushed the thought away.

"I remember doing that when I was a teen." Addy laughed, the sound tight. "Who am I kidding? I've been making myself hard to like for years. It stopped people getting close and seeing the real me and the shame that lived there."

Steph wanted to reassure her, but at the same time Addy's brutal honesty about her past discomforted her. It was information Steph had always thought she wanted to know, but now it hinted at a darkness no one deserved to suffer.

"The real you is amazing and talented and kind," Steph said.

Addy's brows rose. "Did you think you were amazing and talented when you were her age?"

A shiver ran across Steph's skin. "You think something's happened to Zoe?"

"I have no idea," Addy said. "But I think there's more to her behavior than normal teen angst."

Courtney returned clutching her phone. "As expected, they're not with the other girls. Has Zoe called?"

"No," Steph and Addy said in unison.

Courtney tugged at her hair. "Wherever they are, Olivia will be beside herself. I know my daughter and she'll want to be here. She's worked so hard on this project and if someone else jeopardizes it for her—"

"It won't be Zoe," Steph said firmly, surprising herself. "If you'd heard her this morning at breakfast issuing instructions to Henry and me as if we were the kids and she was the adult, you'd know it too."

"Both of them have worked hard," Brenda said. "And I wouldn't normally worry, but Olivia is very reliable."

"Which is why this makes no sense!" Courtney cried.

Steph's phone lit up with Henry's name and she stared at it. Had Kieran broken the speed limit to Four Winds? Maybe Zoe was at home.

"Hey," Henry said, sounding oddly furious and flat. "I've just gotten a text from Jetstar. I think Joanna's on the Sunshine Coast."

Rage blew through Steph so hard it nearly knocked her off her feet. "You've got to be kidding!"

Courtney was saying, "What? Is that Zoe? I want to talk to Olivia!"

"I wish I was," Henry said. "Joanna must have changed the ticket not realizing it was booked through our account and I get notified. God, how can she do this to Zoe? I'm so angry I can't even think. But I don't want anything to ruin Zoe's night so can you tell her the flight's been delayed? That way it won't be as much of a shock when Joanna doesn't turn up."

The significance of Joanna's location suddenly hit Steph like a ton of bricks, stealing the hope she'd been clinging to.

"Henry, Zoe's not here. She and Olivia didn't get off the bus. I assumed they were with Joanna, but Zoe's not answering her phone and Olivia doesn't have one and Courtney's rung the school and the other parents and ..." Her chest was suddenly too tight to breathe and she was choking on tears.

Addy lifted the phone out of her hand and Steph heard her say, "Henry, Kieran will be at Four Winds any minute. Get him to take you to every bus stop between the cove and the school."

"Oh God." Courtney sank onto the chair next to Steph. "We need to call the police."

CHAPTER FORTY-FOUR

WHILE THEY WAITED for the police and Ben to arrive, Marilyn organized cups of tea and sandwiches, but Steph couldn't eat. She continued to check her phone and bargain with a god she didn't believe in. Meanwhile, Brenda had divided the cove into sections and choir members went off in pairs to look for the girls. Even though it was unlikely they were in town, people needed to feel like they were doing something.

Courtney, who'd been panicking from the moment the bus had arrived without the girls, was now oddly calm.

"Wherever they are, at least they're together," she said to Steph.

It was so unexpectedly kind that Steph had no idea what to say to her.

Steph was on her way to the bathroom when Courtney's phone rang. She immediately turned back.

"I don't recognize the number," Courtney said.

"Answer it!" Addy said.

"Hello?" Courtney listened, then grabbed Steph's upper arm, her fingers digging in so hard they hurt.

Steph's heart felt like it had stopped. "Is it them?"

"I promise I'll listen," Courtney was saying. "No, I won't yell. Please tell me so I can help." She was nodding and then she said, "Stay there. I'm coming now." She hung up the phone. "They're at the caves."

"The caves?" Steph repeated blankly as relief stole all cogent thought. "Why are they at the caves?"

"Come on, I'll drive you both," Addy said. "Brenda, can you call Henry and Ben and tell them to meet us there?"

"Leave it with me. Marilyn and I will text everyone to come back to the hall." Brenda put her hand on Courtney's shoulder.

"Give Livvy my love."

Courtney nodded mutely then followed Addy and Steph out to the car.

While Addy drove, Steph grilled Courtney about what Olivia had told her on the phone.

"Most of it was me reassuring her I wouldn't get mad. Oh God."

Courtney's voice cracked. "Is that how my daughter sees me? As someone who goes straight to yelling?"

Steph left that can of worms alone—she was hardly in a position to criticize. Zoe had ignored every text and phone call from her. "At least she called you. Did she say why they're at the caves?"

"I didn't ask," Courtney said. "I just wanted to get here as fast as I could."

Addy pulled up in the parking lot and Steph was out the door before she'd set the handbrake. Courtney was fast behind her and they jogged down the thirty wooden steps onto the hard sand.

"Mum!" Olivia waved, then ran to meet them and threw herself at Courtney.

Courtney hugged her hard. "Are you hurt?"

"No."

"What about Zoe?" Steph asked.

Olivia bit her lip. "She's ... it's complicated. She doesn't want me to tell and she's already mad at me for stealing her cell phone."

"I'm glad you did," Steph said. "Thank you."

Olivia glanced nervously at her mother. "I thought you'd be going off at me."

"Call your dad and Mémé." Courtney handed her phone to Olivia.

"Which cave is Zoe in?" Steph asked.

"The small one," Olivia said.

"Steph, do you want me to come with you?" Courtney asked.

"Thanks, but I think I need to do this on my own."

Steph entered the smaller cave, blinking furiously and willing her eyes to adjust quickly to the inky dark.

"Zoe?" Her voice echoed around the cavern, bouncing back to her.

She waited and listened but there was no reply. The earthy scent clogged her nostrils. *Why the small cave, Zoe?* She suddenly remembered her cell phone had a flashlight app and she turned it on. The light barely spilled beyond her feet.

"Zo, it's Steph."

She listened keenly, willing her to reply. Nothing.

Keeping her head low, she walked gingerly forward, trying not to sprain her ankle on the uneven surface. God, she hated this sort of oppressive darkness. Her breath came faster but she pushed on with small steps, battling her rising panic about the claustrophobic space.

"If you wanted to freak me out it's working, okay. I'm officially freaked. Please give me a sign you're alive."

The silence continued.

Steph waved the phone in useless arcs and muttered, "Don't let there be bats."

Zoe's voice cut through the darkness. "Don't be a wimp. Bats are awesome."

Relief swooped through her that Zoe sounded her normal, snarky self. Irritation immediately followed. What the hell was she playing at, making Steph walk into this confined space when she should be somewhere else?

The conversation with Addy rushed back, stalling her ire. *I've been making myself hard to like for years. It stops people getting close.*

Despite the "whatevs" and "boring" comments, Zoe had never

missed a choir rehearsal and this morning she'd been genuinely excited. Something must have happened to bring the girls here.

Olivia had said it was complicated. Whatever it was, Steph's gut told her it was more to do with Zoe than Olivia, otherwise Olivia wouldn't have taken Zoe's phone and called her mother. For the first time in months, Steph not only wanted to know what was going on, but was determined to find out.

She moved closer to the wall and kept creeping forward, pushing down her panic about the dark so it didn't overwhelm her. The last thing she and Zoe needed was a panic attack. Eventually the light caught and reflected back from Zoe's bracelet—another uniform infringement.

Steph lowered herself onto the sand and immediately felt the dampness seeping into her through the flimsy choir top. She turned off the flashlight app and the darkness pressed in on them.

"Hi." When Zoe didn't respond, she added, "Looks like you got a little bit lost on the way to the hall. Want to tell me why?"

"No."

Don't ask closed questions.

Steph tried again. "I'm interested in why you're here."

"No, you're not," Zoe scoffed.

"Yes, I am."

Zoe snorted. "You're only interested in having another baby and getting rid of me."

The loaded words crashed harshly into Steph, holding a truth she couldn't hide from. "I do want another baby, but it's not the only thing I'm interested in."

Liar!

There was a long silence. "You hate me for making you lose the baby."

Oh, Zoe. "I don't hate you."

"Yeah, right."

Zoe's drawing of the fairy—hands cupping her belly, black tears scorching the ground—flared in Steph's mind. She'd thought it was her, but now she wondered if it was Zoe's pain and guilt. Did Zoe believe she'd caused the baby's death? If she did, Steph had done little to disabuse her.

The realization held up an unforgiving mirror and it was impossible to hide from her own shame. She was the adult and Zoe the child, yet Steph's behavior came close to mimicking immature adolescent blame. It was time to step up and be the mature woman she'd always considered herself to be.

"You didn't make me lose the baby, Zoe," she said firmly. "Us yelling at each other didn't make me lose the baby either. I lost the baby because there was something wrong, *not* because of anything you said or did, or I said and did. It was just an unfortunate coincidence that at the time we were both behaving in a way that was less than our best selves."

She blew out a long breath. "I've been tangled up in my own grief for months and if anyone's to blame for you feeling this way, it's me. I'm sorry. I'm very sorry."

For a while the only sound in the cave was water plinking and Zoe's breathing.

"If you're telling the truth, why do you want me to go back and live with Mum?" Zoe suddenly demanded.

Guilt pierced Steph and she let her head fall back against the cave wall. "Every day you tell me in actions and words how much I let you down by not being your mother. I know you miss Joanna so I thought you'd be happier if you went back to Melbourne."

There was a long silence and then Zoe spoke so quietly Steph strained to hear. "Mum doesn't want me either."

Oh, Zoe.

Steph started to say, "That's not true," then remembered with a stomach-dropping rush where Joanna was. Did Zoe know her mother had ditched her for the sunshine state? Was that why she was hiding here?

"What makes you say that?" she asked instead.

Again Zoe was silent.

Steph was tempted to turn on the flashlight app so she could read the girl's face. She immediately reminded herself that Zoe's face had been closed for months and blinding her wouldn't help. She pinned her hope on the loaded silence reaching capacity and spilling over. She didn't have to wait long.

"She's got a boyfriend," Zoe said.

"That doesn't mean she doesn't want you or that you can't go home."

"It's not home, okay!" Zoe's shout echoed around the cave. "It stopped being home when *he* moved in. I hate him!"

A live-in boyfriend? Steph's mouth dried. "Did he do something to you? I mean inappropriate stuff like touching or—"

"Ew! Gross. No!"

"Thank God." Steph slumped in relief. "Have you told your mother how you feel about him?"

"Why do you think she sent me here?"

Sent. The word punched Steph in the chest, then her rational brain kicked in. Sure, Joanna was difficult to deal with, but Steph had no evidence of Joanna not loving Zoe.

She's putting a boyfriend ahead of her child.

You can talk! You know how tricky Zoe can be.

"Perhaps it was more like a suggestion that you come and live with us for a while rather than being sent away?" Steph said.

"I mean, she bought you the phone so you can talk to her whenever you want, and you do, right? You spoke to her on Tuesday when you asked Dad to book her the plane ticket."

The silence lengthened, only this time it didn't spill. Steph's growing ripple of unease built into a choppy swell.

"Zoe, when did you last talk to Joanna?"

"She texts sometimes," Zoe said softly. "When she wants stuff."

A slew of expletives filled Steph's mouth and she wanted to reach through time and space and slap Joanna so hard she spun. "You mean like a trip to Queensland?"

Zoe gasped. "How do you know?"

Steph sighed. "When you didn't get off the bus I thought Joanna must have picked up you and Olivia from school. Then Henry said he got a text from Jetstar ... It doesn't matter." She reached out her hand and patted the air until she connected with Zoe's leg. "I'm so sorry, Zoe. We thought that even though Joanna wasn't talking to us, she was talking to you every day. I should have asked more questions."

But even as she said it, she knew Zoe wouldn't have told her. Why would she when she felt unloved by both mother figures in her life. When Steph had been so caught up in her own pain, she'd selfishly taken the easy road of ignoring a clearly hurting Zoe. God, did she even deserve to be a mother?

Her mind shied away from that unforgiving truth and landed on the timeline of the last few days. "When did Joanna ask you for the plane ticket?"

"Monday night."

"So you knew about Queensland at breakfast this morning?"

"Well, duh, Steph. It's Thursday."

"Exactly! And even though your mother's let you down and, God knows, I haven't been much better, at breakfast you were excited about tonight. And you're always saying Olivia's a goody-two-shoes, so why did you both get off the bus early and come down here instead of to the hall?"

This time when Zoe didn't reply, Steph didn't wait long. "Zoe?"

"I'm not telling you."

Steph could picture Zoe—arms crossed, mouth a taut and mulish line. She rubbed her temples. "You've just told me so much worse."

"You don't know that!"

"Sorry." She sighed. "I just can't imagine how anything can be worse than you thinking I blamed you for the miscarriage." *Or your mother sending you away.*

"It just is, okay."

"Steph? Zoe?" Courtney's voice called into the dark. "Are you ready to go? If we leave now, we can still make it."

"I'm not going," Zoe said mutinously.

"If you won't tell me, will you tell Henry?" Steph asked her.

"No way!"

Steph instinctively knew asking why wasn't going to get her anywhere. "Is missing tonight fair on Olivia?"

"She can do it without me. I'm not stopping her."

"It's *our* passion project," Olivia called out. "I'm not doing it without you."

"You have to or you'll fail and your mum will literally kill you," Zoe said.

A beam of light appeared and then Olivia and Courtney stood just in front of them. Steph braced herself for the tongue-lashing Courtney was bound to give Zoe.

"God, I hope there aren't any bats." Courtney lowered herself to the ground. "Also I have no plans to kill anyone, literally or otherwise. Of course I want Olivia to do her presentation, but she's adamant she won't do it without you. That's not easy for me to accept, but I'm trying to respect her decision to support you."

"I didn't ask her to," Zoe said quietly.

"It's what best friends do," Olivia said stoutly.

"Friends don't snitch," Zoe said.

"I didn't snitch. You scared me," Olivia countered.

"Sorry." Zoe sounded surprisingly contrite.

"Zoe, I'm guessing something happened at school today and whatever it was it's why you don't want to do the presentation."

Courtney cleared her throat. "I know I wasn't very supportive of your idea at the start, but you and Olivia have been so organized and worked so hard you've changed my mind. I want you both to have the opportunity to show everyone how talented you are."

"Me too," Steph said. "It's pretty impressive the way you got a group of adults excited and prepared to do choralography."

"Addy did that," Zoe said.

"Addy came up with the movements because Marilyn chose the song because she was inspired by your mermaid make-up designs and Olivia's seascape material," Courtney said. "Zoe, I just hate the idea that someone or something is stealing your well-deserved chance to shine. What's the worst thing that can happen if you do your presentation?"

Courtney hadn't turned off her flashlight app and Zoe's face was partially lit. Steph caught the anguish and risked reaching for her hand. Zoe spoke so softly this time she didn't catch the words. "Zo?"

"They'll laugh at me. I'm never going back!"

"If you don't go then I won't go," Olivia said.

"Oh, for heaven's sake," Courtney said, sounding far more like her normal self. "Whether or not you do the presentation, both of you are going back to school tomorrow."

"Did you do something embarrassing?" Steph asked. "We all do things like—"

"It wasn't Zoe," Olivia said. "Tell them, Zo."

"No," Zoe said, but it lacked the previous emphasis.

"Please," Olivia begged. "They want to help. They can help."

Tears slipped down Zoe's cheeks. "I can't show them."

"Can I?" Olivia asked.

Zoe nodded slowly, the movement loaded with dispirited resignation.

Olivia pulled Zoe's cell phone out of her pocket and swiped the screen a few times. A video came up of Zoe in the schoolyard talking to a boy. She looked happy and relaxed—so different from the girl at Four Winds. Then suddenly a donut hit her on the side of the face and jam exploded, dripping down her cheek. Grinning, the boy turned to the camera and gave a double thumbs-up. Girls laughed and voices called out.

"Zoe Sun, you're such a stuck-up little ho."

"You stupid cow!"

"As if Zane would be interested in a yellow dog like you."

Steph gagged. Zoe sobbed.

"That's enough," Courtney said tersely. "Turn it off."

Steph hauled Zoe into her arms and stroked her hair. "You're none of those horrible things they said, Zo. Absolutely none. Don't let their evil words land or stick. And as for that boy, he's a dickhead and not worth your time!"

"There's other stuff too," Olivia said. She brought up text messages and showed Steph.

Ur so stupid

Ur so fat and ugly followed by the vomiting emoji.

Ur so weird

No one likes a chink

Utterly horrified, Steph struggled to speak. "Who would do this?"

"It was Gemma and Ivy and Mia," Olivia said. "That's why I don't want to be friends with them."

Courtney looked shattered. "But they're always so polite."

"Only to adults!" Olivia said indignantly. "They've been mean to Zoe and me and a couple of other girls all year. First they said we were their friends and then they dumped us and told everyone not to talk to us. That's why Mr. Gibbons sent us home. We were sticking up for Daisy and they told Mrs. Delacour we were mean to them! Then one day in art, I heard them talking about a private group on Instagram that the ninth graders have where they share videos. People get points for humiliation and the best ones get uploaded and shared. Everyone at school saw this."

"This is why you don't have a phone!" Courtney said.

"It doesn't mean there isn't a private video of me," Olivia said, sounding far older than her years. "Those girls always giggle when I walk past them. I bet there's something in the privates."

"Zoe, your dad and I are going to sort this out," Steph said. "We'll talk to the principal—"

"No!" Zoe pleaded. "It's already bad."

"Steph's right," Courtney said. "Ben and I will be talking to Mr. Gibbons. I'm on the school council and I know the school has zero tolerance for bullying. As awful as this video is, Zoe, it's evidence of what's going on under the school's nose. And as we can hear voices, we know some of the girls involved. Believe me, they'll be in serious trouble."

"If they were adults, they'd be charged," Steph said, patting Zoe's back. "You don't want this to happen to anyone else, do you?"

Zoe shook her head against Steph's sternum, and Steph welcomed the pain of bone on bone, knowing it was just a hint of the anguish Zoe had endured for months.

That bloody cell phone! No matter which way she looked at it, it represented pain—a mother's rejection wrapped up in a much-wanted gift, and then unrelenting bullying. Steph wanted to throw it into the surf.

You should have known.

Her lack of care tossed her between disgrace and ignominy before trammeling her in remorse.

Steph lifted Zoe's face and wiped away her tears with her thumbs. "When no one stands up to bullies, they cement their power. We're going to stand up to them. And the best way to start is by going to school tonight with Olivia and fifteen adults who are on your side and showing them you don't care what they think."

"But I do care." Zoe's voice, usually so bolshie, sounded small and defeated. "They were so nice at first—I thought they were my friends."

"Of course you care." Steph thought about Addy and how her boss had treated her—friendly at first then gaslighting her. "But they're not your friends and they never were, because friends don't do the things they've done. Friends don't get their kicks out of humiliating you. No one likes being bullied or laughed at and no one deserves to be treated like this. Tonight's all about giving them the bird and not letting them win. I don't know what their passion projects are, but I'm pretty certain they won't feature a choir sounding like a calypso band."

"Yeah, and even though they said they'd laugh at us, they won't do anything in front of the teachers or their parents," Olivia said wisely. "So when we crush it, that will literally kill them."

Zoe managed a snotty laugh. "That sounds dope."

"Thanks, Olivia," Steph said. "Zoe's lucky to have such a good friend."

"Yeah," Zoe said. "Thanks."

"Steph! Zoe!" Addy's voice called from the entrance. "Henry's here."

Steph kissed Zoe on the top of her head. "You ready, kid?" she said, trying to sound like Henry.

"Is there enough time?" Zoe asked anxiously. "It has to be perfect!"

"We've got time if we tweak the plan," Steph said. "You do full make-up for yourself, Olivia and Marilyn. Addy, Morgan and I will paint a sea star on everyone else's cheeks. How about that?"

"And Kieran," Zoe said firmly. "We need a merman."

Steph hugged her, relieved to hear the determination back in her voice. "Sounds like a plan. Now let's go and hug your dad and get this choir on the road."

CHAPTER FORTY-FIVE

MARILYN'S HANDS cut the air and the final sounds of Morgan's and Heidi's voices mimicking a vibraphone faded to silence. The choir took a bow and the school auditorium filled with applause from the parents and whoops and cheers from the students.

Brenda caught Marilyn's gaze and mouthed, "Thank you." Marilyn grinned, then turned to receive a congratulatory handshake from Christopher Gibbons.

As the choir members high-fived one another, Brenda glanced at Courtney. She was hugging Olivia, her smile a mixture of relief and delight. Brenda understood perfectly—the complicated dance of abject fear and chest-bursting pride that accompanied motherhood. Then Ben and Jesse were there hugging them too, and Ben raised his hand and gave Brenda a thumbs-up.

A couple of squealing girls rushed up to Olivia and Zoe and hugged them. "That was epic!"

Christopher Gibbons tapped the microphone. "I think we definitely saw and heard the passion in Zoe and Olivia's presentation. Congratulations, girls. Next up is Noah Ruttan. Noah's passion is magic and he's going to tell us about his research and demonstrate some tricks. Take it away, Noah."

Brenda found Marilyn and they watched the rest of the presentations together. She was aware of Courtney and Ben standing on the other side of the hall and tried not to let disappointment steal the euphoria the singing had generated. This afternoon, when Courtney had turned to her for help, she'd dared to hope their estrangement was over, but of course that was wishful thinking.

When the principal wrapped up the official part of the evening, Marilyn said, "The talent that turns up at these sorts of events always amazes me. As does the teacher dedication. Sissy Delacour deserves a medal doing this year after year."

"Why don't you tell her? She's just over there." Brenda pointed her out.

"Good idea."

The hall was emptying quickly with parents hustling their kids out the door, wanting to get younger siblings home to bed. Courtney would be leading the charge—school nights ran to a tight routine. Brenda glanced around for Ben's height, always an easy marker, but he wasn't in the room and she couldn't see Olivia or Zoe or the Suns.

Kieran walked over. "A few of the choir are going to the Mad Penguin for pizza. Do you and Marilyn fancy a bite?"

"That sounds lovely. Is Addy going?"

He grinned. "It was her idea."

Brenda looked at his dark curls and the silver and gray scales Zoe had painted on his face and knew not just any man would be prepared to go to a pizza joint looking like a merman. Did it mean kindness?

"Kieran, Addy's mother was a good friend of mine. Sadly Rita's no longer with us so I'm her stand-in. Don't break Addy's heart."

His grin smoothed into serious lines. "I don't intend to, Brenda. But what if she breaks mine?"

"Then I'd be sorry for both of you."

Kieran leaned in and kissed her. "Thanks, Ma."

She tried her best at an Irish accent. "Get away with you."

He walked away laughing.

"Mum, are you coming for pizza?" Courtney stood in front of her.

"I thought you'd gone home."

"Ben's taken Jesse home, and the Suns have taken Olivia and Zoe out for ice-cream sundaes."

Brenda stared. "On a school night?"

Courtney laughed, the sound loaded with disbelief. "I know, right? Who'd have thought I'd agree to that, but today's been ... Can we talk?"

In the middle of an auditorium? But Brenda wasn't going to say no. "Of course."

"The rehearsal room's empty." Courtney led the way and closed the door behind them.

Brenda sat on one of two chairs facing each other that looked like they'd been set up for a drama class. Courtney sat on the other one and told her about the video and the bullying.

"I'm terrified of the world Olivia's growing up in," Courtney said.

"From the day she was born, all I've wanted to do is protect her. That's why I'm involved in the school, why I invited those girls over, why I actively discouraged her being friends with Zoe and said no to a cell phone until she's older. But after today, she's never going to be old enough for a phone!"

Courtney's confusion and anxiety circled Brenda. "I know you want to wrap her in cottonwool, but you can't stop her from growing up."

Courtney stared at her lap. "That's what Ben says. But I miss the little girl she was. She used to look at me as if I was the sun, moon and stars and now she tells me *nothing!*"

Brenda stifled a smile, remembering her bewilderment when Courtney hit thirteen. "That's not strictly true. She might not tell you as much as you want to know, but today she recognized she was out of her depth and the person she called for help was you."

"First she told me not to rant!" Courtney sighed. "God, she may have a point. Honestly, I was just so relieved she was safe, I didn't want to yell. I just wanted to hug her and never let her go."

"That never changes," Brenda said.

Courtney stiffened. "I don't remember you hugging me much."

"You turned thirteen and preferred hugs from your father."

Courtney sighed. "Did I? It wasn't a conscious thing, but ..."

Brenda leaned forward, eager to know. "But what?"

"I dunno. Everything with Dad seemed simple."

"And everything with me was complicated." Brenda opened her hands. "I'm sorry that my depression crashed headlong into your teenage angst and you didn't want to have much to do with me. Thankfully you don't have that problem with Olivia."

"I might if I don't back off." Courtney rubbed her face. "I thought by being so involved in Livvy's life I was doing the right thing. I thought it would rustproof our relationship so we'd stay close."

Not like us. The unspoken words hovered between them and an old ache burned.

"Olivia's maturing into a caring young woman," Brenda said.

"She's been a loyal friend to Zoe, and even though you might think that's teenage defiance, from what she's told me Olivia doesn't enjoy going against your wishes."

"And she's been loyal to you. I never expected my teen to teach me things." Courtney's face twisted in an agony of self-awareness.

"I read your letter."

Relief and terror spun on a helix. Brenda didn't dare hope.

Courtney continued. "I've read it a few times. Mum, I had no idea you were depressed on and off for most of my life."

"It wasn't your job to know," Brenda said.

"But now I do and I've been thinking about it. A lot. I've done some reading and what I've always thought of as your detachment and disinterest was probably depression. That's just heartbreaking."

Courtney twisted her fingers. "I know people look at Ben and me and think why does such an easygoing bloke put up with high-maintenance me, but he needs my drive just as I need his calm. But you and Dad never shared anything like it. It makes me mad and sad for both of you. Like you both wasted your lives being unhappy together."

"It wasn't misery all of the time," Brenda said. "The happy memories you have were real, and your father never raised the topic of a divorce. He was a different generation. I honestly don't think he had many expectations of marriage beyond three square meals a day and sex on a Saturday night."

Courtney's cheeks flushed red. "Mum!"

"Well, darling, we obviously had sex at least three times because we had you and your brothers."

Courtney's hands were on her ears. "Lah-lah-lah."

Brenda touched her knee. "I'm glad you and Ben have a true partnership."

Courtney dropped her hands and gave Brenda a long look. "Is that what you have with Marilyn?"

"Yes."

Courtney wrapped her arms around herself as if she needed a hug. "It's just so hard to get my head around it."

"I understand," Brenda said sincerely.

"Yes, but what sort of person am I if I hate you for having what I cherish with Ben?" Courtney's shoulders slumped. "I'm glad you're happy, Mum, I really am. But I don't think I'm ever going to be able to say to people, 'my mother's a lesbian.'"

"That's okay. I still find it hard to say it myself." Brenda dared to slide her hands into Courtney's. "Labels aren't important, sweetheart. What's important is I love Marilyn and I love you and the boys and Ben and all the grandies. For the first time in my life I'm at peace with my truth."

Courtney blinked rapidly and pulled her hands away, searching for a tissue. She blew her nose loudly. "The thing is, the first time I met Marilyn I really liked her. I thought she'd make a great friend, but now I have no idea what she is to me."

"She'd like to be a friend," Brenda said.

One side of Courtney's mouth lifted. "She'd snitch all my secrets to my mother."

"She wouldn't," Brenda said seriously. "Remember the night you both had a drink at the surf club after Livvy was suspended? Marilyn didn't tell me and we argued about it."

Courtney frowned. "Why?"

"I was jealous that you'd opened up to her and not me."

Courtney stared at her as if she couldn't conceive of Brenda being jealous of that.

Brenda shrugged. "Just like you hope to have a close relationship with adult Livvy, it's what I've always hoped to have with you. What I've been working hard on since your father died. But I've learned I can't force anyone to do what I want. I may not always agree with you, darling, and we're probably going to clash as often as we agree, but I'm always here for you."

Courtney was silent for a moment. "I know you are, Mum. And when Livvy didn't get off the bus and I saw you at the hall, all I wanted was for you to hug me and tell me everything would be okay."

Brenda lost the battle not to cry and reached out and hugged her daughter.

She'd just stepped back and wiped her face when Marilyn appeared in the doorway, her brows arching in surprise and question.

"I was wondering where you'd gotten to," Marilyn said.

"Mum and I were just debriefing the last twenty years," Courtney said wryly.

Marilyn gave a quiet smile. "That sounds hopeful."

"I think so," Courtney said. "Marilyn, I'm sorry I didn't cope better with the news about you and Mum. Thank you for making her happy."

"It's my pleasure," Marilyn said. "She makes me just as happy too."

Brenda caught Marilyn's hand in hers and extended her other one to Courtney. "Ready for pizza?"

Courtney breathed in deeply and accepted Brenda's hand.

CHAPTER FORTY-SIX

STEPH AND HENRY sat on a picnic rug under the Norfolk pine, not fully appreciating the warm spring sunshine. Monty was at childcare; Addy was at Four Winds with Alan, applying stickers to circus people and packaging the day's orders; and Zoe was at school.

The morning had been consumed by meetings with the principal and the school counselor. Olivia and Zoe had refused to be separated, and insisted on talking to the counselor without any parents in the room.

While Ben, Courtney, Henry and Steph waited for the session to finish, they'd bonded over the exclusion.

"I'm proud of them," Ben said. "It can't be easy."

"It's going to kill me not asking Olivia what they're talking about," Courtney said.

"'Literally' kill you," Steph said, mimicking the girls. "At least Olivia tells you things. I've got a lot of ground to make up before Zoe trusts me enough to tell me anything."

"She told you a lot last night," Henry said bitterly. "I hate what she's been through."

Steph had hugged him. Now, she handed him a travel mug full of Sven's coffee.

"I think this is the absolute low point of my mothering career," she said. "If it was a paid job, they'd have sacked me and stripped me of all my leave and benefits."

"We've hit rock bottom together," Henry said. "I let Zoe have unsupervised access to the cell phone so she could stay in contact with Joanna. Instead I may as well have opened every window and door in the house and left her home alone. And Joanna—God! What the hell is wrong with her? No one is saying she can't have a boyfriend, but it's like she's decided she's had enough of being a parent!"

"Teens aren't always easy," Steph said.

"Neither are toddlers, but we never think about sending them away," Henry fumed.

Shame burned hot in Steph's chest. "I'm not proud that I asked you to send Zoe back to Joanna."

"You said it in the heat of an argument." Henry turned the cup in his hands and stared at the horizon. "I'm aware that when we talk about the miscarriage and trying to have another baby there are times neither of us are at our best."

That was an understatement, but it was also a whole other topic. Right now, Steph knew to the depths of her marrow that they needed to focus on Zoe.

"Addy said something yesterday about how she'd acted out to keep people at arm's-length. It was a light-bulb moment. Since the miscarriage, I've been in a fog. I've taken Zoe's rudeness and her school behavior at face value and worse, as a personal insult. When I say it out loud it sounds so immature, but all I knew was I couldn't keep my own baby safe and my stepdaughter hated me.

"What sort of mother does that make me? When Zoe was snarky, it was easy to buy into the general consensus that all teens are difficult. It makes me squirm too, because I know not all of them are difficult. I wasn't, and your mum said you were too busy studying to act up. And look at Olivia Burton—she's upbeat and pretty cruisy most of the time."

Steph wrapped her arms around her knees. "Oh, Henry. All these months I've been blaming Zoe for being selfish when she's been crying for help. I was so self-involved I didn't see it. And when you told me you were worried about her, I brushed off your concerns."

He sighed. "You're not totally on your own. I noticed you were distant with her and she was pushing you, but instead of parenting her and calling her out when she was rude to you, I tiptoed around her moods. I've been trying to be her friend instead of her father."

"You nailed the passion project," she said loyally.

"Yeah. But it doesn't make up for not knowing she was dealing with bullying and a mother who'd abandoned her."

Steph sipped her coffee and decided to risk the truth. "Up until yesterday, I always thought of Zoe in terms of your daughter, never mine. And when she only came on vacation with us it didn't matter that you made all the decisions for her, and I stayed just that little bit hands off. But it's not enough now she's living with us full-time. I have to be involved. I want to be involved, but I think we need some professional help to blend us into a family."

"Family counseling?"

"Yes. A lot of stuff came up in the cave. Oh, Henry, she's been blaming herself for the miscarriage."

Henry looked winded. "What? Why?"

Steph didn't want to say the words. She worried how they would sound and she feared Henry's response. But if the last twenty hours had taught her anything, it was that the three of them needed to learn how to communicate.

"When it happened, Zoe and I were arguing. I was so scared, I yelled at her to go away."

Henry dropped his head into his hands and Steph reached out and rubbed his back. "I've apologized. I've told her it's not her fault, it's no one's fault, and that I love her, but I think she's going to have to hear it over and over again. See me show it. She has to learn to trust me—trust us. It's not going to happen overnight."

Henry turned to face her. "All I want is for Zoe to feel loved unconditionally and to know that Four Winds is always home."

Steph thought about Zoe sobbing and snuggling into her yesterday, desperate for love and reassurance. *You're only interested in having another baby.* She flinched. How much damage had she inflicted?

"I want that too," she said. "And I never thought I'd say this, but I think we need to pause the fertility treatment and focus on Zoe."

Henry stared at her, stunned. "Are you sure?"

"I feel I owe it to her. And to Monty and our unborn child. We've been living chaotically for months and we all need time to find our feet." She dug her hands into the sand and watched the grains trickle through her fingers. "I read online today that on average it takes seven years to blend a family."

Henry groaned. "God, by then Monty will almost be a teen."

She laughed and leaned in against him. "We might have gotten our act together by then."

He slid his arm around her. "I want to apply for full custody. Show Zoe she's our priority. Are you onboard for that?"

Steph tried to see the suggestion from Zoe's point of view. "I think we need to ask Zoe if that's what she wants. Part of this whole mess came about because Joanna made a unilateral decision and took away all of Zoe's control."

"Put it on the list for the family counselor?" Henry asked.

"Good idea. And talking lists ..." Was this the time? At least they were alone and actively listening to each other. She sucked in a fortifying breath. "For the last few weeks, I've been keeping a spreadsheet. It's not complete by any stretch of the imagination but ..." She brought up the document on her phone and handed it to him. "Please read it carefully and take your time. No rush."

While he read, she ate an eclair. When Sven had boxed them up and insisted they accept them as a gift, Steph knew she and Henry must have looked utterly shattered. She licked the last of the cream off her fingers and laid down to watch the clouds, knowing Henry needed time not just to read the numbers but to absorb them. It was too important to rush.

"Furniture needs waxing?" Henry asked faintly.

"Wood is a living thing, like shoe leather. It needs feeding."

He started mumbling under his breath. "Designed, ordered, wrote, stamped and mailed ninety Christmas cards. Fifteen appointments for doctor, dentist and haircuts for the kids. Collected the dry-cleaning every week, booked childcare, inquired about swimming lessons, provided homework support, met the bus on wet days, planned two hundred meals out of two hundred and sixty, wrote a hundred shopping lists, packed Monty's backpack for childcare and the beach seventy-five times, bought Monty new clothes when he grew an inch, researched, ordered and wrapped birthday and Christmas presents for all, hung out four hundred loads of laundry, found Pen forty-seven times ..." He ran his hand through his hair. "I thought I did half."

"You do half the cleaning," she said. "You committed to half the cooking and do about a third. You mow the lawns, you make sure the car has petrol and gets serviced, and you do our taxes and pay half the bills, but you don't do any of the invisible stuff like making sure we don't run out of laundry detergent, getting Monty's prescriptions filled, knowing which brand of cheese Monty eats and which days Zoe needs her sports uniform."

"Why didn't you ask? I could have helped more."

She closed her eyes and breathed deeply so she didn't yell. She loved him, but sometimes he was utterly clueless.

"Because asking is just adding to my mental load and it's already sinking me. We both thought working from home was going to be a game changer, and it's been a game changer all right. I've gained more unpaid work, and you've gained time for surfing and band. I don't want to resent you doing the things you enjoy, but I can't get a full day's work done during daylight hours and I'm running on empty. If I'm going to be the mother I want to be to Monty and Zoe, the partner I want to be to you and get a business off the ground, we have to change how we do things. It isn't about helping me, Henry. I'm not the project manager of us. It's about taking responsibility for the boring stuff that I do the bulk of that makes our lives easier."

Henry's look of utter bewilderment reminded Steph of Monty.

"And you're saying this isn't even a complete list?"

"I think we need a full year before we have a comprehensive list. And it will change. For example, once Monty starts school, there's going to be 'wear a color' days and birthday parties and music lessons and whatever sport he wants to play."

"This is a good start," Henry said. "Perhaps we can have a working lunch next week and divide up the jobs according to interest and expertise."

She laughed. "You mean we can flip a coin for most of them."

"Oh, I don't know. I think I have an innate talent for emptying the dryer's lint filter."

She elbowed him gently in the ribs. "Until two minutes ago, you didn't even know such a thing existed."

"This is true, but I do now and I'm on it."

"Great. And talking lunchtime meetings, I'd like to discuss the business. My sales are growing, Henry. Alan's cutting three times a week, and if Addy wasn't doing stickers and packaging, I wouldn't be able to offer the hand-painted boutique editions or do the acrobatic penguins. Which by the way are selling their pants off since Addy made a video with Monty and Pen."

"Well, he is a cute kid and the camera loves him. He takes after his father you know," Henry quipped.

Steph laughed. "And talking of talented Suns, Zoe came up with a great idea. She suggested I make a set of balancing women in non-traditional roles as well as a gender-neutral set. I want to offer those too and see if they meet a need. Mostly, I'm hoping Zoe will get involved and help me design them. I thought it might be something we can do together. Or not. She has to want to do it and I can't force it."

"She's been going to choir with you for weeks," Henry said.

"It was hardly with me. Now we know what's been going on at school, I think choir became her safe space."

"Thank goodness for choir and Olivia," Henry said. "Although knowing how stubborn Zoe can be, she wouldn't have gone to choir with you if she didn't want to. She has let us in now and then; we just didn't understand why she was fighting it so much. Now we do, we won't let ourselves get distracted by her smoke-screens. We'll become one of those families who talk about their feelings."

"Gear up for even more eye-rolling then."

Henry smiled. "I love it when Zoe rolls her eyes. It means she cares."

"It's not just Zoe who needs to talk about how she's feeling."

Steph dug more sand and watched it fall. "Henry, I know I've said for years I've always wanted to run a children's clothing company and so you're confused about Retro Toys. The thing is, when I lost the baby I felt like a failure on so many fronts. I couldn't get pregnant, Monty's been sick on and off for months, and Zoe's been ... well, she's been desperately sad. And I was desperate to succeed with one thing. After Ben's commission, I just fell into toys. But it's not a bit of a sideline, Henry. It's a real business and it's helping me. It's helping Alan and right now it's helping Addy."

She slid her hand into his. "I know I can grow it, but you're the business analyst. I want you to look at the figures and study my business plan. Give me advice on where I can improve and reassure me on what I'm doing right. I believe in Retro Toys, but for it to work, I need you to value it and believe in it too."

He raised her hand to his lips and kissed her knuckles. "Sorry."

But that wasn't enough. "What are you sorry for?"

He sighed. "For putting my job and my hobbies ahead of yours. You're right. The change from baby clothes to toys confused me. I thought you would come out of your grief fog and change your mind so I didn't give you or Retro Toys the support you both deserve."

"After the miscarriage, making baby clothes was too hard," she admitted for the first time. "In a way, it still is."

"Yeah, I get that now." He was quiet for a bit. "So how many hours a week do you want to work?"

"Four full days."

He scratched his head. "How close is Monty to getting an extra two days of childcare?"

"Not that close," Steph said. "There are two families ahead of us."

"What about a nanny for one day and we both work a split shift on Thursdays. You start at 6:00 and I'll start at 1:00? Or vice versa. That way it's only one late night for one of us instead of many late nights for you."

She considered it. "It might work depending on the cost of the nanny and if we can find one."

"I'll run the numbers."

"Thanks."

He gave her an anxious smile. "Steph, I really want what we planned when we moved down here."

"I know, but perhaps it was overly ambitious?"

"Yeah. And you're right—the surfing's gotten a bit out of control. I've been enjoying learning from Kieran, but he's a bachelor not a father of two. I should probably cut it right back."

"I think you need to surf a couple of times a week and take Zoe," Steph said.

"Really? She never wants to come."

"That was before we knew what was going on. Remember when Addy took her surfing last week and Zoe told us it was boring? I asked Addy about it and she said Zoe loved it. She kept at it, determined to catch a wave, and even high-fived Addy and Kieran on the beach afterwards." Steph nudged Henry. "I think she has a crush on Kieran, just like her father."

Henry grinned. "Well, he is an excellent surfer."

"He and Addy are dating," Steph said.

Henry grimaced. "Does he know about Addy's problem?"

"You mean her relationship with alcohol?" Steph gave Henry a long look. "Would you say "problem" if she had rheumatoid arthritis or diabetes or any other chronic illness?"

Henry shifted, clearly uncomfortable. "It's not the same thing."

"I think it is. Addy once told me that a drinking problem is a thinking problem in disguise. I don't know the full story behind why she needed alcohol and, to be honest, I don't think I want to. It's enough to know she started drinking for a reason and now she's getting the treatment and support she needs so she can deal with that reason. It's just like anyone getting help with a chronic illness. She's working bloody hard, Henry. She's been amazing with Zoe and lately an incredible friend to me, so be kind, okay? God knows, we're not perfect."

He nodded, contrition rising off him. "You're right. I think I've got a bit of a thing about people drinking too much."

"She's no longer drinking."

"I know. I have to get over myself," he said.

Steph laughed. "You're not alone there. Yesterday and today I've seen an entirely new Courtney. All that helicopter parenting was her trying to do the right thing, be seen to be doing the right thing, and all the time fearing that she might stuff it all up. God, I wish when we had kids we delivered the placenta and then a manual. Instead we just muddle through and hope for the best."

"So you think you might be friends now?" Henry asked. "Because I really like Ben."

"You can be friends with Ben without me being mates with Courtney." Henry's brows rose. "Okay, fair enough," she added.

"Good, because I think we should invite them over for dinner and a fire this weekend. Jesse will play with Monty. Ben and I will poke the fire with sticks and solve the world's problems. Olivia will be generally enthusiastic and Zoe will roll her eyes then cook the marshmallows perfectly. And Courtney will be intense for the first half-hour then relax."

Steph laughed. "You've got it all sorted."

"We can invite Addy and Kieran too," Henry mused. "You know, some cool adults for Zoe and Olivia rather than just their dorky parents."

"And I'd like to invite Alan. He's got his girls this weekend and it's hard keeping kids entertained in a small apartment."

Henry smiled. "Look at us with a social network in the cove."

Steph thought about everything she'd learned about Zoe and Courtney in the last day and how preconceived ideas had taken her down the wrong roads, stranding her.

"I think the whole bullying situation has bonded Courtney and me. Besides, at the most basic level, we need to be chatting acquaintances because Zoe needs Olivia. Courtney's right," she reflected. "It's important to be friends with the parents of your kids' friends. When Zoe was desperate to be part of the popular group and they welcomed her, then dumped her and bullied her, I hate to think what might have happened if Olivia hadn't stuck with her."

Henry shuddered. "Let's be grateful to Olivia and not think about that."

"Everyone needs a friend," Steph said, and sent thanks into the universe for Addy, Brenda and the rest of the choir.

CHAPTER FORTY-SEVEN

AFTER THE DRAMA of Zoe and Olivia going missing, the endorphin rush of the choir's performance—they'd sounded like they'd sung together for years—and the fun celebration afterwards, Addy had woken with agitation popping in her veins. It wasn't just the remnants of the worry and excitement of the day before that unsettled her—she was still waiting to speak to Heather Lindsay.

When she'd emailed Heather on the woman's second day back at work, an auto-reply had pinged into her inbox. Heather had extended her leave and this time no return date was mentioned. Addy couldn't decide if she should wait until the woman returned to work or intrude on her leave. She swung between the two decisions and made none.

Even the surf had failed her that morning—the bay had barely managed a ripple—so she'd strapped on her walking shoes and marched up the hill to Four Winds. When she arrived, the only person in the workshop was Alan. He never said much, which in an odd way Addy found soothing.

Over lunch, she persuaded him to allow her to film him cutting circus shapes. Then she created an Instagram reel of the entire process, from cutting and the application of the stickers to wrapping and packaging. She used sections of previous videos to add in posting at the store and Monty playing with a set. Fifteen minutes after uploading it, there were two thousand views.

"W-wow!" Alan's face lit up in delight at the finished product.

"C-can I sh-show the kids?"

Addy smiled. "Sure. I'll text you the link. And looking at the success of this reel, be warned I'll be making more."

"Better get my hair cut," Alan quipped without a stutter.

Addy laughed. "You and me both."

By the time she left Four Winds mid-afternoon and walked to the general store to mail the orders, she was calm and content. She was grabbing milk when she saw a tub of fresh mussels. It immediately took her back to happy times around the kitchen table when Rita and Ivan ate them and told stories of growing up in Dubrovnik. Her mother had always cooked their mussels in white wine and garlic. Addy wanted to taste the mussels and enjoy good memories but ...

She texted SCW. *Thoughts on cooking with wine?*

Less than a minute later, replies pinged onto her phone.

Even if you think you won't be tempted to drink it, the taste in the food can trigger cravings

Would you give someone with a peanut allergy satay?

Why risk it? Find another recipe

Addy's gratitude flowed into her reply. *I love you good women. Such great advice as always. Thank you!*

After googling recipes and finding one that was similar to her mother's but substituted lemon juice for wine, she texted Kieran.

Are you free for dinner? I could cook mussels

A thumbs-up emoji pinged onto her phone, followed by: *No surf. Can Fergus and I come early and help you cook?*

Cooking mussels was pretty simple, but she wasn't going to say no. *You can do the garlic bread*

As she walked home she called Steph, filling her in on the workday and receiving a debrief in return about the meeting at school, the counselor and Henry.

As soon as the call was over, Addy texted Zoe: *You rocked last night. Hope those girls get what for*

She gave the bathroom a quick wipe, and was lifting the cooking pot out of the cabinet when Kieran walked through the back door holding a baguette, butter and a head of garlic.

"Oh!" She couldn't hide her surprise. "I was joking. I just meant you could throw the garlic bread from the freezer into the oven."

He shuddered. "Did I not tell you I was a kitchen hand at an Italian restaurant for two summers?"

"You did not."

He grinned. "I'm famous in Strandhill for me garlic butter."

"Just garlic butter?"

"And a few other things. One day we'll visit and the cousins will take great delight in filling you in on all the stories."

Addy laughed, then realized he was serious. She tried the idea on for size and waited for the ripple of panic to hit and grow to a swell. It stirred but didn't grow.

Since Kieran's first invitation to dine at the surf club, they'd done exactly what he'd suggested—some dinners together, the occasional bushwalk when the surf was soup, and he'd surprised her with tickets to a jazz concert at Burnie. While they were at the arts center she'd seen a flyer advertising a touring production of *A Taste of Ireland* in Devonport in a couple of months. Addy wondered if she should surprise him. Would they still be "keeping company," as Kieran liked to call it, by the end of the year?

He was certainly easy to be with, and although he kissed her, casually threw his arm around her when they sat on the sofa, and pulled her up to dance when certain songs played, she sensed he was waiting for her to make the next move. The one that led them to sex.

Addy both appreciated having the control and feared it in equal measure. In her drinking days, sex had been easy—rarely memorable, but easy. Alcohol ramped up desire and diminished inhibitions.

There'd never been any second-guessing. If she met someone she fancied and they felt the same way, she had sex. Even with Jasper, her love affair had always been with the booze and the blessed blackness it ultimately offered her, with or without sex.

But now she was a different person. Accompanying sobriety was an alertness to all stimuli she hadn't experienced since she was a kid. She saw things in body language she hadn't noticed in years, heard nuances in voices, and was acutely aware of the position of her own body in every situation. Sometimes she quadruple-guessed where to put her hands—clasped in her lap, on her knees, across her chest—argh! And in regards to sex, she was overthinking everything.

It wasn't that she didn't want to have sex with Kieran; she did. She really did, but at the end of each date her brain played tennis, lobbing the topic of sex back and forth between the just-do-it side and the what-if-I-stuff-it-up opposition. All her inhibitions that alcohol had masked so well and for so long rushed in. Anxieties about her body. About being naked in front of him. About being clumsy and awkward. About touch. About her debilitating fear of feeling *everything* and being overwhelmed. It was the intimacy that had her running scared.

Her therapist told her these feelings were normal in any new relationship, but that was the problem. Addy had never had a normal sexual relationship. Never had a sober one either. In a way, it was like being a virgin again, only this time she had the choice.

The sound of the bread knife cracking the hard crust of the baguette brought her thoughts back to the kitchen. She visualized what she'd written in her bullet journal: *Be present in the moment.* Right now the moment was food preparation. While Addy made a salad and Kieran buttered the baguette, she let herself relax into his banter and conversation.

She was making a jug of lemonade to drink with dinner and asking Kieran the name of the plumber who'd helped him renovate his bathroom, when her phone rang. She frowned, not recognizing the number.

"You going to answer that or stare it into submission?" Kieran asked.

"Ha ha." She raised the device to her ear and said tentatively, "Hello?"

"This is Heather Lindsay. Is this Addy Topic?" a woman's voice asked.

Addy's heart slammed against her ribs. "Heather, yes. This is Addy."

"Oh, good! I thought I'd give you a call rather than reply to the email you sent a few weeks ago. I'm so sorry I've been slow to respond. My husband came off his bike and things have been a bit chaotic."

"Oh, no!" Addy got an image of a man in the hospital surrounded by machines. "Is he okay?"

"He's home now and on the mend, which means I'm finding snatches of time to clear the mountain of emails. Oh!" Heather sounded surprised. "I confess to scrolling while we've been talking and I've just found an HR bulletin saying you resigned quite a while ago. I guess that means whatever you wanted to discuss is moot. Sorry to have bothered you."

"No! I mean, it's no bother." Addy walked on unsteady legs to the living room and sat down hard on the sofa. "I still have a question I want to ask you."

"Righto, fire away," Heather said in the no-nonsense tone Addy remembered from the audit training.

She licked her lips. "It's about the 2IC job at the Bass campus."

"Hmm," Heather said. "Tell me more."

The job's real. Addy's stomach cramped and she almost cut the call. Only pride kept her on the line. She took a steadying breath.

"You and Scott Matheson were on the interview panel. Apparently you had some concerns about my ability to do the job and you decided not to interview me. I just wanted to discuss those concerns."

The line buzzed with a long silence and then Addy thought she heard the tapping of a keyboard.

Eventually Heather said, "Addy, I'm afraid you've caught me on the hop. I can't find any information about a 2IC position at Bass. However, I was supposed to be on a panel for that position at the Launceston campus next week. Obviously with Eric's injuries I've handed that on to Liberty Blair. I've just checked the applicants and your name's not on the list. Had it been, I wouldn't have any objections to interviewing you. In fact, I wish you had applied."

Addy's heart hammered so fast she became light-headed. *Think!*

"Heather, in mid-February, I was asked to apply for a 2IC position at Bass. The link I was given to upload my application was broken so I emailed it to Grant Hindmarsh. He informed me he'd sent it to HR in Hobart. Later, he told me that you and Scott Matheson would join him on the interview panel."

"But that was before I met you at Wrest Point," Heather said. "Surely you thought it odd I didn't say anything about it to you then?"

Addy tugged on a curl. "I assumed you didn't mention it due to confidentiality."

"I didn't mention it because I wasn't aware there was a job then."

Then? Stay calm. Be coherent. Don't stuff this up!

"Has there been a 2IC job advertised for Bass since?" Addy asked.

The sound of tapping came again. "According to the budgets there's no projection for a 2IC position. Addy, who told you in February there was a job?"

She controlled her breathing so his name came out calmly. "Grant Hindmarsh."

"And who told you I was objecting to your application?"

"Grant."

"And when was this?" Heather asked, increasingly sounding like a cross-examiner.

"Just before I resigned."

"So let me get this straight," Heather said. "You were under the impression you'd applied for a 2IC position in February. Didn't you think it strange there was no interview for the entire semester?"

I missed the signs.

Addy braced herself against the woman's critical disbelief. She needed to come across as credible. "When I inquired, I was told HR were dragging their chain, you were sick, Scott's car had broken down ... There was always a reasonable excuse, and at that point I had no reason not to believe Grant."

"At what point did you stop believing him?"

Go carefully, grasshopper. This wasn't about exposing everything Grant had done to her. That was the job of a lawyer. Right now, she just had to cast doubt on his ethics—sow the seed he'd offered her a non-existent job.

"It's only since I resigned that I've doubted his veracity. The first red flag came when he told me you were unhappy with my work, after you'd been so complimentary after my presentation."

"Hmm." Heather was quiet for a moment. "At this point I only have your version of events."

A slew of negative comments Grant had made in passing about Heather—officious, hostage to detail, pedantic—crowded Addy's mind. Was all that untrue as well? Wariness crawled over her skin and suddenly she didn't know who to trust.

There was more tapping. "Do you have any written correspondence about the job to back up what you're saying?" Heather asked briskly.

Breathe in and out. In ...

"I've got my application, a copy of the key selection criteria he gave me and the email with the attachment referencing the broken link."

"Email them to me, will you?"

Red flags waved wildly and rising nausea made her gag. If she sent them to Heather she'd lose control of them, and she didn't know the woman well enough to glean if she was on her side or against her. After all, she was senior management just like Grant.

Working hard to keep her voice steady, Addy said, "I'd prefer it if you sent me screenshots that prove there isn't a 2IC job at Bass and there hasn't been all year. My lawyer can take it from there."

Addy braced herself for "I really don't think a lawyer's necessary" and marshalled her arguments ready to fire.

"I can definitely do that," Heather said.

"I don't think ... What? Um, really? I ... Thank you," Addy babbled.

Heather's sigh echoed down the line. "Addy, we've had some concerns about the Bass campus for some time now. Nothing concrete, but issues like uneven teaching loads and declining female enrollments in the trades have raised flags. I expected Ravi Bakshi to make a complaint earlier in the year, but perhaps I misunderstood. On the whole, teacher and student feedback has been positive, but I saw the memo from you about the Automotive situation during the audit prep."

Stunned, Addy blurted out, "How did you see that? Grant corrals that sort of information."

"Put it this way," Heather said. "Everyone makes an error eventually and when he attached his figures he forgot to remove your attachment when he forwarded the email."

She cleared her throat. "If you wish to move forward with a complaint there are official forms you need to complete. Be assured, there's definitely some clout in an internal investigation. Bass will be examined very closely from top to bottom and if Grant Hindmarsh is found to have compromised his position by offering you a job that didn't exist, he will go and your job will be restored."

"The gaslighting about the 2IC position is just the tip of the iceberg of a mess of problems at Bass," Addy said. "It needs a new broom, and for the sake of my mental health, I'll never work there again."

"Oh, Addy, I'm so sorry to hear this. The last thing we need is to lose women of your caliber. We pride ourselves on safe and respectful workplaces and, as I said, we'll be investigating thoroughly. Would you consider the position at Launceston? I can promise you, it's a completely different work environment."

It was the job Addy wanted, only at a bigger campus, so a much better promotion and it came with more money. Of course she'd have to move from the cove to Launceston. Due to her sobriety and not working, this house was now only a bathroom renovation away from being an attractive vacation rental. Plus Launceston offered live theatre and music, not to mention the best croissants on the island. But instead of feeling the buzz of excitement and anticipation skittering in her veins, all she felt was a lead weight sitting hard and unyielding in her gut.

You need a job! This is the management job you've wanted for two years.

It was, but with the unflinching gaze of sobriety, she also knew she needed the cove. It was inextricably linked to her recovery. She needed the mood-stabilizing effects of the bush, the beach and surfing. She needed the endorphins the choir offered her through singing and playing the piano, and she definitely needed the choir's friendship and support. She needed Steph's friendship and care and Brenda's mothering. And perhaps, in a way, she needed to live the life in the cove denied to her and, by default, her parents all those years ago.

What about Kieran?

What about Kieran? Where did he fit in?

She instantly rejected any stray thoughts of him being part of her sobriety toolkit. That was a road to disaster. Besides, she'd gotten sober before she'd gotten to know him and she'd learned enough through SCW and her therapist to recognize that building sobriety around any person was dangerous. Sobriety must be hauled from deep down inside her, accompanied by a completely new way of thinking about herself and the world.

You need a job.

I do, but not this job.

Her agitation stilled.

"Thanks for the offer, Heather. As awful as it was to find myself unemployed, it's given me a chance to reassess what I want in a job and out of life."

"Sometimes when change is forced upon us, we feel it's the worst thing, but often the result is an unexpected gift," Heather said.

"I think you're right, although my bank balance may disagree," Addy said.

"Hopefully something that suits your skill set will turn up soon."

"Thanks."

"Based on the presentation you gave in Hobart and your audit reports, I know you're excellent at your job. Please, use me as your reference," Heather said.

Relief made Addy laugh. "Thank you, Heather. I really appreciate your support."

"Anytime. I've just emailed you those forms and the screenshots, and now I'd best go and sort out a meal for Eric. Breaking his hip hasn't impacted his appetite. Cheerio."

Addy lowered the phone, not quite able to comprehend that Heather not only believed her, but was an ally. She stayed seated, churning everything over in her mind before opening her bullet journal and writing: *Reclaim your rights. 9am interview law firms.* She sketched the scales of justice next to it.

A nub of anxiety wrinkled her resolve, but instead of instantly wanting to make it vanish, she sat with it and considered it. No one in her situation would find taking action like this easy. Of course it would be unsettling, but she was done with walking away and letting misogynists not only win but force her onto paths not of her choosing. This time she was standing strong and fighting for herself and her parents. This time she had age, experience and most importantly sobriety on her side. She had the support of the inspiring women of SCW and she had the care and strength of the cove choir. Whatever Grant's lawyers threw at her, she had good people on her side. For the first time in her life, she wanted to let them help her.

Opening herself up to all the emotions, she walked to the piano and sat down. Without second-guessing herself she launched into a very loud rendition of KT Tunstall's "Suddenly I See." For the first time since she'd heard the song on the radio as a teen, she understood the lyrics.

Kieran walked in and jived around the piano, joining her in belting out the chorus. The lyrics took her to a place she wanted to be and lightness streamed through her.

When they reached the final verse Kieran sang the refrain, his twinkling eyes fixed on hers as if he could see into her soul. Of course he couldn't, but he saw things in her that both delighted and terrified her. Overwhelmed, her gaze slid away. But instead of it giving her space to regroup, she immediately missed him.

Suddenly I see.

She lifted her head and met his gaze full on, riding out the mix of fear and embarrassment. The world didn't stop. Kieran sang the words back to her, his accent turning her limbs liquid.

He was closer now, his breath warm on her skin. Delicious sensations tingled all over her, joining the singing endorphins party. She sang the last line with a belief that had been missing almost as long as the life of the song.

Kieran grinned at her. "I can never decide if you're sexier when you surf or when you sing."

She laughed. "With you, it's a toss-up between hammering in nails or cooking for me."

"And here I am thinking it was me in my wetsuit that made you notice me."

"Oh, it was." She stood up and wrapped her arms around his neck. "But you're so much more than a body. Not that I don't want to explore it."

His eyes darkened. "So that is something you'd like to do?"

"It is," she said.

"And would it be sooner or later?" he asked, his tone gently enquiring.

She buried her hands in his hair. "Most of me says right now."

He studied her closely. "And the rest of you?"

She gave him a wry smile. "Is a mess of neuroses I'm trying hard not to listen to."

"Good idea."

"So how about you, Kieran? Would you like to ..." She swallowed hard and got out of her own head. Then, embracing her nerves and excitement, she tried flirting. "Would you like to explore me?"

He bent his head and kissed her in a way that left her in no doubt.

Addy lay on her bed grinning at the ceiling, reliving every kiss, caress and exquisite torment. "Well, that seemed to go pretty well."

Kieran laughed. "Glad I could surprise you."

She rolled over and cupped his face, loving the feel of his stubble on her palms. "Kieran, you were never in doubt." She thought about the intensity of what she'd just experienced—not just her orgasm but being present the whole time. "I surprised me."

"Believe me, Addy, you have nothing to be in doubt about. You're wonderful," he said softly before giving her a wide grin. "And to be sure, we were bloody brilliant together."

"Bold words," she teased. "I'm sure we'll improve with practice."

His eyes twinkled with delicious intent. "Well, I wouldn't be objecting to that."

She kissed him then snuggled into him, reveling in being in the moment and aware of every part of his body touching hers. With her ear on his chest, she relaxed into the rhythmic lub-dub of his heart and the rise and fall of his ribs. Warm and relaxed, she could stay here forever in this safe cocoon. Her eyes fluttered closed.

Suddenly she was being pushed sideways. Her eyes whipped open to see Kieran on his feet. Frantic barking echoed down the hall and an ear-piercing shriek sliced the air. Kieran ran.

Addy pulled on a T-shirt and picked up his boxers. She found him in the kitchen, naked except for an oven mitt, and waving a tea towel furiously toward an open window. The garlic bread lay on the tray, a black lump of charcoal.

"I forgot about the bread," he said regretfully.

She tossed him his boxers. "I think I've got my first Kieran story to share with the Strandhill cousins. The naked chef with his famous burnt garlic butter."

"Aw, you wouldn't."

She laughed, loving that she was sober and able to remember every single detail of the moment. "I think I might."

He reached for her with his oven-mitted hand and she dodged him. Fergus barked. Addy ran.

And, thankfully, Kieran followed her back to the bedroom.

EPILOGUE
A YEAR LATER

ADDY STOOD IN THE SUNSHINE, welcoming its warmth on her face.

The fifteenth eisteddfod—the second since Marilyn had resurrected the choir—was almost over. While the judges were sequestered deciding the winners the choirs had spilled out of the cave and onto the beach. This period before the winners were announced was always tense. There was little mixing between choirs—that would happen at the afterparty in the hall. Right now, there were many sideways glances and hushed animated discussions. The coffee truck at the top of the stairs was doing a roaring trade.

Addy was looking forward to the party, especially since Zoe and Olivia had secured some local funding and they'd interviewed choir members from each choir. Henry had set up computers and screens in the hall so the video could run continuously. Addy was sure it would be a hit, as well as a balm to remind everyone why they loved to sing whether they'd won an award or not.

Right now, Addy's job was taking photos for the eisteddfod's Instagram page. Unlike the social media marketing she did for Steph's Retro Toys, Sven's café, the cove market and half a dozen other businesses along the coast, her work for the eisteddfod was a labor of love. Ethical Online Marketing had been born out of the help she'd given Steph with her website and social media, her business degree and all she'd learned writing and teaching the social media marketing course. All of it had given her the confidence to start the business, and the photography aspects helped fill the creativity well she'd run from for years.

Addy had also started teaching music. When Zoe had asked if she'd give her singing lessons, Addy had panicked, then thought about it for a week. Kieran had suggested she tell Zoe the truth—that she'd never taught singing before and didn't want to get Zoe's hopes up then let her down if she didn't enjoy teaching. Henry, delighted to see Zoe's enthusiasm, had suggested a trial lesson and Addy had discovered that the past stayed where it belonged and she loved teaching music.

She'd pinned up a flyer on the hall noticeboard and contacted the schools. Now, five students played Rita's piano in a light-filled room each week, and three singing students stood by the window with a glimpse of the sea. Most importantly, working for herself gave her the flexibility to block out times for self-care—surfing, walking, journaling and her check-in counseling appointments.

She snapped a photo of Zoe and Olivia cheek to cheek, each girl pointing to the red heart stenciled on her face, then gotten their permission and uploaded it to Instagram stories. Although she'd posted formal photos of each choir, she loved the fun aspect of stories and the way it gave a snapshot into the emotions of the competition.

She'd gotten a great shot of some worried choristers from Burnie— they'd won the previous year so they had the most to lose.

"Look at the surf," Kieran lamented as even sets rolled in.

"Poor you," Addy teased. "Torn between your two great loves of singing and surfing."

He pulled her in close and whispered, "You know my real love is you."

In their early days together, him saying something like that would have made her squirm in embarrassment and she'd have said "Enough with the blarney." But now, knowing he spoke the truth, she lay her head on his shoulder, her heart full.

After a year together, during which she'd weathered an inquiry, a defamation case and unwanted media attention, there'd been times when it had taken every tool in her sobriety kit not to break, not to walk away from the fight. But with Kieran's support, and the support of the cove, she'd stayed strong. She knew with absolute certainty that Kieran's love for her was loyal and unwavering. Equally important, she recognized she deserved that kind of love and returned it to him wholeheartedly.

Her phone beeped with a message and she checked it.

"What is it?" Kieran asked. "You've got your lawsuit-grimace face on."

"The money's being deposited tomorrow."

Grant Hindmarsh and Jett Longeron had lost their jobs. That had been enough for Addy, but the court case had come with a financial settlement. It was ironic that the money she'd lent to Jasper had proven too difficult to recover, but now she was custodian of a far greater sum. She planned to donate a large chunk of it to a fund for women fighting sexual harassment in the workplace.

Kieran kissed her. "It's officially over. I'd be lying if I said I wasn't pleased about that. Tonight, we're celebrating."

"I hope we're celebrating more than that." She checked her watch.

"Surely the judges have made up their minds by now."

"I'll go and see what I can find out."

♫

When Steph returned to the beach, coffee in hand, she needed some reassurance and walked straight to Addy. "I think I hit a few bum notes. Will it ruin our chances?"

Addy hugged her. "I didn't hear them. Besides, Stanley's 'Somebody To Love' was truly impressive."

"And the harmonies in Devonport's 'True Colors' made me cry. Mind you, I cry at the drop of a hat."

Addy stared at her. "Are you telling me you're on fertility drugs or is it even better news?"

Once the question would have gutted Steph, but not anymore.

"We've decided not to try IVF."

"But I thought you were just delaying—"

"Of course I'd like another baby," she said quickly. "If it happens it happens and we'd be over the moon. But remember how I went a bit nuts on the clomiphene? And the IVF drugs are worse. I'm not prepared to risk my and everyone else's mental health after we've worked so hard and come such a long way this past year. Zoe's finally in a good place—well, most of the time. She's pretty good at talking to Henry and me now, but I hate that we can't wave a wand and make Joanna the mother Zoe wants her to be."

"She's got you now," Addy said.

Steph squeezed her hand. "And she's got you too and the women in the choir. The poor kid's got mothers coming out her ears, but that doesn't fix the fact she misses the one who refuses to put her ahead of a complete dickhead."

"I totally get it," Addy said. "But Zoe's strong and she has solid support networks now. Occasionally when we're out in the swell, she'll say something so profound I have to remind myself she's not even fifteen."

"If you want to be reminded, drop into Four Winds when she's tired, hungry and has history homework. Believe me, it's drama, drama, drama." Steph laughed. "Monty's our secret weapon. He has a sixth sense for when she's stressed or sad and he walks up to her and presents her with Pen. Zoe laughs and hugs him and the storm's over."

"True sibling affection."

"It goes both ways. When his asthma plays up, she sits with him and watches a heroic amount of *Bluey* or she reads to him. It's all wonderfully normal."

"Normal is bliss," Addy said. "By the way, have you had time to read that email I sent you from the ABC?"

"Yes!" Excitement skittered through her. Steph's Retro Toys had continued to grow and, with Henry's support and some financial backing, she'd moved it off the kitchen table and into a repurposed shed she was renting from Ben Burton. "I can't believe the timing. It's almost as if you organized it to coincide with the growth in retail accounts."

"Well, I have been sowing seeds for a few months," Addy said. "But mainstream media do their own thing on their own timeline."

"I spoke to the reporter and she wants to do a piece on why retro toys are so popular, with a special focus on the modern take of gender-neutral and girl-power toys," Steph said. "Zoe's pretty pumped."

"I bet. It will give the business some great exposure and hopefully that means lots of sales so you can continue to afford me," Addy teased.

Steph looked at her friend's relaxed face. "I know you think working for me saved your sanity after the mess at the college, but you've helped me as much as I've helped you."

Addy raised her hand in a high-five. "Then let's keep doing it."

The happy shrieks of a child made Steph turn. Kieran was spinning Monty around and around.

"He's great with kids, isn't he?" she said.

Addy's gaze was fixed on Kieran, her mouth curved in a soft smile. "He is."

"So have the two of you had the conversation yet?"

"Which one?"

Steph nudged her. "The baby conversation."

"Oh, that one." Addy sighed. "He's super keen. I'm terrified."

Steph laughed. "So situation normal. You overthink everything, Addy. Remember how worried you were about moving in together? It's been six months and you've never looked happier."

Addy gave her a wry smile. "Yes, but he has a house he could return to if it was a complete disaster. I can't give back a baby."

"Even on the tough days, you won't want to. At least not after a quick breather away from them to regroup," Steph said. "And I know you've been borrowing Monty to practice on. Besides, it's all about sharing the load. Someone wise gave me a great tool for that."

Addy smiled. "I have the occasional brilliant idea."

"Seriously, I think it saved us as much as family counseling did," Steph said. "It makes Henry and me pull together as a team. When we're tempted to play the "I work harder" card, it reminds us we're both working hard. I've given Kieran a copy so he knows exactly what he's in for as a dad."

Addy laughed. "You're a true friend."

Henry joined them, a megaphone in his hand. He was master of ceremonies for the eisteddfod and he took his duties very seriously.

He slid an arm around Steph's waist. "The choir sounded amazing. You're amazing. Zoe's a songbird and I teared up. If you don't win, it will be a travesty."

Steph laughed. "Any chance you're just a teeny bit biased?"

"One hundred percent." He raised the megaphone to his mouth and turned toward the crowd. "Ladies and gentlemen, please return to your seats. We're ready to announce the winners."

♪♪

The audience filed into the cave first and then the choirs gathered down the sides and at the back, filling all the available space. Brenda squeezed Marilyn's hand as nerves jittered in her belly. Unlike last year when the cove choir had decided only to host, this year they were competing.

"Sweetheart, you're hurting my hand," Marilyn said.

"Sorry." Brenda released it. "I don't know if I'm more nervous or excited."

"I'm excited at the crowd and the nice healthy profit," Marilyn said. "This year the hall can have a facelift to match its beautiful gum-green Colorbond steel roof."

The chair of the judging committee took her place on the stage.

"What a great afternoon of song we've been treated to. There's so much talent up here on the north-west coast and I hope all the choirs will consider entering the Festival of Voices in Hobart next year." She smiled at the crowd. "Choosing winners isn't always easy and today was no exception, but it's a competition so winners there must be. Congratulations to Burnie on third place with their creative rendition of 'Africa' by Toto."

The audience applauded, the Burnie choir tried not to look too disappointed they'd slipped from first to third, and their conductor graciously accepted the award.

Brenda bit her lip, shared a glance with Marilyn and crossed her fingers.

When the Burnie conductor left the stage, the judge leaned into the microphone again. "Second place is awarded to Devonport for their rendition of 'True—'" But the whoops and cries of "Yes!" drowned her out. Obviously Devonport had brought their own cheer squad.

Unease dragged at Brenda. She'd thought the cove choir had a shot at second or third place, but first? That seemed like punching above their weight.

This time Marilyn's hand squeezed hers tightly.

"Goodness," the judge said when the boom of applause finally faded. "Such enthusiasm. And now, the winning choir, whose name will go on the honor board and who will be custodians of the perpetual trophy for a full year, is ..." She paused for dramatic effect. "Stanley with 'Somebody To Love' by Freddie Mercury."

Marilyn sighed and dropped Brenda's hand to applaud. "It was pretty amazing," she conceded.

"Yes, but we had heart," Brenda said, unable to suppress her disappointment.

"Obviously it wasn't enough," Marilyn said glumly.

During Stanley's acceptance speech, Brenda's mind turned to the mini quiches and sausage rolls in the hall kitchen that Ben had promised to heat up and not burn. She was expecting Henry to thank the organizers and invite everyone to the hall for celebratory drinks and nibbles, but although he was on stage, he was in deep discussion with the second judge. She was waving a piece of paper at him. Eventually he accepted it and handed it to the first judge.

"Attention, everyone," the woman said. "I'm terribly sorry, but I appear to have missed a piece of paper. This year, two new awards have been added to the mix."

The crowd settled, eager with curious anticipation.

"What awards?" Brenda asked.

Marilyn shrugged. "Addy was in charge of that."

The judge held up a conductor's baton. "The best conductor award for arrangement and choralography goes to ..." She consulted her clip-board. "Marilyn Rennie."

Brenda squealed and gave her a smooch on the lips. "You clever thing!"

Marilyn laughed. "I don't know what's shocked me more. Winning or you kissing me in public."

"I've surprised myself," Brenda admitted, not being someone who showed affection in public. "But get used to it, darling."

She gave Marilyn a pat on the behind and gently pushed her toward the stage. Then she glanced at her family to see how they were coping. After all, none of the Lambecks were particularly demonstrative in public, and she and Glen had hardly been role models in that department. Richard gave her a thumbs-up. Colin didn't appear to have noticed and Courtney gave her a resigned shrug. Brenda laughed and savored the continuing freedom of being herself.

"You're a legend, Marilyn!" Courtney called out.

"Mum! No ... stop. That's too weird," Olivia said.

Courtney smiled and sneaked in a stealth hug. "That's my job."

Marilyn accepted the baton and adjusted the microphone. "I wouldn't have won this award without the love and support of my partner, Brenda, or the commitment of the Rookery Cove choir. I want to give special thanks to Addy and Kieran for their input on the musical arrangement and choralography, and to Zoe and Olivia for keeping us hip."

She waved the baton in the air. "This award belongs to all of us. Thank you so much."

When the applause died down, the judge said, "That leaves the people's choice award. Each ticket holder was asked to vote for their favorite choir ..."

"That means Devonport will win," Brenda said as Marilyn rejoined her.

"... and the Rookery Cove eisteddfod's inaugural people's choice award goes to the Rookery Cove choir with their rendition of the Pretenders' 'I'll Stand By You.'"

"Oh my God!" Stunned, Addy turned to Kieran, tears brimming. "I don't believe it."

"Believe it, darlin'." He stroked her hair. "You sang it with your heart outside of your chest and it was amazing."

"I sang it to the choir." She swiped at the now spilling tears. "And I sang it to you."

"And I did the same." His love for her was clear in his eyes. "And then everyone joined in with their own take on love and support. It's a bloody tear-jerker and we should have won first prize. We were robbed!"

She laughed and hugged him, embracing the joy of the win and acknowledging the heartache that Rita and Ivan weren't here to share it with her. For so long she'd shied away from hurt and pain, but now she accepted it was as much a part of life as the exhilaration of happiness and the daily sameness of routine. The key was to let all of the emotions visit, but not allow any to overstay their welcome. The sadness at the absence of her parents was lifted by knowing how proud they'd be of her and how glad she was happy. Most importantly, she was at peace with herself. It was a constant surprise how much that peace opened her to positive experiences and made her want to give back in return.

Then arms were being thrown around her and Steph was hugging her, then Courtney and Brenda.

Marilyn's voice boomed in the cave. "Cove choir, get yourselves up here and close the eisteddfod so we can party."

As Addy took her place on the stage and the opening bars of Randy Newman's "You've Got A Friend In Me" played, she grabbed Steph's and Brenda's hands and sang.

♫

Video Interviews of the Choirs of the Rookery Cove Eisteddfod by Zoe Sun and Olivia Burton.

"When I arrived in the cove I only knew Brenda," Marilyn said. "I wanted something we could do together and help the hall get a new roof. Singing's great exercise. It improves breathing, posture and muscle tension and it releases endorphins, which make us happy. Not many activities can boast members from thirteen to seventy-nine. I'm very proud of that."

♫

"Ready, love? I'm Stan so I suppose I should be in the Stanley choir, but I live in Devonport so I'd be run out of town. I belt out tunes in the shower so I don't know why it took me forty years to join, but when my wife died, I took the plunge. Best thing I ever did."

♫

"I've always loved singing, Zoe, dear," Vera said. "And it's lonely living on your own, so it's nice to get out of the house. Learning all the lyrics to the songs keeps my brain active. Is that the sort of thing you're after?"

♫

A laughing couple in their seventies looked straight at the camera. "When the cove started up the eisteddfod again and we saw Stanley's name on the honor board from back in the day, we knew we had to get the band back together."

♫

Heidi's face filled the screen. "Singing fills me with joy. Even if I wasn't in the choir, I'd sing."

♫

"I was hoping I might meet someone special!" Morgan laughed. "And I did. Sixteen really great people, including you and Olivia."

♫

Fern peered into the camera, her face serious. "Did you know, Zoe, that Buddhist monks chant to prepare the mind for meditation?"

♫

A woman with short purple hair and rainbow glasses looked confidently into the camera. "Burnie's got its own musical eisteddfod, but we like to support the smaller towns in the north-west. And we love the acoustics in the cave!"

♫

"Me ma told me I came out singing." Kieran laughed, then sobered. "For me, singing's sharing a story and sharing the love attached to it."

He leaned in and gave a conspiratorial wink. "Plus Addy's gorgeous so that was an added incentive to join."

♫

"I joined the choir because it was the one place Mémé and Mum were in the same room," Olivia said. "And because I thought your idea for the passion project was epic." She stretched out her hand for a high-five.

♫

"W-when I s-sing I d-don't s-stutter." Alan took in a deep breath. "Bri and I joined the choir. We have dinner first and then we sing. It's helping. We've been talking about getting back together and I never thought that would happen."

♫

"I only joined the choir because Dad said I might be able to do make-up for the passion project. I thought everyone would be old and boring, but they're interesting and pretty nice. I mean, everyone can be annoying sometimes. Even me." Zoe smiled. "I didn't think I'd like singing, but some days when stuff gets to me, I sing. Like Addy says, it won't fix the problem, but it will lift your vibe so you can see if it's your problem to fix."

♫

"Why did I join the choir?" Brenda mused into the camera. "Initially I joined to support Marilyn. She was so keen to get it up and running again and I love her enthusiasm for life. I'm so proud of what she's achieved. What we've all achieved, really."

Steph's face appeared onscreen. "If you'd asked me this last year, Zo, I'd have told you I joined the choir because I desperately wanted a couple of hours to be me. But thankfully a lot's changed and now, walking out the door on a Tuesday night with you is special. I love we're sharing the drama and the fun that's choir. Although thankfully there's been almost no drama lately and a lot more fun. I'm never going to be as good a singer as you, but at least I can hold a solid harmony." Steph clasped her hands to her chest. "I was so proud when you sang your first solo."

"You cried and missed your cue." Zoe's voice came from off camera. "Embarrassing!"

Steph shrugged and smiled. "And I'd do it again."

Addy brushed a curl out of her eye and smiled at the camera. "I know I did the work, am still doing the work, but in so many ways choir saved me. It forced me out of hiding so I had no choice but to face my reality. Now, it provides me with great friendships and a sense of belonging, which is something we all need, right?" She moistened her lips. "Growing up, my mother was the choir conductor and this new choir connects me to her in ways I didn't know I needed. It's restored my joy in music and helped me reclaim how I want to live my life. For that I'll always be grateful."

She laughed and her cheeks pinked. "Sorry, was that too schmaltzy? Should I tell a joke?"

"No, that was epic," Zoe said. "Choir rocks."

ACKNOWLEDGMENTS

This novel was written on Wadawurrung and Eastern Maar land. I pay my respects to the First Nation Peoples of this land as custodians of learning, literacy, knowledge and story.

Back in 2020, when I started this book, a COVID-19 vaccination was being approved and I thought we had the virus on the skids. However, we hadn't reckoned on a variant so I am asking you to dream of a time when singing in a group is allowed and embrace the idea of a choir. Fingers crossed, community singing will once again be a part of our lives soon.

Writing the acknowledgments in each book is an honor and a joy as it reminds me how lucky I am to have so many people who happily help me on the winding journey each book takes me on. People often say "I didn't help much" but when an author needs information for authenticity, it's gold. If it takes a village to raise a child, it takes a team to write a book.

Thanks to long-time writing mate Rachael Johns for brainstorming with me when the only thing written on the whiteboard was "Escape." Huge thanks to my talented and hardworking cousin Anne Tonkin for her advice on audits and quality assurance in the tertiary education sector, and to Kim Hainsworth for chatting about the administration side of things. Fortunately, they work in far better workplaces than my fictitious community college! Thanks to Sarah Marlowe for guiding me through the language of the LGBTQIA+ community. Personal preference always plays a role. Any mistakes are mine.

Thanks to Gayle Narita for sharing her perspective and social experiences on being alcohol-free. Thanks also to Caroline Collet for sharing her community choir experiences. Penny and John Radalj helped me with some Croatian words, and Dr. Lianne Wong assisted with some Chinese words. Rose, Belle and Zara Goodall-Wilson "literally" kept me up to speed with 2022 teen-talk.

Thanks to Chrissie and Conn Mios for answering my questions about how much a new hall roof would cost; and to doctor and keen surfer Angus Ewing for offering to proofread my surfing scenes. Not only can he surf, he's got a nice literary touch. For all things Irish, a big shout-out to Dee Swinburne, a reader who discovered my books over in Ireland and offered to help me with expressions and music. Massive thanks to Norma Blake for her assistance in 'Americanizing' this edition and converting slices to bars, meters to yards and a thousand things in between. If you wish to read the Aussie edition, listen to the audio

Huge thanks to Erica and Gabi Mansfield who answered all my Tassie north-west coast questions, from the price of coffee to internet issues in the hinterland, and put me in touch with people if they couldn't answer the questions.

My eldest son moved to Tasmania for university and thus started our love affair with the island state. Part of his time there was spent on the north-west coast. We enjoyed many happy hours exploring the stunning coast between Devonport and Stanley so it felt only right to set the book there. If you haven't visited, put it on the list!

The team at HarperCollins Australia do an amazing job, reassuring me when story ideas won't gel, smoothing out my writing, designing wonderful covers, generating buzz and getting the books out into the world. Thanks go to Rachael Donovan, Annabel Blay, Nicola O'Shea, Jo Munroe, Karen-Maree Griffiths and Emily O'Neill.

The Lowe Team have once again supported me in getting this book into your hands. Thanks to Barton for the cover design of this edition, all the banners, slide-shows and website maintenance. Thanks to Sandon for always being happy to brainstorm book ideas and plot problems. And last but not least, thanks to Norm for the meals, the laundry, being the driver on research trips, the massive conversation task from Australian punctuation to US-style and always being in my corner. And HUGE thanks to you, dear reader, for spending your precious time reading *A Family of Strangers*. The choice of books is enormous and the book budget limited, so I appreciate it very much. I love meeting you on book tours, Facebook, Instagram, TikTok and email. Please stay in touch; your enthusiasm keeps me writing.

ABOUT THE AUTHOR

FIONA LOWE has been a midwife, a sexual health counselor and a family support worker; an ideal career for an author who writes novels about family and relationships. She spent her early years in Papua New Guinea where, without television, reading was the entertainment and it set up a lifelong love of books. Although she often re-wrote the endings of books in her head, it was the birth of her first child that prompted her to write her first novel. A recipient of the prestigious USA RITA® award and the Australian RuBY award, Fiona writes books that are set in small country towns. They feature real people facing difficult choices and explore how family ties and relationships impact on their decisions.

When she's not writing stories, she's a distracted wife, mother of two "ginger" sons, a volunteer in her community, guardian of eighty rose bushes, a slave to a cat, and is often found collapsed on the couch with wine. You can find her at her website, fionalowe.com, and on Facebook, TikTok, Instagram and Goodreads.

BOOK CLUB QUESTIONS

*When I started writing *A Family of Strangers*, I had one word on my whiteboard: *Escape*. Does the idea of escape come through in Addy's, Steph's and Brenda's stories? What other themes do you see in the novel?

*Moving house to the seaside or countryside is an increasingly popular lifestyle choice in Australia. Do you know anyone who has done it? Were they truly prepared, or did they struggle in their transition from big city to small town retreat?

*Blending a family, whether it's gaining in-laws or a child, is a huge task that most people underestimate. Steph struggles with her relationship with her stepdaughter's biological mother as well as her relationship with Zoe herself. Are there other relationships within blended families that are challenging? Who is responsible for those relationships?

*Women's alcohol consumption rates are fast catching up to men's; and studies during the Covid-19 pandemic showed women to be drinking more than men. Why do you think these changes are happening?

*Scroll through social media and you'll find jokes like "It must be five o'clock somewhere!" or someone telling you "Have a drink, you deserve it!" What is our culture's relationship with alcohol that makes it more socially acceptable than prescription or illegal drugs? Is alcohol any less dangerous than drugs?

*Part of Steph's anguish as she tries to juggle work and home is a common frustration for women. Who carries the mental load in your household? Have you tried to shift it or share it? How did you go about it?

*Although bullying in the workplace can happen with workers at the same level, it is often a power dynamic. Why do you think it is so under-reported? What role does the fear of losing a job and income play in how someone deals with the situation?

*Despite many young people coming out on the spectrum of sexuality and gender, there are still those who keep their true selves hidden. How does hiding your identify affect your health?

*Is it easier to come out today or does it still present challenges? What do you believe are the best conditions to foster someone's coming out within a family?

*What were Addy's, Steph's and Brenda's reasons for joining the choir? Do you think belonging to a group is important for mental health?

*Group dynamics can make or break a group. What do you think are the important elements that enable a group to function?

CPSIA information can be obtained
at www.ICGtesting.com
Printed in the USA
LVHW101020150822
725922LV00007B/25